HARBOR OF SPIES
A Novel of Historic Havana

ROBIN LLOYD

Guilford, Connecticut

An imprint of Globe Pequot

Distributed by NATIONAL BOOK NETWORK

British Library Cataloguing in Publication Information Available

Library of Congress Cataloging-in-Publication Data

Names: Lloyd, Robin, 1950- author.
Title: Harbor of spies : a novel of historic Havana / Robin Lloyd.
Description: Guilford, Connecticut : Lyons Press, [2018]
Identifiers: LCCN 2017045172 (print) | LCCN 2017041220 (ebook) | ISBN 9781493032273 (ebook) | ISBN 9781493032266 (hardcover : acid-free paper) | ISBN 9781493032273 (e-book)
Subjects: LCSH: Ship captains—Fiction. | Havana (Cuba)—History—19th century—Fiction. | GSAFD: Historical fiction. | Spy stories.
Classification: LCC PS3612.L69 (print) | LCC PS3612.L69 H37 2018 (ebook) | DDC 813/.6—dc23
LC record available at https://lccn.loc.gov/2017045172

For my wife, Tamara

Preface

This novel is a work of fiction. Most of the characters are invented, as are all of the situations. While the story is a product of my imagination, it is my hope that the book provides a reasonably accurate depiction of Havana as it was in 1863 at the height of the US Civil War. Some of the Union blockading gunships and blockade runners mentioned in the book are actual vessels. The diplomatic envoys based in Havana for the United States, the Confederacy, and Great Britain are real, as are the two Spanish slave traders. The details surrounding the actual murder of the English diplomat George Backhouse in 1855 were researched from newspaper articles and letters to his widow from the British Consulate in Havana.

Part One

CASTILLO DEL MORRO

The masts of the immense shipping rise over the headland . . . we steer in under full head, the morning gun thundering from the Morro, the trumpets braying and drums beating from all the fortifications . . . while the broad sun is fast rising over this magnificent spectacle.

—Richard Henry Dana Jr.
To Cuba and Back

1

*

January 30, 1863

A lighthouse gleamed over the massive stone fort like a Cyclops peering out to sea. They'd seen its beam thirteen miles away when they were halfway between the Salt Cay Banks and Matanzas. The young man on the American merchant schooner *Laura Ann* was standing by the foremast, his hands resting on the ratlines. He rubbed his cheeks where a stubbly beard had started to grow in. He felt awkward and undeserving, calling himself captain. He had signed on as first mate in New York, and now, two weeks later, he was the ship's captain. His change in status was not a promotion but a necessity, and it did not make him feel proud. Alone on deck, Everett Townsend was doing the first anchor watch. It must have been near midnight. He breathed in deeply, and then exhaled with a sigh as he turned toward Havana harbor, which was a welcome sight after a damnable voyage.

Townsend cursed himself and ran his calloused hands through his dark curly hair. The howl of the wind and the roar of the waves had been deafening on that stormy night a week ago. What could he have done? They were sailing downwind, wing and wing, riding gale-force winds directly into the Gulf Stream current. The huge boom of the schooner's foresail had swung out of the darkness, smashing Captain Evans in the head and sweeping him overboard. They had turned back as quickly as they could. All night long he had called the captain's name into the wind and the waves. They had waited until morning, but it was useless in the storm. The man was gone, swallowed by the night one hundred miles off the coast of North Carolina, a familiar graveyard for so many sailors. Townsend kept blaming himself. Maybe he was the ship's Jonah? The old tars said it only took one bad sailor to curse a ship.

A fish jumped, startling him from his memories. The beam from the lighthouse tower slithered over the glossy blackness of the water. Townsend looked up at the grim stone walls of El Morro Castle. He knew the Spanish word *morro* meant headland, and he'd read that this castle was partially hewn out of solid rock, and modeled after a Moorish castle in Lisbon. There was a mysterious darkness about it. He could see the outline of a sentinel next to the shape of a cannon on El Morro's parapets. A fitting portrait, he thought to himself, of this Spanish colonial fortress city. He shifted his gaze to the naval gunboat disappearing into Havana harbor, its paddlewheels thumping and throbbing. The gunship with its deck guns fully manned had passed by earlier on night patrol, and its captain had told him he was too late to enter the harbor. Townsend understood Spanish, but he pretended he didn't. The Spanish captain then picked up his sea trumpet and repeated his commands in English, making his meaning loud and clear. He pointed to El Morro Castle. No boat was allowed to pass into Havana Bay after the signals had been dropped after sunset. The captain barked that he must head back seaward or wait at anchor outside the harbor until sunrise. Those were the orders of the Captain of the Port of Havana.

The strident tone of the man's voice left a bitter taste in his mouth. Townsend had no love for authority. He'd almost started an argument, but then reconsidered. Going back to sea was not an option. The Confederate gunboat, the *Florida*, was somewhere off the coast of Cuba on a rampage, burning American-flagged merchant ships. No, they would not be claimed as a Confederate prize, particularly as they were an unarmed vessel flying the Stars and Stripes. Townsend felt lucky to reach Havana without an encounter. He knew the crew was anxious to get ashore. Even after the accident, storms had stalked them most of the way from North Carolina down past Abaco Island and into the Bahama Bank. The voyage had left its mark on all of them.

Townsend had given an order to anchor the *Laura Ann*, a two-masted, double topsail schooner, just five hundred yards to the east of the fortress. He'd made soundings and they were in about eleven fathoms, some sixty-five feet of water. The ocean floor outside Havana harbor was known to have poor holding ground. He walked toward the bow where the riding light illuminated the thick anchor cable on the drum of the windlass. He pulled the hemp line, which was not only taut, but quivered with tension, much to his relief. The other anchor on the port side was ready to be dropped if they started to drift. He was taking no chances, not after what had happened on this voyage.

Townsend scanned the worn, yellow pine decks of the ninety-three-foot-long schooner. They were covered with a cargo of Maine lumber. Somehow in all the stormy weather they hadn't lost even one plank of wood. He could hear one of the men snoring inside the forward house, the beams creaking as another sailor moved restlessly about in his berth. Townsend looked down at his bare feet and imagined what he must have looked like to that prim Spanish naval officer. He was more like a fisherman than a ship captain. Not only was he barefoot, his dirty shirt was open at the chest. Tar-stained overalls hung low around his waist and were two inches too short. He had a Bowie knife in a leather sheath on his belt. No one would have taken him for the shipmaster. It wasn't just his appearance, but his age. He was only nineteen years old.

Townsend clenched the staysail boom tightly as he thought of his many mistakes. Until a month ago, he thought he would be a naval officer. His quick-flare temper had gotten him into trouble before. It wasn't that he resented all authority. He just rejected it when he felt the person was in the wrong. He thought of his father back in Maryland at their home in Havre de Grace who by now had probably heard the sudden and unexpected news of his son's dismissal from the Naval Academy. Maybe he'd received a copy of the same letter Townsend was given. "Midshipman Everett Townsend: General Conduct: Not good. Aptitude for Naval Service: Poor: Not recommended for continuance at the Academy." The words stung. He imagined his father cursing his oldest son for bringing disgrace to the family.

His gloomy thoughts were interrupted by a figure with a floppy hat emerging from the forward cabin house. Clyde Hendricks carried a kerosene lamp in one hand and the coffee pot with two cups in the other.

"Midnight now, Cap'n," the cheery Bahamian sailor said in his lilting island accent, and handed him a cup. "How the ship anchor holdin'?"

"Like molasses on a jackasses's tongue," said Townsend with a smile.

"You bes' get something more than molasses to plug up them Irish sailors' muzzles. They be honkin and braying like true jackasses, I tellin' you."

They both laughed. Hendricks bunked in the forward cabin house with four Irish sailors on lumpy mattresses filled with straw or what they called "donkeys' breakfast," and he was always grumbling about the snoring.

The two men sat at the stern of the boat on the raised "boot heel" quarterdeck, talking quietly as a silvery slice of the moon crept up in the sky. Hendricks reminded Everett of the Negro sailor who had taught him to work the foredeck on several of the Chesapeake Bay schooners owned by his father. Hendricks was a man of about forty, he guessed, but he looked younger, hardly a furrow in his sloped-back forehead. His wide-set eyes were oddly mismatched: one hopeful and sparkling, the other, sad and distant. He was a skilled sailor with a quiet manner. After they lost the captain, the two of them had sailed the boat together through several days of heavy weather. The crew, most of whom were Irish immigrants trying to escape forced conscription into the Union army, had huddled below deck, fearful that the ship was cursed. But Hendricks hadn't hesitated, tending halyards and jib sheets like a nimble acrobat. Once they reached the Bahamas, he had shown Townsend his shoal water skills by climbing up to the foremast head and helping him pilot the boat through the shallows with simple hand signals. Hendricks was a man Townsend thought he could grow to like, but he knew their paths would probably separate in Havana. The schooner was to be sold to the Havana merchant house receiving the cargo, and they would all soon be looking for another ship.

The two men fell into silence and looked out at the dark silhouette of El Morro Castle and the clear, starry skies. Both were lost in their own thoughts. There was not a sound to be heard now except for the waves gently rolling ashore. A cool breeze brushed against Townsend's face. He guessed it was below 65 degrees, cold for the tropics, but balmy compared to where they'd come from. Just thirteen days ago they'd left New York harbor, catching the last sight of Sandy Hook lighthouse and saying farewell to the leafless trees and snow-covered hills of New Jersey. With that fading landscape, he had lost contact with the news of the Rebellion, and he was eager to get to shore to hear what the latest developments were.

Just behind the fort, Townsend could make out hundreds, maybe thousands, of sparkling lights. There was Havana, the city of his imagination. Just the name made him think of gold-laden treasure ships, explorers and pirates from centuries past. He was suddenly excited, but then the reality of his situation came back to him. His mother was Cuban, born and raised on the island, but she had rarely spoken much about her past or her family. When she did say anything about Cuba, it was always in whispers to his father as she choked back her sobs. Townsend knew his parents had met in Cuba, but not much more than that. She'd spoken in Spanish to him and his brother when they were little, but as they got older she mostly spoke in English. Now she was gone forever from his life. Two months earlier she had died from pneumonia—leaving him to ponder why she had been so secretive—and why she had left Cuba, never to return. He sighed and looked upwards as he wondered for the hundredth time if he'd made the right choice to come here.

At the sight of three bright stars directly overhead, Townsend nudged Hendricks. "Orion's Belt?" he asked. From his studies at the Naval Academy, Townsend was pretty sure it was.

Hendricks looked up to the sky and nodded. "Yeh, mon, you right."

"What about the Southern Cross?" Townsend asked. "Can you see it from here?"

Hendricks shook his head and gestured toward the harbor. "Bes' way to find south at night is to sail for El Morro lighthouse. Once you see dem lights of Havana you know you can't go no futher south. You mus' sail east or west. Dis a big island, you know. More than seven hundred miles long."

At that moment, Townsend heard splashing, something thrashing about in the sea.

"What in tarnation is that?" Townsend cried out. Hendricks was silent, but went up to the bow to try to get closer.

Then they heard a muffled cry.

Townsend rushed over to the stern rail. The yawl boat had already been readied for use, and was now hanging outboard on the davits. He unfastened the block and tackle line from the cleat, dropping the small boat with its oars into the water. Hendricks threw a rope ladder over the bulwarks, and they both leaped in, rowing out away from the ship toward shore. Townsend felt for his knife in the sheath at his side. It was still dark but they were getting closer. Now they could hear a man shouting for help. Townsend caught a glimpse of a black shadow on the surface of the water, passing within an oar's length of them.

"Did you see that, Hendricks! Some kind of fish."

"Lawdy, da ain' no fish. Das a shark," Hendricks yelled out.

Townsend could now see a white blur swimming quickly toward him, a pale, silvery face of a man with an expression of terror. The black fin was already circling back. They pulled with greater strength toward the splashing. The man was punching the water like a madman. All around him were the silhouettes of a half-dozen shark fins and an orgy of glimmering phosphorescent light. Townsend threw a line toward him and watched as the man reached for it, grabbing the rope with one hand even as he fended off a shark with the other. Townsend pulled him in, the man's body twisting through the water like a twirling corkscrew.

Suddenly an ominous black dorsal fin passed within a yard of the boat's stern. The fin came right for the man's arms. Townsend reached for his knife, but Hendricks had already leaned over the gunwale and stabbed the back of the shark. The dorsal fin abruptly veered off in a swirl of phosphorescence, and the surface of the water erupted into an explosion of thrashing. The sharks were attacking one another. Hendricks stabbed and plunged his knife into the dark frenzy of twisting and tearing. Townsend reached out and grabbed the man's flashing arms and hauled him aboard with a sudden jerk, falling backwards in the process.

Breathing heavily and shivering, the man looked at Townsend with bulging, fear-stricken eyes, and then collapsed in the bottom of the boat, his body heaving and twitching. The revolving beam from the lighthouse streaked across his face. The man looked like an emaciated survivor of a shipwreck with unkempt curly hair, a scraggily beard, his clothes torn, revealing bruises and welts on his skin.

"Bloody hell! Close . . . close call. Thank you," he finally gasped. "Damn! I thought I was a dead man."

"You're a lucky man, I will say that," Townsend replied. "What in blazes were you doing out here at night?"

The man remained silent, still breathing heavily, shivering and shaking. It was as if he didn't hear the question. Finally he looked up at Townsend.

"Look here my man, I need your captain."

"Certainly," Townsend replied, noting that this man they'd rescued had an English accent, and a refined one at that. He was no rough sailor from the East End of London.

"Can you take me to him?" the man asked, a plea in his fearful eyes.

"You're speaking to him."

The man looked at him first with astonishment, then relief.

"Please hide me," the man asked, and suddenly collapsed. He was bleeding from a shark bite on his calf. They rowed back to the schooner and took him below into the captain's cabin. The crew was still sleeping. Hendricks stitched up the wound on the man's leg, painted it liberally with Lugol's iodine solution from the ship's medical kit, and bandaged it tightly. Townsend handed him some dry clothes to put on and a warm blanket. They gave the man a heavy dose of Dover's Powders for the pain and told him to rest.

Hendricks pulled Townsend aside and whispered to him.

"What you gon' do with this man? He gon' cause trouble. You know dat?"

"But he needs help," Townsend replied.

Hendricks shook his head. "I tellin' you he gon' cause big trouble. We talkin' about Spanish Cuba. T'ain' got no justice here, none a' t'all." But Townsend simply looked away.

An hour later, the same Spanish steam sidewheel patrol boat cruised by. Townsend got a closer look at it this time. It wasn't much bigger than the *Laura Ann*. Sharp bow, rounded stern with a large cabin house. Two light cannons in the bow and two in the stern. The Spanish flag flying from a stern pole. He could see the Spanish naval officer standing on top of the paddlewheel box searching the waters with his spyglass, a cloud of angry black smoke rising above him. He felt a sudden wave of doubt, bordering on panic, and it increased as the gunboat came closer. The thin-faced captain picked up the ship's trumpet and asked in Spanish if they had seen anything unusual. He repeated the same question in English. The Spaniard was staring suspiciously at the yawl boat still in the water with the oars all askew, and the rope ladder dangling from the side of the schooner. Townsend's head swam. He grabbed one of the stays with a tighter grip. For a brief moment, he thought about telling the Spaniard about the swimmer, but it was something about the captain's unpleasant expression that made him shake his head. He put his hand on his knife as a way to bolster his confidence.

"Only fish," Townsend stammered, wondering if he would regret those words. "Nothing unusual."

The Spanish captain hesitated. Even in the dim light, it was clear from his posture he didn't believe or trust Townsend. The Spaniard loudly announced he would be boarding the schooner. Townsend pretended he couldn't hear what the captain had said. He was glad the shadowy darkness cloaked his unease. The next thing he heard was a command in Spanish to drop the gunship's launch boat into the water.

"Prepárense para bajar la lancha. Vamos a abordar la goleta."

In a panic, Townsend shouted a reply in English.

"You are welcome aboard, Captain, but you should know we have a sick man aboard. Some kind of fever. We hope it's not yellow fever." Townsend was surprised at how easily the lie had flown out of his mouth. A weighty silence between the boats greeted that announcement. Finally the Spanish captain rescinded his order, and informed Townsend the search could wait until tomorrow morning when the young captain would need to present his ship's papers to customs immediately upon entering the harbor at sunrise. It was then that Townsend understood that his unexpected guest might be a fugitive from Spanish authorities. He looked up with trepidation at the looming walls of El Morro, and then at the departing patrol boat, which had left behind a faint residue of sooty smoke clinging to the Laura Ann's mastheads.

2

Dawn arrived with a thundering cannon blast from the Morro fortress, signaling the opening of Havana harbor. In the distance, Townsend could hear the clanging of church bells and gunfire. He grabbed his spyglass and scanned the fortress walls and then the rocky plateau east of El Morro. He was looking for a search party or any soldiers gathering, but all he could see were a few cows and goats grazing on the hillsides. The ocean was like glass with not even a whisper of wind. The silhouettes of the tall palm trees that dotted the hillsides were still as statues, providing no hint of an incoming breeze. He had suspended the Stars and Stripes ensign from the end of the jib boom as required, but so far no harbor steam tug had come to offer them assistance.

Barefoot, Townsend crept silently to the door of his cabin, listening for any sounds of the crew stirring. He had told Hendricks to say nothing of their nighttime visitor to the crew. It was still quiet. From outside his cabin, he whispered, "Are you there?" As he opened the door slowly, it occurred to him he didn't even know the man's name. The stranger was on the bed where he'd left him, sound asleep. He'd given him some of old Captain Evans's clothes. The shirt and pants were too big for the man, but at least they were dry.

The early morning sunlight streamed through the porthole, allowing Townsend to take measure of his guest. The man's face was swollen. His body was lean and bony. He had bruises all over his wrists and ankles. Townsend guessed he was a man in his late forties with early streaks of gray in his unkempt dark hair and beard. With his pale complexion, he looked English, maybe Welsh. Townsend shook him, but the body was limp. He shook him again for what seemed like a solid minute. At last the man opened his blue eyes, and sat up bolt upright.

"Where am I? Who are you?" he stammered, clearly disoriented. He was shivering like a leaf. "You're not Spanish."

"I am the captain of the American schooner, *Laura Ann*. Captain Everett Townsend. You're in my cabin."

The man nodded, and allowed himself to relax in a slump.

"I'm sorry. Forgive me. For a moment there, I didn't know where I was."

"Who are you?" Townsend asked, lowering his voice to a softer whisper. "Speak softly, I don't want the crew to know you're here."

"The name is Abbott," he whispered hoarsely. "Michael Abbott, I am from England." He paused. "I should be cautious about what I say."

"Go on," Townsend urged.

The man looked at the young captain suspiciously and after a few moments said, "Let me just say I am here doing an investigation, a private investigation." His voice was now calm and resolute. "A matter of injustice. A most sordid matter. I'd rather not say more."

Townsend's eyes narrowed. This was no time for evasiveness.

"You asked me in the boat when we rescued you to hide you. Hide you from what?"

Townsend realized that Hendricks was likely right. The man would be trouble. He wanted to be rid of him, the sooner the better. Perhaps he should just turn him over to the Spanish and be done with it. But then he remembered that he had already lied to that Spanish captain. He could feel the tension building in his forehead.

"Look here Mister, what in hell's name is this all about? I have no need to put myself and my ship at risk."

"Please Captain. You must trust me."

Michael Abbott stared into the sunlight streaming through the porthole. He was sitting quietly on the bed, his bare feet held close together. Captain Evans's shirt hung loosely on him like bed sheets on a clothesline, making his face seem even more haggard than the night before. He spoke in a whisper, but his voice became surprisingly steady.

"I was locked up for the past two weeks in an underground dungeon. The Spanish authorities said I would remain there until I stood trial before a military tribunal. I am innocent. Please trust me. My only crime is to have spoken my mind. They accused me of conspiracy against the Spanish government."

Townsend fidgeted with the handle of his sea knife. He was having a hard time controlling his growing agitation. The man nodded with a somber look on his face.

"I need your help— "

Townsend cut him off. "What exactly did they do to you?"

"I was questioned harshly. To put it more plainly, I was tortured. They wanted me to confess that I was an English spy. Crikey, for the sake of all things decent, I implore you, Captain. Consider what hell I have been through. They would have killed me."

Townsend flinched, and began shaking his head from side to side as it dawned on him just how much trouble this man might be.

"How did you escape?"

"Last night I pretended to be dead. The guards swore and kicked me. Then left to fetch the doctor. They left the cell door open. I suppose they thought a dead man couldn't escape."

Above him, Townsend heard the shuffling footsteps of someone washing the deck and the sides of the cabin house. He knew he should go. It was time for him to make an appearance, but he wanted to hear the rest of Abbott's story. If the wind picked up, the other sailors would alert him. He heard more water being sloshed around above their heads. Through the porthole, he could see a mop and hear a sailor's voice. Abbott looked alarmed.

"Can they hear us through the porthole?"

Townsend quickly closed it.

"Finish your story."

"I walked out of the cell in a daze. I saw what they call the *carreta de muertos*, the deadmen's cart, a large wooden box with two handles at each end. There were already three bodies in it under a dirty piece of canvas. I jumped in beside the dead men and threw the canvas cloth over me. I heard voices. I prayed it wasn't the guards. They would have sounded the alarm as soon as they saw the empty cell. The voices came close and the cart was lifted up, carried up some steps. The three corpses were already stiffening, and the smell and the cold flesh made me sick. I started to gag, but fortunately the men were talking and laughing. We were in a damp passageway, and then I felt a cool sea breeze. They grabbed my feet and arms. I had to remember to stay limp. I opened my eyes slightly and caught a glimpse of the top of a wall. Next thing I knew I was flying through the air. I imagined falling on the rocks. I thought this was the end, and I braced myself for the pain."

The man closed his eyes for a moment, and then shook his head back and forth.

"Don't turn me over to those animals. I beg you, Captain! It would mean a death warrant."

"How far did you fall?" Townsend asked.

"Must have been forty to fifty feet. So dark I couldn't see. I hit the water with my feet. I swam underwater away from the land. I came up for air. That's when I saw the light at the front of your boat and I set out to reach you. It was my only hope. I thought the worst that could happen is that I would be turned away."

They were interrupted by a knock on the door. It was one of the Irish sailors, a strongly built man by the name of O'Toole from Cork, who had red whiskers all around his face. Townsend met him at the door to block his view inside.

"Breeze up, Cap'n. Might be enoof wind to raise the sails."

"I will be there shortly," Townsend replied, and then shut the door. He turned to Abbott. "Get cleaned up. I'll think of something."

Townsend watched the man quickly shave and wash his face at the washbasin. He mentally conjured up the ship as he tried to think of all potential hiding places. Since Captain Evans's death, he had become familiar with the man's cabin. It was not large, but it was bigger than his old cabin on the other side of the schooner. There was an elevated bed with drawers underneath, a chair, a small area for books, and a full-length closet for oilskins. In the back of that closet there was a hidden compartment used for storage of storm headsails and staysails. The young captain opened the door to the crawl space and signaled to Abbott where he could hide.

Townsend left the Englishman in a dark, airless space leaning up against the interior planking, his arms folded, his knees touching his head. Their eyes met briefly, and Townsend whispered to him, "The crew won't come in here. But what happens when we get into the harbor is another matter. We must get you on shore secretly. Once ashore you'll be on your own."

Townsend decided he had no time to judge the merits of what he was doing. Abbott's story had frightened and troubled him, but he was inclined to help the fugitive. He surfaced on deck. The sun was rising. Townsend could feel the blast of heat on his face. In the distance, he could see Havana's towers and domes rising above the city of ships in the harbor. A faint breeze was sliding off the hills, slow and easy from the east.

"Winds making up, let's get along," Townsend cried. The men hauled up first the mainsail and then the foresail and then began raising the anchor.

With a faint, light easterly breeze still holding, the *Laura Ann* sailed through the narrow mile-long entrance into Havana harbor without any need to signal for assistance from a steam tug. The young captain stood at the helm, steering with one hand, his eyes darting back and forth as the schooner glided by the thick-walled Morro fortress looming above on the port side with its signal staffs and gun ports. Directly opposite only a few hundred yards away, another smaller fort armed with heavy gun fortifications clung to the rocky outcroppings that lined the shore. All Townsend's senses were on full alert. He'd heard El Morro was protected by a battery of high-caliber cannons, each named after one of the twelve apostles. Even as he monitored the schooner's progress, part of him was absent. His inner thoughts remained on the unseen man crouched directly below him in the dark storage area below deck.

As the schooner sailed by the cannons, Townsend took a look through the telescope at the protected bay that widened out ahead of them. It was some three miles wide, surrounded by hills on all sides. Ahead of him to the east, three-masted merchant ships, flying flags from a half-dozen countries, were anchored off a wharf lined with warehouses. To his right, the twin towers of the city's ancient cathedral rose over a patchwork of brightly colored houses. Spread out before him in the early morning light was the centuries-old city of Havana crowned with the glimmering tips of church spires and belfries. For that brief moment as Townsend caught his first sight of Old Havana he forgot about his troubles, but then that moment was gone.

"Watch yourself, Cap'n!" Hendricks cried out.

Townsend shielded his face from the unrelenting glare of the sun. For a moment, he was disoriented, blinded and immobilized by the light. The bow of a dark gray ship emerged from behind several anchored vessels.

"Oly mother av Jesus, we are gonna be hit," cried out one of the Irish sailors.

Townsend faltered at the sight of a two-masted paddlewheel steamer churning toward them. Hendricks motioned for him to tack, and the young captain snapped out of his paralysis.

"Ready About, Hard Alee!" Townsend called out, spinning the wheel sharply to port.

He gestured to Hendricks at the bow and without a word spoken, the Bahamian back winded the staysail, helping the schooner to change direction. A faint steady breeze now filled the sails, and the *Laura Ann* crept forward even as the steamer's paddlewheel box clunked and thumped directly off the schooner's stern. The angry faces of the men on board glared at Townsend. He started to yell at them to slow down, but then he saw the Confederate Naval Jack on the stern flagpole.

Blockade runners, he hissed to himself. He remembered Captain Evans telling him that Havana was now filled with ships running the Union blockade into the Gulf of Mexico. He'd called it a rebels' nest, and had tried to convince Townsend that it would be a good business. Spanish Cuba, he'd said, was now a major depot of war contraband. All around him Townsend heard a chorus of ships' whistles and cheering as the Confederate steamer chugged its way out of the harbor, its funnel belching out black clouds of smoke and coal ash. He could see Confederate blockade runners had plenty of supporters in Havana.

Townsend turned the spokes of the wheel to starboard as the schooner gradually rounded up into the wind, the sails fluttering lazily in the light breeze. They were about four hundred yards off the central wharf area. Some fifty sailing ships with different flags were tied together at the docks to form a thick forest of spars and rigging along a mile-long landing. Within moments they were surrounded by a flotilla of small awning-covered rowboats, with shirtless boatmen of all colors and shades wearing straw hats selling bananas, pineapples, and coconuts.

One of the Irish sailors threw the lead line and called out, "There be t'airty five feet ov water, Cap'n."

Townsend called for the anchor to be dropped. He heard the rush of the hemp cable coming out of the hawse holes and the splash as the big anchor plunged into the murky water.

It was then he heard Hendricks's warning.

"A Spanish longboat comin' from one of dem warships, Cap'n. An' they got plenty men with guns."

He turned to look at a long rowing boat with six oarsmen, all Spanish navy sailors with their flat-brimmed straw hats marked with the name of the ship, blue shirts, and white duck pants. There were several officials seated in the stern next to a fluttering red and yellow Spanish flag. A thin man in a dark blue navy coat with a sword at his belt stood erect like a flagpole. Townsend lifted the telescope to his eye. As he suspected, it was the captain from last night.

"Put out the rope ladder," Townsend told one of the sailors. "We are being boarded, and I suspect they have more in mind than checking our papers."

The Spanish navy captain came up the rope ladder first, followed by several armed soldiers from the *Guardia Civil* with their heavy black boots. The thin navy captain, one hand resting on his sword, introduced himself as Captain Reinaldo Gómez of the harbor patrol gunboat. He was much shorter than Townsend had thought. He spoke in Spanish, and after introducing the health official and one of his military companions, Captain Alfredo Vásquez of the *Guardia Civil*, Captain Gómez switched to English. He was curt and to the point.

"I am here, Captain, to ascertain if your ship should be quarantined. Where is the sick sailor?" he asked with brusque formality. "The health officer will examine him now."

Townsend looked down at the upturned face of the small Spanish captain. He had suspected this would happen, and he had already prepared an answer.

"As good fortune would have it, Captain Gómez," Townsend said with poker eyes, "the sailor miraculously recovered this morning. We gave him a strong dose of lobelia and Dover's powder last night. Must have been nothing more than ague. No reason for any concern now."

The Spaniard glowered at Townsend.

"I am so pleased to hear that, Captain. Your sailor must have a guardian angel. I hope you understand that we will still need to search your ship."

"As you wish," Townsend said. "May I ask why?"

"A dangerous man escaped from El Morro prison last night. If he did not drown, he may have sought refuge on your boat. Your schooner was strangely close to shore."

The Spanish officer had a curious smile. Townsend's mouth quivered as he looked directly below him into the man's bird-like face. The horrors Abbott had described in a Spanish prison flashed through his mind's eye. He thought about telling the truth, but then he realized he would have to admit to hiding a fugitive. His only object at that moment became to fend off any leading questions.

"I think I told you last night, Captain, we saw nothing. Perhaps your prison escapee is hiding in the rocks near the castle?" Townsend said with a thin veneer of mock concern. "Maybe he has run into the hills?" Townsend relished the height advantage he enjoyed over this arrogant Spanish captain. He was suddenly aware that he felt a curious link with Abbott, some kind of mysterious empathy. He didn't know what the Englishman had done or whether he was guilty or not, but instinctively he knew justice would not be served by handing him over to the Spanish.

Captain Gómez scanned the ship's deck, surveying the Irish sailors. Townsend could tell the naval officer had an inherent distrust and hostility toward foreigners.

"We are looking at all alternatives, Captain, but the most likely possibility is that the prisoner jumped off the walls into the ocean. One of the night sentries reported hearing a lot of splashing over the noise of the waves after the man was reported missing by the guards. The sentry even thought he heard yelling, perhaps by more than one person. Last night when I came by your ship, Captain, I could not help but notice your yawl boat. The oars were askew like they had been left there in haste, and the boat was filled with water. Can you explain that? As I said before, you were anchored suspiciously close to shore."

Townsend pretended to be disinterested even though he felt his voice tremble slightly.

"We had some trouble with the anchor line. Nothing serious. We did hear splashing. We assumed it was fish. Perhaps your prisoner was attacked by sharks?"

Captain Gómez curled his lip, and looked at Townsend with grim menace.

"Search the ship," he shouted to his men in Spanish. Townsend furrowed his brow. He was furious at these Spanish officials, but his best hope was to be midshipman-disciplined, and keep his short-fused temper in check. His anger helped him control his nerves.

The two Spaniards walked up forward and poked their heads into the damp, cramped space of the cabin where the crew slept on simple stacked berths. Finding little of interest in these dark, dank quarters, they walked back to the main cabin house where Townsend showed them the galley, pantry, and storerooms. Unlike most schooners, the *Laura Ann* had the galley in the main cabin, not the forward deckhouse. This is where the crew ate, at a table alongside a coal-fired stove.

Townsend offered them some coffee, but the Spaniards refused. He led them aft to look at the two staterooms for himself and the mate, mindful of how their eyes had now focused in that direction. He raised his voice, hoping Abbott would hear, as he told them how modest his cabin was. Both captains followed him into his quarters, and gazed around the small ten by twelve foot space. They opened the closet door and felt around and then began pulling the coats out. Townsend's mouth felt parched. He watched helplessly as they looked into the closet. Suddenly he heard the latch open. They had discovered the hidden door to the sail locker.

"*Son velas,*" he heard one of them say to the other.

Sails, they had discovered the sails. Townsend braced himself for a shout of surprise. He heard them rummaging through the sails, cursing the small opening as they tried to pull the heavy canvas out to get a better look inside. Should he run before they made the discovery? He tried to move his legs, but they had no strength. To his surprise the swearing stopped and they turned around. They'd seen nothing. Michael Abbott had vanished.

Both captains came up on deck and the navy captain indicated he would be going back to his ship now. He blew a whistle and called out his ship's name, and then an order. Townsend tried to read the man's face to see if he had found more than he had let on, but Townsend couldn't discern anything.

As the longboat was brought alongside the schooner, the captain said goodbye to Townsend with strict Spanish formality.

"*Por lo visto*," he said as he took one more mistrustful look at the schooner's sailors lined up on the quarterdeck. "It would appear that we will have to declare this prisoner's disappearance a tragic suicide."

Then he pointed to Hendricks.

"By the way, is this your slave?"

"No, he is one of the sailors. He is a free man."

The Spanish navy captain looked at his fellow officer and the captain of the *Guardia Civil* on cue addressed Townsend.

"I should inform you Captain, here in Cuba, all Negro sailors on foreign flagged ships must remain on board the vessel until they leave port."

Hendricks glared at the Spaniards but said nothing.

As soon as they'd gone, Townsend rushed below to his cabin, and yanked open the closet and pulled the latch into the secret compartment. He poked his head inside the dark space. He looked around, but saw no one. The man had disappeared.

"Are you there?" he whispered anxiously. A pale hand suddenly emerged. Abbott had buried himself deep underneath a pile of canvas in the darkest corner of the locker. "Yes, I am here" came the tentative answer. "I fear I may need more pain medicine."

3

Night was falling, and down below in the hot cabin Townsend could feel the cooler air coming in from outside. He had released the crew for shore leave in the late afternoon so he and Abbott were now alone on board ship, along with Hendricks. Abbott was still in his cabin, hidden. With another dose of Dover's Powders for the pain, the Englishman was able to walk, although with a slight limp. He said he wanted to be taken to the boarding house in Havana where he had been staying before he was arrested.

"I have to retrieve my belongings."

Townsend ran his hands through his tangled hair. "A risky venture, for sure. There are police all over the docks."

"It's only six or seven blocks from here. You must help me. I can hardly walk."

Townsend looked at the desperation in Abbott's eyes. He rubbed the stubble on his chin as he thought of the danger. He and this mysterious Englishman were two strangers in a strange land brought together by circumstance in a tide of darkness. He'd already decided he would help the man, but he hadn't specified how. He knew he needed to take careful measure of the risks.

It was pitch dark when Townsend stepped out of the cabin house and onto the shadowy quarterdeck. He made no effort to hide himself from any prying eyes along the crowded waterfront. Ships were moored in tiers, a sprawling web of hemp ropes and wooden planks, scraping and twisting together in noisy harmony. A soft land breeze now wafted by, but along with the dusty scent of the earth came a rank whiff of sewage, a reminder that this was a city of more than 150,000 people.

On either side of him were vague, solitary figures, dimly lit by the faint glow of ships' lanterns. These were sailors on adjacent boats who had been left behind as guards. Townsend knew there were likely other unseen faces nearby with unfriendly eyes, watching and waiting. The police had a high-profile presence on the wharf, and he presumed his new Spanish friends from the morning would have informants eyeing the boat.

They had brought the *Laura Ann* to the docks in the late morning to un-load the lumber, clear customs, and complete the paperwork with Morales & Co., the Havana shipping company. There were dozens of fees to be paid: not just customs duties but everything from wharfage dues, to the captain general's fee, a six-dollar arrival charge, and a two-dollar fee for the interpreter. Townsend had never been in a foreign port before, and all of this was new to him. Nothing had gone as planned. Everything from the lizard smiles of the Spanish customs agents to the outstretched hands of the port officials seemed designed to complicate the clearance process. Customs officials thoroughly checked the ship's cargo to see if it matched the manifest. Townsend had stood by nervously as they counted out the number of boards. The customs commander warned him with a faint smile that if there were any variance, he would have to pay a stiff penalty.

All day long Townsend had listened to the sounds of a military city, the rattling of drums, the braying of trumpets, and the marching of soldiers in the nearby Plaza de San Francisco. As if that wasn't a sufficient show of military force, the end of the day was marked by a crescendo of cannons fired from El Morro's walls. It seemed like Havana was a city drunk with the love of gunfire at all hours. He was told he still had paperwork to complete related to the death of Captain Evans. The Spanish officials had taken down his declaration, but now wanted to see the ship's logbook. He knew tomorrow he would also have to present the ship's papers at the American Consulate and submit a full report about Captain Evans's death. The shipping company in New York would have to be notified. So would his family. Townsend knew the old captain was married with three grown children. He thought he'd mentioned a home in Staten Island, but like many lifelong seamen, the grizzled old veteran had not said much. He had lived his life on the water he sailed on. His home in New York was merely an interlude, a rest stop in between voyages.

Fortunately the crew had somehow managed to oversee the stevedores unloading the cargo. Forty thousand feet of ⅛-inch boards of spruce and white pine from inland Maine were now stacked on the wharf alongside the schooner waiting for inspection by the merchant house. At the going rate in Havana of twenty-five dollars per thousand feet, Townsend knew what price he should be getting for this fine quality lumber. What he wasn't sure about was how he and the crew would be paid. He knew the ship was to be sold to Morales & Co., but he had no idea of its exact worth. He thought five thousand dollars was the lowest he should accept. An even bigger concern was he hadn't been able to locate the consignee. There were still more fees to be paid, and he was counting on their assistance. At the offices of the Captain of the Port, he'd been warned if he couldn't pay all the dues soon, the schooner would be seized. Those were the rules.

Even as Townsend worried about all the unfinished paperwork, his mind was on the man in the cabin house. He thought of the arrogance of the Spanish navy captain, which was partly why he had decided to help Michael Abbott. But there was something else. Something about the man's description of what he'd been through triggered his sympathy. It brought back memories of so many of those desperate moments when as a boy he had watched his father secretly load the runaway slaves, shivering with fear, onto one of the freight-carrying scows going up the Susquehanna River on their way to find freedom.

Havre de Grace was a stopover on the Underground Railroad. His mother and father had helped the fugitive slaves by hiding them in some of the outbuildings on their property. His mother would cook for them and bring them food. His father would help the runaways get to safety, sometimes on one of the barges. He'd told him, "Boy, always remember to give a helping hand to those who are underneath because those on top don't care a lick." His father was a stern man, originally from Massachusetts. A real Yankee, from one of the early American families. What would his father have done in this case?

Townsend put that thought aside at the sound of Hendricks emerging from the forward cabin house in the bow. He watched the shadowy form of the Bahamian walking back to the quarterdeck.

"Is it time yet?" he whispered. Hendricks shook his head. "Not as yet, but de man should be comin' directly."

To avoid being seen by any police on the landing, he and Hendricks had devised a plan earlier in the day. They'd hired one of the banana vendors with the awning-covered rowboats called bungo boats to come back to pick Abbott and him up when it was dark. For extra money, the Cuban boatman had agreed to let them have his boat for a couple of hours. They had told him to come with no lights.

Surprisingly on schedule came the creaking of the oars against the wooden thole pins. Somewhere in the unseen darkness Townsend could hear a voice speaking in Spanish.

"*Aquí está el bote. ¿A dónde voy?*"

"Over here," Townsend whispered into the night. "Come over to the starboard side."

It was darker there, and they were able to pull the rowboat into a swath of blackness alongside the schooner. From the top of the bulwarks, Townsend leaned over and looked down at the dim outline of a man in the shadow of the ship's side, a drop of six feet. He pretended he was buying bunches of bananas and sacks of oranges, but he quietly and secretly exchanged hats with the Cuban fruit vendor, and then, in the midst of the confusion of lifting cargo onto the schooner, they switched places. No one saw another shadowy figure as it slid through the freeing port in the bulwarks below the raised quarterdeck, hidden by several clusters of bananas.

Townsend now found himself in the unlikely disguise of a Havana boatman wearing a straw hat in an old wooden boat infested with fruit flies. He began rowing away from the schooner into the darker areas of the inner harbor. Abbott stayed hidden, hugging the soggy floorboards, quietly cursing the flies. Not far away, a squeaky fiddle traded melancholy notes with someone strumming a guitar. From another ship he heard the cracked voice of an old Spanish sailor singing a forlorn ballad. Ahead of them in the distance, Townsend could see the golden beam of Havana's lighthouse. He heard a sentry's cry piercing the night.

"*¡Centinela alerta!*"

Across the harbor entrance from another fortress came the reply.

"*¡Alerta está!*"

On hearing these cries, Abbott squirmed as he tried to crawl underneath some clusters of bananas. Within minutes, they arrived at the small docking area at the city's fish market where they quickly tied the boat up to a rusty iron ring embedded in the stone. The fish market was built on top of the wharf, and the ocean water ran underneath it. The air was ripe with the fetid smells of old fish left too long in the sun. Townsend gulped back his nausea.

They walked up the well-worn stone steps into the empty market, and were confronted with the frightening form of a strange figure standing motionless like a statue. He was dressed in a long, thick dark coat, carrying a lantern in one hand and a spear in the other, a pistol around his waist. This apparition blew a whistle and began to knock his pole on the ground, yelling something unintelligible. Townsend shrank back, prepared to retreat to the boat, but Abbott didn't seem to be bothered.

"It's a *sereno*, a night watchman," he whispered. "Not to worry. Every half-hour they call out the time and the weather. They are all over the city."

They passed outside the pillared arches of the market, and quietly slipped into the gas-lit alleyways of the old city. Above him, he could see the silhouettes of bell towers off to his right. As he walked along the cobblestone streets, Townsend glanced over his shoulder nervously, expecting that they would be followed. The street traffic thickened. Soon they were caught up in Havana's nighttime activity, dodging ungainly carriages with oversized wheels that threatened to knock them over. The sidewalks were so narrow, two people couldn't pass each other. He felt a hand catch his arm and he jumped. Crouched by the wall was a black woman with the stump of a large cigar in her mouth. He turned away, but the woman's deeply wrinkled face and sad eyes stayed with him.

They turned onto a street that ran parallel to the wharf. It was mostly commercial buildings, stores and merchants' offices, but there were residences as well. They passed dark wooden doors with iron spikes, barred windows of houses open, floor to ceiling. He saw a pretty girl with her hands on the bars looking out onto the street like a bird in a cage. They passed a large house and were startled by a voice coming out of the darkness.

"¿Quién vive?"

They didn't reply, and didn't stop walking. It was a military guard armed with a musket. The man stepped forward into the streetlight. He had a black hat, a white jacket, and black boots.

"¡Alto! Alto!" They heard a whistle blow repeatedly, and then footsteps.

"Hurry, we're almost there."

Abbott grabbed Townsend's arm and they ran.

Breathless, they rested underneath a shadowy arcade where they knew they would be out of sight. Somehow they had eluded the guard, but Abbott admitted in his panic he had turned the wrong way. The Englishman gestured toward the interior of the old city and muttered, "Havana Street and San Juan de Dios. Let's go! We have to get to Mrs. Carpenter's boarding house." Townsend thought about leaving him at the arcade, but he knew Abbott might not make it. They walked for several more blocks, until Townsend finally saw the name of the boarding house near the gray stone walls of an old church. It was a flat-roof, three-storied building with a stable to one side. They banged on the front door's brass knocker and were let in by a maid. They stepped inside an airy, cool interior. A marble staircase with balustrades also of marble wound its way up to the next floor. He could hear the melodic sound of a violin echoing through the house. Behind the staircase Townsend spied an open veranda and a small courtyard. His eyes turned as a tall, full-figured woman, strong-jawed but with comely features, purposefully walked down the staircase. She had thick, wavy dark hair streaked with gray, all neatly tied up in a business-like bun. She looked to be in her late forties, not much older than his mother was.

Abbott spoke in a soft whisper to avoid being overheard.

"Eleanor, I am afraid I had an unpleasant encounter."

"Yes, indeed," she said as she examined the bruises on his haggard face. "I would say you did have a bit of unpleasantry. What on earth happened?"

He didn't answer, and instead continued, now speaking in a louder, more formal voice.

"Allow me, Mrs. Carpenter, to introduce you to my young companion, Everett Townsend, an American ship captain. He has just arrived here in Cuba. He has kindly come to my assistance."

Townsend bowed slightly as he'd been taught at the Naval Academy.

"Delighted to make your acquaintance, ma'am."

She acknowledged Townsend with a nod, and a warm smile. She turned back to Abbott. "I am afraid we had to give up your room, Mr. Abbott. You were gone so long. I hope you understand."

Abbott didn't reply. The violin seemed to grow louder as Townsend listened. It sounded like Mozart, his mother's favorite composer. When would it be appropriate for him to bid his farewell? He had done the right thing.

"We have no rooms available, Mr. Abbott. Otherwise I would certainly offer you one. We could, however, provide you with some basic accommodation in the storage area. It would just be for one night until you can find other suitable lodging."

"No, I must go. I just need a small bag of clothes. I do not wish to trouble you further."

"Are you certain?" she asked softly. Townsend couldn't tell if she was sincere or not.

The Englishman nodded.

"Alright then," she said, "let me have Emma show you where your belongings are being kept. She is entertaining some of the guests at present." She called out Emma's name and Townsend heard the sweet sound of the violin abruptly stop. He was about to take his leave when he spotted the young woman gracefully walking through the library. She was a slim brunette, her long, wavy hair slightly pulled back to reveal a high forehead and a thin neck. Her brown eyes were framed by high cheekbones and arched eyebrows. She smiled shyly at Townsend, and he allowed his gaze to linger on her. She was clearly Mrs. Carpenter's daughter, a much slimmer and prettier version than her mother, but she shared that same purposeful stride and look of determination.

Emma appeared shocked to see the Englishman. She looked at Abbott, and their eyes met. It was just a glance, a momentary gesture made between them. To Townsend, it appeared almost as if they shared a secret. Mrs. Carpenter introduced her daughter to Townsend, and then instructed her to take Mr. Abbott to his belongings.

Townsend was left with the older lady, who led him out onto the veranda where there was more privacy. At first, he was reluctant to say much of anything about himself, but she was persistent. He told her a little bit about his story, his arrival in Havana, how he saved Michael Abbott from sharks off El Morro, their close call on the boat. At the mention of El Morro, Mrs. Carpenter grasped at her necklace, shifting uncomfortably. Her voice was now reduced to a hushed whisper and she leaned closer to him.

"Michael Abbott stayed with us for a month. He's been missing now for some two weeks. We didn't know what had happened. Usually bad news travels fast in this city, but we never heard anything. It never occurred to me he would be imprisoned in El Morro."

Townsend nodded. "That's what he said."

"Oh Lord, have mercy. Poor Mr. Abbott. It is probably best that I not hear more of this story. The less I know the better. To tell you the truth, I feared something like this might happen. I was afraid to make any inquiries. I hope you understand, Captain, as a foreigner living in Havana I must be very careful. The Spanish government hears all."

Pausing for a moment, she then leaned in closer to his ear. "Tell me, am I to believe then that Mr. Abbott is now a fugitive?"

Townsend didn't reply. He had already said too much. But his face must have given him away.

"Oh, Merciful heaven," she sighed. "This indeed is disturbing news." She again fingered her necklace and then turned away to speak quickly to one of the maids. Abbott reappeared shortly afterward. He was carrying a small bundle.

"Shall we go, Captain Townsend?"

Townsend hesitated. Didn't the man understand he would be heading back to the docks now? He'd fulfilled his promise. Before he could say anything, Mrs. Carpenter spoke up.

"Mr. Abbott, have you considered seeking help from the British consul general? Given your circumstances, it might be . . ."

"No," Abbott replied tersely. "I cannot do that. I should not say more, but that is not advisable. Thank you, Mrs. Carpenter. I will contact you with a forwarding address. Come, Captain Townsend. We must go."

A dark cloud came over Townsend as they left the house. Something snapped. He felt he had done enough to help this man.

"See there now, I told you I would get you to your boarding house," Townsend said, stopping Abbott to look him squarely in the eye. "I have done that. This is as far as I go."

Abbott's eyes fell to the ground. Townsend wavered as he looked at the man's pained face. He started to walk away, but stopped at the sound of running footsteps. He wheeled around to come face-to-face with Emma, who stole a quick glance at him before turning toward Michael Abbott.

"I am so glad I caught you, Mr. Abbott. I wanted to say goodbye. I apologize for my mother. If it were up to me, I would insist you stay. There would be no question. Where will you go?"

"Some of my colleagues in London gave me an address of a safe haven. They may have a bed for me. Thank you for your hospitality, Miss Carpenter. I will always remember you kindly."

Emma nodded, her eyes lingering on Abbott for a moment before she looked over at Townsend.

"Mr. Abbott is so fortunate, Captain to have you helping him."

"Well, not really," the young captain mumbled. "I'm actually just—"

"You are truly a good Samaritan," she said with a faint smile.

Townsend bit his lip. He almost said he was going back to his ship, but as he looked at Emma he choked back the words, his eyes drawn to her. Her lustrous brown hair and clear olive complexion glowed in the mottled light from the street lamps. Her brown eyes sparkled like river stones, and her smile disarmed him.

She wished them both a good night and went back inside.

Abbott made a gesture to Townsend.

"We need to go!"

Townsend shook his head at first, but then took Abbott's arm to help him down the steps.

He could hear in the distance the steady beat of rhythmic drums, along with chanting and singing. It was unsettling. He was pleased when they turned away from the drumming, and the music faded in the distance. Townsend kept looking over his shoulder to see if they were being followed. After walking for a half an hour, they arrived outside a looming stone church with a high belfry tower. Even in the shadowy light from the street lamps, Townsend could tell that there was something ancient about it.

"What is this place?" he asked Abbott.

"It is the Church of St. Augustine, a centuries-old monastery now run by the Order of St. Francis. I have the name of a monk I must see. Wait for me."

Abbott walked into the front door of the church. Townsend was left standing in the shadows of the towering building, staring at the thick arched wooden door framed by ornate stone medieval frieze carvings on the building's façade. Dusky figures with heavily laden yokes around their necks passed by in silence, the water pails on ropes swinging back and forth like off-tempo pendulums. Dogs barked in the distance. The clanking of wheels on stone announced the arrival of a donkey cart followed by the ghostly shapes of hooded monks. It seemed like he had stepped back into the dark ages.

Then suddenly he heard a crowd chanting in Spanish. He darted to the side and hid as a group ran by. They were all Negroes. He tried to listen. "*Avanza, Lincoln, avanza, tú eres nuestra esperanza.*" He translated to himself, "Forward, Lincoln, forward, you are our hope." He jumped at the sound of someone whispering in his ear in Spanish, "Tell Mr. Lincoln to come free us." He wheeled around to see who it was, but it was too dark, and the figure had run away. He heard whistles and heavy footsteps running down the street, and he ducked back out of sight to wait for Abbott in the safety of the gloomy walls.

When Abbott reemerged from the wooden door, he looked worried. He shook his head. He leaned against the wall of the dark stone building. Townsend could tell the man needed a doctor.

"What happened?" Townsend asked.

"I was turned away. The man I was looking for was not there. He was out in the community, I was told. I asked if I could wait for him." Abbott's voice cracked. "But the *padre prior*, who was in charge, told me I would have to come back tomorrow. I told him I needed a place to stay, but he just shook his head."

Out of the corner of his eye, Townsend caught a glimpse of a ghostly bearded face with sharp features looking at them intently through a barred window. Townsend beckoned him, but the mysterious onlooker pulled a brown hood over his head and disappeared back into the darkness behind the barred window.

Abbott groaned, "So thirsty. Need to rest." Townsend walked with him to a tavern. An awkward silence enveloped the room as they entered. The place was full of a lower class of rough Spaniards, who clearly weren't accustomed to newcomers. Townsend could feel the cold, furtive stares, and hear the unfriendly whispers in Spanish about *los perros Yanquis*, Yankee dogs. Once again he heard the disquieting sound of drums.

"What is that infernal drumming?" Townsend asked.

"Slaves, dockworkers," the Englishman replied. "Around New Years the Spanish allow them to practice their rituals."

They ordered a bottle of cheap wine from the Canary Islands that proved to be so bitter and brown that Townsend only sipped at it. Abbott downed several glasses. Townsend gave him what was left of the Dover's Powders from the ship's medicine kit, and they sat together without speaking until the wine had settled their nerves.

"Mr. Abbott, I would like to know why are you here in Cuba?"

"I told you. I have come as part of an investigation."

"Of what? Surely you can tell me more? Are you a policeman?"

Abbott paused and fidgeted with his empty glass. Finally he looked earnestly at Townsend.

"Never mind what I am. I have come here at the request of an English widow to investigate the murder of her husband. He was brutally stabbed to death in their house in Havana eight years ago under mysterious circumstances. This poor woman has suffered ever since. Every year for the last eight years on the 31st of August, the day her husband was killed, she goes to our church to pray on what she calls her day of sorrow. Suffice to say, the mission I am on is a righteous cause."

Townsend said nothing. Abbott almost sounded like a missionary, zealous and principled.

"Eight years. That was a long time ago."

"Yes, but there is new evidence. Possibly a witness. She begged me to help. She said she is desperate to put this to rest."

"Presumably the Spanish authorities would want to hear that new evidence."

"I don't believe the Spanish want to hear anything."

"Why?"

The Englishman laughed darkly.

"How can you ask that, Captain, after what you've seen already? There is no justice on this island. I have told you enough, Captain Townsend. More than enough."

Abbott averted his eyes and downed a last drop in his empty glass. They could hear the beat of drums now coming closer.

"Perhaps it would be best to accept Mrs. Carpenter's offer to stay in her storage area, at least for the night," Townsend said. Abbott only nodded. The two of them walked out of the tavern to a chaotic scene. Crowds of dancers were leaping in circles, moving like marionettes to the beat of drums. The street was swirling with dark people, lost in a wild frenzy, chanting something in an African language. The warlike drumming was hypnotic, and Townsend was mesmerized as men with conical-shaped hoods over their heads moved toward them menacingly, beating drums made from logs, snapping whisks, and shaking rattles. He thought he heard a shot behind him, but it was only the echoes off the old walls. When he turned back around, he had no time to think before he was swallowed by a mass of muscular arms and bare torsos sweeping him down the street like a fast-moving, outgoing tide.

Townsend looked frantically for Abbott and spotted him trying to push away a man with an African mask. Suddenly Townsend saw the glint of a knife. The hand holding the knife was white. Townsend's warning shout was too late. Abbott grimaced in pain, and fell to the ground. Another hand grabbed his bag. And then Townsend felt a crushing pain in his head and felt himself falling.

When he woke it was still dark and he was staring up at a sea of concerned faces. The air was thick and ripe with the dusty smells of the unwashed street. Someone was throwing cold water over him. He lifted himself up, and winced at a sharp pain in his head. He was confused. And then he remembered.

"Abbott, where is . . ." he muttered. He looked around and noticed he was surrounded by a pool of blood. He touched his head. It hurt but there was no wound, just a large bump. He touched his stomach, his legs. No sign that he had been knifed. It must be Abbott's blood he was sitting in. He tried speaking in Spanish. "*Mi amigo. ¿Dónde está mi amigo?*"

He heard someone call him *un borracho Yanqui,* a drunk Yankee. A pair of black boots in stirrups came into view in front of him. A uniformed man on a dapple-gray horse blotted out the sky. He heard the shaking and clanking of iron chains.

"*¡Póngale grilletes y cadenas!*"

"*Sí, Capitán.*"

Unseen hands picked him up from behind and began shackling his wrists and his ankles.

"Wait . . . What are you doing? What in blazes—" Townsend cried out in alarm. "You have no right!" he shouted as he struggled to free himself. "I am an American. *Soy Americano. Capitán de barco.* A ship captain. I demand to speak to the American consul general. I have done nothing wrong!"

He felt a blow to the temple. "*¡Cállate cabrón!*" They put a hood over his head and threw him in the back of a horse cart. His arms and legs were shackled together so tightly he couldn't move.

"*Llévalo a la cárcel,*" he heard.

They were taking him to a prison.

4

Dark, stagnant air filled Townsend's lungs as he paced the floor of his small cell like a caged wild animal. The only window was a grated hole twenty feet above his head. He was what the prison guards called an *incommunicado*, locked up in solitary confinement. He had no chair, no bed, just the stone floor to sleep on. It had been over a week, although it already seemed like an eternity. He had no way to get word to the crew, or anyone else for that matter. All around he could hear the cries of other inmates, the cursing, and the fighting.

All he knew about his prison was that the soldiers called it the *Cárcel Real*, the Royal Prison. It was Havana's main prison. All week the rank smell of raw sewage assaulted his nose. He spit out the rancid food, a yellow starchy mush that had the flavor of mold and made him gag. He cursed the Spanish and lamented his decision to help the Englishman. He started beating the wall with the palm of his hand. He had been a fool. He should have listened to Hendricks when he warned him the man was trouble. It was unbearably hot, and he lay down shirtless on the stone floor to try to sleep. His unsettled mind refused to grant him an escape into the welcome oblivion of sleep. All he could think of were the beads of sweat that meandered down his spine like sap from a tree.

Townsend had demanded to see the US consul general, but the prison officials had laughed and told him he was a *filibustero Yanqui*, a Yankee filibusterer, sent to Cuba to plot another military expedition, and as a result had no rights. His interrogators wanted to know about the Englishman named Abbott, the man he'd helped to escape. At first, they had just asked him questions, but the interrogations had gotten more intense. Every day his handlers tied him to a chair, naked and exposed. They prodded and taunted him, and one of them kept asking him questions. The prison official's black eyes seemed to seethe with resentment. They wanted to know, what was the Englishman doing in Cuba? Who did he meet with? Who were his contacts? Frightened and disheartened, Townsend told them what he knew, or most of it. He continued to pretend he didn't speak the language. He lied and said he had no idea what had brought Abbott to Cuba. He could tell they were suspicious. From listening to some of their private conversations in Spanish, he kept hearing the word for liar, *mentiroso*. It was clear they were referring to him.

To escape the horrors inside the prison walls, he had come to recognize the sounds of life he heard from the outside. In the morning and the evening, a symphony of church bells rang from every part of town, calling people to mass. Even the firing of the cannons from El Morro, marking the beginning and end of each day, had become welcome. But then he would hear the soldiers marching outside, the roll of drums and the firing of guns, and his throat would tighten and he would struggle for breath.

"Listen for the drums," the chief interrogator told him, his voice full of menace. "When you hear the braying of the trumpets you will know there is one less prisoner on death row." They reminded him that the Spanish had executed scores of *filibusteros Americanos* who had invaded the island in 1851, led by the Spanish traitor, Narciso López. "Spain will defend herself against all her enemies, and Cuba will remain *siempre fiel a España*, forever faithful to Spain."

To further heighten his unease, his prison handlers seemed to take delight in explaining the other form of capital punishment, death by the *garrote*. Those sentenced to death were placed in chairs with an iron collar around the throat. A screw is slowly turned from behind, which chokes the person and finally crushes the spinal cord. Townsend tried to shake away these thoughts, but he couldn't. His palms were moist with fear. He desperately needed to sleep, but like a sudden gust of wind his tangled mind instead took him where it wanted to go.

Lying there, eyes wide-open, he felt a sudden pang of sadness as he recalled Captain Ebenezer Evans. Once again he recognized the familiar bitter taste of guilt in his mouth. It was a night that had shaken him to his core, and he didn't want to think about it. What could he have done? The block for the boom tackle on the foremast had broken under the strain of the heavy winds. As first mate, if only he'd given the order to install a replacement preventer on the boom, the tragedy might never have happened. If only. . . . Maybe he never should have trusted the sailor at the helm. If only Townsend had taken the wheel, the ship might never have veered off course. If only . . . but then, how could he have known the captain would walk out of the cabin house unannounced and then go up forward for no apparent reason? And how could he have known that a rogue wave was about to hit them broadside? He was left with the echo, if only . . . if only. It was all a blur, lost in a mixture of ocean spray, white foam, and darkness.

Surrounded by the blackness in the cell, Townsend cursed himself. They didn't make men like Captain Evans anymore, more at home on the sea than on land. He didn't know the man well. Evans had been a blue water seaman with the Black Ball Line sailing from New York to Liverpool for over thirty years. That much he knew. They'd had some conversations about the war. Mostly the old ship captain wanted to talk about the blockade and how foolish it was for the Federal government to think they could close off the entire coast of the Confederate states, three thousand miles of shoreline with scores of ports, harbors, bays, and inlets. They didn't have the gunships, he had declared. It was a fool's errand. Townsend could tell that Captain Evans liked him. Perhaps he even respected him because of the formal education Townsend had received which Evans never had.

"Might be I'd like to try runnin' through the Union blockade from Havana. Care to join me, son? I could use a first mate like you. Don't want to waste all that good learnin' you got."

Townsend had never given an answer. His own view about the Rebellion was that the Southern states were foolish to secede, but they did, and that was that. As a Marylander, he'd grown up with hot-headed firebrands who resented Northerners. He understood Southerners and their longing for a separate identity, but he couldn't comprehend their call to arms. Once they'd fired the first shot, they forced Lincoln's hand, and the war was on. As for slavery, he thought the sooner that evil institution was done away with, the better.

It was all too much. The war between the states, Evans's death, his imprisonment. He tried to turn his troubled mind to more pleasant memories. He conjured up the vision of a formation of honking Canada geese flying over a small island of loblolly pines and wild asparagus. Suddenly he was on a Chesapeake Bay pungy. He was just a boy. He and his family were going to Smith Island to attend a wedding. It was a crisp, late October day, the breeze coming slow and easy out of the west. They sailed by a stately plantation home with a recently harvested cornfield sloping down to a hidden blackwater cove. It was a special occasion because his father rarely took time off.

As a local merchant and ship owner on the upper Chesapeake Bay, he was forever preoccupied with affairs of business.

At the helm, his father had a carefree look as he glanced up at the sails. His mother, so lovely with her sharp features and deep brown eyes, had put a bonnet over her head as a shade from sun and wind. They were all laughing and enjoying the beauty of the day. Even his younger brother, William, who hated sailing because he got seasick, was beaming. His mother, normally tense and stern in her demeanor, had relaxed, and she teased her husband about the amount of gray in his beard.

Townsend gulped as he felt the pain, the realization she was gone. He had never been able to say goodbye. He was not overly religious, so he took little comfort in the Bible's promise of the life hereafter. His only solace was the deep memory of his mother.

The last time he had seen her, he was about to set out to Annapolis to join the Naval Academy. They were in the parlor room. She had just finished playing a beautiful Schubert sonata on the piano. She rarely talked about her private thoughts, but she had turned to him that evening and said, "It's important to know yourself, *mi hijo*, and be comfortable with who you are. Never lie to yourself, son. Promise me that. I am just reading some of Emerson's latest essays. I think you might like them." She handed him Emerson's new book, *The Conduct of Life*, as a gift.

She had paused and looked at the flickering flames in the fireplace and said more softly almost in a whisper, "It's important to find your own way, *mi hijo*. The world is constantly trying to make all of us into something other than what we are. Remember life is what you make it. Emerson writes some nice words in the book I gave you. 'Live in the sunshine, swim the sea, drink the wild air's salubrity.'"

Rank prison air entered his lungs like a poisonous cloud. His mouth felt dry and swollen. His head throbbed. Again he moved restlessly on the stone floor and tried in vain to find a comfortable position. He thought back to the year leading up to the war. He'd been thrilled to escape the small-town life in Havre de Grace. The first year at the Naval Academy, he was in Annapolis, but then, once the war had started, the students and the faculty were moved to the school's temporary home in Newport, Rhode Island. They had all made the sea journey together on board the historic USS *Constitution*. The housing in the dank quarters at Fort Adams had been horrible. A typhoid outbreak in Newport caused much panic throughout the town, and he and his classmates were never happier than when they were moved to the Atlantic Hotel. In those early years, Townsend had been praised by his teachers for his quick mind, his aptitude for tackling navigation computations, and learning about steam engines and the new class of heavy, shell-firing naval cannon.

Perhaps his schooling there had been a blessing. He remembered the Naval Academy Band, and the charismatic German bandleader, Mr. Zimmermann, whose passion for music had inspired them all. The constant drilling in the early morning, the gunnery training and the rigorous classes that included mathematics, ethics, and Spanish had kept his mind fully occupied. To fill the desperate need to get officers to sea quickly, the Naval Academy had dramatically shortened the four-year program. That intensity and the summer sea trials prevented him from seeing much of his family. He was not sure what he would have done had he known that William intended to run off to volunteer with Lee's Army of Northern Virginia. Maybe it shouldn't have surprised him. His brother had always been drawn to a different crowd, angry and rebellious. When Townsend eventually found out his brother had enlisted in the Rebel forces, he had kept quiet about it. The mood at the Naval Academy at the outbreak of the war was tense. Fistfights among students broke out almost daily. Many of the upperclassmen had left to join the South, and these divisions were a source of constant friction.

Then word had come of his brother's death at the battle of Antietam, and his mother's surprise illness and death shortly afterward from pneumonia. A double tragedy. Instead of grieving, Townsend had grown morose and incommunicative. Word leaked out about his brother, and his fellow students whispered rumors that Everett Townsend was probably secretly a "secesh" just like his brother. That constant whispering rankled him. Still, he never should have let his anger take over. He remembered the last letter he'd gotten from his father. "Mark my words, son," he'd written, "the Confederacy is on the wrong side of history. Your brother was a fool to be caught up in the fiery rhetoric of these zealous secessionists. His foolhardy thinking cost him, and he paid the ultimate price. I hope you won't act as rashly."

Those cautionary words still stuck in his throat like a sharp fish bone, threatening to choke him. What had he done? True, he'd been drinking. All the students had been drinking that Thanksgiving night. The regulations didn't stop them from roaming the streets, drinking in the taverns, and staging noisy mock assaults and howling outside of windows. But what he had done had crossed the line. Even he knew that.

Townsend wiped the perspiration off his forehead. His eyelids were wide open in the unseeing inky darkness. Outside the cell, he could hear the faint cry of a *sereno* calling out the hour. With no light in the cell, that distant voice was haunting. He tried to think of something else to distract his mind, but he kept coming back to his final weeks at the Naval Academy.

In retrospect, it seemed like Angus Van Cortland had wanted to pick the fight. He was two classes ahead of him and had always disliked Townsend. Mostly he'd been bragging about being called into service early. He was on leave from serving on board a Union steamship on patrol along the coast of Texas and Louisiana, searching for Confederates running the blockade. His ship, the USS *De Soto*, was under repairs at the Philadelphia Navy Yard, and Van Cortland had returned to the Naval Academy to see his own younger brother.

Van Cortland had strutted his own accomplishments. He kept provoking Townsend, questioning him about his own views. In front of his classmates, he accused Townsend directly of being a Rebel spy.

"You're not only a spy for the Rebs, but I hear tell your mother was a Cuban whore."

Townsend had responded in a spasm of anger and punched Van Cortland in the face. They'd gone at each other in what the superintendent wrote in his report was "a knock-down, drag-out fight." Even worse than that, when he was called before the superintendent, Townsend had called the portly and aging head of the Academy a dunderhead to question his loyalty to the Union. That effrontery sealed his fate. As soon as the report from the Academy's superintendent had reached the desk of the secretary of the Navy, Townsend was informed he would not be allowed to continue at the Academy. He was labeled a troublemaker, unfit to be an officer of the US Navy. Van Cortland's barbed slur had found its mark. He should have walked away, but the simple truth for Townsend was any mention of his mother by a stranger triggered an explosive mix of emotions.

His dark thoughts now settled over him like a storm cloud. He had known there would be stern words or worse from his father if they had come face-to-face. So he had decided he would go his own way. After he was dismissed, he jumped on a small trading schooner bound for New York and had aimlessly wandered the South Street docks. He hadn't intended to go to Cuba—at least not consciously. He just wanted a ship, any ship to take him to sea, away from his profound emptiness and his anger. He was also hardheaded, and determined to succeed, and if the Navy felt he wasn't good enough, he would go elsewhere. If there was one thing he knew about himself—if he was knocked down, he would get back up. As soon as he had spotted the *Laura Ann* tied up at the New York docks near Peck's Slip with her familiar Chesapeake Bay lines, her tall two-topmast rig with a slight rake and her sharp clipper bow, he wanted to be on that ship. It was like going home.

Still, when Captain Ebenezer Evans had told him he was leaving for Cuba the next day, he had hesitated. Even without the verbal assault by Van

Cortland, he knew there were dark secrets about his mother's past in Cuba. She had never spoken about her family or her childhood except for her rare but intense angry outbursts about her own mother. She'd mentioned a place located near a city called Matanzas. He thought she called it something like Mambi Joo, but he wasn't sure because she would say it in passing or in whispers to his father. He had asked her about a family name he had heard her mention, Carbonell. His mother said it came from her grandfather, a Frenchman, who had fled to Cuba from Haiti at the time of the slave uprisings and massacres there. Sometimes Townsend had overheard his mother recalling some aspects of life in the Cuban countryside, but it was usually a memory about someone or some place that meant nothing to him, and his parents never bothered to explain.

Once at dinner, he and his brother had asked if they would ever meet their grandmother. He would never forget the heavy silence that fell over the table. His father looked like someone had hit him unexpectedly. His mother was suddenly combative. She glared at him. "That woman doesn't exist for me," she had cried out. "She is an evil woman. All she ever cared about was herself. She lied and manipulated the truth, all to satisfy her own greed. She will never be allowed to see my two sons. Never! ¡Nunca!" She had stormed away from the dining room table with a strangled cry and gone to her room, and their father had followed behind. He and his brother had heard them talking behind the closed door, the tearful whispering, the faint sobbing and his father's quiet measured voice trying to console her.

Their father had given each of them a thrashing for upsetting their mother. After that outburst, they never dared mention or ask questions about their grandmother or anything about Cuba. He and his brother realized at a young age that something terrible had caused their mother to leave the island, but they had no idea what it was. Cuba was a closed door, a forbidden topic never to be discussed. They didn't even know their grandmother's full name. Their mother just called her la bruja, the witch.

By his estimation, it was late morning when he heard the rattling of the heavy prison keys being inserted into the lock on his prison door. He looked up at two silhouettes that now stood at the entrance to his cell. A guard entered with a lantern, and handed another man his own light. The two guards marched into his cell and yanked him up. He struggled, but it was useless. One of them put a hood over his face. He felt his hands being pulled together and then shackled to the iron belt around his waist. They told him to walk and he hobbled forward, barefoot with the shackles around his ankles.

Townsend felt a surge of panic. He started gasping. It was difficult for him to breathe. The hood was suffocating him.

The two men on either side of him tightened their grip on his shoulders. "¡Cállate, perro! Que no tienes por que saber nada."

He understood what they said. They had told him to shut up. They had called him a Yankee dog and said he didn't need to know anything. He thought about pleading in Spanish, but he had second thoughts. These were not people who would show him any mercy. A crushing fear overwhelmed him as he realized he had no means of escape. He wondered if he was being taken to a firing squad or whether he would be garroted. He now understood why Abbott would lie next to dead bodies. He struggled again and this time they struck him with a stick. He heard people pass by on either side of him, soldiers drilling outside, and then the firing of a volley of guns.

5

After walking what seemed like a mile through damp tunnels, going through door after door, the guards stopped, as one of them unshackled Townsend's arms, and then his legs. Townsend felt the circulation return to his limbs. He was no longer breathing the foul prison air. They didn't say a word. He expected any moment to hear the roll of drums and the command in Spanish to prepare to fire. He told himself this was the end and he needed to face it like a man. He breathed in deeply and waited for the end of his life. But instead of a volley of rifle shots, he heard a voice say they could take the hood off now.

Townsend stood there blinking in the blinding glare of the light, disoriented, terrified. He couldn't see.

"Don't shoot," he cried out. "I have done nothing wrong."

There was silence and he braced himself again for the bullets he imagined would soon tear through his chest. But then his eyes adjusted to the light. Slowly he began to focus on his surroundings. The room had red Spanish décor tapestries on the wall and dark furniture. A well-dressed man stood in front of him, medium height and slight build. He wasn't a policeman. He looked more like a businessman with his formal coat, light blue waistcoat, and black satin tie. The man took off his flat-brimmed hat, and asked one of the guards to bring in two chairs.

"Do sit down," he said to Townsend.

Townsend stumbled to the chair. Before he sat down, he caught a glimpse of himself in a gilded frame mirror on the wall. He stood transfixed at what he saw—a shaggy-haired, dirty man in stained cotton prison rags. He brought his right hand up to his unshaven face. It was like looking at a stranger. He became aware of a stale, sharp odor, and he realized he was smelling his own urine and vomit-soaked clothes. He suddenly felt a deep shame. He tried to straighten up like a midshipman, but his shoulders slumped over when he was jolted by the pain in his spine.

"*Buenos días, Capitán. Por favor, siéntese.* Take a seat," the man said as he pointed to the chair.

Townsend warily sat down. He looked more closely at the man across from him. He had a full head of hair, slicked back tight against his skull. His finely chiseled features were framed by a well-trimmed beard and moustache with a slight touch of silver-gray. He spoke with a clear and crisp Castilian accent, but when he sat down directly opposite Townsend, he addressed him in English—a flawless English with no detectable accent.

"Let me introduce you to something peculiar to Cuba, *una cosa cubana,*" the man said with a smile as he pulled out a large seven-inch cigar from his coat pocket. "In Cuba, smoking cigars is as fundamental as eating and drinking. Everyone here smokes cigars, even the ladies."

He cut the tip of his cigar and handed it to Townsend. "*Tome uno,*" he said politely with a smile as he scrutinized Townsend's face. Townsend shook his head.

"*¿Habla español?*" the man asked as he raised one bushy, black eyebrow. Townsend lied, and said he didn't. He feared the worst. Maybe this man is the military judge who would soon sentence him? He looked back at the two guards. He felt his body tremble, an inner shudder running through him— he was utterly powerless. The Spaniard lit the cigar with a Lucifer match. Townsend noticed for the first time how pockmarked the man's face was.

"This fine cigar is a Regalía Imperial of the Fígaro brand," he said as he puffed on the cigar several times to see that it burned well. "I am Don Pedro Alvarado Cardona. I am a Havana merchant. And you are?"

"E. J. Townsend, American ship captain of the schooner *Laura Ann,*" Townsend replied warily.

"E. J.?" he inquired. "That seems so formal. What is your first name?"

"Everett," he replied.

"I see," said the man smiling broadly. "I like that name. You have a touch of the Southern in your manner, but your accent also has a tinge of the sharp clip of a Boston Yankee."

"My father is from New England."

"I see. From your manner of speaking, you seem like a well-educated young man. Where are you from?"

Townsend was reluctant at first to say. He was confused. He felt tired and weak from exhaustion and hunger. He was sore from sleeping the last eight nights on nothing but the stone floor. He felt his head spinning, and he thought he might pass out.

"Havre de Grace, Maryland," he finally mumbled.

The man looked at him in a long and penetrating, almost intimate way, as if he suddenly recognized him.

"Then you are a Southern boy. That is good to hear. Captain Townsend, let me get to the point. I have come here after speaking with the agents at Morales & Co. They have informed me of your dilemma and I believe I can help you immeasurably."

Townsend sat up with a start. These were the first kind words he'd heard from a Spaniard. Still he was wary. The man was pleasant enough, but there was something veiled about him, something hidden.

"You see, I deal with the transaction of all business related to shipping. I specialize with foreigners who have troubles here in Cuba." The man took a puff on his cigar and watched the smoke rise above his head.

"As you may know, the island of Cuba is a province of Spain. A most faithful colony, I might add. As we say, *siempre fiel a España*, always faithful to Spain. The man in charge is appointed by Her Majesty, Queen Isabella II, and ultimately only answers to the Crown. His rule is absolute here on the island. The current captain general is his Excellency, Don Domingo Dulce, who only recently arrived here to assume his duties. I have been to see his Illustrious Excellency about your predicament, and he has explained to me the seriousness of your situation."

Townsend raised his eyebrows in response to the Spaniard's sharper tone of voice.

"As you know, you are charged with helping a prisoner escape. Make no mistake, Captain, that is a serious charge."

Townsend nodded, his lower lip quivering.

"The government has already taken possession of your ship, and they have deported your crew as undesirable foreigners."

"My crew has been deported?"

"Yes, all of them."

"I see," Townsend replied soberly. "But I was not deported. That does not sound promising."

"Believe me, Captain, it is not. Under Spanish law, you will be required to appear before a military tribunal soon."

There was a heavy silence. The Spaniard paused as if to add weight to what he had to say.

"You could be sentenced to death."

Townsend gulped. So they were going to execute him after all. Townsend looked at the man with a glazed stare and wiped his moist brow with the back of his hand.

"I have not even been allowed to speak to anyone since I was brought here," Townsend blurted out angrily. "All I want to do is get out of here."

He noticed that the Spaniard never stopped smiling even as he studiously puffed on his cigar.

"I believe that is exactly what I can do for you. I can get those charges dropped."

As if on cue, a guard showed up with a plate of food, far more appetizing than what Townsend had been fed. The tangy aroma of fried fish floated into the room like a fresh sea breeze filling a limp, windless sail. Townsend breathed in deeply, the rich smells so tantalizing and tempting. He had not eaten for days, and what he had eaten he had thrown up. Townsend took the plate with the cooked fish and garlic, rice, and plantains and began wolfing it down as if it were his last meal.

"Let me explain, Captain, what I have in mind. It is a business proposition, a serious proposal. First, let me say that I greatly admire your schooner. I spotted her when you sailed into the harbor and was impressed with the way you avoided that Confederate steamer."

Townsend nodded cautiously, but didn't respond.

"Before I say more about what I have in mind for you, I should mention that I have already acquired your schooner from the Spanish government. The *Laura Ann* is now a Spanish-flagged vessel under my firm's name."

Townsend put the plate down. The Spaniard flicked his ashes into a metal bowl.

"I see I have your full attention now. Let me get right to the point then. I have two schooners already and with yours I have a fleet of three. All are centerboard schooners and can easily cross the shallow bars of most rivers along the Gulf Coast. Less danger of running aground, as you know."

Townsend wasn't sure what this had to do with him.

"As a captain working for me, you will have wealth and adventure, a chance to smuggle valuable cargoes of cotton and war materials in and out of the South."

Townsend spat indignantly. "You have taken my boat and now you want me to do what? Run through the Union blockade?"

"Exactly right, Captain. I want you to take my cargoes through the blockade into Texas, Florida, or Alabama. I need a competent captain."

"There are plenty of good captains in this city. Ask one of them."

"I'm afraid I've made my choice. I want you for many reasons, chief among them your experience. I spoke with the sailors on your crew before they were deported, and they had only good things to say about your seamanship. It appears you are an excellent navigator, not as common a skill as you might imagine."

"That may be true, but I am no smuggler," Townsend said emphatically. Pressure began building on his forehead, and he knew he would have to restrain himself.

"I would think a young man like you would find it an enjoyable occupation. It is not as perilous as it may sound. The fact is the Union Navy doesn't have enough gunships, particularly here in the Gulf of Mexico. Far too few ships to adequately patrol the shoreline from Florida to the Rio Grande, far too many harbors, inlets, and passages."

"Go find somebody else. I have no interest. I won't run the Union blockade. I have no desire to sail for the Rebel cause."

"Indeed."

The man's smile was ever present. The merchant paused as he relit his cigar, all the while glaring at Townsend.

"I'm afraid, Captain, what you want to do is not important. I may be your only choice to save yourself."

Townsend felt the walls closing in on him. Sr. Alvarado Cardona kept smiling. Only the slight twitch of the moustache revealed the man's true feelings.

"I will pay you an acceptable rate of six hundred dollars round trip. You will find that is competitive with other schooner captains here."

Townsend could see he was dealing with a man of business, but every word made him feel sick inside.

"The profit from the cargo of course is mine initially, but as captain, you will get a percentage profit from the cargo of cotton on the return trip. I will pay you seven dollars per bale of cotton you bring to Havana, a very generous gesture on my part. Again you will find my offer is more than fair."

The merchant took several appreciative puffs on his cigar. He cocked his head at the two guards who were still there with their guns and the shackles. Townsend caught that look, and even though he felt his anger rise, he told himself to calm down.

"And if I don't agree to your terms?"

"Well, naturally I don't know what a military tribunal might decide about your case, but as I said earlier, you might never leave this place."

"Why would you trust me?"

"In your case, it is my hope, necessity will lead to trust."

"But I could just sail away."

"I hope that eventually you will see what a promising business opportunity I am offering." He paused and pulled something out of his coat pocket.

"Here is our contract. I took the liberty of writing it up. It only requires your signature. Should you fail to comply and attempt to run off, it clearly explains that the Spanish navy will pursue you and should you flee to the United States, the Spanish captain general will request your extradition as someone guilty of crimes against Spain, and Cuba. If you sign it now, you are free to walk out with me."

Townsend took the contract in hand. He wanted to tear it up and then stuff it into this arrogant Spaniard's mouth, but he forced himself to stiffen his back, and look directly at the man in front of him.

"All charges dropped and I will be released right now?"

"Yes."

Townsend picked up the pen, his fingers trembling. He had no idea who the man was or why he had so much power. He felt his self-respect slipping away. He thought of his dead brother. His father would have two Rebel sons now. He forced himself to sign the document. The two men shook hands. Townsend noted the firm handshake and the man's lingering stare even as he felt helplessly ensnarled in a situation he was powerless to change. He was close enough to notice that the man had an odd, musky sweet smell, and as he looked more closely at his slicked-back hair he guessed the strong scent came from his hair oil.

"My congratulations, Captain Townsend," said the Spaniard, shaking his hand. "I know we will have an excellent relationship. By the way, please call me Don Pedro from now on. Most everyone does."

The guards escorted him out of the prison. They gave him back his old clothes, still crumpled and stained with Michael Abbott's blood. The sight of the now brown stains brought back the horror of that night, and he shuddered as he tried to forget the sight of the knife, the drums echoing in his head. He felt vulnerable, like a mouse cornered by a cat. Now he was to be a blockade runner, a hired man working for a Spanish merchant from Havana on the Rebel supply line. It seemed surreal. He and his new employer walked out into the open courtyard outside the yellow limestone prison building in the midst of a military ceremony. Townsend felt the warmth of the hot sun on his face and he took a deep breath of sea air. Off to his right he caught a glimpse of the Gulf of Mexico and a small fortress, but the sound of trumpets brought his attention back to the prison yard.

There were hundreds of soldiers in formation lining the perimeter, all dressed in their narrow striped blue and white jackets, flashy red cockades, and carrying their Belgian-made rifles. It looked like an entire infantry regiment in addition to some cavalry with their blue linen uniforms and palm leaf hats. He could hear the roll of military drums as several robed priests carrying a crucifix walked slowly toward an elevated platform where a chained man in a white shroud and wearing a white cap was seated. On the platform behind the seated man was a large black man wearing a hood over his head. Townsend didn't need to be told what he was looking at.

"What good fortune," the Spaniard exclaimed. "You will see the *garrote* in action before you leave the prison."

He pointed to the large hooded man.

"I should tell you the story of the city's executioner. Some years ago he was a slave, sentenced to death for killing a man. In return for his life and his freedom, he agreed to take on this job and become the state's executioner. I am told he finds it to be a suitable arrangement."

A suitable arrangement indeed, Townsend thought. His contract with Don Pedro sounded much the same. He watched as the priests finished crossing themselves, and then there was a drum roll. Suddenly the convicted man in the chair cried out, "*¡Viva Cuba Libre! ¡Muerte a los Peninsulares!*" It was a cry for an independent Cuba and death to the Spaniards. Townsend watched in horror as the executioner stepped up quickly to the chair and began twisting and turning a lever, tightening the iron collar around the prisoner's neck. The man's neck was thrust forward, his body twisted and writhed for what seemed like an eternity. He tried to shout again, but no sound came out. The spinal cord snapped and the prisoner's head fell to the side. There was a moment of silence and then the trumpets sounded, announcing the news to the city that another death row inmate had been eliminated.

Townsend looked over at the stiff profile of Don Pedro, whose chin was slightly raised as he scanned the line of infantry that now stood at attention.

"A quick death for a filthy Creole traitor," Don Pedro said with conviction in his voice.

"What was his crime?" Townsend asked somberly.

"I believe he tried to help a Negro escape from the island."

Townsend knew from the man's cry there was more to it than that, but he said nothing. He felt an unease inside his skin, a sense that he was no longer quite the person he thought he was. As they walked toward the thick outer walls of the prison, Townsend could hear the noises from the open street. The prison guard at the arched entrance door looked at him suspiciously, but at a signal from Don Pedro the man motioned them on. As Townsend passed the guard, he uttered a silent prayer that the officer would not call him back and tell him there was a mistake and he must return.

6

February 12, 1863

Townsend had gotten used to the pungent smells on the docks, an odd mixture of dried fish, human sweat, and tobacco smoke. He had been living aboard the *Laura Ann* tied up at the wharf since his release. He rubbed his stubbly chin and combed his curly hair with the fingers of his right hand. He had cleaned himself up as soon as he got out of prison, but now his beard was growing in again. He knew he needed a shave, but he didn't much care. It had felt strange at first, returning to the schooner, empty of all the crew. He'd heard the Spanish police had deported them to Key West on the regular mail boat that came into Havana. None of the Irish sailors meant that much to him, but he would have liked to say goodbye to Clyde Hendricks. He had asked Don Pedro if he had any information about him, and the Spaniard had just shrugged off the question.

Outside the ship's cabin, Townsend could hear the rhythmic work songs of the slaves and the wheeling of crates on stone. He walked up the schooner's companionway out onto the raised quarterdeck, and looked out at Havana's main docking area where all the trading schooners and three-masted tallships came to load and unload cargo. He scanned the landing, or *muelle de caballería*, as it was called. He was looking for any sign of Don Pedro. The Spaniard had asked for a full report on the condition of the ship's hull. Townsend had spent most of the morning inspecting the schooner's musty cargo hold area. The scurrying of small feet and the squeaking in the darker corners had told him there were plenty of rats that no doubt had boarded the schooner before they left New York. But rodents were not his major concern. He'd spent several hours poking his knife into a particularly wet area in the midsection of the ship's hull where he'd found large areas of rotting wood. Many of the planks were so soft and punky he could put his finger through them. The schooner would have to be hauled out of the water onto a railway for some major repairs. He knew he needed to let Don Pedro know as soon as possible.

Not too far away, Townsend could see the two men assigned by Don Pedro to be his watchdogs. They were leaning on some hogsheads of molasses, glaring at him as if he were a newly acquired dog. They hadn't let him out of their sight ever since he got out of prison. Don Pedro had introduced them as his "business associates." Any problem you might have, he told him, they can help you. Townsend particularly disliked the smaller of the two men. Arturo Salazar was short and thin with a narrow face and a scraggily beard. He was dressed in a rumpled, tan linen suit and a matching flat-brimmed hat. His eyes were a cold light blue like the Gulf Stream, unusual for a Spaniard. Don Pedro said he was from La Coruña in northern Spain where some Galicians have light-colored eyes. The other man, Manuel Rodríguez, went by the nickname Nolo. He was a powerful, thick-set, darker-skinned Spaniard with a sloped-back forehead, and a hawk-like nose. Don Pedro said he had been brought to Cuba from Spain as an orphan from the interior of Cataluña. Both men spoke some English, and it was clear from the familiar way that some of the police and other officials greeted them that they were well-known figures on the docks.

Townsend averted his gaze from his two watchdogs as he continued to scan the crowded wharf. The frenzy of the day's buying and selling was well underway. The main landing was a swirling mix of disheveled sailors, shirt-less slaves, donkey carts, and stacks of everything from lumber and bricks to wooden kegs filled with incoming turpentine and outgoing rum. Off to one side, squads of soldiers and police stood ready to quell any disturbance. Underneath the shady arcade of the warehouse buildings, well-dressed merchants haggled with each other, but there was no sign of Don Pedro. Amid all the activity, Townsend couldn't help but notice that the quays were piled high with cotton bales. The warehouses were crammed full of wooden crates awaiting export to Texas, Alabama, and Florida, everything from British-made Confederate uniforms, ammunition, and guns, to medicine. It was no exaggeration to say Havana had become a huge foreign supply depot for the Confederacy.

The aroma of garlic wafted over the ship's decks, signaling Townsend it was time to eat. He'd become a frequent customer at some of the cheap taverns in the back alleys near the docks that specialized in plates of fried fish, yucca, and *ajiaco* stew. He'd grown to like swilling down his meals with dark rum or red wine and a cup of *café fuerte* or a pot of hot chocolate afterward, all for less than a sixteenth-ounce gold coin. By now, Townsend had become familiar with the currency in Cuba. The Spanish doubloon, or *onza* as it was often called, was worth seventeen dollars, the other smaller coins just fractions of that amount. There was no problem changing American coins. It was easy to go to one of the many *Cambio de Moneda*, currency exchange shops scattered around the city and get his half doubloons changed into silver *reales* and *pesetas* or American dollars.

As Townsend stepped off the boat onto the docks, he was quite aware of his two minders. He made no effort to hide his resentment toward these men with their ominous scowls. The idea that he was forced to become a hired captain to run the Union blockade increasingly grated against him, shortening his temper. He swore silently that he would try to escape Don Pedro's clutches as soon as he could.

As an experiment, he walked away from the docks toward the *bodegas* and taverns without checking with them first. The two Spaniards caught up with him and held onto him as if they were placing him under arrest.

"*¿A dónde va?*" Salazar asked, first in Spanish and then in English. "Where are you going? You know the rules."

Salazar tightened his grip on Townsend's left arm even as Nolo placed himself squarely in front of Townsend to block his path.

"Do you want to go back to prison, *Yanqui?*" Nolo added with a sneer as he put his face close to Townsend's. "*¿Quiere volver a la cárcel?*"

The young captain pushed them both away and cursed at them. Nolo grabbed him with an iron-fisted grip, and Townsend wrenched free. Before it turned into a fight, Don Pedro, dressed in his formal dark business suit, seemed to emerge from nowhere, and began to smooth things over. As usual he was smoking his signature full-length cigar.

"*Cálmense, muchachos*, he said to the two Spaniards. "*Yo me encargo de Townsend.* I will take care of this." After calming down Salazar and Nolo, he explained to Townsend again how he had assigned the two men to the *Laura Ann* just for his personal safety, and naturally the protection of the ship.

"As you know, Havana has a knife-prone waterfront," Don Pedro said with barely hidden malice.

Townsend tried to tell him about the survey of the ship, but the sound of cannons being fired from El Morro caused the Spaniard to rush off to see what was happening. Two Confederate-owned schooners flying the Stars and Bars Rebel flag were just entering the harbor, having run the blockade.

They were out of the Sabine River area in east Texas. The schooners were so heavily loaded they looked like floating piles of cotton under sail. A Spanish navy screw-propeller frigate fired off one of its cannons to show its sympathy and support for the incoming ships, which set off copycat gun salutes booming out from the walls of El Morro. The smell of gunpowder hung in the air.

Townsend had seen enough to know that the Spanish claim of neutrality was somewhat of a charade. From reading the conservative newspaper *Diario de la Marina*, he knew the Spanish sympathies lay solidly with the South. He had heard relations between the Spanish and American governments were still tense ever since a month earlier when the Spanish authorities allowed the Confederate sloop-of-war, the *Florida*, to run into Havana harbor. Not only was the gunship allowed to recoal and resupply, but then the commanding officer, Lieutenant John Maffitt, was permitted to exchange intelligence with Confederate representative Charles Helm. Forty-eight hours later after leaving Havana, the Confederate gunship destroyed seven US flagged merchant ships off the coast of Cuba and the Bahamas. Tensions had grown worse when three days later a Spanish navy gunboat fired two shots from its deck guns at a small US mail steamer leaving Havana for Key West. The stated offense was that the US Army mail tug handed off some intelligence information to an American war steamer within Spanish territorial waters. Many in Cuba thought the US Navy might retaliate, but nothing had happened. The latest news in the Havana newspapers was adding fuel to the fears of another flashpoint between Spain and the United States. The Rebel gunboat CSS *Alabama* had burned and sunk three American merchant ships off the coast of Haiti, and rumors were already circulating that this screw sloop-of-war might soon come into Havana Bay to recoal.

As soon as the two cotton-laden schooners tied up, a small army of Negro stevedores stood ready to begin work. Townsend could see the overseers, whips in hand, moving out of the shade under the arcade, and the merchants from the M.A. Herrera house that managed many of the Confederate shipments checking their inventories. The unloading and loading of the newly arrived blockade runners would soon begin. To ensure order, Spanish soldiers and police clustered along the edge of the quay, conspicuous in companies and squads near the San Francisco Plaza.

Amid grim threats and menacing shouts from the overseers, the shirtless Negro stevedores trundled down the gangways, pushing their bulky cotton-laden drays, sweat running down their backs and faces, their arm muscles bulging. Each bale of cotton weighed from four hundred to five hundred pounds, or twenty *arrobas*, the Spanish unit of measurement. What was it that Don Pedro had called the dockworkers who killed at night? *Ñañigos*.

He repeated that word silently to himself, and remembered what his new employer had told him after he'd asked him about Michael Abbott.

"What happened to the Englishman I was with?" Townsend had asked. "Do you know?"

Don Pedro had almost seemed not to hear the question. He paused for a moment before answering.

"It was the *ñañigos* who probably attacked you."

"Who are they?" Townsend had asked.

"Slaves, *negros*, dockworkers mostly. *Ñañigos* wear the devil costumes of the Abakua. It's a secret society that goes back to the Calabaris in Africa. You and your friend, that Englishman, were just in the wrong place at the wrong time."

For a moment, Townsend had thought he would argue with the Spaniard— at least two of the attackers that night were white. Instead he had stayed quiet. Don Pedro looked away but abruptly turned back to Townsend.

"Concerning that Englishman," Don Pedro said, his tone suddenly more aggressive. "I would hope you will forget that man ever existed. He was trying to interfere in Spanish affairs. In Cuba, you must be careful who you help, my friend. Foreigners are welcome here, but they must respect our laws. Just a bit of advice."

It was early in the afternoon when Townsend again spied the slender figure of Don Pedro walking in the hot sun alongside a well-dressed gentleman with a top hat and a sparkling white linen suit. The two crossed the landing over to where Townsend was standing near the boat, weaving between a stacked labyrinth of crates and kegs. Townsend winced as a passing donkey cart lost one of its wheels and overturned directly in front of the two men, causing several hogsheads of semi-refined melado sugar and molasses to break apart. Don Pedro cursed the black driver and the two men gingerly walked around the mess.

A Spanish merchant began beating the driver with a cane, and a white overseer walked toward the accident with a team of black workers in front of him. A squadron of police was not far behind. Despite all the hubbub, Townsend's gaze was drawn to the broken hogsheads. Mounds of different types of sugar poured out onto the stone, all different shades, from light to brown and finally from the bottom of the barrels came a deep molasses black. The different shades and colors reminded Townsend of the patchwork of humanity that surrounded him in Cuba—the races mixed and mingled, but remained separate and unequal. Moments later, Don Pedro broke his reverie and with great fanfare introduced him to "my good friend, The Honorable Charles Helm, the Confederacy's representative and special agent in Cuba."

Townsend quickly assessed the Confederate representative. He looked to be a man in his mid to late forties. He had no hair on his face except for a curious, lonely tuft of curly, dark brown hair tucked neatly under his chin like a clump of moss. Dignified and well dressed, he had the look of a man accustomed to the world of cigars and politics.

Don Pedro gestured toward the *Laura Ann*. "This schooner is my latest acquisition and Townsend here, is its capable captain. As a gentleman from Kentucky, Colonel Helm, I know you would appreciate that Captain Townsend is a true son of the Chesapeake."

Townsend blanched but said nothing. Helm smiled and reached out to shake Townsend's hand.

"It is indeed a pleasure to meet you, sir," he said with a cavalier Southern drawl. Again Townsend said nothing but took the man's hand. Helm looked over the schooner, taking out a small pad to jot down some notes. Don Pedro explained to Townsend that the colonel was a decorated war veteran in the campaign against Mexico. Just two years ago, Helm had finished a three-year stint as consul general for the United States in Havana during the Buchanan Administration, so he was a well-known figure in Cuba, and highly respected by the Spanish government.

Helm beamed at Don Pedro, and gave him a look of steadfast determination.

"On that political note, Don Pedro, I want you to know I have had an audience with the newly appointed captain general of the island, His Illustrious Excellency, Don Domingo Dulce, whom I know you hold in great esteem. He has told me the palace doors are open to me at all times as the representative of the Southern States. He agrees we would all be beggared if we give up slavery. The institution is for our convenience and our interest. So I am hopeful that Spain will soon see fit to recognize the Confederate States of America as a separate nation."

"That is gratifying to hear, Colonel Helm," replied the Spaniard with his stony black, poker eyes.

Helm gestured toward the boat.

"I am most pleased to see, Don Pedro, that you are now acquiring sailing ships. By my calculations, most of the two hundred ships that ran through the blockade here in the Gulf last year, either from Nassau or Havana, were schooners just like the *Laura Ann*. They say the entire coast of Texas is so full of blockade runners now it looks like squirrels runnin' up an oak tree."

Don Pedro chuckled, and turned toward Townsend.

"You should know, Captain Townsend, that Colonel Helm lists every cotton ship that comes into Havana. He records the date, cargo, name of the ship and he knows every ship carrying arms and ammunition across the Gulf of Mexico into Confederate ports."

Helm nodded his appreciation and closed up his notebook.

"When will your vessel be ready for sea?"

"We will be running the blockade shortly to Mobile," Don Pedro replied. "No doubt some patching and painting will be necessary. What's your survey indicate, Captain? How soon will we be ready to go to sea?"

Townsend lifted his eyebrows and cleared his throat.

"I'm afraid the ship is in worse shape than I had imagined," Townsend replied. "Some rotten wood in the planking midsection needs to be replaced."

The Spaniard frowned at this unexpected news, but then quickly restored his ever-present smile, and vigorously began puffing on his cigar.

"That's not a problem. *No hay problema.* My friends at the shipyard will give us prompt attention, I can assure you, Colonel. This schooner will soon look like new. We will be glad to take whatever supplies are needed for the cause, with the regular reduced freight charges naturally."

"Excellent. Excellent," said Helm with a smile. "I am preparing to speak with our British suppliers again. The British consul general in Havana, Mr. Crawford, as you know, has been our warm, ardent friend from the beginning of the war. It is vital we get the next shipment through as one of our schooners was just captured by the enemy off the coast of Texas. Five tons of much-needed gunpowder were seized."

"What cargo will we be carrying into Mobile?" Don Pedro asked.

"Four hundred British Enfield rifles with bayonets, another three hundred Belgian rifles, five hundred cavalry swords, fifty boxes of ammunition and gunpowder, and naturally some items greatly esteemed by our military officers—two dozen boxes of brandies and wines that as per usual should be labeled as medicine. Discretion in such matters is important, as I am sure you can appreciate."

The Confederate agent laughed, and then stroked the tuft of hair hanging under his chin.

"Speaking of discretion, I am sure I don't need to ask, but I presume, when you leave here you will be notifying port authorities that your destination is a neutral port like Belize or Matamoros, Mexico?" Helm winked at the two of them. "For the purpose of keeping up appearances, we do want to respect Spain's claim of neutrality here. Just a formality, you understand."

"But of course, Colonel Helm. *Como siempre.* As always."

"Good. Excellent. That's why I like Don Pedro," Helm said to Townsend with a smile and a nudge. "I have known him a long time, and I believe he could talk a cat out of a tree."

Helm laughed at his own joke. Townsend politely smiled.

"You can, of course, expect to receive the most favorable, cordial reception in Mobile from our Confederate officers. They will provide you with as much cotton as your schooner can hold. How does that bit of fair dealin' sit with you, Don Pedro?"

Townsend could see the Spaniard was pleased. The Confederate portion of the cargo was large, but it was far from filling up the hold of the schooner. He would still be able to make a valuable profit by shipping food items like coffee and tea, which the blockade had cut off and made extremely costly. And for the return voyage, the promise of a ready supply of cheap cotton was clearly what the Spaniard had hoped to hear.

Don Pedro pulled out of his coat pocket a bundle of long cigars and handed them to Helm. The Confederate agent thanked him for the gift, and looked from Don Pedro to Townsend with zealous, forthright eyes. He said he was headed to inspect the latest batch of cotton that had just arrived on the docks from Texas. As he walked away, Don Pedro smiled, an even broader grin than usual.

"You called him Colonel," Townsend remarked. "Is Helm a military man in the Confederate army?"

"No, that's just a symbolic title. A bit of puffery, you might say. *Pura paja. Pura apariencia.* Others call him Major Helm. I have no idea what his military rank is. I like the sound of Colonel, and he's never corrected me."

Don Pedro held his cigar up as he continued to look in the direction the Confederate agent had gone.

"Just think of the profits, my young friend. One bale of cotton purchased in the South is worth eight times that price by the time it reaches England. They say Helm is sitting on a treasure chest of four thousand bales of cotton here on the Havana docks, right now. That is all part of an emergency Confederate fund to pay for all these weapons, cargo we will soon be carrying into the South. It appears this American war is what we call here in Cuba, *una espléndida bonanza,* an excellent opportunity. The clink of gold is as sweet a sound here as it was in the days of Spain's glory years in the *Siglo de Oro.* Only now the gold is cotton."

Alone on the ship, Townsend sat down at the small desk in his cabin. He
pulled out a sheet of paper and began thinking about what he should write.
He wasn't sure how to express himself, but he knew he should let his father
know where he was. With some hesitation, he began writing.

Dear Father,
I am writing to tell you that I have arrived safely in Havana where I have been
given employment . . .

Townsend abruptly stopped and put the pen down. "Hang it all!" He
crumpled up the paper into a tight ball, and threw it against the wall. "What
in tarnation is the use of writing," he said to the empty cabin. He banged
his fist on the table. After what had happened, he was probably as good as
dead to his father. His once-promising career as an officer in the Navy and
his ambitions were over. Perhaps for now it was better not to write. If his
father were to learn what he was doing, it would only worsen the situation.
He sighed. His life had been turned upside down. He felt the stubbly black
hair on his cheeks, scratched his dirty scalp. He knew he looked no better
than many of the rum-soaked sailors that wandered the docks. A wave of
melancholy fell over him. He felt alone and lost.

But he was out of prison—it was a start. Townsend shook off those dark
thoughts, and began writing up the list of the ship's needs. Before leaving,
Don Pedro had told him to draw up a complete inventory of items needed
for the boat to present to the Cabarga's ship chandlery several blocks away
at #7 Obispo Street. With that in mind, Townsend inspected the ship's deck
for caulking needs as well as the condition of the ratlines, fastenings, and
the rigging. He made a note of every halyard and sheet that was in need of
repairs. As he finished surveying the sails in the sail locker, he stopped to
look at a small shelf where Captain Evans had kept his collection of maritime
books. *The Atlantic Navigator* was a favorite of the captain's. He'd seen him
reading that book before they left New York. He leafed through the large
volume. Then he picked up Maury's study of the wind and currents of the
North Atlantic, and finally Blunt's updated edition of *American Coast Pilot*.

In each of these maritime books, the old sailor had written his name on
the inside of the front cover. Townsend noticed there was also a stack of navigational charts of the Gulf of Mexico done by the US Coast Survey. Some
of the charts had rhumb lines drawn in with pencil of possible blockade-

running routes from Havana to several Southern Gulf ports, from Galveston to Mobile to St. Mark's, Florida. How ironic and tragic, Townsend thought. It would be he, not Captain Evans, who would be running through the Union blockade. He would be the one following the rhumb lines, the footsteps of another man's dreams. He felt a twinge of sadness for the old sailor.

Townsend tried to assuage his own troubled conscience by telling himself that fate alone decides when the time has come. Man is powerless to stop the unseen hand of destiny. Life is nothing but a puff of wind, gone before you know it. He whispered to himself the Spanish word to live, *vivir*. He savored the vowels, and then spoke out loud the Spanish word to survive, *sobrevivir*. How curious, he thought. The word *sobre* meant "on top of." If you separated the word into two words, *sobre vivir*, it could be interpreted to mean "to be on top of life." He allowed his troubled mind to wander further. To be on top of life was to overcome one's miseries, the sadness, the fears and the loss. Perhaps life is nothing more than each person's story of confronting these many challenges. Perhaps the only value and meaning in life is the struggle to survive. *Sobre vivir*, he whispered to himself.

Townsend felt the load of Captain Evans's sudden death descend on him. He thought of the loss of his mother and his brother. That too was a heavy weight to bear. He looked again at those pencil lines on the charts, and he shook away his melancholy. He took a deep breath and stood up straight. Life was also about hopes and dreams, he told himself, even if they never become reality. He gave a quick look at some of the routes the old captain had drawn and put them aside where he could readily find them.

The inventory job, tedious as it was, gave Townsend an idea of how he might escape the scrutiny and prying eyes of the two Spanish watchdogs. He wanted to tell Mrs. Carpenter and her daughter what had happened to Abbott. Townsend realized he was the only person who might give them the sad news that in all likelihood, Michael Abbott was dead. In the back of his mind, he knew there was another motivation. There was no denying he felt an attraction to Emma Carpenter. Try as he might, he couldn't stop thinking about the young woman. He couldn't stop humming the melodic strands of Mozart that he'd heard her play on the violin that night.

7

Townsend heard a shout from behind him, someone yelling in Spanish, "¡Atención! ¡Atención!" And then the loud clip clop of horses' hooves and the clattering of wheels getting nearer. Fearful he was being followed, he whirled around to see two fast-moving horses come around a corner, and charge directly at him. The horses were pulling one of the strange-looking Cuban carriages called *volantas* with their huge six-foot-high wheels and the sixteen-foot-long shafts. With a flash of silver mountings on the open chaise body and the gleam of silver spurs on a black-booted Negro postilion, the carriage swept past him into the old square and clattered by the city's cathedral. Inside he caught a glimpse of a man in a top hat smoking a cigar next to two well-coiffed Spanish ladies dressed with black lace mantillas over their heads and shoulders. Townsend breathed a sigh of relief. It wasn't anybody he knew.

The captain was headed for Mrs. Carpenter's boarding house. It was the first time he had left the docks unaccompanied by his two minders, and he walked with a quick light step, enjoying the freedom. He'd told Salazar he had to go to the ship's chandlery. The Spaniard had been too distracted by the arrival of the 220-foot blockade-running steamship called the *Alice* that had just come in from Mobile after a fast run of two and a half days. Salazar hadn't noticed that the normally shabbily dressed young ship captain was wearing a clean pair of duck trousers and a light blue cotton shirt. The new clothes had belonged to Captain Evans, and they hung loosely on his slim frame. They were too big for him, but it was as good as he could do. He'd also shaved and combed his hair.

As Townsend walked through Havana's narrow streets and arcades past announcements of lottery drawings and bullfights, he couldn't help noticing the sharp contrasts. Beggars were on every corner with their hands outstretched. Men in elegant French top hats and formal black dress coats walked side by side with shirtless street peddlers pulling donkeys and mules. It seemed like almost every other person, rich and poor, was smoking a cigar. Townsend met the sharp-eyed stare of one of the Spanish shopkeepers who had picked him out of the crowd as a person of interest. The man, dressed in a rumpled white linen suit, had the lazy gaze of a businessman not overly encumbered by scruples. With a gamy poker smile, the man solicitously beckoned him to come over to his clothing store. To Townsend it was a reminder that in Havana there were always people watching, looking for opportunities.

Moments later, he heard the whistling of a bamboo cane, the cruel crack of a whip followed by the gruff commands of soldiers. He stopped abruptly, his neck stiffening. These sounds were all too familiar. It was the prison chain gang trudging by on their way to clean out sewage from the street gutters. A small regiment of soldiers armed with pistols and swords surrounded them to make sure they didn't escape. In prison, Townsend had often heard these poor souls painfully shuffle by his cell, but he'd never seen them from his solitary confinement. Each one of the men had an iron band riveted around his ankles and his waist with chains dangling between them. He pulled his hat down and turned away as he listened to the scraping of chains on stone pass him by. He found himself staring at the doors and windows of the thick stone buildings around him. They all had iron bars. At that moment, he felt as if he were back in the prison, shackled and under interrogation. A sudden panic swept over him.

Townsend turned to run, but then he heard a shrill whistle and peals of laughter. A pretty coffee-colored woman dressed in a bright yellow blouse with a tray of sweet pastries balanced on her head was laughing at him. He quickened his step to a fast walk until he arrived at an open-air market in the Plaza Vieja. There in the middle of the noisy market he lost himself in a crowd, a dizzy blur of smiling eyes, straw hats, and red and yellow turbaned heads. The shouting and yelling of buying and selling competed with the clanging and chiming of church bells. Flies swarmed everywhere, from the meat counters to the garbage bins to the faces of small barefoot and naked black children picking up scraps on the street.

"¡Naranjas! ¡Naranjas!" cried an approaching toothless black woman who was vigorously sucking on an orange as she pushed her way through the crowd. The oranges were selling for ten cents a half-dozen. Another woman was selling custards made with coconut milk, and a mixture of tropical fruits he had never heard of, *guayaba, zapote,* and *mamey.* He shook his head and walked away, swatting the flies that had now discovered him. So this is Havana, he said to himself, the tropical crossroads in the Gulf, one of the few remaining footholds for the Spanish in the New World. He looked inside one of the grated windows he passed. A young woman was seated in a cane chair. She was sewing. He stopped to look at her. For a moment, with her sharp features and thin face, he thought she looked like his mother. But when she looked up at him, he realized it was only the black hair that was similar. He wondered if he would ever discover what kind of life his mother had here in Cuba, or why she had left with such anger.

Townsend breathed a sigh of relief as he stepped into Mrs. Carpenter's boarding house. It appeared so different than it had at night. He was immediately struck by how much sunlight filled the high-ceilinged rooms. He looked around the place. The floors were a black and white marble, the rafters some twenty feet above him were painted a light green, and the huge windows were open to the floor. He felt as if it were a refuge from the steamy cauldron of humanity outside. A violin accompanied by a piano played in another room. He followed the music into the central living room, passing a table with bowls of oranges and pineapples. This path took him through wide semicircular arcades that led out to an interior courtyard.

There on the covered veranda a small group of guests were seated, watching and listening to Emma on the violin and a man next to her at the piano. He recognized the music as a sonata his mother had played. He stood at the edge of the courtyard, enjoying the cool breeze and the music. He didn't see Mrs. Carpenter. His eyes focused on Emma's tilted brown head and the fluid movement of the bow as her right arm expressively played the familiar melody. She was a gifted musician. He wondered if she could feel the intensity of his gaze.

Soon it was over. Amid much polite applause, Emma warmly greeted the audience. They were all the new arrivals who had just come off the English passenger steamship, the *Corsica.* Men with gray moustaches, women with flowing black silk dresses, an Old World dandy wearing a gold mounted eyeglass—they circled around the veranda taking measure of one another. Emma announced that she would now take the opportunity to play a favorite violin solo of hers, Bach's Partita #2 in D minor.

With the precise yet lilting sounds of Bach in his ears, Townsend ambled back inside. He could see that a fine buffet was already being set out in a room adjacent to the covered veranda. An older Englishman with a round, bloated face and a protruding stomach was filling his plate even as a waiter was attempting to refill his glass of claret.

"I love listening to Bach in the tropics, don't you?" the Englishman said as he addressed a short woman dressed in a voluminous blue silk dress and a gauzy hat.

"It is such a relief to hear civilized music," she replied with a toothy smile as she fanned herself.

"Quite so," the Englishman replied. "I am so tired of these Africans with their horrific drum beating. Some believe the blacks now outnumber the whites in Cuba. Imagine that! This could be another Saint Domingue, another slave uprising. It is no wonder the Spanish have so many soldiers here. Some say as many as forty thousand armed soldiers."

"Oh, my," said the woman in blue. "This certainly is a garrison city."

Townsend stopped eavesdropping and turned to go back into the library where he spotted Mrs. Carpenter. She was busy scolding some of her maids, most of whom appeared to be Irish. Townsend noticed that some of the young girls with their light blue eyes and freckled faces were scowling at her.

At that point, Mrs. Carpenter spotted Townsend, and turned her attention to him.

"Why, Mr. Townsend how pleasant to see you. These young girls are such a problem. They need so much guidance and training. I pay them seventeen dollars a month, you know when, in fact, they should be paying me. I like to say my small hotel is the best run of any in Havana. Of course, Mrs. Almy down on San Pedro Street might disagree. But then so would some of the other American lady innkeepers like Mrs. Bremer and Mrs. Cutbush."

She pulled him off to another room where there was nobody within earshot, and spoke in a hushed whisper.

"How is poor Mr. Abbott faring?"

Townsend relayed to an incredulous Mrs. Carpenter what had happened to Abbott and himself—the attack by the hooded devil figures, and then Townsend's own imprisonment in the Havana City Prison.

"Heaven help us. Truly, I am speechless," she said as she reached for a handkerchief. "Havana is not a safe place. I am so sorry to hear this troubling news, Mr. Townsend. Her voice cracked slightly. "I don't even want to ask. Is Mr. Abbott . . . I mean is he . . . ?"

Before he could answer, Emma walked into the room. From the concerned look on her face, it was clear that she had overheard some of the conversation.

"What has happened to Mr. Abbott?" she demanded quietly.

"I don't know exactly," Townsend said, slightly flustered at the sight of her. She was even prettier than he remembered. He shook his head. "I mean . . . I was just telling your mother—"

Eleanor Carpenter interrupted and pulled her daughter closer.

"He was knifed in the street, Emma," she whispered.

"Lord have mercy!" Emma clutched her hands to her chest.

"I am sorry to have to tell you this," Townsend said softly. "As I was recounting to your mother, he was stabbed. We were surrounded by this mob of costumed street dancers tromping and beating their drums. I was knocked out, and when I came to, there was no sign of him. I woke up on the street in a pool of blood, presumably his blood. That's really all I know."

"Could he have escaped?" Emma asked.

"I suppose so," Townsend said with an uncertain shrug. "I suppose it's possible."

Emma turned away, looking at the wall. Her eyes were red and moist. After several seconds of awkward silence, she spoke softly to her mother.

"Mother, you don't suppose this could have been the work of—"

Mrs. Carpenter gave Emma a look of warning.

"Shush. Sometimes it's best not to talk about these things. . . ."

Then she turned to Townsend, speaking in a controlled whisper. "Remember the walls have ears here. May I ask, sir, how did you gain your freedom? Are you a fugitive?"

"No, I was released, but I will tell you I feel lucky to be alive."

Not wanting to upset her or Emma, Townsend said little of his own trauma in the jail. The government had seized his ship and deported the crew. He told them he'd been freed thanks to a Spanish merchant who had purchased his ship from the government and had now hired him as the captain.

"So that was the condition of getting released?" Mrs. Carpenter asked.

"Yes, I had no choice. Circumstances obliged me to take the job."

Townsend didn't want to say much else. From her accent, he knew she was a daughter of the North.

"And who is this merchant of mercy?" Mrs. Carpenter asked with a barely disguised note of sarcasm.

"Don Pedro Alvarado Cardona."

"Alvarado Cardona," she repeated. "No, I don't think I know that name, but you should be careful with any of these merchants here in Havana. They are the money lenders, the island's bankers, an unscrupulous bunch. Not to be trusted."

She paused and took a deep breath, trying to collect her thoughts.

"Do be careful, Captain. You know scarcely a night passes here when a murder or a robbery isn't committed, and, I might add, never reported. As for Mr. Abbott," she sighed as she wiped her eyes, "let us hope and pray for the best. We must believe God is looking out for him."

Townsend looked from Mrs. Carpenter to her daughter. He could tell from their uneasy expressions that they knew more than they were saying.

"Mr. Townsend, you must excuse us. I don't mean to be rude, but Emma and I must see to our guests now."

"Yes," said Emma. "Let me see you out." As they walked through the house, Townsend looked more closely at Emma. He thought he caught her stealing a glance at him, once or twice. It was her eyes that captivated him, a cinnamon brown color, almond shaped with a slight upward slant. Cat-like, framed by dark eyebrows, they commanded attention.

"What are your plans? I assume you will be leaving Havana soon?"

"We are readying the schooner to go to sea."

"Oh," she said with some hesitation in her voice. "You're not one of those blockade runners are you?"

Townsend's face reddened at the directness of her question.

"No, of course not. I mean . . . I haven't been told where we will be sailing."

Townsend didn't know why he lied, but he had, and that was that. He looked down and scuffed his feet on the floor.

"I hope you will come and visit us again, Captain. Perhaps on Sunday, when we will have fewer guests and won't be so busy."

On his way out, Townsend noticed some pencil sketches of Havana on a side table, all finely drawn with dark and half tone shading, some with colorful splashes of watercolor. One was of a harbor scene depicting the loading of cotton onto a blockade runner. He leaned over to look more closely. The artist had captured a moment of cruelty on one of the ships. A white man with a harsh and ruthless face was kicking one of the black stevedores. But what stood out were the expressions of the onlookers, smiling, leering unsympathetic faces yelling encouragement. At the bottom was the title, "Applause for the Devil." He noticed the signature at the bottom right. Emma Carpenter. So she was a sketch artist with a sharply observant eye as well as a fine musician. He wondered what more she knew about Michael Abbott, and hadn't wanted to say in front of her mother.

8

It was 7:00 a.m. and the early morning bells were ringing from all sides of the city. Townsend stepped onto a ferry boat that would take him across the harbor from Old Havana to the working class town of Regla. The schooner had been pulled up on a marine railway at a local shipyard there. Townsend was going to oversee the scraping and the painting, and to assess the condition of the ship's wooden hull. The sun was rising over the land as the small steamer chugged and thumped its way across the bay. The young captain pulled his flat-brimmed hat firmly down on his head. The weather had warmed up considerably, and he could feel it was going to be another hot, windless day. He looked over toward the west side of Regla at the long row of sugar warehouses that lined the deep-water docks there. He'd counted them, some fifty-eight in all. This was where the island's big-money sugar crop came in by railroad to be loaded onto the ocean-going ships. Don Pedro called it Havana's Brooklyn. Now the wharves were filled with not only thousands of hogsheads of sugar and sacks of coffee, but mountains of cotton bales brought in from the southern Gulf states by the blockade runners.

As the ferry boat slid up alongside the main landing at Regla and thudded against the stone, Townsend could hear the screeching of cranes and the rhythmic songs of the Negro stevedores. The day's work had already begun. He stepped out onto the wharf and walked by the Confederate sidewheel steamer, *Alice*, where the stevedores continued to unload the last of its cargo of cotton. The large blockade runner had its steam up, and was clearly hoping to load a new shipment and make another run through the Union blockade. Farther away he could see the large bluff bowed freight steamers from England where the cranes were unloading crates of war supplies. He felt torn and conflicted. Just two months ago, when he was still in the Naval Academy, he would have been repelled by what he was now doing. Now looking at those crates of arms and ammunition headed for the South, he could feel his inner turmoil mounting.

A broad hot sun was rising over Havana Bay as Townsend joined the other workers painstakingly scraping and chiseling away at the heavy layer of barnacles on the schooner's hull. Like most schooners, the bottom was not copper sheathed so the wood was vulnerable to sea worms, and even a month in Havana's murky, polluted harbor left a ship's bottom covered with sea moss. With each stroke of the mallet onto the chisel head, Townsend felt he was chipping away at himself, layer by layer. It was as if he were a different person. A part of him wondered if inside his skin he was being transformed like the boat—or was he more like a chameleon that only changed colors outside to blend in with his surroundings? He wasn't sure. The boat was all he had of his previous life now, but with each scrape and chisel of the old paint he felt a pang of unease.

Townsend took a deep breath of sea air as he surveyed the ship standing upright out of the water. Some of the schooners in the harbor had definite sags at the bow and the stern, and were said to be "hogged," a sure sign of old age. Fortunately, he didn't see any obvious signs of that on the ship. Don Pedro had changed the schooner's name along with the registration. Her new name was *Gaviota*, which was seagull in Spanish, and her new homeport was Havana. She was now flying the broad red and yellow stripes of Imperial Spain. He touched the schooner's white oak planking, now exposed wood, and he felt a controlled burn of confidence inside of him. He looked up at the wide loblolly pine masts above him. He and the boat shared the same heritage. They were Chesapeake-born. A different flag and a new name did not change the identity of the boat, he told himself, and the unfortunate circumstances he found himself in did not change who he was.

At the sound of cannons being fired from El Morro he jumped. He scanned the harbor entrance and saw a funnel with billowing black smoke. No doubt another blockade runner arriving with more cotton. He shook his head as he realized just how easily he became startled. Never far from his mind were the menacing voices of his interrogators as they kept asking him about Michael Abbott, their probing, accusatory stares, the fusillades of rifles. Some nights he would wake up in a cold sweat. It was always the same dream. He was back in prison, walking barefoot with a hood over his face, his heart racing at the roll of drums, the blare of bugles. Then he would wake up with a shout, and lie there in his bunk breathing shallowly, his body drenched in sweat, trying to be calmed by the rhythmic sounds of the rigging slapping against the masts.

Townsend didn't understand why Michael Abbott was so important to the Spanish authorities. He couldn't imagine how this Englishman could be a threat to the island's security. He needed to find out more about Abbott and why he came to Cuba, if only to protect himself from whomever the Englishman's enemies were.

He thought about going back to the cathedral where Abbott had sought assistance. He hoped that after being stabbed, the Englishman had been able to drag himself there. But then Townsend remembered the frightened face of the robed man looking at him through the barred window. The religious man had turned away when Townsend had beckoned to him. No, it would be too risky to go there. Far better to find out what more he could from the Carpenters, mother and daughter. Mrs. Carpenter clearly had not wanted to reveal much, but that was understandable. Emma seemed to care a great deal about Michael Abbott. She might know more. He would have to go back to the boarding house. That thought brightened him.

The grinding whirr of saws and the banging of mallets brought his attention back to the ship up on the rails. The other workers, most of whom were from the Canary Islands, were beginning to scorch the bottom of the hull with blazing torches to kill any sea worms that had penetrated the wood. Townsend thought about the changes that would soon be made to the schooner. He and Don Pedro had met at Cabarga's ship chandlery to discuss them. While the chandlery's clerks carefully measured out lengths of rope for sheets and halyards for the *Gaviota*, Don Pedro had introduced him to one of the old grizzled men there who sat at a corner table, an American by the name of Thomas Godfrey, originally from Newburyport. Godfrey had been a slave captain, a coal trader operating from Havana. Townsend marveled at the number of connections Don Pedro seemed to have, everyone from high-ranking Spanish officials and diplomats to slave traders.

The old captain had given Don Pedro and Townsend a list of ways to camouflage the ship. Some of the tricks of the ebony trade, he'd said, would apply just as well to running the blockade. It was all about eluding capture. The tops of the masts should be painted a dark green-black to make them look like the tops of pine trees. The white canvas sails should be soaked in a black coal ash slush to turn them a dusky dark color, difficult to spot at night. And most importantly, as soon as the scraping and burning of the worms was done and the hull re-caulked, the ship should be repainted gray to make it less visible at sea. All that needed to be done before the schooner would be ready.

The sound of women chanting in the distance caused Townsend to stop his chiseling and look up. A procession of black women with their bright-turbaned heads sang and wailed as they marched from the road and waded into the sea. He asked the man working next to him what these women were doing. The Spaniard looked at him with a pair of deep-set, sorrowful eyes.

"*Quieren regresar a África*," he said in the quick-fire Spanish that was common among the Havana boatmen. The man laughed drily and went back to scorching the wood. "*Puras tonterías de los esclavos*, just slave nonsense. They are asking Yemayá, the African Goddess of the Sea, to take them home, back across the ocean, back to Africa."

Townsend lingered as he pondered this poignant sight, admiring the harmony of their voices. The women were waving their arms back and forth as they sang and swayed. Like him, he thought to himself, these Africans had no way back. Yet they sang and they prayed. They held onto some distant hope. They were trying to keep alive their memories. Next to the women, a familiar profile of a man stood stiffly erect at the wharf's edge. From the slender, stiff shape of the body he knew who it was. Salazar.

Townsend had confronted Don Pedro about the two watchdogs, and asked him to call them off. The merchant had shrugged with a resigned but steely look on his face and said, "It is for your own protection and naturally my insurance policy. I don't want to lose my ship captain, and the authorities don't always make inquiries about dead sailors." What was not stated but understood was that Don Pedro didn't trust him. Townsend turned back to the ship and continued his work with the chisel and the mallet. The afternoon sun felt as hot as a blacksmith's furnace.

Tired and dirty, Townsend walked into the bar to the sounds of a slow-picked guitar. A Spanish woman was singing a mournful love ballad. Sailors' bars in Havana all looked similar, with a labyrinth of small dark rooms. Drunken tars over the years had scrawled notes and scripture on the greasy walls. The words were like sailors' epitaphs. He stopped briefly to read one in large letters, "May the Lord, Jesus take me from this forsaken, unholy city. Look down upon me with forgiveness for the evil deeds I have done." The place was called *El Toro del Mar*, or Bull from the Sea. It was one of Havana's many fandango taverns. Don Pedro had suggested he start looking for a crew, and this was a rowdy dive in the San Isidro section of the old city, known as a popular watering hole for those who favored the Southern cause.

Before sitting down, Townsend took a good look around. Grim-faced men slouched over the tables. Sullen and resentful, they looked at him like cornered, kicked dogs. There was a scattering of fleshy women in cheap chiffon perched on the laps of sailors. These women wore low-necked dresses, and high-heeled shoes. Their eyebrows, arched and plucked, only served to make their eyes seem more cold. Besides the Spanish singer, the other voices he heard in the noisy din of the tavern were English. He'd come to the right place. At one of the breaks in the music, a rum-faced ship captain got up on top of a chair and raised his glass. He announced that he was a Scottish veteran of a Louisiana Volunteer Infantry Regiment who was now running the blockade with his own schooner.

"Dram up lads. Ah have an important toast tae mak'."

"Hear, hear. Let's hear it."

"I'm wantin' ta wish ye all some luck. Let us in the business o' blockade running toast the Southerners fur producing the cotton."

"Hear hear!"

"The Yankees fur blockading the ports."

"Hear hear!"

"And the English fur keeping th' price of cotton up!"

"Hear, hear!"

"Here it is, a toast ta all three. May the war between the North and South continue!"

The barroom broke out in cheers and calls for more drinks. A group of Southerners began singing "Bonnie Blue Flag." A heated discussion was going on among some of the more serious drinkers at the bar. Experience told Townsend to move away from the sounds of trouble. He sat down in a shadowy corner. From there he could watch the spectacle. Confederate loyalists at the bar wearing ragged gray uniforms or butternut jackets were giving a few sailors a hard time.

"Don't give them a drink, bartender. They've just delivered cotton that's going to supply the Yankees. They're Yankee spies off that steamer *Alice*."

"All we did is deliver the cargo," one of the men protested.

"Liars! You're getting paid with Yankee money. That cotton you brought in is going to New York. You're sellin' cotton to the enemy!"

It looked like there would be a fight soon. Like the calm before a storm, the music and the singing stopped, and conversation at the other tables went suddenly silent. Townsend noticed there was a contingent of police at the door watching and waiting. The noise must have attracted them. His first instinct was to get up and run out the back door, but then he noticed there were police standing there as well.

"What's all this about?" Townsend asked the man next to him, a big man with a weathered face, bushy bright red beard, and coarse skin like sand. He spoke with a gravelly Southern drawl that conveyed many years of chewing and smoking tobacco.

"Case of spy fevah, I reckon."

"What's that?" Townsend asked.

"Somethin' that people git during a war when they're lookin' for scape-goats. The blockade is tightenin' up like a prison gate. The Federal Navy has two whole blockading squadrons now covering the Gulf Coast. With N'Orleans in Federal hands, it's not as easy to get through as it were before. These Southun boys heah are lookin' for someone to blame."

Townsend could see a large knife under the man's old waistcoat. By Span-ish law, sea knives were supposed to be left on board ship, but most of the foreign sailors in Havana ignored this regulation.

"Heh, you sodbusters. Leave them alone!" shouted the man as he tugged at his leather suspenders. "I know those sailors and they ain't done nothin' wrong."

The silence deepened. One of the Confederate troublemakers flaunting secession insignias walked over to where they were seated.

"So, you boys traitors too? How much they paying ye to spy on us," he hissed as he spit a gob of tobacco juice on the floor in front of them.

"You white-livered, low-flung half-breed," exclaimed Townsend's new acquaintance as he jumped up, almost falling when his feet slid on the slimy gob of tobacco juice on the stone floor. At that moment, the police stepped in and hauled the Confederate man outside for questioning. To smooth over the dispute, the bartender called over about a half-dozen of the bar girls who were serving drinks, and motioned for them to mingle with the men.

Townsend's new acquaintance was a man of few words at first, but they eventually struck up a conversation. His name was Tom Withers, but he liked to be called Red Beard. He was a native of Texas. He looked to be about thirty years old. He'd started out in a cotton screw gang in Galves-ton and learned how to load cotton. He had been employed most of his life on cotton packets and then more recently on small cargo schooners and brigs on the Gulf. When the war broke out he became a pilot for the Confederate States Navy on board one of the sea steamers assigned to the Defense Squadron on the Mississippi. He found that after completing his one year of conscription, he didn't much care for his superior officer or the Confederacy.

"I guess there are those who might say I weren't loyal to the Confederit cause," Red Beard chuckled, running his hand through his whiskery beard.

"Truth is, I believe I done my share. I don't much care beans about this war one way or the other, not a single old red eyed bean."

"So what will you do now?" Townsend asked.

"I'm fixin' to run the blockade. I'm just lookin' to make some money. I got no family obligations. No home. I know these waters better than most. I been haulin' cotton ever since I was a boy in every ragtag cotton hole from Sabine River to the Brazos River on the other side of Galveston."

Townsend described the *Gaviota*, but Red Beard just had one question.

"What she draw?"

"Five and a half feet of draft with the centerboard up. Sixteen feet with the centerboard down."

He nodded approvingly. "Right pretty shoal draft boat. That'll do to git into any number of the bayous and bays along the Gulf."

Townsend offered him a higher than normal salary for a first mate. Thirty dollars in advance and another thirty dollars when they got back to Havana.

"I reckon that's fair dealin'," Red Beard said as he held out his hand. As he shook the man's calloused hand, Townsend noticed how strong his grip was.

"If you're lookin' for other sailors, try that fellow over thar. See the one who's eyeing them dark-eyed sirens."

Withers pointed to a husky man at a table surrounded by four young Spanish women who he was busy charming.

"I ain't a gamblin' man, but I'd be willin' to bet my salvation he would go with you."

The man had a big beaming smile and an even deeper baritone voice that cut through the din of the tavern. He looked to be around twenty-five with an angular face and a full beard. His tangled hair was slightly receding, but despite that flaw, he clearly had what some women find attractive in a man, a broad chest with an equally broad, roguish smile.

"Go on," Townsend said. "What else can you tell me?"

"His name is Pierre Bertrand. He goes by either name. I don't know much about him exceptin' he's lookin' for a berth on a blockade runner. He says he's American, but he speaks English like one of them Frenchies, you know, zee this and zee that. I can tell you he can speak the Spanish. The bartender told me that fellow had grown up as an orphan boy in one of them N'Orleans cathouses on Bourbon Street in the *Vieux Carré*. I reckon that's whar he git his gift with languages, from those handsome Creole gals."

Townsend walked over to introduce himself. Bertrand smiled easily and openly. He spoke English with a French accent, frequently mixing the two languages. He told Townsend he had learned the sailors' trade when he was crimped as a boy and put on board a cotton ship, which sailed from New

Orleans rounding the horn to Valparaiso. He was full of bluster and bravado, but at brief moments, Townsend could see a glimpse of someone else. He noticed a dull, fearful look that spoke of pain and hardship. He offered him the job and when Bertrand accepted, they called Red Beard over, and the three of them ordered a bottle of rum.

It was early in the morning but still dark when Townsend headed back toward the docks. He and his recruits had found themselves in a back room with a second bottle of rum and a cluster of lusty wharf women who wanted to know if they were *Confederados*. It was the first time Townsend had ever heard the Spanish translation of Confederates. He had left his two new crewmembers passed out in some cubicle in the back area of the bar. He was still pretty drunk, and the past few hours had now blurred into a fuzzy memory of dangling gold earrings, heavy wavy hair, and the strumming of a slow-picked guitar. He dimly remembered talking with one of the women. She was a Chilean actress brought to Havana and then abandoned by her lover. She was trying to get enough money for a passage back to Chile. Hearing this story, Bertrand had lied and told her he was the owner of a tallship bound for Valparaiso, and was the one who could help her. Townsend hoped she wasn't that gullible. He'd already gotten a good sense of the man's character. Flattery and falsehoods poured out of Bertrand like stormwater running downhill. He was someone who treated most impediments as opportunities, and that included charming any attractive woman who might resist him.

Townsend listened to the crunch of his own footsteps on the cobblestone streets. He kept looking over his shoulder, and steering clear of the shadowy figures huddled against the dark walls. Even at this late hour, there were open windows with dimly lit lamps swinging from the ceiling. He could see brightly dressed ladies through the iron bars. From the satin and lacy dresses they wore he guessed these were the higher class of working women. Townsend thought of Don Pedro's warning that almost every morning in the harbor a body floats by with its pockets turned inside out. He was learning that Havana's streets had its share of dock rats that drank by day and prowled by night.

He was headed for the rooming house he had found off Jesús María Street. His simple room just had a bed with a straw-filled mattress, a chair, and a table. It was all he needed. And it was cheap at twelve dollars a month, much cheaper and cleaner than staying at the roach-infested boarding house of

Miss Gilbert's down at the docks where some of the transient sailors booked rooms. The cheapest hotels in Havana cost two dollars a day, and the nice boarding houses like Mrs. Carpenter's were more like twelve dollars a week.

Around the corner a block away, he caught a glimpse of someone familiar out of the corner of his eye. Whoever it was didn't want to be seen. The figure had ducked behind a royal palm tree in a small park. He grabbed his sheath knife and walked cautiously over to the tree. There was no one. He couldn't be sure but he thought the figure he'd seen was Nolo. He may have been followed, or perhaps this was a delusion. He was too drunk to know. A mangy skeleton of a dog, slinking away from a pile of garbage, crossed the street in front of him, growling but with its tail between its legs. Someone had once told him you can judge the cruelty of a culture just by observing how the people treat their dogs. By that measure, Spanish Cuba was not a kind place.

9

On Sunday afternoon Townsend eluded his two bodyguards by ducking into a clothing store. He watched and waited until one of the cumbersome *volantas* negotiated a turn around a street corner with difficulty due to a *guajiro* poultry vendor on horseback. The man from the country was carrying two dozen live chickens, strung together by their legs and tied to the horse's neck and withers. The long shaft of the *volanta* snared the rope holding one batch of squawking chickens, setting the birds free and causing the poultry man to begin hurling threats and accusations. This created a useful distraction for Townsend. He boldly walked out a side door. He turned and got a quick glimpse of Nolo standing outside the front door of the shop. He wanted to make sure he didn't follow him to Mrs. Carpenter's boarding house.

When he arrived, Townsend could hear the soprano notes of Emma's violin accompanied by the rich resonant tones of a cello. Mrs. Carpenter seemed happy to see him. She took him to the outdoor courtyard. One of the Irish maids brought out some Earl Grey tea and a plate of molasses cookies. Mrs. Carpenter told him that Emma would join them shortly.

As she poured them both a cup of tea, Mrs. Carpenter seemed intent on finding out more information about him and his background. She had already asked him where he was from, and was trying to learn more about his family. Townsend wondered how he could persuade her to divulge more information about Michael Abbott. He tried a couple of times to suggest he would like to talk about Abbott, but both attempts were unsuccessful. She ignored his hints, and he ended up boldly asking her how she had come to live in Cuba.

Mrs. Carpenter seemed to tense up at that question, but then after a brief moment of silence, she told him how she had been brought to the island from Philadelphia as a young bride. She was married to a Spanish merchant by the name of Enrique Lozada. They had two children, but then a few years after Emma, the third child, was born, he had left to go back to Spain.

"Oh, I see," Townsend said awkwardly, noticing that her voice had taken on a sharper edge. "That's terrible. I'm sorry."

"Well, that was more than fifteen years ago. Ancient history, I suppose. You are probably wondering why I don't use the name Lozada? Legally that is my name, Eleanor Carpenter de Lozada, but with my guests, I prefer the name of Carpenter."

She looked at him with a solemn face, somewhat vulnerable, and Townsend realized he might have trespassed into too-personal territory.

"I bought this boarding house as a way to support myself," she said proudly. "And I raised Emma and her two older sisters here."

"Did you ever contemplate returning to Philadelphia?"

"Why, Captain Townsend you certainly are an inquisitive young man," she said, arching her left eyebrow sharply. But with a deep breath, she continued talking.

"Yes, as a matter of fact I did think of going back, but I quickly dispelled that notion. Given my status—I mean the awkward situation with my husband, it would have created difficulties. I'm not sure I would have been accepted back readily into my family's circle of friends, certainly not without a great deal of harmful gossip. So I stayed in Havana against the advice of my mother and sister in Philadelphia. There was a growing community of expatriate Americans here, more than five thousand. I suppose that's why I remained on the island," she mused. "I always thought it was inevitable that Cuba would one day be American."

Eleanor Carpenter pursed her lips as she poured them both another cup of tea.

She offered him a molasses cookie, looking at Townsend closely, seeming to study his face and his clothes.

"But enough about my life. Let's talk about you, Captain Townsend. You seem well educated, and well spoken, not like some of the dregs you find on the docks. I'm surprised you aren't in the Navy."

"I was a midshipman at the Naval Academy . . . but Navy life didn't agree with me."

"How extraordinary! You were a midshipman? What didn't you like about the Navy?"

"It wasn't for me."

"I see. So you left the Navy to come here to Cuba, and now you're a hired ship captain on a trading schooner."

"I suppose it does seem strange—but circumstances, as you know, obliged me."

Townsend could now feel Eleanor Carpenter's fixed gaze on him, making him feel vulnerable and uncomfortable.

"And where do you sail on your next voyage?" she asked pointedly.

Townsend muttered that they were repairing and refitting the schooner. He was still trying to pull together a crew, but that he had heard Mexico mentioned. Townsend hesitated, and then replied defensively. "Matamoros probably."

"Running the blockade then, are you? I had surmised as much."

"No, no, not really," Townsend stammered, caught off guard by her directness. He knew where Emma had gotten it from.

"Oh come now, Captain. Everyone in Havana knows the merchants and ship owners here file papers clearing for a neutral port, when in fact they're headed for Galveston or Mobile. These days the profits lie in getting through the blockade. Just about any ship that can float here in Havana Bay is being readied to run the blockade."

Townsend muttered that all he knew was that they were headed north into the Gulf.

"Mr. Townsend. I wasn't born yesterday so stop the pretense." Mrs. Carpenter arched her left eyebrow and gave him a skeptical look. "Given your new profession and your Maryland roots, might I assume you are of the Southern persuasion, Captain?"

Townsend tried not to squirm in his chair. He could tell from the stern tone in her voice that she had no love for the Southern cause.

"I consider myself a Southerner, but I grew up in a home that had no use for slavery. My father is a Yankee with little regard for the institution."

"I see. And your mother?"

He paused before answering.

"My mother is . . . or rather was . . . she died recently. She was from here originally."

"Your mother was Cuban? Where from?"

"Matanzas, I think. I'm not really sure."

"You're not sure?"

"My mother never wanted to talk about her past, so sadly I know little to nothing about her life in Cuba."

"I see," Mrs. Carpenter replied, her eyes sparkling with interest at all this new information.

An awkward silence settled in between the two of them. Townsend could tell she wanted to ask another question, but she didn't. After another sip of tea, Mrs. Carpenter suggested they move farther into the garden where there would be more privacy. They sat at a table next to a small water fountain that splattered and splashed noisily into a Moorish-style blue and white tiled basin. She leaned toward him and began speaking in a soft voice.

"I know you want to talk about Abbott. I didn't want to say anything before. Some of the servants might be eavesdropping. The Spanish government is always listening, and even among my staff I never know whom I can trust. Here we should be out of earshot. After your last visit, Emma and I felt we should tell you more about Michael Abbott. We both are worried you could still be in danger, particularly if Abbott is alive. What do you know about him?"

Startled by this unexpected turn in the conversation, Townsend replied, "I know almost nothing. He told me he was investigating an unsolved murder . . . some man who was stabbed to death eight years ago. That's about it."

Mrs. Carpenter looked around her to see if any of the maids were approaching. Satisfied that they were alone, she once again leaned in closer.

"Michael Abbott is a detective from London. Or maybe I should say, was. . . . He came here to investigate the Backhouse murder."

Townsend stared at her with sudden interest.

"Yes, he was investigating the murder of George Backhouse . . . British diplomat. He was Her Britannic Majesty's judge in Havana. Knifed in his own house by what they said was a gang of men. Eight years ago but never brought to justice."

She paused for a moment and patted her hair before continuing.

"We foreigners all knew them. An attractive young couple. George Backhouse was only thirty-seven years old when he died, in his prime. His wife, Grace, could be a bit temperamental at times, but she had a group of friends among some of the other British and German wives. I must admit she wasn't enamored with Cuba. She thought the men were dishonest and the women wore dresses that were provocative and too revealing. She found the city to be dirty, and she hated the pervasive African music. She and her friends would come down here to have tea and some of my coconut lime pie. She seemed more relaxed then. I must say she was always very gracious to me and extremely kind to my daughter. Emma was invited to their home once a week to play the violin. Grace loved her piano, and she and Emma would play duets. She wanted to expose her young daughter, Alice, somewhat of a tomboy, to Mozart and Bach. I think Grace Backhouse missed England terribly. Emma said that she had covered the walls of their house with paintings of the English countryside. She was always talking about returning home."

"What exactly did George Backhouse do here?"

"He had judiciary powers over captured slave ships. By treaty law, he could imprison slavers. An important job."

"But he's a foreigner. I don't understand how. . . ."

Mrs. Carpenter cut him off. "Let me explain. By treaty with England, the Spanish Crown agreed to abolish the slave trade. This was decades ago. The result was the formation of a Joint Commission made up of Spanish and English representatives. But to those of us who live here, this Commission was, and still is considered somewhat of a shameful farce. The fact is slave trading to Cuba has only grown. No one knows for sure, but they say ten to twenty thousand new African slaves are landed here each year. The Spanish government routinely thumbs its nose at the British, and breaks the laws it promised to uphold."

"And Backhouse?"

"Well, as British representative he was supposed to enforce the treaty. As soon as he arrived here, George Backhouse made it clear he took the job seriously. He was no fire-breathing abolitionist, mind you, but he was committed to enforcing the treaty's laws to end slave trading."

"But why investigate this now if the murder took place eight years ago?"

"I asked Abbott the same thing. All I know is what he told me. Grace Backhouse told him she needed to find out once and for all who killed her husband. She had received some new information about the murder and wanted to know if he would help her. He said she was desperate to put the murder to rest. Put it behind her. Truthfully, I fully understand. I can't imagine living with that tragedy. Never knowing who did it, I mean. Thankfully she remarried recently, Abbott said, to a minister, but for all these years, he said she's been nearly destitute, barely scraping by on a budget of one hundred pounds per year. He said her appeals to the British government for further assistance were largely ignored. Frankly I don't know how she managed all these years to bring up those children alone."

Mrs. Carpenter took out some slightly faded and folded newspaper clippings from England and the United States, holding them out to him.

"Abbott took most of his documents with him but he left these old clippings behind in his room. He must have brought them with him from London. I'm not sure what newspapers they came from."

Townsend picked up one slightly crumpled article from September of 1855, with the headline "Murder of Mr. G.C. Backhouse." He read how Backhouse and his dinner companion, Thomas Callaghan, were attacked the evening of the 31st of August after dinner by "a gang of negro ruffians accompanied by two white men" and in the struggle, Backhouse was knifed on his left side, "the knife passing through his lungs and spleen and in about four hours he died."

"Here's another one," Mrs. Carpenter said. "This one has more details about the attackers." Townsend glanced quickly at this other article. It was from London's *The Examiner* dated October 8, 1855. He read how Mr. Callaghan "was thrown on the ground, his arms tied and his watch taken from his person." The article said Backhouse fought back, and "made an manful struggle . . . tried to throw his assailant on the ground, but he was too powerful a man . . . he attempted to take away the monster's knife." That's when Backhouse was stabbed. The article went on to say that the "murderer and all his confederates were captured."

He looked up at Mrs. Carpenter.

"So they caught the assailants?"

"Well, they made arrests. The newspapers made it sound like the police had found the culprits."

Townsend read another account that stated there was reason to believe "there was sufficient proof to condemn at least two of them," and concluded "before this month is over they doubtless will be garroted."

"We thought there was going to be a trial, but then the suspects were mysteriously released."

"Why?"

"Insufficient evidence."

"And what about the investigation?"

"The newspapers here weren't informative, but that's not surprising given the general government censorship in Cuba. The investigation came to a halt. The truly astonishing fact was that the British government did next to nothing."

"How surprising!"

"All we ever heard is that the British consul general, Joseph Crawford, offered a small reward for more information, and that was it."

"Crawford?" Townsend looked at Mrs. Carpenter. "Do you remember when you suggested that Abbott should go to the British Consulate to speak with the consul general?"

"Yes," she said. "I do remember. He wouldn't go."

At that point, Emma walked out into the courtyard with a graceful swish of her long skirts. A faint flush filled her face as she swung her hair back so that Townsend couldn't help noticing her thin neck. She asked what they were talking about. When she heard they were discussing Michael Abbott and his strange refusal to seek help from the British consul general, she gave her mother a long, lingering stare.

"What is it, Emma?" her mother asked.

Emma looked around, pausing before she spoke.

"Mother, I know you don't know this. Mr. Abbott told me not to say anything, but you might as well know. About a week before he disappeared, he tried to speak with someone at the British Consulate. When he mentioned the Backhouse case, he was politely told that the consul general was ill and unable to see him. He went back another day, and was told again that the consul general was indisposed."

"So he was turned away from his own consulate?" Townsend asked.

"Yes, apparently so. He was quite distressed. He thought the British consul general would be eager to help him. After all, Mr. Crawford had worked with George Backhouse. He also thought he might be able to talk to some of the consulate staff. Perhaps uncover some clues about what happened all those years ago. He said he wanted to tell the consul general face-to-face that Grace Backhouse still strongly believes her husband was killed because of his job . . . that he was the victim of a conspiracy."

"Pshaw," exclaimed Mrs. Carpenter as she shook her head. "We will talk about this later, Emma. You know my concerns." Her face was taut and strained. "If you'll excuse me, Captain. We have guests arriving on the New York bound steamer from New Orleans."

After she left, Townsend could hear her shouting at the maids to get the rooms ready and put new linens and mosquito netting on all the beds. Emma seemed not to notice. He took a deep breath and decided he would ask a sensitive question.

"If it's not overly presumptuous to ask, Miss Carpenter, what can you tell me about Michael Abbott? Did you know him well?"

"I would describe him as a highly principled man," she replied. "Earnest in his beliefs. Firm in his resolve. A decent man."

"You seem to have been fond of him?"

"Yes, he was so nice to my mother," Emma replied. "So charming. She told me Mr. Abbott reminded her of a true Philadelphian gentleman of the old variety, so polite and refined, even though, of course, he was English. I thought maybe Michael Abbott was the one."

"The one?" he asked quizzically.

"Yes, the one," she said with a smile.

"The one . . . for you?"

"No, no," she laughed. "Not for me. For my mother, you silly, of course, my mother. Not me. Why would you say that?"

"Oh, I thought maybe . . ."

She laughed lightly even as a slight crease appeared between her dark eyebrows. With a deep breath, her voice turned serious.

"Mr. Townsend," she said. "Let me tell you something. I am not usually drawn to older men."

Townsend smiled awkwardly. She grinned, clearly enjoying his obvious discomfort. She looked away, and the smile faded.

"No, I liked Mr. Abbott because he was kind to my mother. It was the first time I had seen her interested in anyone since my father left us. She doesn't like to talk about that—but my father abandoned us after squandering all her money. As you may have noticed, we don't use his name. Like my mother, I go by Carpenter. Legally Lozada is my last name, but I never use it. It has been hard for my mother, raising three girls on her own. With Abbott, she was a different person, laughing and smiling here in the boarding house, even treating the maids kindly. Imagine, she wasn't even shouting. The two of them were going on evening walks down at the Cortina de Valdés to see the sunset and the harbor. I thought she had finally found someone, but then that all changed."

"Why? What happened?"

"He confided in her about why he had come to Cuba. She got scared and told me I should stay away from him. She said he was a danger to himself and to anyone who got too close to him."

"I'm presuming you didn't listen to your mother."

"No, I ignored her, of course. Abbott cared for my mother. I could see that. They were in love. I was trying to mend their relationship, and I suppose that is why Abbott took me into his confidence."

"Did Abbott tell you anything more about his investigation?"

"He said Grace Backhouse had received a letter from someone in Cuba. She read it to him in tears, and begged him to help. Abbott told me that she called on him in London and asked him to go to Cuba. 'Not just for my sake,' she told him. 'It's for my former husband, George.' That's what she said to Abbott. 'George is lost to history. No one in England even remembers who he was. He lost his life in the service of his country, but his murder has been forgotten.'"

Townsend was about to ask her what she knew of the letter when a volley of rifle shots and a drum roll broke the peaceful quiet. He leapt out of the chair. His head was filled with the sound of throbbing drums. He could feel his face pounding. He saw the glint of the knife blade and Abbott's body crumbling forward. His throat tightened. He felt a wave of mortal dread sweep over him.

"Are you all right?" Emma asked. "Just a passing regiment of soldiers. Nothing to be concerned about."

"I am sorry," Townsend stammered holding his hand up to his neck. He told himself he must remain calm. This would pass.

"I felt something caught in my throat." His hands shaking, he poured some water into a glass, and took a long drink. "I will be fine. Will you have some water?" he asked her politely.

She shook her head. "No, thank you."

The water, which had been cooled in a clay jug, soothed his throat. He breathed in deeply. He decided he would not ask Emma anything more about Abbott. Maybe he would be better advised to forget the man. Hendricks had gotten it right. The man was trouble, and this Backhouse story made him uneasy.

Townsend turned to face Emma. The beauty of her face and the curve of her neck somehow calmed him. His gaze lingered. He asked her about her music, and she began telling him a little bit about herself. She had taken violin lessons ever since she was a little girl and had trained for several months with the famous composer Louis Moreau Gottschalk when he was living in Havana.

"I love playing the violin," she said. "It's been a companion, always there to comfort me. But my real passion now is sketching."

"I saw some of your drawings the other day. They're good. Quite good, in fact."

"Thank you so much. I want to be an artist," she exclaimed. "I spent a year in Philadelphia where I stayed with my aunt while I attended the Philadelphia School of Design for Women. The experience forever changed me. I met one of the editors of *Frank Leslie's Illustrated Newspaper* there and he admired my sketching. He was very encouraging."

Townsend couldn't stop looking at her broad smile and her beaming face. He could tell that she liked the attention he was giving her.

"I have always wanted to get underway on a ship," she said. "Tell me about your schooner. How big is she? How many sailors do you have on board?"

Surprised at her interest in ships, Townsend told her a little bit about the *Gaviota* and how a schooner of her size would normally require five or six in the crew. Then there were the two shipping representatives, which would make it seven or eight men on board.

"Do you have separate cabins?"

"Only the captain and the supercargoes. The sailors are in stacked berths. Not exactly an appropriate place for a lady."

"Oh," she replied and then was quiet.

"Well, I would love to see more of your drawings, particularly of ships," Townsend said.

She smiled and nodded. She took him inside the house over to an easel where she'd been working on a drawing of a blockade runner under sail entering Havana harbor.

"That's really quite good," he said as he scrutinized the sketch. "You've even drawn in all the proper shrouds and halyards, all the rigging details."

"That's high praise from you, Captain. Growing up here you might say I have always been drawn to ships and the sea. I'm an island girl, born and raised in Cuba, *una criolla de La Habana*."

Townsend stepped back to admire it from a distance.

"I would like to see this view of the harbor. It's quite a good vantage point."

"I'll show you."

As they climbed three flights of stairs, he studied her figure. She was slight and dressed in the thinnest of white linen dresses, which seemed to follow her body with every movement. He could almost see through the hoopless dress, her slender shape, her hips, her narrow waist. They surfaced at the rooftop terrace surrounded by a low parapet on which there were gray stone urns. The sun was just beginning to touch the horizon. He took in the rich panorama of flat roofs and church towers everywhere, the massive stone buildings painted in faded colors bleached by the hot sun and rain. He could see the water crashing against El Morro, the walls momentarily gilded with light. It was a beautiful view of the city and the harbor below, the masts of all the ships at the main landing, framed by the tower at the Plaza de San Francisco and the old cathedral. He could see the tiny figures of fashionable Havana parading at the water's edge on the Cortina de Valdés promenade.

She pointed to a telescope mounted on a support, and he realized this was her studio. He bent down to look through the glass. His eyes followed a newly arrived square-rigger as it drifted gracefully toward the southern end of the city and crossed the paths of some of the harbor ferries. From this high point he could now see the extensive shoaly area empty of larger ships, which extended off the eastern section of the Regla docks. There were four or five of these shallow areas scattered around Havana Bay, but none of them seemed to pose any risk to the scores of small sailboats crisscrossing the bay like white seagulls circling over the surface of the water.

Townsend stepped away from the telescope. The air was mild, and he breathed in deeply. The sky was now a faded red. He turned to look at her face lit up by the softer light. He could see that her deep-set, cinnamon brown eyes had tiny flecks of green. With her glossy brown hair and dark eyebrows, she was Spanish-looking, but American as well. To Townsend, she seemed refreshingly genuine. Like the palm fronds rustling back and forth in the wind, she was a free spirit. A risk taker who did not seem to worry what others thought. She clearly was someone who spoke her mind.

Emma returned his stare.

"The editors of Frank Leslie's Illustrated Newspaper wrote me they have a writer in Mobile now doing a story about blockade runners," Emma said as she brushed a strand of her hair back in place. "They would like to look at my illustrations of Havana harbor."

"That's wonderful," he replied. "But I wouldn't advise going to Mobile now. The only ships going in are the blockade runners. That would be dangerous."

She looked disappointed but said nothing. She pointed to the pale full moon slowly rising. She smiled at him coquettishly.

"Did you know, Mr. Townsend, that moonlight on this island is considered dangerous? Some Cubans don't dare to venture out in moonlight without covering their heads. It's just a superstition. I guess they are afraid something bad will happen to them."

He touched his bare head. He had left his hat on the veranda.

"Does that mean we're both in danger?" he asked jokingly as he looked at her and then up at the moon.

Before she could answer, they could hear Mrs. Carpenter calling. "Emma, where are you? I need you."

"I'll be right there, Mother," Emma replied.

"Some of our guests want to hear you play a Mozart sonata."

Emma smiled at Townsend as she turned toward the stairs.

10

The *Gaviota* had been launched that afternoon, and she was tied up at the shipyard's wharf at Regla ready to be rigged. The last five days of feverish painting on the ship's hull had been difficult for Townsend. Like many things in Havana, the work was of good quality but it was slow. Don Pedro wanted to be ready to sail as soon as the Confederacy's shipment of weapons came in from Liverpool. Helm had received word that the shipment had left England for Bermuda, and once offloaded there it would be on its way to Havana. In addition to the Confederate cargo, they would fill the ship with boots, hats, hosiery, all of which sold in Mobile for three to four times what they cost in Havana. Molasses cost twenty cents a gallon in Havana. It was an unbelievable seven dollars per gallon in Mobile. Coffee was also going for three times the price it was selling for in Havana. Townsend was getting an idea of the profits Don Pedro was contemplating, and that was before he even loaded up the ship with cotton for the return trip.

The postilion's whip cracked in the air with a sudden snap, and the two gray horses began pulling the open-bodied carriage forward. The gaudily dressed postilion with his silver-trimmed light blue jacket and top hat cracked the whip again, and the horses began to pick up their high-stepping gait, prancing even faster. Townsend was surprised at how gentle and easy the motion of the *volanta* was despite the awkward appearance of the huge cumbersome wheels. It had rained the night before and the streets in Old Havana were filled with mud holes and flooded with pestilent standing water.

As they passed the tobacco factory of La Honradez on Sol Street, Don Pedro handed him a top hat and a long coat to put on, and said he was going to take him to see the finer sections of the city where it was important to dress in formal attire.

"I think you've earned it," he told him. "I am afraid our streets are in need of repair. When it rains in Havana, we live in the midst of mud and filth, but in the *volanta* we should be quite dry."

Townsend looked over at Don Pedro puffing on his cigar. He was taken aback at how chipper the Spanish merchant was today. Normally he was stiff and tense, rigid like a ship's anchor line. But in the carriage he seemed almost like a friendly uncle, more casual and relaxed and less secretive. Don Pedro joked with him about spending too much time eating and drinking at those roach-infested bodegas, and asked him lightheartedly what harbor vermin he was associating with. He wanted to know all about the work on the schooner, and how Townsend was faring pulling together a crew. Townsend told him he still needed to find a couple more sailors.

They passed a *guagua*, one of Havana's omnibus wagons that provided public transportation for up to a dozen people. Some of the passengers waved at them as they went by. Townsend waved back. Soon they were approaching the main gate of Old Havana, and the thirty-foot-high mustard yellow walls that surrounded the old city. Don Pedro, smiling as usual, told him that the massive five-foot-thick walls with their medieval-looking bastions, watchtowers, and gates would be demolished this year to accommodate the growing city. He had come to Cuba just in time, Don Pedro said. "In another year, these two-hundred-year-old walls will have disappeared along with all the history they have witnessed. Havana is rapidly growing into a modern city to rival the great European cities."

A soldier was on guard as the carriage passed through the heavy Monserrate gateway and ambled across the small bridge over the moat into a vista of wide boulevards and gardens. It was five o'clock, and the quiet siesta hours of the afternoon were over. The hot, tropical sun was quickly going down, giving way to the cool evening sea breezes. The relatively new city outside the walls, *extramuros*, as the Cubans called it, was coming alive with prancing horses and glittering carriages. Soon they were on the Paseo de Isabel II. This wide boulevard with its tree-lined promenade was filled with men in top hats and women in fine evening dress with parasols. Don Pedro pointed to a small stocky military man on horseback with a hawk-like nose and a prominent black moustache. He was wearing a tassled cocked hat and dressed in a gaudy military uniform with high black leather boots.

"That is His Excellency, Captain General Domingo Dulce," he said with pride. Watching the Spanish military man nod to some of the well-dressed passers-by with an air of nonchalance seemed to Townsend like being transported back to medieval times when the king stood on a platform, acknowledging the knights and ladies of his court.

It was an island of sharp contrasts—the beauty and the cruelty he had seen, the wealth and the poverty so visible throughout the city. The richly decorated carriages glided by, pulled by high-stepping horses snorting and prancing along the wide double road. The young women perched on seats between two enormous wheels looked like princesses, dressed in the finest brightly colored silks and cotton, their black hair done up in elaborate dangling curls and ribbons.

They were so different from Emma. It had been days since he had seen her. She was never far from his mind. He would close his eyes and find himself back on the terrace roof with the sunset light playing on the rooftops and the cooling sea breeze fanning their cheeks. It was a magical moment. He wondered if she had felt the same way. Perhaps he felt the connection because they both were half Spanish, half American, but then he had no reason to believe the attraction was mutual. She had seemed more interested in her sketching and reaching Mobile than anything else. He knew he should probably forget her. He would soon be far away at sea.

Townsend gazed at broad avenues of tall palm trees, marble statues, and fountains. He wondered if his mother had come here when she was a young girl. He found it hard to imagine his staid, practical mother in this formal Old World display of wealth and class. He supposed his mother's life here would remain another unsolved Cuban mystery.

Don Pedro waved his hands around at the scenery. He pointed out some of the fine homes and mansions of the wealthy planters near the Campo Marte, the military parade ground, calling them the city's monuments to sugar.

"*Mira quien viene*, look who's coming in our direction. My good friends."

He had the postilion pull up alongside an entourage of ladies and young men who were walking behind two older, fastidiously dressed men. With their white pants, colorful vests, dark, long coats, and black top hats, the two men had the look of powerbrokers. The small parade of parasols and bobbing hats behind them paused as the two men walked up to the carriage, twirling their canes.

Don Pedro tipped his hat to the two men, and greeted them formally, exchanging pleasantries. Townsend was struck that Don Pedro made no effort to introduce him. It was as if he were invisible.

"Who were they?" Townsend asked after Don Pedro had signaled the postilion to move on.

"*Venerables caballeros de Habana*. Two of our city's leading citizens, both extremely wealthy and well-respected gentlemen," Don Pedro replied. "Don Francisco Marty y Torréns, and Don Julián Zulueta. They have done much for the island's economy. They both pioneered bringing Chinese field workers to Cuba. Between the two of them they own at least six or seven sugar plantations on the island. Don Julián may have the most African slaves of any other single plantation owner on the island. Some fifteen hundred slaves, I've heard. The older man, Don Francisco, friends call him Don Pancho, is an institution on the island. He owns the *pescadería*, the fish market down by the wharves. He also built our *Teatro Tacón*, one of the finest opera houses in all of the world. There look, you can see it over there. We are just passing it."

Townsend followed Don Pedro's extended arm. He could see the stately opera house just a short distance away with its high-peaked roof and grand arcades. It was guarded by mounted gendarmes dressed all in white. Several dozen carriages and *volantas* were clustered around a nearby busy cafe called the *Louvre* and one of the top hotels in the city, *Hotel Telégrafo*. Fine hotels, restaurants, casinos, and an opera house, Townsend mused. This was a far more elegant Havana than he had seen before.

Soon they were on the Paseo del Prado heading north. A dusky twilight dropped over them like a gauzy mantilla of Spanish lace. Don Pedro saluted the shadowy silhouettes of passers-by with a gracious wave of the hand and a nod of the head. He turned his attention to two eye-catching young women in a carriage dressed in light, open-necked dresses with fluted ruffles. Their wavy black hair was decorated with flowers, their faces powdered chalky white with something called *cascarilla*, a Cuban custom.

"Do you see how they hang the skirts of their silk dresses over the side of the *volanta*? It's like the birds with their feathers. They're signaling us," Don Pedro said with a wink.

As their carriage crossed the other *volanta*'s path, Don Pedro leaned forward and said "*adiós, guapas*," drawing out the words in a suggestive way that was clearly a practiced and familiar ritual for him. He gave them a lazy, predatory smile as he looked them up and down appreciatively. He wasn't even subtle. Townsend imagined how offended American women would be if they were approached this way by a leering stranger, but he noticed as they passed by that these young Cuban ladies were smiling and giggling behind their rapidly fluttering fans.

The fading light sparked the lighting of gas lamps all along the boulevard. A larger Victoria carriage with two elegantly dressed women passed by and then stopped. Don Pedro got out of the *volanta* to speak to the two women privately. It seemed like they had expected to meet him as they showed no surprise. One was an older dignified woman, dressed in a long flowing light blue dress of linen and silk, and a half-dozen strands of pearls. Next to her was a stunning, much younger woman. Townsend couldn't say what her age was, certainly older than he was, but that was part of her attraction. Their postilion servant on top of the horse was dressed garishly in a green coat and a pink vest.

Both women were looking at Townsend with interest. The older lady in particular seemed to be focused on him, her gaze lingering with a certain probing intensity. Maybe it was his imagination, but were they talking about him? Don Pedro walked back to the *volanta*.

"The two ladies find you pleasing to the eye, Captain. They asked me to introduce them to the tall, well-built and handsome young man with the curly black hair. I believe they are referring to you," he said with a laugh. "I have told them you are my newest ship captain, a well-learned and skillful seaman, who will soon run the blockade. Come, let me introduce you."

Townsend walked over with Don Pedro and was presented to Doña Cecilia de Vargas and the Comtesse Angélica Fernández de Buisson, or the Condesa as she liked to be called. The older woman in particular seemed to examine him closely with a haughty droop of her eyes. A strange, almost invasive look, he thought, that made him uncomfortable. He looked away. She spoke with a disarmingly thin voice, a slight Spanish accent, but otherwise perfect English.

"It is nice to meet you, sir. You are so young to be a ship captain. What did you say your name is?"

"E. J. Townsend," he replied. "From the Chesapeake Bay."

She nodded in a knowing way, but didn't say anything more.

Then it was the other woman's turn. He found himself meeting her intense gaze, so filled with life and energy. She had sparkling black Spanish eyes that flirted openly with him, and rich full lips that were hard to ignore. This woman could probably have any man she wanted. Her red silk dress was the latest Paris fashion, displaying an open neck, her shoulders and arms bare. She had a scarlet ribbon over her forehead, the dark brown hair, long and flowing, curling down the side of her neck. Her voice was deeper and had a more sultry tone, with a mixed French and Spanish accent.

"*¿Qué le parece nuestra Habana?* What do you think of our Havana? *¿Bonita, verdad?* Beautiful, don't you think?"

"Yes, very pretty, *es una ciudad muy linda.*"

"Ah, I see you can speak some Spanish. And are you staying long, Captain?"

"He will be leaving soon to run the blockade," Don Pedro said proudly. "On my new schooner, *Gaviota.*"

"Oh!" she replied. "How adventurous, and how gallant. It seems such a shame that you will be leaving us so soon. But they say ship captains are like driftwood. They never stay on shore long." She smiled coquettishly. "Don Pedro must show you the sights of Havana at night. We are at the end of Carnival now, you know. It is the height of festivities. Everyone will be out on the streets. Don Pedro should take you to one of the masked balls."

"Masked balls?" Townsend asked curiously.

"The masquerade dances. *Los bailes de máscaras.* It is a tradition here. I believe there is one tonight. Not the formal ball at the Tacón theater. There is another one, much more lively where there is *música habanera.* Don Pedro knows the place. Come after eleven. The fun will only just have begun."

Townsend looked over at Don Pedro, but the Spaniard didn't say anything. He was looking at the countess with an inquiring but bemused expression.

"¡Ay, *es una maravilla!*" she said in Spanish and then switched to French, "*une folle nuit de danse.* It is quite exciting. You don't know if you are dancing with a saint or a devil. All masked dancers, twirling like planets to the Cuban rhythms. And no one knows who the other is. They are strangers to each other."

Townsend felt his face flush.

"And if you go, Captain," the Condesa began with a mischievous laugh as she leaned over toward him. He couldn't help gazing at her bare neck. "You should know that it is against the law here to take the mask off your dancing partner. Don Pedro will tell you all about it."

Townsend had never encountered a woman, clearly older, so openly flirting with him. He wasn't certain how to react.

"*A ver si se animan y vienen a las máscaras.* We shall see if you both have the energy to come. *¿Me promete un baile?* Will you promise me a dance, Captain?"

"*Por supuesto,*" Townsend responded eagerly, without even realizing he was speaking Spanish.

As they drove off, Townsend didn't take his eyes off the departing carriage. "Who were they?" he asked.

"Two ladies of high society here," Don Pedro replied. "The Condesa returned to Cuba about a year ago. She was raised here but her parents sent her to France where she married a French count, Le Comte Henri de Buisson. She is not popular with many of the society ladies here in Havana."

"How so?"

He smirked.

"Some of the married women here call her "*La cazadora*," the huntress. I suppose they think of her as Diana, the huntress of Greek mythology. Only she hunts men for game. She lives here without her husband. It seems they have an accord. The old count has remained in Paris with his mistress. And she stays here in Havana. She is, as they say, more Parisienne than Havanese in her manner."

"But she is married."

"Ah, but this is Havana, and that distinction does not necessarily make a difference. To some Spanish gentlemen, it makes her even more desirable."

"And to her?"

"I believe she enjoys a conquest. She has told me she views Havana like a river that is abundantly full of men who always rise to a pretty feathered lure. Some of the wives call her bad names, but as she is quite wealthy, she can do what she pleases. She is beautiful, is she not?"

"What about the older woman? She seems quite distinguished."

Don Pedro looked at him searchingly.

"Doña Cecilia is a woman of considerable influence from one of the older plantation families. Her husband, Rafael Espinoza Vargas, died many years ago leaving her a widow and the owner of her family's sugar estate in the Yumurí Valley. She has been helpful to me over the years, shall we say." Don Pedro's gaze didn't move off Townsend's face. "I see she left an impact on you, or perhaps it is la Condesa you are thinking of. *Es una mujer magnífica. ¿Verdad que sí?*"

Without thinking, Townsend nodded, as he inadvertently translated what Don Pedro had just said.

"Yes, she is quite stunning."

"You speak Spanish better than I realized, Captain. You're a quick learner or perhaps you're getting lessons in some of those dockside fandango bars."

Don Pedro laughed deeply, and pulled out two of his trademark Fígaro Regalía Imperial cigars, offering one to Townsend. This time the young captain accepted.

"How do you like our young women, Captain?" Don Pedro asked pointedly. "You must have your opinions. *Son hermosas de buen ver*, are they not?" he asked with a lascivious grin on his face. "*Guapas. ¿Verdad que sí?*"

Without waiting for an answer, he continued.

"I have always felt that full-bodied women and full-bodied cigars go together." He struck a Lucifer match and puffed on his cigar. "You might be interested in knowing that the best tobacco in Cuba comes from the southwestern part of the island, the area known as *la Vuelta Abajo* in Pinar del Río. The tobacco leaves are selected for their good color and their elasticity."

The Spaniard cocked a bushy eyebrow and puffed before continuing.

"In my opinion, this region is also where Cuba's most beautiful women can be found. Who knows why. It's just been my personal experience. Maybe it's something in the soil? Both the women and the tobacco are richly flavored and delicate, but once lit, they are slow-burning and hard to extinguish."

Don Pedro laughed at his own joke. Townsend smiled politely.

"You should know here in Cuba, people judge you by the way you handle your cigar. Among the finer class of people, the smoker should always present the lighted end of his cigar to the guest."

Don Pedro handed his lit Fígaro Regalía to Townsend so that he could light his own cigar.

"Now you should return it, holding the burning red tip away from your host. An intricate custom perhaps, but this is an important demonstration of courtesy here on the island. Unlike you Americans, we have more Old World customs here."

"Thank you for the advice," Townsend said as he puffed on the large cigar, and watched the light gray smoke curl upwards into the dark sky.

Townsend breathed in the cool night air. He could hear the whisper of palm fronds rustling somewhere high above him in the wind. It was shortly after eleven o'clock, and Don Pedro was walking toward the sound of music. Townsend's head was spinning, and as he stumbled along he realized he was drunk. Dark shadows and mottled light from the scattered gas-lit street lamps marked the way. They'd been drinking at the crowded Dominica Café near the Plaza de Armas where the evening regimental military bands were playing. The Dominica, as Don Pedro called it, was a meeting place for everyone from money-lenders to gamblers and diplomats. It was located right across from the gloomy walls of a convent for Dominican nuns. Townsend's blurry mind was filled with images of swaying hips, fluttering ladies' fans, mixed rum drinks, all lost in a smudgy veil of tobacco smoke.

He could now hear the clattering of carriage wheels on the cobblestones, and the jingling of harness bells. Masked men with dress coats and top hats and women clutching their long flowing robes and trailing skirts swept by, the women giggling with excitement. He heard a steady rhythm of dancing music spilling out into the street. For a moment, he thought he saw Emma.

She was with a crowd of young people ahead of them. But then he looked again and she wasn't there.

They walked into a large stately house where he heard what sounded like a string quartet with a piano and a rhythmic beat. The air was a potent blend of tobacco smoke, perfume, and rum. Don Pedro handed off some money to a man at the entrance who whispered something to him. Townsend soon found himself amid a crush of people being directed to what was clearly the bar area. Don Pedro headed for a marble-topped table presided over by a silver-haired man with a snow-white moustache. It was the British consul general, Joseph Crawford. The distinguished diplomat was seated with two other gentlemen holding their masks and surveying the dance floor.

Don Pedro called out to the consul general, but instead of greeting him, Crawford pretended not to see the Spaniard.

"Mr. Crawford, when do you expect Her Majesty and Mr. Palmerston to finally recognize the Confederacy? Rumors are it will happen soon."

"Pshaw," Crawford replied. "I have nothing more to say to you, Sr. Alvarado Cardona."

Don Pedro insisted on introducing Townsend to Crawford as the captain of his newest ship. The British diplomat reluctantly acknowledged the young captain, and then turned away. It was clear to Townsend there was a hostility between the two men. Don Pedro ignored the snub and turned to Townsend, speaking loudly enough so that Crawford could hear him.

"Mr. Crawford is an ambitious man with many irons in the fire. My informants tell me he is hoping to be named the first British ambassador to the newly formed Confederate States of America."

Just then, a finely dressed Negro servant squeezed his way through the crowd and whispered something in Don Pedro's ear. The man had a silver-laced green jacket with a jaunty pink vest. Don Pedro nodded with a smile, and handed the black man some money. He laughed as he bought Townsend another rum drink, and they both turned their attentions to the dance floor. The saloon area was a mob of twirling masked dancers, a noisy din of music, cries, and calls. The orchestra was made up of all black musicians wearing finely tailored clothes. They were playing piano, cello, violin, and flute. The music was like a waltz, but what made it different was the thumping deep baritone from the bass, and the scraping of gourds called güiros.

Townsend had never heard music like this before. He'd been taught how to dance the waltz, but this was far different. The dancers shuffled their feet, moving at a slow pace to the scratchy rhythm of the scraped gourds. Young ladies dressed in brightly colored muslins, neck and arms bare, yellow silk roses in their hair, were spinning round and round the dance floor with men in formal coats, jewel-colored vests, and bow ties. Everyone had masks, and Don Pedro quickly handed him one, a striped orange and black tiger mask. It covered his eyes, nose and forehead. It even had tiger ears. Don Pedro put on his own mask, a smiling court jester's face all in white with red and green trim.

"This is Cuban dancing, *la danza criolla*. Remember the usual courtesies don't apply at a *máscara*, and here especially. Now that we are in Carnival, more liberties are allowed. Ladies need no introduction to invite a masked gentlemen to dance, and it's against the rules and considered a grave offense to try to forcibly remove the mask from someone else."

He started to turn away, but then quickly turned back.

"Be careful," said Don Pedro behind his smiling mask. "Keep your hand on your money. There are plenty of light fingers and dangerous hands on the dance floor."

Don Pedro approached one of the *décolleté* masked women standing nearby, and he soon was swept away into the swirl of silk and linen. Townsend watched mesmerized as the dancers, all masked, moved in perfect rhythm. White porcelain faces with yellow lips and gilded cheeks moved by red devils with black horns and silver lips. Cheek by jowl the couples moved as one with perfect precision and grace, following formal steps but moving sensually with their hips to the raspy tempo of the gourd, and the beat of an African drum.

Townsend's eyes focused in on the fast moving yellow-gloved fingers of the pianist as they traveled across the white and black piano keys. His head swam and he felt like he was floating into a carefree euphoria. The flutist pierced the air with a high note. Suddenly he found himself in the arms of an unknown woman wearing a full-faced cat mask with glittery golden whiskers and ribbons adorning her hair. There was no introduction. No talking. She moved naturally with the music almost with no effort. Her steps flowed like water, shuffling to the tempo, sweeping him along.

At first he moved awkwardly, but then he let the music flow through him, feeling the scraping of the gourd in his feet. Acting on impulse, he pulled his dance partner closer, placing his left hand on her waist. He pressed his fingers against the curve of her lower back. All he could see through the mask were the eyes, dark mahogany hair, and a beautiful smile. She was young, and slender. Her perfume was a scent he found familiar. She tried to whisper something in his ear, but he couldn't really hear. She spoke louder.

"You are a quick learner, Mr. Townsend."

Startled, Townsend leaned back to look at his dance partner. All he could see through the mask were her brown eyes.

"Miss Carpenter? Is that you?"

His dance partner leaned in closer. "I need to tell you something about—"

The music suddenly became louder. Before he knew what was happening, all the dancers switched partners. Townsend found himself twirling away with another woman who was wearing a full-faced white Venetian mask with red glitter around the eyes. Again no words were spoken. This woman was more confident, and more bold. Her black hair tumbled down her neck in curls onto her bare shoulders. Her shiny curls were only enhanced by a necklace of diamonds perched strategically above her low-cut formal dress.

He felt the rounded curves of her body, and breathed in the sweet scent of her perfume. Any caution or reserve slipped away as this mystery woman pressed against him. He felt the strength of her arms and the warmth of her hands as they twirled to the other side of the dance floor. The sway of her well-rounded hips moved like an undulating stream. Not a word was spoken until the end of the dance when she leaned into him so he could feel the soft cushion of her breasts. He instinctively pulled her closer. Through her mask Townsend could see dark Spanish eyes and below the mask, rich full lips. His mind was a blur. His only thought was how much he desired this woman. She breathed into his ear in Spanish, "*Venga conmigo.* Come with me."

Townsend was still quite drunk, and had only a faint idea of what he was doing or where he was going. She took him outside onto the street where her closed carriage was waiting. He heard the crack of the man's whip and the jingling of the carriage's harness as the wheels moved forward. No one could see in or out. The woman pulled off her mask and removed his, and he found himself in the arms of the Condesa. She laughed mischievously as she pressed her lips to his face and began breathing into his ear.

"This is the end of Carnival," she whispered to him, "and the priests say we are permitted to sin."

11

The wheels creaked and groaned as they clattered along the stone. The Condesa's fingers slid underneath his shirt, and she began caressing his chest. He was uncertain what to do, awkwardly responding to her touches. The few women he'd known were working girls, and there had been no romance in those encounters. Here he was with an older woman, a Spanish lady. A married woman of high society. As drunk as he was, he knew these were treacherous waters.

Hang it all! I won't follow my judgment, Townsend thought. He knew he couldn't stop anyway.

"Don't worry, Captain. No one can see us. My postilion will make sure no one comes near us. No prying eyes will get too close. Just relax."

In the darkness of the carriage, he sensed her burning gaze even as he felt her caressing hands. She began breathing into his ear again, whispering what she wanted him to do. His hands traveled up under her petticoats, sending a shudder through her body. She pulled his head to her breasts. Townsend needed no encouraging now. He began helping her to undress. He slid his hands over her bare hips and thighs and then the full length of her body. She was clearly experienced in the ways of handling strange men. She helped him undress, pausing for several seconds to make sure he put on one of those new "French safes" made of rubber, a new experience for him. He felt the soft touch of the carriage's leather seats on his bare skin. Then a body on fire wrapped around him, vigorous and desirable. She was breathing rapidly into his ear. He felt the gently moving carriage, her caressing hands exploring his body. He hardly knew what he was doing, but he didn't care. He could smell the perfume in her hair. Her moist lips had the taste of flowers. He felt the driver pull the horses to a stop, and then heard the roar of the ocean in the background.

Townsend woke up to the sound of waves and the unsettling roar of breakers. At first he had no idea where he was, but as he looked around the dark confines of the enclosed carriage, he remembered. He looked over to see her shadowy silhouette set against an inky mauve sky. She was leaning out the carriage window smoking a cigarette attached by small claws to a golden tong with a ring that fit over her left forefinger. She was looking away from him with a dull stare at the waves crashing against the shore. Her brightly colored, *décolleté* ball gown of blue and green muslin now seemed incongruous. Her carefully coifed black tresses had drooped into a state of disarray. The silence between them in the carriage had settled like a windless fog.

His head throbbed, and he was still woozy. His memory was a blur, filled with the night's intoxicating music, the swirling masked dancers, the Condesa's deluge of shiny black hair, and the sweet scent of gardenia. He remembered how drunk he was. He remembered the carriage rocking, her warm breath in his ear. And then it was as if he were falling into a void, only to be awakened and aroused again.

His reverie was interrupted by the Condesa's sensual voice.

"*Me encanta el cielo negro-gris, el aire fresco justo antes del amanecer*. I love the black gray sky and the cool air just before dawn, don't you? Even though the sun's trumpet blast is near, the night still rules."

The Condesa inhaled deeply and then blew the smoke out into the night air. Her eyes glided his way, giving him a brief sidelong glance before turning her gaze to the ocean.

"The early dawn is a time for all the night birds to find their homes. Where would you like to be taken, Captain?" she asked in an impersonal tone. "The docks, I presume?"

"I have a rooming house," Townsend replied. "Can you take me there?"

She nodded and he gave her the address on Jesús María Street. Soon the carriage was ambling along the oceanfront road. He looked outside. He could see hardly anything, not even the glint of stars. They were along a stretch of road he had never seen before, facing the north coast. It was a deserted promontory, and the waves tumbled toward the shore, breaking onto the rocks with an explosion of spray. He looked over at the Condesa's contemplative face. She was cold and distant, as if last night had never happened. With her *cascarilla* white powder smudged, she looked older than he had thought. Perhaps it was the emerging fan of small wrinkles on the outer corner of her eyes that gave her away. She was still beautiful, but he could see that those intense Spanish eyes had lost some of their youthful luster.

"I apologize for my behavior last night," she finally said with a faint smile, one eyebrow arched upwards.

"No apologies necessary," Townsend replied.

"I am not always a demure lady." She propped up her chin with her hand.

Her husky voice was subdued, but in her eyes he saw something different, some kind of silent satisfaction, a mischievous glint. They gleamed like black river stones.

"You were fine," he replied. "Better than fine. You were good, I mean—"

"I should have resisted your advances, but I let you have your way with me," she said with a small smirk as she brushed aside wisps of her hair hanging down her face.

Townsend raised his eyebrows, but said nothing. Even now he could feel how seductive this woman was. He found himself hypnotized by her mysterious indolent stare. Could he have forced himself on her? Had he done something terrible? He knew he'd been drunk, but that was not the way he remembered it. He could still hear the raspy scratching of the gourds on the dance floor, and feel her body molded to his, their faces close together. She had known it was him behind the mask. He was sure of that. She had chosen him as her dancing partner, but he had followed her willingly.

"The fact is I am a woman who follows her impulses. *Comme on dit à Paris, je suis portée sur le sexe.* It is not fair is it? Men with a certain appetite are applauded, but women are punished, branded with a label, *femmes légères de petite vertu.* I sometimes wonder if society will ever look upon both sexes impartially."

A troubled crease deepened between her eyes. She looked away in silence. More details of the night came to him. He remembered her unbuttoning his trousers, and helping him undress.

"I don't usually allow myself to be pursued by ship captains, no matter how handsome they are, Captain, but Don Pedro knows that I like my evening entertainments and he thought I might enjoy meeting you. It was amusing last night, *n'est-ce pas? Notre petite aventure.*"

"What does that mean?" Townsend asked. He didn't speak a word of French.

"Our little adventure of the night," she said. She smiled, this time more coyly. "Don Pedro assured me you were from a respectable, genteel family."

Respectable, genteel family. That remark gave Townsend pause. What did Don Pedro know about his life? He doubted the man knew anything about him.

"What do you know about my family?" he snapped.

"Nothing," she replied as she turned away.

"What does Don Pedro know?"

She shrugged. "I have no idea. Don Pedro is a merchant, a trader of many things, and one of the commodities he trades in is information. He gathers secrets even as he keeps his own well hidden."

"What else can you tell me about him?" Townsend asked.

"I believe he was sent away to school in New Orleans, and then to New York. That's why he speaks English so well. He came here from Spain as a boy. I've heard it said that he had an important benefactor, a sugar planter in Matanzas who helped him get started as a commission merchant."

Townsend sat up at attention. His mother had grown up in Matanzas. It was the first time he had heard any mention of it, the place his mother was from. His chest ached at the thought of her. The carriage had reached the north gate into the old city. Off to one side he could see the shadowy figures of the destitute crouched up against the walls.

The Condesa lit another cigarette. Her manner had softened, and she continued to tell him more about the Spaniard.

"Don Pedro is well connected here in Havana. He travels in many circles, and because of his business has many connections abroad. I used to see him more often, but we both are a little like stray cats. He has a reputation in town as a *búho licencioso*, a night owl who likes to spread his wings. We both enjoy our independence. I find I still have an attraction to him, but I don't quite know why."

"What other reputations does he have?"

"I would be misguided if I said much more. He told me you had the misfortune of falling into the wrong hands when you arrived here, and that he saved you. Is that right?"

She smiled as she puffed on her cigarette.

"I suppose you could say that," Townsend replied.

"You should be pleased. I think Don Pedro sees you as a promising young man with great potential. I believe he hopes you will decide your future lies here in Cuba. Above all, he values faithfulness. *Siempre fiel*, he often says. Or as they say in France about loyalty to the Emperor, *toujours fidèle*."

She paused thoughtfully. "Unfortunately our evening together must remain a secret."

Townsend was startled to hear her speak so plainly. The Condesa looked out the window and continued talking as if she was talking to herself. She began telling him about Paris. She was sent there as a young woman and traveled in lofty circles. She became good friends with the French Empress Eugenie, who was Spanish and a distant relative, and through her had met the French emperor.

"For a short time, I became one of the emperor's *petites distractions*. But this must be boring to you."

"Not at all. On the contrary," Townsend replied. He was intrigued. Havana was a place filled with secrets and surprises, and this woman had plenty of both.

"I felt badly about betraying my friend, of course, but I had fallen under the spell of her husband, the emperor. When he tired of me as he did of so many of his mistresses, I married the count, but after one year we both realized that we would live largely separate lives. The emperor and I would see each other now and again. When he heard I was returning to Cuba, he asked me to keep an eye on his political interests and the war between the North and the South. I suppose I am unofficially the French agent here in Havana, behind the scenes, of course. The emperor is quite keen on creating an alliance with the Confederate states, but he does not want a war with the North. The French armies have taken Vera Cruz and they are marching towards Mexico City. Soon the Emperor will control Mexico, but that's not all he wants. He would like to reclaim *La Louisiane* for France, everything from northern Florida to Texas."

She laughed at his wide-eyed reaction.

"Some of the *crème de la crème* here might unkindly call me a spy. Others whisper worse things, but I am no different than most who keep their eyes and ears open. Havana is a city where spies and emissaries rub shoulders, and the delicate game of gaining secrets is frequently played to the sensual rhythm of *una danza criolla*."

She laughed again and held up her finger to her mouth.

"Remember, all this is only for your ears. I would ask you to say nothing of our little affair, even to Don Pedro. He may suspect something, but he doesn't know what went on between us in the privacy of my carriage."

A chorus of roosters were crowing when Townsend alighted from the carriage outside his rooming house just before first light. The postilion driver opened the door and let him out. He stopped to look at him. The man had seen this before, the flirtation, the conquest, and the farewell, all in the darkness of night. Townsend remembered him now. He was the well-dressed Negro he had seen at the masked dance with the silver laced green jacket and pink vest whispering to Don Pedro. Townsend's throbbing head ached even more than before. The Condesa had told him he could add her to his many conquests, another notch on his belt. He knew it was just the reverse. He was the one who had been conquered, not her, and it was her belt that must be heavily notched. It was clear to him that she'd had her dalliance and now it was over. He felt a certain unease under his skin, a sense of being violated. He looked back once to see if she would wave, but the carriage was already moving away. He remembered what Don Pedro had said about her, *la cazadora*, the huntress.

He climbed up the wooden stairs to his room with its bare whitewashed walls. He opened the only window that looked out to the harbor to let in a cooling sea breeze, and threw himself down on the straw-filled mattress. The screeching cries and whistles of the early morning street peddlers now filled his room along with the clattering *volantas* carrying merchants to work, and the barking dogs. A lottery vendor directly under the window called out, "*¡Lotería! ¡¡Lotería!*" The morning milkman with his cow and its muzzled calf, beat on his bucket and shouted out, "*¡Leche! ¡Leche!*" The man's parrot squawked and then echoed the same refrain. Townsend leaned his head out the window and shouted in Spanish at the man below to shut up and go away.

He slammed the heavy wooden shutters closed and put a pillow over his head. This strange city was corrupting him with its dishonest ways, the sleazy glamour, the women. A *sereno* cried out the hour. A donkey brayed. The city's church bells clanged from all directions, calling people to morning mass. Today was the last day of Carnival, and it seemed like the Catholic priests were summoning the sinners early. Townsend quietly cursed the city. His head throbbed. He thought of Emma. He kicked himself. The woman whom he had first been dancing with. He knew it was her.

12

March 9, 1863

Townsend spent the next few weeks working on the boat at a wooden wharf across the harbor in Casa Blanca, a small fishing village on the eastern edge of Havana Bay. It was a hot, windless place that stank of fish and sewage from the nearby La Cabaña barracks, but the repair work helped him forget his troubles. The town was a sordid place of storehouses, ship-repairing establishments, and working wharves filled with boats of all shapes and sizes. All day long he could hear the banging and sawing of ship carpenters. In the distance, the constant sound of marching and drilling mingled with sporadic cannon fire reminded him that the heavily fortified La Cabaña fortress was nearby. Despite its many drawbacks, Casa Blanca was a place where large shipping supplies of all kinds could be found in storehouses—wooden spars, canvas sails, sheet copper, large iron bolts—and Townsend found it practical to be there. Halyards for seven sails had to be run up the mast and tied down to sets of wooden pins on the bulwark rails. With the two topmast spars in place, the ship would have more than five thousand square feet of sail.

Townsend, Red Beard, and Bertrand lived on board the *Gaviota* along with a new crewmember, whom they had found recently at the *Toro del Mar*. His name was Nils Olsen. He was a bony, garfish of a man with light blue eyes, smudgy from the sun, and thinning silver blond hair tied back in a ponytail. He was a little old, in his fifties, but Townsend had picked him because he had been the cook on board a Danish government mail and passenger schooner that ran between the islands of St. Thomas and Santa Cruz. He spoke English well, but with a slight lilt.

Red Beard had started calling him a Dutchman or just "Dutch" because of his strange accent. This didn't sit well with Olsen. He said he was from the Danish island of St. Thomas and didn't even speak Dutch. He explained he came north to Cuba to make some money running the blockade because even in Copenhagen's island colonies to the south, the effects of the American war were visible. Townsend had to admit the rough old fellow, stubborn and argumentative as he was, did have some of the characteristics of what sailors called a "rusty guts" Dutchman. He could see from his bulbous red nose and bloodshot eyes that Olsen liked his rum, but there was something about his rough-hewn hatchet face that made Townsend believe the man knew his way around boats.

Even with his new crew to keep him company, Townsend's thoughts kept returning to Emma. It had been more than ten days since the masquerade dance. He thought of dancing with her. Memories of their brief dance together haunted him. How light she had felt, her steps and rhythm so perfectly timed to the music. The dance had been so short. If only he had turned the Condesa down when she lured him outside. He had been a fool, a drunken, lusty fool. Now he was suffering the consequences. He had walked by Mrs. Carpenter's boarding house several times and had almost walked into the lobby, but each time he couldn't summon the courage. He hoped Mrs. Carpenter would send him an invitation, but none came. He consoled himself by thinking that she was probably busy with guests, and had forced Emma to work. But he knew that was probably not the case. He knew his decision to go off with the Condesa had dashed any hopes of winning over Emma's affections.

At dusk, he told the other three they could finish staining the decks with turpentine and linseed oil tomorrow. He would meet them later at a favorite hangout for blockade runners in the old city called *Las Ninfas de Oro*, the Golden Nymphs. Once the others had gone, he sat down in his cabin to write a letter to Emma. He wanted to beg her forgiveness and ask her to give him another chance. He wanted to tell her how beautiful she was. That he was drunk that night of the masquerade dance, that he could not explain the reasons for his actions. Instead, he told her about the new crewmembers and the work being done to rig the boat. How he wished he could come and see her but he was very busy. That they would be leaving as soon as the cargo came in from Bermuda. He thought about admitting to her that he was going to run the blockade, but then decided against it. He signed it "respectfully," even though for a slight moment he thought about writing "fondly."

After the ritual sunset symphony of cannon blasts and church bells had subsided, he left the ship. He looked around to see if one of his bodyguard shadows was watching him, but he saw no sign of Nolo or Salazar. As he sailed across the harbor on a hired boat, he heard the cannon blasts from El Morro and saw the Navy steam corvette the USS *Huntsville* steam into port. She was a wooden screw-propelled steamer, a three-master with a stubby-nosed bow built by the renowned Westervelt yard in New York. As a well-known fixture of the US Navy's East Gulf Squadron in Key West, the USS *Huntsville* was rumored to be assigned to patrol the coast of Cuba westward and to the north of the Tortugas islands—the exact route most of the Havana-based blockade runners took on their way to the Texas ports. He knew he might be seeing something of this ship.

Townsend took out his glass and scanned her decks. She had at least one sixty-four-pounder smoothbore gun and two thirty-two-pounders. He knew that these weapons would be devastating because they could skip shells and shots across the water over long distances. She dropped anchor next to a small two-masted Navy brig flying the Stars and Stripes. He could just barely make out her name on her transom, the USS *Leopard*. He watched as the blue-uniformed Navy sailors with their flat-topped hats jumped into longboats bound for the wharf area adjacent to the main docks. They were singing a sea chantey he recognized as they were rowed ashore.

"Oh, we're rollin' down to Cuba to load up sugar, boys!

Haul away, boys, haul away!"

Townsend knew there might be trouble ashore from this group. Neither the Spanish nor the Confederates had any love for Yankee sailors. There were several blockade-running steamers in port—the harbor was filled with Confederates. Word was that two battalions of Spanish infantry were to be dispatched soon to Santo Domingo to help quell a full-scale revolt against Spanish rule, so Spanish navy sailors were also on edge.

As he dropped off the letter outside Mrs. Carpenter's boarding house, he stopped to watch the house. There was no glimpse of Emma, but then he saw her familiar profile pass by a window. He waved at her enthusiastically. She nodded back. He took it as an invitation, scooped up the letter, and stepped inside the boarding house.

Townsend looked around to see if her mother or any of the maids were there, but it appeared they were alone. She met him at the door. Instead of a warm smile there was now a frosty formality.

"Good evening, Captain Townsend. I saw you pass by the window," she said as she gave him a sharp, stony look, her eyes narrowed. "How can I help you?"

"Uh, I wrote you a letter," he stammered. "In fact, here it is. I want to apologize—"

"No need for apologies, Captain Townsend." Her voice dipped with indifference.

"I mean about the dance. That was you in the cat mask, wasn't it? I was drunk, you see, I—"

"No need for explanations Captain. You are certainly a free man to do as you please."

"I know you were trying to tell me something."

Her eyebrows lifted slightly. She paused and pursed her lips.

"What I wanted to tell you is that a letter came from London for Mr. Abbott. It was from Mrs. Backhouse." She pulled a letter out of a pocket in her dress. "My mother didn't want to open it, but I did anyway. I wanted to get your opinion."

"Of course."

"Clearly Mrs. Backhouse has heard nothing from Abbott. In her letter, she writes she hopes he is making progress, and mentions she received another note from Cuba enclosed. See for yourself."

Emma handed him the piece of rough brown paper. Townsend began reading silently. It was dated January 15, 1863.

Dear Mistress Backhouse,
Like I wrote before, tell the man you sendin' to wear a black top hat with a red feather. That way I gon' know who he deh. He must come to Matanzas. I am on a plantation that uses English speaking slaves. That is where he will find me. Twenty-four years I been a slave now. I was a free man in Jamaica. Then they kidnapped me. I knew your husband. He was a good man. He wanted to see justice done. He said he would get me freed. Now I fear I have been forgotten.

Townsend looked up at her with a furrowed brow.

"No name, and no signature. I am afraid there is little to be done," Townsend replied with a resigned sigh. "Maybe write Mrs. Backhouse to get more information about this man?"

"But it will take weeks to get a response," she said. "I think we should go to the US Consulate here. My mother knows the acting consul general. He and his wife know me as well. He would talk to us."

"I'm not sure I want to go to the US Consulate," Townsend said nervously.

"Because you're a blockade runner?"

Townsend looked at her with surprise.

"Yes, my mother told me. She suspected it all along. You weren't honest enough to tell us yourself. That doesn't speak highly of you, Captain."

Emma's expression was dark.

"Whatever your principles, I need your help. I think we should pursue this. At the very least we should try to find this poor unfortunate man who is enslaved."

Townsend just shook his head. "It would be like trying to find a needle in a haystack. And not just any haystack, I might add, but one filled with sharp pitchforks and crawling with poisonous snakes. It would just lead to more trouble, Miss Carpenter."

"Perhaps we should go to the Church of St. Augustine then . . . didn't he have a contact?"

"I don't think that would be wise," Townsend replied. "Look, I helped Abbott, that is true, but that doesn't mean his cause is mine. Perhaps the best thing you could do is to write Mrs. Backhouse and tell her Mr. Abbott may have been killed on the streets of Havana. I do not see what else can be done, not here on this island."

"I'm sorry you feel that way," she shot back angrily, making no effort to hide her scorn.

Townsend replied softly. "Abbott knew the risks he was taking. I think we need to accept the fact Michael Abbott is probably dead, and so is his investigation of the Backhouse murder."

"We do not know Abbott is dead!" she snapped, her eyes filling. "We've got to find Abbott and help Grace Backhouse discover who killed her husband."

"I'm afraid what you suggest would be too dangerous, Miss Carpenter. Our efforts would most likely lead nowhere, and get us into trouble—you are too naïve about the reality of the situation. Your mother is right. Abbott's cause is a danger. You are too young—"

She interrupted him. "And you are too young to be without hope and so easily scared off! When you helped Abbott that night I thought I was looking at a true Samaritan. I thought I could trust you. You were a good person. Now I see I was wrong. It seems your new life as a blockade runner has changed you. You told my mother you were against slavery, but how do you really feel supplying the Confederacy with guns and supplies, funding their war effort by bringing out their cotton. That makes you a supporter of this hateful institution of slavery."

Townsend squirmed in his seat and looked away into another room to avoid her contemptuous stare. "No, I don't believe so."

"Then why are you helping to supply the South?"

"You know I am not a blockade runner by choice."

"Then what are you, Mr. Townsend?" she asked bitterly. "What would you like to be called? I understand you tried and failed at your endeavor to become a naval officer. A man's principles don't drop off all at once. They creep, slide and slip like mud on a riverbank. What's apparent to me is that you are not the man I thought you were."

It was a cruel, biting remark and she knew it. Townsend stared at Emma with a forlorn look.

"Miss Carpenter, I just—"

"I have nothing more to say to you. Please show yourself out."

Dejected, Townsend stumbled along on the streets. He cursed Emma. He was angry with her, but also angry with himself. It was over. Whatever spark there had been, it had gone. He would probably never see her again. And it had been his fault. But he saw nothing to be gained in pursuing a dead man's dangerous mission. He had already faced enough misfortunes trying to help that Englishman. But her barbed remarks about his identity had found their mark, and his mind was filled with dark thoughts.

The pungent smell of dried fish and garlic wafted out the open windows of some of the bodegas even as the rank smell of urine assaulted his nose on the street corners. He passed some drunken sailors staggering and cursing, drowning their sorrows with their rum bottles, lost in their self-pity. At that moment he felt a certain kinship, lost as he was in his own world of shame and regret. All he wanted to do is forget what Emma had said, and forget the situation he was in.

When he got to *Las Ninfas de Oro* and walked through the doors, Townsend was greeted by the sound of wooden sandals called *chancletas* clacking like gunshots. A Spanish girl was dancing on stage, her arms over her head, her dress provocatively slit down the middle. He could see the cubicles wallpapered with old newspapers on either side of the bar. Girls were slipping in and out of there with their companions with some frequency. The place was filled with a familiar mix of boozy sailors and gamy land sharks, who were all there for the same thing—drink, song, and women. He looked around the bar for his crewmembers, but he didn't see them.

The music suddenly changed to a slower tempo. Townsend gave the dancer on stage a lingering look when she started to sing with a surprisingly hoarse and raspy voice, deep and earthy. Like so much of this Cuban music, the words were often about pain, lover's grief, and sexual innuendo. He watched her face contort with emotion as she sang the words about her lover, the watchmaker. "Whenever he comes to see me, Ay, se le para el minutero, the minute hand goes up." Townsend smiled at the not-too-subtle lyrics.

The bartender asked what he was drinking.

"Un ron blanco," Townsend replied. "Uno doble."

The bartender poured him a generous glass of the new distilled clear Bacardí rum from Santiago de Cuba. Townsend downed it in one gulp, and then asked for another. He could now feel the strong undertow of the sensual music carry him along. As the bartender poured, Townsend felt a gentle touch on his arm, the smell of perfume, and then heard a tantalizing, sultry voice whisper in his ear.

"¿Festejando algo, marinero? Are you celebrating something, sailor?"

Townsend turned to come face-to-face with a dark-haired smiling temptress who was smoking a cigar. "¿O ahogando las penas? Or just drowning your sorrows?" She moved closer so that her body leaned into his. He felt her hand touch his side.

Just then, he heard his name being shouted. It was Red Beard calling him to the back of the tavern. Townsend turned around to look at the girl, but she was already talking with another sailor. Red Beard introduced him to a hulking man with powerful shoulders, a bushy beard, and tangled hair. He looked to be in his thirties.

"Higgins here is on the run from the blue bellies," explained Red Beard. "He's an assistant engineer who jumped off the USS Huntsville. Seems they wouldn't give him shore leave so he took it anyway. You should talk to him."

The man's full name was Ezra Higgins. Townsend decided he liked him immediately because of the straightforward way he looked him in the eye.

"I reckon Higgins here chews his own tobacco, as we say in Texas," Red Beard said. "An independent man."

The Texas sailor laughed and took a bite off a plug of tobacco and began chewing vigorously. They were drinking a mixture of molasses, rum, lime, and ginger, and Townsend called out to the bar maid to bring over another round.

"Higgins has been telling me he wants to set sail with some real sailors," Red Beard said. "Wants to join the chase across the Gulf. Make some money from running the blockade."

Townsend studied the man as he lit one of the cigars Don Pedro had given him.

"How did you become a Navy man?" Townsend asked.

"Not too sure," Higgins replied. "Someone in a South Street grog shop in New York doped me up. The next thing I knew I woke up on a Navy gunboat headed for the Gulf."

"He may not be a cotton man who knows the Gulf waters, Cap'n, but he knows all about the Navy's tricks," Red Beard said enthusiastically. "He could be useful to us."

Higgins began talking about life on board ship. He described everything from the boredom to the horrible diet of salt meat, hard tack, and dishwater coffee. "The only reason the Navy doesn't have more desertions is the prize bounties," he said. "It's a powerful lure. Each time they capture a blockade runner, the shipmasters, officers and crew, they all get some of the money from the prize court."

Townsend got a sense that something was wrong when Higgins suddenly slouched over, grabbed Red Beard's floppy hat, and pulled it down over his own head. He turned around to see a group of six or eight US Navy men walk in through the bar. Judging from the double-breasted coats, there were several officers, including a master at arms, a warrant officer, and a couple of junior officers off the two Navy ships in port. They went to the bar and asked the bartender questions. It was quite clear they were looking for someone. Townsend told Higgins to slip out the back. Without thinking of the consequences, he then jumped up on stage.

"*Vamos a bailar*," he told the woman singing. "Let's dance." He started clapping his hands, and surprisingly the musicians continued playing. Soon he was dancing with the woman, her wooden sandals clacking away, and the entire tavern was cheering him on. Out of the corner of his eye, Townsend caught a glimpse of Higgins slipping out the back door. He started to make a quick exit himself when he heard his name.

"Everett Townsend! Well, if that don't cap all. A butternut hiding out in this rum-soaked hellhole. Looks like you got yourself a new job as a Spanish fandango dancer." Townsend knew that voice. It was Angus Van Cortland, the source of his troubles. "What are you a blockade runner now?"

Townsend turned to look squarely at the man addressing him.

"Or are you just a lowly trading skipper?"

Van Cortland still had that look of an arrogant New York patrician. A big, clean-shaven face, curly yellow hair with bushy sideburns and a large thin nose, all set on a short round neck. Townsend's head pounded at the sight of this man, and he stood stock still. The musicians stopped playing and an awkward silence hovered over the bar. Van Cortland signaled to two of the Navy men. They jumped up on the stage and marched toward Townsend.

Townsend was taller than Van Cortland, so he looked down at the man's large head, stocky chest, and thick legs in blue uniform trousers.

"So you are a cotton runner then," Van Cortland hissed. "A filthy grayback, just as I suspected."

Townsend stepped closer to Van Cortland, but then he shook his head and stepped back.

"I am not going to fight you, Van Cortland."

"No, I imagine you wouldn't. Afraid to get yourself bloodied up." He turned to his fellow officers. "I want you to know that this is one of the Rebel traitors who got expelled from the Naval Academy. He was a spy in our ranks, a traitor. His brother was a Reb too."

"Van Cortland, you better shut your trap."

Townsend noticed Van Cortland's blue officer coat, and he could see his shoulder patches with a silver anchor in the center and two gold bars at each end.

Van Cortland noticed where he was looking.

"That's right, Townsend. You can call me Lieutenant Van Cortland now. I am no longer on the USS *De Soto*. I have my first command, the gunship *Leopard* here in Havana, a captured Rebel brig. Most of my graduating class skipped the grade of master to become lieutenants. It's a shame you will never have that privilege."

At that point, the Spanish proprietor intervened, and approached them on stage.

"*¡Fuera, Yanquis sinvergüenzas!*" the man shouted to Van Cortland and the other Navy men. "*¡A la puta calle como lo que sois, perros!* Worthless Yankees, get out of here. Go to the fucking streets like what you are, dogs."

Van Cortland waved the man off. "Keep to yourself, Sancho Panza. This man and me got unfinished business." He then turned back to face Townsend.

"Townsend, I want you to know nothing would give me more pleasure than to seize your ship as a prize and send you north to Elmira Prison in New York along with the other Confederate prisoners."

"See there now, the only place you and your ship are going to end up, Van Cortland," Townsend shot back, "is pitched up high and dry on a reef in the Tortugas."

This comment set off large guffaws of laughter in the bar, and then some cheering. "Hear, hear!"

"You're just like your dead brother, Townsend," Van Cortland shouted. "Nothing but a filthy Rebel traitor!"

"I don't need to fight you, Van Cortland. Let's save it for the open sea."

There were more boos and catcalls from the barroom floor, and cries to "send the blue belly lubbers back to their ship." Townsend breathed deeply to contain his anger. Van Cortland, who had clearly been drinking heavily, seemed to enjoy making the crowd of Southern sympathizers even more rowdy.

"And this grog house of low-life, rum-bud Rebels is probably where your father met your mother. No doubt this is where your father first grabbed her cat-heads."

Van Cortland never saw it coming. Townsend's right fist found Van Cortland's eye and a second later his left fist came up under his jaw. He soon had him on the floor. Navy officers started clubbing Townsend from behind, and the young captain might have been in trouble if Red Beard and Bertrand hadn't hurled themselves up on the stage and joined the fight. A full brawl ensued. The small contingent of Yankee officers might have paid a costly price if not for the sound of the police whistles. Sailors scattered, and moments later the police along with a small force of the *Guardia Civil* led by a saber-wielding Captain Vásquez marched into the fracas. Soon the Spanish police had surrounded and corralled the entire bar, including Townsend, his crew, and all the Navy officers and had begun making arrests.

Townsend was shaking he was so angry, and Red Beard had to restrain him from taking another swipe at Van Cortland's battered face. It was then he saw Salazar and Nolo speaking with Captain Vásquez and the next thing he knew he and his crewmembers were being released. He never thought he would say it, but he was glad to see the faces of his watchdogs. He hoped Higgins had managed to get out. It was with some satisfaction that he watched the US Navy officers being dragged off to jail, although he knew they wouldn't be kept there long. Even though Van Cortland was under arrest, he hissed a farewell as he was led away.

"I'll be looking for you, Townsend. I will find you and haul you and your ship into Key West. You're going to end up in chains."

Part Two

Blockade running was not regarded as either unlawful or dishonorable, but rather as a bold and daring enterprise . . . those who attempted to brave it, did so at their own risk, subject by the laws of war to be fired upon . . . killed or wounded in the course of the capture.

—William Watson
The Civil War Adventures of a Blockade Runner

13

March 15, 1863

With the winds gusting as they were, Townsend was restless to get underway. He picked up his telescope and scanned the rain-swept harbor. The
normally calm bay was churned up with angry whitecaps, causing the boats
at anchor to bounce and heave like a herd of bucking horses. Wild gusts of
winds caused the crowns of palm fronds on the coconut trees along the coast
to wave like angry windmills. Over at the docks at Regla, a few of the larger
blockade-running steamships like the 250-foot *Cuba* were loading crates and
boxes of arms and ammunition with the help of a large metal crane. There
was no sign of the distinctive sharply raked masts of the USS *Leopard*. She
had left days earlier, presumably with Van Cortland as her shipmaster.

Van Cortland's words had seared into Townsend's skin, burning like a
red-hot branding iron, steeling his resolve to run the blockade. Before the
barroom fight, he had been conflicted, pondering Emma's words, but once
he felt the sting of Van Cortland's accusations, he knew what he wanted
to do. He would show those Navy gunship captains what seamanship really
was. But even as his mind was made up, he couldn't rid himself of a gnawing unease. He could hear his father now, principled, fixed in his opinions
and blunt in his criticism. He would say blockade running was trading with
the enemy. Townsend put the image of his father out of his mind, or at least
tried to.

In the pelting rain, the young captain helped direct the cargo into the dry
sections of the hold. He was glad he'd put his oilskins on early. He and his

four rain-soaked crewmembers were using the foremast halyard with a large eight-inch-long three-sheaved block and tackle to hoist the heavier cargo aboard ship. Red Beard showed off his singing skills, teaching the others some of the chantey-man songs he had learned as a young man in the Gulf.

> Seven dollars is a white man's pay
> For screwing cotton ten hours a day.

Ezra Higgins had signed on as a crewmember, joining Red Beard, "Dutch" Olsen, and Pierre Bertrand. Townsend could have used one extra man, but he had told Don Pedro he was happy to sail with the four sailors. Salazar and Nolo were coming with the vessel as the merchant's representatives or super-cargoes as they were called, but they were not part of the crew. He watched as the two Spaniards guarded a section of the cargo as if it were a shipment of gold. He could barely read the marking on the wooden crates. The words had been partially painted over, but he could still make out some of the black stenciling, "London Armory, Her Majesty's Service." He presumed this was the military cargo Helm had procured for the Confederacy from British suppliers.

A small group of *Guardia Civil* officers with their broad-brimmed felt hats purposefully walked toward their ship. The heavy wall of rain made it difficult to see who it was. He thought he could make out the small stocky figure of Captain Vásquez with his dark blue coat and white pants out in front. He and his men were dragging along a black man, a familiar sight on the waterfront as the police were frequently arresting slaves on the docks. Since his release from jail six weeks before, Townsend had gotten to know Captain Vásquez. The Spanish official was ever-present on the docks, and he seemed to show a special interest in Townsend. Bertrand had advised him to frequently slip the man some money as a good faith gesture. The Cuban custom of handing out *sobornos*, or bribes, was the only way to get anything done on the docks.

As the small group got closer, Townsend gasped. The black man in custody was no dockworker. It was someone he had never expected to see again. He rubbed the water off his eyes to try to get a better look, and held up his hand to shield his face from the stinging rain. There was no mistaking the man's features. It was Clyde Hendricks. He'd been beaten up pretty badly, eyes swollen, but his old shipmate smiled hopefully. Townsend wanted to greet Hendricks, but he resisted the urge and held his emotions in check.

Vásquez nodded to Townsend.

"Muy buenos días, Capitán. Siempre es un placer verle por aquí."

Townsend nodded, and said the feeling was mutual. He had become accustomed to the formal introductory remarks of Spanish officials. The protocol demanded a pleasant greeting, which was then followed by the business to be discussed. It was all a façade of politeness.

"¿Conoce a este negro, Capitán? Do you know this Negro?"

"Why do you ask?"

"He claims he came to Cuba on board your ship a few months ago."

"Yes, I know the man. He sailed south with me to Cuba."

"Is this the Negro we deported to Key West along with the rest of your crew two months ago?"

Townsend nodded. "Why have you arrested him?"

"As you should know by now, Captain, we do not take kindly to black foreign sailors on Havana's docks. And this Negro has returned to Cuba illegally, and by law will suffer the consequences. He is headed for the chain gang, and then perhaps to the cane fields."

Townsend looked at Hendricks who was literally shaking. "What can I do to change your mind?" Townsend asked suggestively, smiling as he put his hand in his pocket and began jingling some coins ever so gently.

The trace of a smile crept over the Spaniard's face. Vásquez adjusted his hat and pulled Townsend away from the other officers so they couldn't hear what he was saying. He switched to a mixture of Spanish and English.

"Usted es un buen hombre, Townsend. You're a good man and I like you. As you are now the captain of a Spanish-flagged ship, I am prepared to make an exception and release him to you." He lowered his voice to a hushed whisper. "But if you do not want him, as you well know, Cuba is always in need of more *bozales,* more Africans to cut the cane. And slaves who speak English are hard to find. They go for a high price."

Townsend nodded, and discreetly handed Vásquez a small handful of half-ounce gold coins. He was about to turn away when the Spaniard grabbed his arm, and spoke into his ear. He said he needed to talk to him about another delicate matter. *"Se trata de Pierre Bertrand."* Townsend groaned. What had Bertrand done now? "We know the woman he is currently seeing," the Spanish official said. *"Una mulata de rumbo."*

Townsend had heard that term before. It meant a classy, good-looking woman of mixed race. The seductive stroll of these women on Havana's streets was like a siren's call for many Spanish men.

"Ella está prohibida," the Spanish captain said in a stern voice.

"Prohibited?" replied Townsend. "Does she have the French pox?"

"She has another man, an important man who wants her attentions."

"I see," Townsend said, relieved it wasn't the other possibility. "No doubt he is your superior, Captain?"

Vásquez glared at him with his gamy, distrustful eyes, and Townsend knew he'd guessed correctly. Secret affairs and mistresses were as common as spies and drunks in Havana.

As soon as the Spanish captain had disappeared from sight, Townsend went below. He found Hendricks in the galley in the main cabin. The Bahamian was seated at the large kitchen table that was fastened to the starboard bulkhead where they had hung several string bags filled with green coconuts, oranges, and pineapples. Hendricks was hunched over a cup of coffee. Townsend threw more coal in the stove and poured himself a cup. They stood and stared at each other silently. No words were necessary. Townsend could tell Hendricks was quite shaken. One of his eyes was swollen completely shut, and he looked like he was in pain.

Townsend opened the cold storage locker and chipped off a small piece of ice, a valuable commodity on board ship.

"Here, put this on your eye. It might help reduce the swelling. Looks like you got what the Cubans call *un trancazo*, a hard blow."

"Da ain' no lie. I tried to jump ship, but the Cap'n, he ain' like that. It got violent, you see, and he bust up me face bad."

"How and why in tarnation did you come back here to Cuba?"

Hendricks then explained what had happened to him over the past month and a half. He and the other Irish sailors had been dropped off in Key West, and the Navy had put him to work shoveling coal.

"Them Union boys treat me like I deh a runaway field slave. Deh call me a contraband. Deh make me a coal heaver. So after weeks and weeks of shovelin' coal, I jump on a steamboat headed for St. Thomas. De captain put me in the boiler room with all the other negroes. Das a mean job, I tellin' you. Hot like the devil's own place. Smellin' bad too. The engine clankin' and hissin'. When we stop in Havana to pick up coal, I see the old *Laura Ann* tied up at the docks. And then I see you. I tried to run, but they grab me, and mash me up good."

Hendricks flicked his right hand quickly back and forth, his index finger slapping against the second finger, making a noise that sounded like someone getting a whipping. "Yeh mon, they wup me up bad. I tellin' you. Then they hand me over to them Spanish, and I got some more licks."

Townsend was silent at first, and then spoke in a more somber voice.

"You realize we are now running the blockade."

"You mus' be jokin'? For true?"

"Not by choice," Townsend replied quickly. "I've had my own trouble. The man you warned me about—the one we saved. Well, that same night he got a knife in the gut and I got arrested. The Spanish kept me over a week in a dungeon. I thought I was a dead man. I had to decide—make a deal or die. Make no mistake, I have no love for the Confederate cause," Townsend said defensively. "It's just a job."

Hendricks looked at him, his brow furrowed.

"That ain' jus' any job. That's a dangerous job. I seen the captured boats and the prisoners in Key West. The Navy sends many of dem blockade runners north to prison in New York."

"I could use your help," Townsend insisted. "We're headed for Mobile."

Hendricks raised his eyebrows skeptically.

"We're shorthanded. You'll get the same pay as the other men."

Hendricks looked at him strangely. Townsend wasn't sure what the Bahamian was thinking.

"You suppin' with the devil now, you know. With them Spanish you bes' have a long spoon." Hendricks paused for a moment and then finally shook his head in resignation. "But then I s'pose I ain' got no choice. I gon' go with you. You tellin' me same pay, right?"

Townsend nodded, and they shook hands on it, just as Red Beard called for him from above. It was Don Pedro, who wanted to know if they would be ready to leave before dusk. Townsend nodded. They had already been cleared to leave the harbor. Even though they were intending to run into the blockaded port of Mobile, he had cleared for Matamoros, technically a neutral port in Mexico, just a stone's throw across the Rio Grande from Texas. The Spaniard smiled reassuringly, and handed him a recent Blunt's survey of Mobile Bay and a booklet with the secret code of flash-light night signals used by the Confederates along the coast near Mobile. "A gift from Mr. Helm," he said with a smile. Before leaving, Don Pedro handed him a note.

"I almost forgot to give you this."

Townsend looked at the small folded piece of high-quality linen stationery with apprehension. It was sealed with red wax. At first he thought it might be from his father, it was so official-looking, but the florid handwriting was not his.

"Open it," Don Pedro said with a smile. "It's from one of your new admirers in Cuba."

Townsend unsealed the letter and began reading.

I want to wish you a safe voyage, Captain Townsend, and a speedy return. I hope you will come see me at my estate in the Yumurí Valley as soon as you are back in Havana.
    Respectfully, Doña Cecilia de Vargas.

"It seems Doña Cecilia has taken a liking to you," said Don Pedro as he lit one of his Fígaro Regalía cigars, his drooping, black eyes gleaming like river stones.

"Where is the Yumurí Valley?" Townsend asked.

Don Pedro puffed on his cigar. "Near the city of Matanzas."

Even with the wall of windswept rain, Townsend could make out the blue Confederate Navy Jacks quivering and snapping on several ships' masts, cracking like distant artillery fire. It might be terrible weather for loading cargo, but these were good conditions for running the blockade, as long as the wind held steady. Townsend looked over at the flagstaff at the Captain of the Port's office. The half-blue and half-yellow triangular signal fluttered ominously, warning that the bad weather was worsening. With darkness so close, Townsend gave the order to raise the sails.

"Ready on the mainsail throat! Ready on the peak!"

Olsen and Bertrand stood on the starboard side holding the peak halyard. Hendricks and Red Beard were on the port side ready to pull up the throat halyard.

"Heave. Heave. Get the jaws all the way up!"

"Heh yah, Ho yah."

The foresail went up next with a squeal of blocks, clicking of mast hoops, and a flogging of canvas, followed by the jib and the boomed staysail. The sails stained with coal ash fluttered and then filled in, the boat suddenly straining to be free of the docklines. The rain had let up, but the winds were still strong. The storms were rolling through in a parade of squalls.

"We'll pay off on the starboard tack," Townsend cried out. "Cast off and sheet in."

With a steady southeasterly wind gusting at twenty miles per hour, the lead-gray colored schooner quickly gathered headway. Two other schooners running the blockade for the T.W. House Company of Houston and the R. and D.G. Mills Company of Galveston were right behind them. A Confederate-flagged sidewheeler tugboat was just off their starboard bow. The entire fleet of blockade runners got a warm send-off with many of the anchored ships blowing their horns in support. A few boatmen waved the Confederate flag, and yelled out, "¡Vivan los Confederados!"

Townsend could see the blue coats of some young Navy officers standing on board an anchored Federal gunboat. It was a big screw-propeller steamship. The officers watched through their glasses. Townsend had learned the rules of engagement in this so-called neutral port. The Navy's East Gulf Blockading Squadron with its fleet of warships based in Key West could enter Havana for recoaling and repairs, but international law prevented them from chasing any ships inside or directly outside the harbor. They could do nothing to stop them, not yet. Townsend wondered if any of the Navy men could have been at the Academy with him. As he looked at their blue uniforms, he realized he was still resentful, still angry about what the Navy had done. He felt a tightness in his stomach. He didn't want to be seen by anyone from his old life.

Townsend looked back over the city's old wall toward the rooftop of Mrs. Carpenter's boarding house, and raised his glass to his eye. He thought he saw a lone figure standing next to one of the urns looking out to sea, but when he looked again the figure was gone. He felt a sharp tinge—sorrow and regret for what might have been. Red Beard's nudge snapped him from his reverie. He turned to see the first angry puffs of black smoke coming out of the funnel of the Navy ship they had passed.

"She got steam up, Cap'n. Looks like she may be fixin' to give chase. Might be we'll see her out thar in the Gulf."

Booming cannons signaled their approach to El Morro Castle and the line of guns known as the twelve apostles. In the fading light, he could see the armed sentries and gunners above him waving their black caps in support. The irony didn't escape him. He had been imprisoned by the Spanish, and now, sailing under the Spanish flag, they saluted him as a hero with their cannons. He had never been celebrated for anything, but here he was the focus of admiration and adulation for a cause he didn't believe in. He felt a strange mixture of pride and unease run through him. Behind him, through the stormy haze, he could just make out the skyline—Havana's domes and steeples. It hardly seemed possible that he was leaving this city.

As the schooner cleared out of the harbor, Townsend stood at the wheel and felt the heavily loaded ship lean into the wind. He admired the graceful sheer of his boat from the raised quarterdeck to the long bowsprit and jib boom thrusting out an additional forty feet from the bow. At that moment, the *Gaviota* felt like a small clipper ship to him. With the wind getting stronger, he did a visual check of everything on deck. The large twelve-foot launch boat had been tied down forward of the main hatchway, the panniers of live chickens placed under the boat for protection. All the other hatches were battened down, portholes dogged, lines coiled, and all gear including the freshwater barrels securely lashed on deck. He looked through the telescope and could see far in the distance the heavy gusts blowing against the Gulf Stream current, creating steep, jumbled whitecaps, and scuds of sea spray flying in the air.

"I reckon it will be a wet ride," said Red Beard. "Should be foul weather at least as far as the Tortugas, and I don't doubt we'll be tolerable busy looking for smoke on the distant horizon. What's our course, Cap'n?"

"West toward the Yucatan banks," Townsend replied. "Then before reaching Bahía Honda and the Colorado reefs, north towards the Tortugas. We want to get as far out to sea as possible before daylight."

"That's about when we might see if any Navy gunship came after us," Red Beard said.

Townsend handed the helm over to his first mate, and then steadied himself like a gimbaled lantern, seesawing back and forth with the pitch and roll of the waves as he looked up at the sails and the rigging. He breathed in deeply and smelled the salt in the air. The clouds of misty sea spray seemed to wash away the tensions and restlessness that haunted him ashore. As he reacted to the familiar heave and roll of the ship's deck, Townsend suddenly felt free of the land, like a gliding seagull in the sky. But then he saw the shadowy figures coming up the companionway steps. The two supercargoes, Salazar and Nolo, emerged onto the quarterdeck. Townsend clenched his teeth and felt his stomach tighten.

14

It was midnight and pitch black when Townsend took his turn at the wheel. With the wind almost dead astern, the schooner was sailing wing and wing, with the foresail on one side and the mainsail on the other. He peered out into the darkness. The weather was still thick with gusty winds so he decided to keep the schooner under a reefed main and foresail. To stay clear of the Gulf Stream current, they hugged the Cuban coast, judging their distance off shore by observing huge fires on land, presumably from some of the seaside plantations. They were well within the six-mile territorial limit claimed by the Spanish, so they were in little danger of being spotted by a Navy cruiser. For safety, Townsend had installed a reinforced boom tackle to both the fore and the main to prevent jibing. He told the crew to leave the tackles on a semi-permanent basis, ready to be rigged at any moment. After what had happened to Captain Evans, Townsend was taking no chances with the boom swinging over at night.

As he watched the dark, unknown shoreline pass by, Townsend saw in his imagination the cane fields, coffee plantations, and lush tropical forests, the land of his mother's childhood. He wondered if he would ever see the farm where she grew up. He thought of the letter he had received from Doña Cecilia de Vargas. It struck him as strange that this refined woman of the Cuban upper class would invite him, a young unknown American ship captain, to her plantation. He assumed it was because of her friendship with Don Pedro. Perhaps he'd find that place called Mambi Joo his mother had spoken of. Perhaps he could find a distant relative. He looked out into the blackness. Answers about his mother's Cuban heritage could be out there.

He thought of his mother's lithe, slim figure and her thick black hair. Her sharp, perceptive eyes had a way of seeing through people, detecting their flaws. She could pick the honest ones from the scoundrels and the frauds. She had always called his well-meaning father a fool for trusting people. He hoped he had inherited some of her keen sensibilities in judging character. He was beginning to feel that some of that skill had rubbed off on him, not just her hot-headed temperament, an unfortunate trait he knew he shared with her. He suddenly felt a deep pang of sadness, an oddly specific emptiness knowing she wasn't there anymore. Thank goodness, she didn't suffer the shame of hearing about his dismissal from the Naval Academy. Poor soul. They said it was pneumonia, but he thought she'd died of a broken heart from the news about the death of her younger son.

Townsend looked over at Hendricks. He had chosen the Bahamian as his watch partner because none of the other sailors knew him. He wasn't sure about the mindset of these men, how they would react to a Negro crewmember, and he wanted no problems on board ship. You could know a man on land, but at sea was a different story. As there was no space in the cramped forward cabin house, Hendricks was sleeping in one of the available pipe berths in the galley area, not far from his quarters. It would be safer that way.

Some fifty miles down the coast, Townsend had Hendricks loosen and detach the preventers. They both sheeted in the main and foresail, and the schooner headed on a northerly course away from the treacherous Colorado reefs off the Cuban coast into the open Gulf. The dark distant shore of Cuba soon faded into blackness. The only light on board was the glimmer from the compass light. Townsend had no way to do a sighting, so he was charting a course by dead reckoning. He thought about these men he had chosen. They were all hardened sailors with rough-hewn, weather-beaten faces to prove it. The steely eyes of Higgins, the whiskery jaw of Red Beard, the tangled hair of old Dutch Olsen, and the roguish smile of Bertrand, all told a story of men who had seen too much to be overly hopeful about life's rewards. What he liked was they might have their sympathies about secession and the war, but they were all outsiders. No Southern fire-eaters among them, as far as he could tell. Nor were there any true believers. They sailed for adventure and money. Higgins had deserted from the US Navy and it sounded like Red Beard had done the same from the Confederate States Navy. Maybe they were all running away from something, forever drifting, like sun-bleached driftwood, beaten and battered by life's storms. Havana just happened to be where they washed ashore for a time.

In some ways, he told himself he was no different. He was an outsider like them, someone whose only creed had now become the art of survival. He had told them about doing prison time in Havana for helping an Englishman escape, and this had earned him respect. None of them cared much for the Spanish. They all knew about him getting kicked out of the Naval Academy. After the bar fight with Van Cortland, he had explained what had happened. They understood. He was young, younger than all of them. He remembered what Higgins had told him. He'd said he would sail with him because he wasn't just another pig-snouted bookworm full of useless information. What mattered to these hardened sailors was that he knew his way around boats, and was well trained in navigation as well as gunnery—experience and knowledge they didn't have. If they had any doubts, they kept it to themselves. But he knew they would be watching him. He remembered what one of his instructors had said about leadership back at the Naval Academy. "Show no fear and do what it takes to get the job done. Be tough with your men, but respect them and above all, never humiliate them."

Townsend handed over the wheel to Hendricks and stepped down into the main cabin house. The schooner was now heeling over sharply as the bow heaved into the waves. They were battling the strong currents of the Gulf Stream, and he wanted to consult the charts that Don Pedro had given him. He was surprised to find Salazar and Nolo sitting up at the table, leaning over buckets with faces of despair.

The two Spaniards were bunked together in the stateroom opposite his quarters. They had been below in their cabin ever since they left Havana. It was clear they were in dire straits from seasickness. He saw that both Spaniards had retched volumes onto their laps before they'd found the buckets. Townsend bit his lip to hide an unkind smile and gave each of them some ginger lozenges, feigning sympathy.

He went into his cabin and began pouring over the charts. One of them was an old survey done by Josiah Tattnall in 1830 for the US Navy, a thorough guide to the chain of sandy islands that made up the Tortugas. One quick look at the different charts, including the ones Captain Evans had left behind, told him these were tricky waters filled with treacherous shoals. His gunnery professor had ominously called this tiny archipelago "Land's End." He noted the location of the tall 150-foot lighthouse, recently built on Loggerhead Key. He knew he wanted to sail west of that island, not only to avoid the risk of running aground on a particularly dangerous shoal called the Quicksands, but also to stay well out of reach of the powerful guns of Fort Jefferson. He was counting on the *Gaviota*'s camouflaged gray sails and hull to allow them to pass undetected before the early morning light would strike their sails.

Townsend had learned about this massive sea fortress at the Naval Academy. The Federal government had started building Fort Jefferson in 1846 as a way to protect shipping in the Gulf. It was a six-sided, four-tiered brick fort built on a sandy island called Garden Key. It was being used as a Union prison for deserters, but Townsend knew the fort was also well fortified, with everything from forty-pound James rifles to the long-range eight- and ten-inch Columbiads that could fire shell and shot two to three miles away.

Just before four o'clock in the morning, Townsend roused Red Beard and Higgins. It would soon be time for their watch. When he came back, Hendricks was shaking his head.

"Gulf Stream too strong. We bes' head off further west."

"See there now, I know what I'm doing," Townsend snapped.

"I tellin' you," the Bahamian insisted. "We gon' run into problems. The current pushing us too far to the east."

"Heigh-ho!" Townsend said. "Never mind, just leave the calculating to me."

Hendricks shrugged his shoulders, surprised at Townsend's uncharacteristic reaction. He was about to say something, but perhaps out of deference to the captain or fear of being rebuked, he remained silent.

It seemed as if Townsend had just laid down on his bunk when he was jolted awake by Higgins at the door, tense and agitated, his brow furrowed.

"You need to see this, Cap'n."

Townsend grabbed his telescope and ran up the small stairs to the deck. One look at Red Beard's shadowy face at the helm and he knew something was terribly wrong. The first mate pointed 30 degrees off the port bow.

"Look yonder," he said with his Texas drawl. "It's the onliest light out thar."

Townsend had expected to see the Tortugas lighthouse off to the starboard to the east of the schooner, but instead the gleaming light on the horizon was on the port side of the boat to the west. The realization hit him like a heavy blow to the head. Hendricks had been right—the current had swept them much farther off course than he had calculated.

"I reckon yer miscalculatin' has gotten us into trouble, Cap'n," Red Beard snapped. He bit off some tobacco from a black plug and began chewing.

Townsend didn't like the surliness in Red Beard's voice—he knew he might have a problem with this man. He picked up his telescope again and scanned the western horizon. It was still dark and the sky was hazy from the storm. The winds remained south, southeast. He thought he could see a faint tip of what could be a sail, and not too far from that a suspicious splotch of darkness that could be black smoke from a steamship. He knew there were Navy cruisers patrolling off the Tortugas. Higgins clambered up the ratlines and agreed there was something shadowy on the western horizon about seven miles away that could be smoke from a steamship.

"Fall off one quarter so we are sailing north, northwest, and then hold course," said Townsend, trying to sound as confident as he could. His mouth had become parched and he tried to moisten his dry lip with his tongue.

Red Beard looked at the young captain with a stubborn set of his jaw, and then back down to the compass. "That course will take us directly to that fort! As soon as those bluebellies see our gray sails, they'll know for sure we're a blockade runner, and they'll blast us out of the water like ducks in a pond."

Townsend felt his temper rising. He told himself he needed to maintain a quiet, calm manner to project confidence.

"The garrison is not likely to fire on us," he said steadily.

"How you calculatin' that?" Red Beard snapped back. "What in thunder do you mean!"

"With our Spanish flag, they will likely assume we are legal traders headed for Mexico."

"I hope you're right," grumbled the Texan as he pulled at his beard.

Townsend turned away from the brooding face of the first mate and looked over at Hendricks, acknowledging his mistake with a shake of his head. The Bahamian responded with a nod of confidence. That's what he liked about Hendricks. So much could be said without words.

"How soon before the sun comes up?" he asked the Bahamian.

Hendricks looked up at the sky and said, "I gon' guess one more hour."

"Keep her good full on this course, Red Beard."

"Aye, Aye, Cap'n," the Texan said with an edge in his voice.

It was a gray black sky when they caught their first good look at Fort Jefferson, some four miles away. No one spoke as the grim fortress seemed to rise out of the dark sea as they sailed closer, like an ominous ironclad warship made of rusty red bricks. In the gray light it was still mostly in shadow, but the size of the fort left them speechless. Through the telescope Townsend could see the red and black sea buoy marking the entrance to the South East Channel.

"What is the range of these guns?" asked Bertrand as he nervously pulled on his beard. "*Quelle est la portée?*"

"Two miles for the Columbiads," Townsend replied matter-of-factly, causing Red Beard to frown.

"How many guns them blue bellies got in that fort?" asked the Texan.

"Better than fifty," replied Townsend somberly, glad for the darkness that kept a nervous twitch in his face from being seen. "The fort is manned by about two hundred men."

"*Mon Dieu,*" whispered Bertrand.

"No way around it. We're in the devil of a hobble. We'll be comin' in range shortly," said the Texan.

"Hang it all!" Townsend said angrily. "Let me reason with you, Withers. Hitting a vessel as small as the *Gaviota* at that range will be like you swatting a fly with your tallywacker."

The entire crew stood watching in awed silence as they drew closer to the giant walls bristling with destructive firepower. A desperate calmness hung over them like a dark cloud. Between them and the fort were reefy shoals, bare sandy islands, and waves dashing up against the walls. Off to their right, they could barely see a hint of foaming breakers, pelicans diving into the water and more sandy islands. Beyond that lay the passage north to the open Gulf.

Townsend pulled out one of his Havana cigars and began chewing on it. The dull black of the night had given way to the smudgy gray of early morning. He could hear the muttering and mumbling around him. He knew there was a shiver of disquiet on board ship.

"Hendricks, how many minutes before sunrise?"

"Com'n soon Captain. . . ."

Townsend pointed to a sandy bump on the ocean's surface with scraggy vegetation, barely visible some three miles off the starboard bow.

"That's East Key. Sail due east toward that island," Townsend instructed Red Beard.

"Why in blazes . . . that will take us outside the channel. We'll be in the shoals. We'll run aground," the Texan grumbled. At first, the first mate looked like he would refuse the order, but then one look at Townsend's wild and determined face made him pause. He turned the wheel so that the ship's bow pointed at the small island, all the while muttering to himself. "Dad-burned fool idea if I ever saw one."

Just then, Higgins cried out from his perch in the masthead. "Smoke to the east, southeast, steaming in our direction. Looks to be a Navy gunship."

Townsend swung around, holding the glass to his eye. He'd almost forgotten the danger from that gunship they'd seen in Havana harbor. He could see the smoke on the horizon and the gray outline of a warship. It was coming directly toward them, steaming into the Gulf Stream current. He estimated it was three to four miles away.

"She just fired at us, Cap'n," Higgins shouted.

Townsend felt the grim tension even as he fought against the cross current of fear and anticipation running through him. He kept looking at the ship through his telescope as if that would make it go away. He heard the first report and saw another flash of a bow gun. They were well out of range so there was no immediate danger. He knew the Navy gunboat was probably firing its cannons to alert the gunners at the fort.

"Keep your eyes on the fort, Higgins," Townsend shouted.

At that moment, the sun peaked up from the horizon exploding in the eastern sky like a trumpet blast, blinding everyone on board. Townsend looked back toward the sunlit fort where he now could detect the gleaming black muzzles of scores of cannons and small figures running on the parapet, gesturing and signaling.

"Steer due east into the sun. Hold course."

"I can't see a solitary thing," Red Beard exclaimed as he held up the palm of his hand to his eyes.

"Never mind," Townsend said. "Just hold your course, damn it. You can't see, but neither can those gunners on the fort. So hold your tongue. It's waggin' like a mangy dog's tail."

"Doomed. We're doomed," declared Red Beard and he spit a gob of tobacco juice onto the deck.

Moments later a ball struck the water about a quarter of a mile ahead of them, sending spray everywhere. Townsend looked back and saw an ominous yellow muzzle flash and then the report from a heavy gun. It was the flat dull boom of a smoothbore.

Soon dozens of guns were firing, and the buzz of round shot could be heard overhead. Spouts of water shot up all around them, blasting spray over the schooner's decks.

"Set gaff topsails," Townsend cried out, a sudden urgency in his voice. The glare from the sun was so bright his eyes hurt.

Bertrand scrambled up the ratlines of the foremast some seventy feet to the hounds to set the topsail. Higgins, who was already high up the mainmast hanging onto the topmast shrouds and backstays, maneuvered an unwieldy pile of lines and canvas into position to raise that sail. Just then a black streak screamed over the two men's heads with an ear-splitting rush like a freight train, causing them both to cry out. Townsend knew these were explosive shells fired from rifled guns, and were far more dangerous to a wooden-hulled ship than shot. If the fuses were timed correctly, the shells would explode on impact.

"I jus' see the yellow flash again Cap'n! Watch yeself!" Hendricks cried.

Townsend heard the high-pitched crack. He threw himself on the deck just as he heard the roar overhead. The shell plowed into the main cabin, blowing off the roof in a shower of splinters. A second later the water ahead of them erupted in a geyser-like explosion.

"Check the two Spaniards down below," Townsend cried out to Olsen. Townsend breathed deeply and looked around at the shattered deckhouse. After a quick check, Olsen reported that Salazar and Nolo had some splinters but nothing too serious. Townsend sighed with relief that no one was seriously hurt. He estimated that they soon would be out of range of the fort's guns.

The schooner headed directly into an enormous sun that swallowed the horizon with an explosion of gold. The glare was so bright the silhouettes and cries of the birds helped to guide them toward East Key. From studying the charts earlier, Townsend knew the water around East Key was quite shallow. There were no channel markers here, no way to know where the dangerous shoals and sand banks were. They would have to navigate by sight. Townsend nodded to Hendricks, and without saying a word the Bahamian sailor quickly climbed the ratlines. When they'd sailed through the Bahamas, Townsend remembered how Hendricks had piloted the boat through the shoals by conning from aloft. As soon as the Bahamian reached the foremast head, he began signaling to Townsend.

"Fall off one quarter," Townsend shouted to Red Beard. The Texan turned the wheel quickly and the bow of the ship veered off to port. Off to the starboard side, Townsend could see how shallow the translucent water had become. Brown and red shapes were visible just three feet from the surface. Coral heads, he whispered to himself. They were big enough to have ripped a hole in the ship's hull. He breathed out deeply to calm himself. He looked up to Hendricks for further guidance. The Bahamian was now signaling to turn more sharply west. Again Red Beard adjusted course. Hendricks and Higgins slacked the sheets of the foresail and the jib to help the bow of the schooner swing over more quickly. Off the starboard side, Townsend looked down through the glassy water at the shallow sandy bank they'd almost struck. They would have run hard aground. Another close call.

Soon they cleared East Key, and the ocean became a darker blue, indicating deeper water for the moment. The boom of cannons could still be heard, but most of the shots were falling far behind them. Townsend could barely make out the foaming white water in the distance that marked more shoal areas. The old charts from 1830 had told him there would be two more sandy islets, but as he looked through the glass there was nothing there, just break-ers and diving pelicans to mark where the sand once had been. He thought to himself this indeed was Land's End, a watery world where the small strips of ever-shifting sand remained permanently under siege.

At the sound of another cannon, Townsend swung around and looked back at the fort. They were well out of range now. From the faint smiles on the crew's faces, he guessed he might have won a grudging nod of respect from these men. Perhaps they had fewer doubts about his seamanship. Still he was aware they'd been lucky. His underestimation of the strength of the Gulf Stream current had been a serious navigational error.

Townsend looked up at Hendricks. The Bahamian again signaled more shallow areas ahead, but Townsend knew from the charts that they were isolated spots, and they should be able to dodge their way around them.

"Lay two points closer to the wind, Red Beard."

"Aye, Aye, Cap'n."

"Stand by to work on the wind's eye with short tacks," he called out to the crew.

Later that same day, they spotted a billowing column of black smoke from a steamer coming from the west. It was just six miles away. Townsend guessed it was that same gunship from Havana. The big Navy ship had been forced to go around the fort to the west as they were unable to follow them through the shallows away from the deeper channels. Townsend ordered the sails to be dropped, and he pointed the bow of the schooner in the direction of the passing ship. This was a trick Townsend had heard about from some of the blockade runners in the bars of Havana. As long as the steamship did not come toward them, all they would see on the horizon would be a stick in the water. He didn't think it would work, but amazingly, they were never spotted. In the mauve sky of dusk, the low gray hull and the bare black poles of the *Gaviota* never stood out enough to catch the attention of the Navy lookouts.

15

Townsend imagined what death would have been like if they had been hit by one of those explosive shells: a blinding flash of light and then nothing. He shook that thought away. Standing with his feet spread wide apart for better balance, he felt the reassuring rolling motion of the deck. The stormy weather had given way to clear skies, and the southeasterly breeze now continued fresh and steady. The darker shade of blue of the sea and the more responsive heel of the ship told him they were in much deeper water. He grabbed one of the windward stays to steady himself, and looked around at the crew.

One of the first things they'd done after leaving the Tortugas was to rebuild a temporary frame over the splintered main cabin roof. He had watched with satisfaction as the crew came together to do what needed to be done. They all knew the "A-Roving" chantey, and sang it as they covered the gaping hole with a canvas covering.

> She swore that she'd be true to me
> But spent me pay day fast and free.

When they got to the chorus, "I'll go no more a-roving with you fair maid, no more roving with you," they pulled the canvas tight and lashed it down to brass fastenings on the deck. He knew they'd been lucky to escape from the Tortugas. He'd been too proud to listen, and he hadn't shown the men enough respect. His carelessness had put them all in danger. He was trying to learn from his mistakes, but he knew he was still on trial, particularly with Red Beard.

At night they kept the same watches. Townsend and Hendricks both enjoyed the middle watch, the dark shadows and the silence of the night. They sailed with no lights so the *Gaviota* moved through the water like a ghost ship, invisible from a distance. The only light was the schooner's frothy wake, the waves alive with silvery phosphorescent stars. With the sextant, Townsend took star sights each night of Sirius, Capella, and Canopus, and then carefully marked those positions on the chart. During the day at first light, he confirmed those star sights, and took another reading at noon to confirm the latitude. He would not make another navigational error like the last one.

He recalled some advice he'd gotten back in Havana from an old veteran in one of the bars. The man had told him how the captain of a blockade-running schooner needed to be a good navigator, but mostly he needed to think more like a rabbit than a fox. "Check your navigation," the old captain had said, "and stay vigilant."

As part of that strategy, Townsend insisted that one of the men be up the masthead at all times, looking out for white sails or black smoke on the horizon. To make it comfortable for the man on watch, they furled the fore topsail and arranged the canvas around the shrouds and the spring stay to make a crow's nest perch. Each time they spotted a suspicious sail or a cloud of wispy black smoke on the horizon, they would change course and move away from it. Townsend had learned his lesson.

It was a blustery afternoon with the winds blowing a steady twenty knots when Townsend faced his next test. They'd been at sea for four days, and the day had started like the one before it. Life on board ship had fallen into a familiar pattern. Before dawn, the crew bathed on deck. Each sailor would stand naked on the foredeck while one of the others threw buckets of cold sea water on him. Olsen got the coals burning in the stove at first light, and with the first blast of the sun, the smoke would be curling up through the stovepipe to the upper deck. Breakfast, usually hard biscuits and the occasional fresh eggs from the shipboard chickens or line-caught fish, was served at sunrise. That afternoon Hendricks had just earned praise from everyone with his line fishing skills by pulling in several beautiful gold and green fish the Cubans called *dorado*. They were busy scaling and gutting the fish on the deck when Higgins cried out from the masthead.

"Sail on the horizon. Looks about seven miles away." He pointed to the south at a distant white speck, its low-lying hull barely visible, and its sails seeming to touch the water. The distant ship was making good progress with the winds behind her. At times it was hidden from view by the waves.

Townsend climbed halfway up the shrouds and took a look through the glass. It appeared to be a two-masted brigantine, and from the faint line of her raked masts, Townsend suspected he knew the ship. He felt a hot shiver of excitement and anticipation. It was the *Leopard*. She may have been sent into the center of the Gulf to look for them.

"Hold course, northwest by north, one quarter north," he called out. "Keep the wind blowing on your shoulder."

"Aye, aye, Cap'n," Red Beard said.

Two hours later the brigantine was just three miles away and with her skysails and royals set, she was closing fast under full sail. It was clear they had been spotted and would soon be in range of her guns. They tried the old trick of throwing water on the sails to make the canvas more supple to hold the wind, but to little effect. Townsend started doing short tacks, close to windward, forcing the larger square-rigged brigantine to try to follow. From his frequent sightings, he knew they were about one hundred miles due west of Egmont Key on the Florida coast, some 220 miles southeast of Mobile. He believed they could escape at night if they could get close in to shore. If they could stay out of range of the Navy ship's guns, he thought, they might be able to escape into the shallows as soon as it was dark.

But just before dusk, the wind faded. There was an eerie silence and calm as the two boats floundered in the open Gulf, adrift with their sails limp, floating less than two miles apart. Townsend's hopes sank as he watched through the glass the Navy sailors drop anchor in what was probably more than sixteen fathoms of water. It was so quiet he could hear the distant clanking of the ship's anchor chain. With the sun below the horizon, Townsend grimly observed the sailors lower the two launch boats, each one filled with a half-dozen armed men all wearing the Navy's flat beret-style hats.

The sailors quickly rowed in their direction, and he noticed the commanding officer standing in the lead boat with his billed cap pulled down. Angus Van Cortland's round head, clean-shaven face, and short round neck were unmistakable. He was standing erect, looking directly at Townsend through his glass with a determined gaze. It was clear he intended to capture them as a prize, and his men seemed eager. The sixteen dollars per month salary paid to Yankee seamen could be handsomely supplemented by the capture of a blockade runner. When a prize court auctioned off a seized ship and cargo, 44 percent of the prize money was distributed to the captain, officers, and the sailors. It could make them rich, all from an afternoon's work.

"Should we break out the Enfield rifles we got in the cargo hold, Cap'n?" asked Red Beard. "We can fill 'em full of lead in short order."

Townsend thought about that, but then shook his head.

"Take out the sweeps," he called out. "Let's try to move away from them. Keep the sails up. Maybe an evening breeze will come up and fill 'em. We can hope. Start whistling, Bertrand."

The men unlashed the four sixteen-foot-long oars tied to the stays and fit them through the holes in the railing. Townsend told Higgins to bring up the two supercargoes from their cabin and put them on one oar. The two Spaniards, still looking fragile and sick, were dragged up to the deck and told to row. They were too weak to protest. All five sailors and Townsend joined together, two men at each oar, as they tried to make some headway and pull the heavy schooner forward.

"Row! They'll be on us shortly. Put your backs into it." Townsend felt beads of sweat on his forehead and the burn in his shoulders and back.

The *Gaviota*'s oarsmen pulled and dipped the oars in the water as the big, heavily laden schooner crept forward. But the two Navy boats kept gaining ground. They were now just a quarter of a mile away. He could hear the shouts of the Navy sailors, the rapid creaking and splashing of their oars. Just then, Townsend felt a nudge. He looked over at Hendricks, who with a simple gesture of his head told him to look over the side. Townsend gazed out over the glossy surface of the water and saw a steady line of ripples quickly moving toward them from the north. The ripples signaled an incoming breeze.

Moments later, he felt the first faint hint of fresh air fanning his cheek. Van Cortland had clearly spotted the ripples as well, and Townsend could hear him urge his men to row harder.

"Pick up the stroke, men. Pick up the stroke."

They were just several hundred yards away. Suddenly he heard Van Cortland's voice, booming across the water like a cannon shot.

"This is an order to the captain of the Spanish merchant ship, *Gaviota*! Strike all sails or we will commence firing!"

A darkening ripple of wind was now rapidly moving toward them with an ever-wider swath. It had just reached the schooner when Townsend heard Van Cortland's next command for them to throw a line or they would fire. The two Navy boats were now almost alongside the *Gaviota* and several of the sailors were standing with their rifles raised and ready to shoot. Townsend glanced at the guns pointed in their direction and threw up his hands. He nodded to Van Cortland and threw him one of their docking lines.

"Make the line fast and strike your sails, Townsend," Van Cortland demanded, waving his Navy Colt pistol in his hand. "You and your men are now prisoners. Your ship is a captured prize of the USS *Leopard* and will be taken to the adjudication court in Key West."

Townsend did as he was told and tied the line to the stern quarter bitt even as he could feel the wind filling in more briskly, the ship's hull creaking in response. From the safety of his spot behind the dinghy hanging off the stern, Townsend spun the wheel hard to starboard as the full breeze kicked in and the schooner began to heel over. He shouted for the men to sheet in the sails.

"Move to the lee side. Take cover."

Then he turned the wheel hard over to port, causing the booms of the two masts to come crashing over with a crack. With all that confusion, the sailors in the launch boat were thrown off balance. Van Cortland fired his Navy Colt pistol at Townsend, but missed. He began screaming to his men to fire their rifles, and a volley of wild, misdirected shots soon peppered the canvas sails. Hendricks and Higgins from their prone position in the bow managed to pull tight some of the sheeting lines of the headsails, helping the boat to pick up headway on its new tack.

With the schooner responding to the freshening breeze and the sails beginning to fill, the *Gaviota* started to make headway. The Navy launch, which was still attached to the schooner by the tow line, careened along some thirty feet behind, wobbling and tipping from one side to the other. One of Van Cortland's men managed to hurl a grappling hook that caught onto the *Gaviota*'s taffrail. Hand over hand, the desperate Navy sailors began pulling their launch close enough to the schooner's stern so they could board her. A sharp breeze filled in from the east, and the *Gaviota* heeled over sharply in response, carving its way through the water. With his pistol holstered, Van Cortland scrambled to the bow of his launch boat, bringing his face up to the cap rail of the schooner's stern. Townsend and Van Cortland were now just several feet apart. For several seconds, their eyes remained locked together.

"You're my prisoner, Townsend," Van Cortland shouted. "Surrender now or we will shoot."

"Then fire away," Townsend said.

Van Cortland cursed and reached for his holstered pistol with one hand even as he tried to pull himself up on board the *Gaviota* with the other. Townsend leaned down and grabbed the pistol by the barrel before Van

Cortland could react. He stuffed the gun in his belt and then yanked off the emergency ax fastened to the wheelhouse, raising it over his head.

Townsend looked down at his rival, who was struggling to keep his balance. With some satisfaction, he watched the man's beet red face change in expression from anger to disbelief and then to panic. Townsend wanted revenge, and for a brief second he thought about splitting Van Cortland's head in two like a coconut. He swung the ax down, but instead of striking his foe, he brought the blade of the ax down on the grappling line. The Navy launch, now free of the grappling line's restraint, hurtled backwards until the tow line snapped taut like a bow string. The launch boat careened from one side to the other, taking in water over the gunwales. Van Cortland, who had been perched precariously at the bow of the launch, flew into the water. As more sailors fell overboard, Townsend quietly untied the tow line and watched as the swamped Navy boat began to sink, surrounded by the bobbing heads of sailors screaming for help.

In the fading light of dusk, Townsend could see Van Cortland and the others pulled to safety on board the other Navy boat. Darkness soon enveloped them, and the *Gaviota* disappeared into the quiet of the night with a good sailing breeze astern. Townsend steered by the compass, taking comfort in looking up at the sky to find the North Star, the way north to the Alabama coast. He spotted the Big Dipper in the northern sky and remembered what his father used to tell the runaway slaves about that constellation. Follow the drinking gourd in the sky, he would say. That will take you to the North. Townsend handed the wheel over to Red Beard, who began singing one of his cotton screw gang songs.

> Were you ever in Mobile Bay
> Screwing cotton by the day.

Townsend pulled out one of the Upmann cigars he'd bought from a store in Havana. By now he realized how many types of cigars there were available in Havana. Imperiales, Regalías, Conchas, Brevas, Londres to name just a few. He lit one of the Lucifer matches and with the sudden blast of light looked at the label. These cigars were called Cazadores, or Hunters. How aptly named, he thought to himself. He puffed appreciably on his cigar as he imagined how angry a soggy Van Cortland would be returning to his ship. He would have to suffer the embarrassment of looking his men in the face, acknowledging failure. He smiled contentedly as he flicked some ashes over the side, and then picked up Van Cortland's pistol. He walked down into the cabin. He held the gun up to the lamp and admired the elegant walnut pistol grip and the engraved scene on the revolver's cylinder. It was an 1851 Colt Navy six-shooter, a big gun, fourteen inches overall, .36 caliber. It would serve well as the ship's gun.

Later that night Hendricks knocked on his door. The Bahamian told him he had walked by the Spaniards' cabin. He had brought them some soup for their supper. He was about to knock on the door of their cabin when he heard them talking. He didn't understand a word of Spanish, but he did hear them mention Michael Abbott's name several times, followed by Townsend's name. Townsend flinched at the unexpected mention of Abbott's name.

"Abbott? They mentioned Michael Abbott? What in blazes did they say about him?" Townsend felt a shiver run down his back.

Hendricks shook his head, and explained, as he didn't understand or speak Spanish he had no idea, but when he knocked and opened the door they gave him a menacing stare.

"I left the soup, and they told me to get out the cabin. Deh were cussin' me in Spanish. Deh look like deh were gon' kill me."

16

April 13, 1863

The nearly three weeks they spent tied up at the docks in the blockaded port of Mobile Bay were mostly a blur to Townsend. They'd gotten through the blockade without any trouble, coming in at night undetected through the shallows of the eastern approach. Once within the protective reach of the guns of Fort Morgan, they were hailed by a Confederate gunboat and given clearance to sail on. It was a moment to celebrate. It had been more than seven hundred miles from the stone walls of El Morro to the Confederate fortifications at Fort Morgan, close to eleven days at sea. Since then Townsend had mostly stayed on board ship. It was clear that Nolo was under orders to watch him closely. The sharp-nosed Catalan was always nearby, whittling a piece of wood with his double-edged, long-bladed knife.

The Spaniard followed him wherever he went. Any lingering thought Townsend might have had of trying to escape in Mobile, he now quickly dismissed. When he'd been forced to sign that contract with Don Pedro two months ago, he had sworn he would try to run off the first chance he got. Now, he realized, his thinking had changed. He supposed it was the loyalty he felt to the crew that made him want to stay with the boat, or maybe it was the satisfaction he got from outwitting the Navy. Whatever it was, he was not going to try to escape, at least not yet. He wanted to return to Cuba.

Salazar made it clear to the military commander in port that he and Nolo were the sole business agents for Don Pedro Alvarado Cardona. In their talks with the Confederate Quartermaster Corps, the two Spaniards never acknowledged Townsend, dismissing him as nothing more than a hired hand whose only job was to attend to the ship. Townsend swallowed his pride and held his temper in check, but his anger was mounting. Even though he was kept away from all business negotiations, the young captain energized himself by learning about cotton. He watched in one of the work sheds as the huge unwieldy bales were first compressed in cotton presses, squeezing the soft fiber together until a bale was half its original size, almost as hard as iron. The two Spaniards had made sure they only took delivery of pressed bales. The more cotton they could carry, the greater the profits. Cotton cost eight cents a pound on the Mobile docks, but in Havana each bale fetched a hefty price of thirty-six cents per pound. In Europe, the price skyrocketed to double or even triple that.

Townsend and the crew used the time in Mobile to rebuild the main cabin house with the help of a local carpenter. The tap-tapping of mallets and the sawing of wood blended in with the braying of donkeys on the wharves and the bawdy songs of screw gangs. All around them were acres and acres of cotton bales stacked on the waterfront waiting to be loaded on ships. There was everything from flat-bottomed Texas shoal draft schooners to wide-beamed Biloxi traders, to old river sidewheelers and light draft towboats that looked like they were barely seaworthy. From almost every mast, the Confederate Navy Jack and the Stars and Bars snapped and fluttered to the roll of drums and the rhythm of soldiers drilling.

When it came time to load the *Gaviota*, Red Beard found a good chantey singer and with four other men who made up the screw gang joining in the chorus, they pulled at the jackscrew handles, tightening and jamming the cotton into every corner of the ship's cargo hold, inch by inch. With each turn of the big screws came another chorus of one of the cotton chanteys. The screw gang squeezed three bales into a space that would normally only hold two. It was a tedious, somewhat boring process to watch, and Townsend's gaze wandered. He noticed a well-dressed man with a wide-brimmed slouch hat in white pants and a dark brown jacket, sitting on a barrel busily scribbling in a notebook. He was tall, looked to be in his late thirties, with black, curly hair, and a small beard covering his face and chin. Townsend watched him for a while. At the end of the day he decided to find out who he was. As he got closer, the stranger looked up and extended his hand.

"I take it you are Captain Townsend."

"Yes," Townsend responded cautiously. "And you are?"

"The name is Stringfellow, James Stringfellow, I am with Frank Leslie's Illustrated Newspaper."

"I see. And what is it I can do for you? You've been sitting here spying on my schooner. I assume there's something you want."

"Lookin' for passage to Havana, that's all."

Townsend pointed off to the south at the steamship docks where black clouds of smoke spiraled skyward from a blockade-running steamship.

"Why don't you try one of those fast sidewheelers down the bay. The *Alice* is loading cotton now. They'll get you to Havana much faster. Two to three days."

"No, only a cotton schooner will do," Stringfellow replied.

"I don't see your point," Townsend said suspiciously.

"My publication has a strong interest in blockade runners, particularly the cotton schooners. We did a story on Fort Jefferson just last year, and our readers are quite intrigued about the blockade here in the Gulf of Mexico."

Townsend pointed to three other schooners tied up next to them.

"Why don't you try the *Elizabeth Moose* or those two Confederate-flagged ships, tied up alongside us, the *Clementina* or the *Magnolia*."

"The truth is, Captain Townsend, I would prefer to sail on your ship. I should explain. You see you have come highly recommended by Miss Emma Carpenter of Havana."

"By Jupiter!" Townsend exclaimed. "She sent you? When? How?"

"I can see you are acquainted with the young lady. I am so glad I was not misinformed. She wrote she had met you and could vouch for your seamanship. She has done some illustrations of Havana harbor, and my publication is hoping to purchase the rights to use them. So I need to get to Havana, but I also need to write about running the blockade on board a cotton schooner. That's why she suggested your name."

"Hang it all!" Townsend ran his fingers through his uncombed hair.

"We only just received her letter. She wanted to come to Mobile herself, but that clearly would not have been wise for a young lady given the dangers of the blockade."

"That certainly is good judgment," responded Townsend.

"I will, of course, pay for the passage," Stringfellow added. "Be assured, I don't require commodious accommodations of any kind, and I can dispense with all need for ablutions."

Townsend rubbed his stubbly chin. He looked down and scuffed his feet on the ground as he contemplated the man's persistence. He found him to be somewhat affected, but the man's connection with Emma made him put aside his reservations.

"Come along then, Mr. Stringfellow. Get your kit together and come on board. We have a small pipe berth in the galley. We leave as soon as the next blue norther comes in."

"Blue norther?" Stringfellow inquired as he stepped on board with his small black trunk and carpet bag. "I am not familiar with that term."

"You will be soon. Stormy weather from the north. High winds and bone chilling cold. We have a south wind now. The Spanish sailors in Cuba have a saying, *Sur duro, Norte seguro*. When the south wind blows strong, a norther will be 'ere 'fore long."

With cotton loaded below decks, stacked and firmly lashed down above decks, they were soon ready to go. It had taken them three days to load 225 bales of cotton. Townsend had made sure the bowport openings were heavily braced and caulked so there was no chance of leakage. The cotton was piled so high on deck, it was hard for Higgins and Bertrand, who were the shortest in the crew, to see the ship's bowsprit unless they stood on the quarterdeck. The sky had an ominous dull blue-black sheen as they left the docks. By the time the *Gaviota* neared Fort Morgan at the mouth of the bay around midnight, the weather had changed abruptly. They battened down the hatches and dogged the portholes, everything on deck thoroughly lashed. It wasn't long before the heavy rain came lashing down. The blue norther had arrived with a vengeance, and the two Spaniards retreated to their cabin, but his new passenger, James Stringfellow, stayed close beside Townsend on the quarterdeck. He said he wanted to experience it just like a normal sailor.

Townsend had gone over the charts with Red Beard and the others before they left the docks. Instead of going out the Swash Channel to the east, the way they came, they were going to sail right into the Middle Channel, directly through the gauntlet of blockading ships that formed part of Admiral Farragut's West Gulf Blockading Squadron. The night was dark. With the heavy rain there would be no visibility, and the howling of the wind would muffle any noise they might make. He knew what they were facing. There were as many as six gunships anchored in a semicircle about three miles from Fort Morgan, well out of reach of the Confederate guns. They all kept steam pressure in the boilers so they could quickly give chase. No doubt there would be a warship stationed at both the westward and eastward entrances to the harbor, and at least one twelve-oared launch on picket duty, deployed for reconnaissance work. Two other vessels were patrolling somewhere offshore.

According to the intelligence he had gathered before leaving Mobile, one of the steamships anchored in the main channel was the 158-foot USS *Kennebec*, a Unadilla class schooner warship built for the Navy at the outbreak of the war. Townsend had studied these ships when he was at the Academy, so he knew they would be facing a gauntlet of deck guns, everything from Parrott rifles and Dahlgren smoothbores to twelve- and twenty-four-pound howitzers. The senior naval officer for the blockading squadron was a relative newcomer, Captain John Goldsborough. He was on board the three-masted steam screw frigate, the USS *Colorado*.

Just before one o'clock as they were about to sail out of Mobile Bay into the Gulf, Townsend suddenly turned the wheel and luffed the ship up into the wind, pulling into a small protected cove in Bon Secours Bay.

Red Beard looked at him with a puzzled frown. "What in tarnation you doin', Cap'n?"

With the schooner's bow now rising and falling to meet the waves, the spars banging back and forth in complaint, Townsend quickly explained his plan to Red Beard and the others. Before leaving Mobile, he had bought six dark blue Navy uniforms and anchor caps from a Confederate captain who had captured and commandeered a Navy sidewheeler tugboat called the *Fox*. The captured Yankee crewmen had defected to the Southern cause, and they were selling their old Navy uniforms. Townsend bought all of their clothes— blue caps, trousers, and coats, along with some pyrotechnic flare sticks and the Navy's signal flare code book, all thrown into the sale for just two dollars.

"They were practically giving them away," Townsend said as he pulled out the uniforms. "How do all of you feel about the color blue? Navy blue."

The rain pelted the decks and the blackness of the night prevented Townsend from seeing any of their faces. In the cabin house, there was much joking, mischievous smiles, and good-natured commentary as the sailors stripped down. In the relative comfort of the dimly lit cabin, the weather-beaten *Gaviota* sailors set aside their heavy cotton trousers and shirts and were soon all dressed in snappy blue uniforms. Red Beard, who had worn Confederate gray, looked like he'd just been forced to put on a woman's petticoats. Olsen and Bertrand could barely squeeze their stomachs into the pants. Higgins and Hendricks were the only ones who looked remotely comfortable in uniform. Townsend couldn't stop laughing at the sight of all this discomfort.

But his smile quickly turned to a frown when it came time for him to put on his own uniform. He looked at the lieutenant's rank insignia on the jacket, and he suddenly felt a huge weight descend on him, pulling him into despair. At that moment, he felt like two people stuck in the same body but with different faces. He kept buttoning and unbuttoning the coat and adjusting the hat to try to square it properly on his head. He looked at himself in the cabin's small mirror, but in the dim light all he could see was a dark shadowy figure. Townsend swallowed hard as he left his cabin and turned to face the men huddled together in the galley.

"Remember, our story is we are Navy sailors off the *Leopard* and we were thrown off course by the storm. The *Gaviota* is our captured prize. We thought Mobile Bay was New Orleans. We are now headed to New Orleans to turn the schooner over to the adjudication courts. Understood?"

There were no questions. Back on deck, with the cold rain now stinging their faces, the sailors gathered in the darkness of the quarterdeck. The night sky was an ominous black. Gusty winds whistled through the rigging, making the luff of the sails snap and vibrate. He couldn't see the men, but he could feel the tension in the air. He sensed rather than saw their doubts and fears.

"Reefs out," Townsend cried.

The men all understood the urgency of that command. They would need full sail to get through the blockade. Townsend watched as white-knuckled hands shook out the reef lines of the mainsail and foresail even as others grabbed the inch-thick lines of the throat and peak halyards to haul the big sails higher up the mast. The schooner was soon off before the wind, the sheets on the mainsail and the foresail squealing through the blocks with a huge sudden force. A wild gust of wind came upon them suddenly as they cleared Fort Morgan and entered the choppy waters in the Gulf, causing the heavily laden schooner to dive and heave into the waves. With their cargo of some fifty tons of cotton, the schooner's hull was now riding lower in the water by a foot or more. It would be a wet ride. Townsend looked over at the iron rod for the centerboard that was to the left of the small stairway down to the main cabin. Hendricks had already read his mind.

"Centerboard all de way down, Cap'n."

"That's good," he replied. "We will need it with this heavy load of cotton. We're riding low."

Townsend clutched the wheel tightly with both hands as he felt the whole body of the ship groan. Somehow the storm set him free—an illusion, he knew, but it strangely relaxed him, allowing him to forget momentarily the dangers that lay immediately ahead of them.

17

Cold and shivering, Townsend breathed in the stormy air. He knew this was madness. The hard reality of what they were doing suddenly descended on him. The schooner was barreling toward a staggered line of blockading gunships anchored off the harbor. One shell from a Parrott gun would blow them out of the water. Nothing could be seen in the blackness, just a faint gleam of curling white water on the leeward rail, and the beady drops of icy rain on the binnacle. He told himself that the violence of the storm might cause the Navy to assume no ship would try to escape in this weather.

Townsend could barely make out the shadowy form of Red Beard, clutching the stays with both hands on the lee side of the forward cabin house. He'd sent the Texan and Olsen up to the bow to keep their eyes peeled. Hendricks stayed back in the quarterdeck along with Stringfellow, who was writing in his notebook in the darkness. Bertrand and Higgins were amidships. They were at least one mile off shore and would soon sail into the anchored gauntlet of Navy ships. He knew that despite the storm the Navy would still be waiting and looking, cannons ready to fire. Townsend braced himself.

He heard a muffled cry. He gripped the wheel tightly as he swiveled his head from one side of the boat to the other. His immediate thought was that a Union gunboat was bearing down on them.

It was Bertrand. The sailor staggered back to the quarterdeck, clutching the stays for support.

"C'est moi, Capitaine. We need to go back."

"What? Have you gone off your chump, man? You're daft!"

The New Orleans sailor cupped his hands and shouted into Townsend's ear that they had a black cat on board. It was perched near the hen coop under the launch boat amidships.

"I tried to catch it, but it disappeared and hid behind the cotton bales. *Que faire, Capitaine?*" Bertrand wanted to know what to do. Townsend shook his head in amazement, and told Bertrand to forget the cat and get back to his station.

Townsend signaled Red Beard to set off the flare signals. Two white and a green. That meant "enemy headed to the right." Townsend hoped that this false signal would divert some ships away from them. He held his breath as he looked out into the darkness. Out at sea, he spotted a splotch of red, then white and red. The senior officer's ship had received the fake communication. No doubt they would send one of the blockading ships to investigate.

Moments later, Olsen spotted the first Navy ship. He gestured off the port bow. Less than a hundred yards away, Townsend could see the dark blue-gray wall looming over them. There were no lights to be seen. He recognized the familiar profile of the schooner-rigged steamship with the single funnel and two masts. It looked like the USS *Kennebec*. They were so close that even with the sound of the wind and the rain, he could hear the clanking of her engines and the squealing complaints of the anchor chain as the warship pitched and heaved in the waves. The faint shouts of the man on watch penetrated the night. Townsend couldn't hear what he said.

Within seconds they passed that ship and spotted another right behind it, this one a large three-masted frigate also with steam up. He could hear the intermittent thumping of her engines. Suddenly a blood-curdling howl tore through the night, followed by Bertrand cursing and screaming.

"What in Satan's hell is that!" Townsend cried out.

"*Merde!*" yelled Bertrand. "The cat, *Capitaine*. I step on the cat! *Je suis desolé*. I am sorry."

"Quiet," he hissed.

But they'd been spotted. A white explosive flare went off to the starboard that lit up everything around them like a bolt of lightning. In that instant, Townsend caught a glimpse of a Navy picket launch off to the starboard side with a boatload of surprised sailors in oilskins peering up at him through the rain. The Navy men were clearly astonished by this ghost ship that had appeared out of nowhere. In the rain and the dark, they had not seen the schooner bearing down on them.

The signalist on the picket boat pointed his flare gun upwards and fired off another explosive that lit up the cotton-laden decks with an even brighter flash of light. Townsend took quick measure of the launch boat. It was about thirty feet long, four oars on each side. Two men with pistols. They were clearly rowing back to their ship because of the stormy weather. It was too dangerous in the storm for them to remain on picket duty. The junior officer on board began yelling orders to Townsend with his ship trumpet.

"Come up into the wind and drop sails, or we'll fire."

Townsend looked at all the blue uniforms on the *Gaviota* through the wall of rain and for a brief moment allowed himself to think he was a US Navy lieutenant. He wasn't sure what had come over him, but suddenly he wanted to confront that junior officer. After all, with his lieutenant's uniform he outranked the man. With great difficulty he wrestled with the wheel and luffed up the schooner near the picket boat, almost capsizing it. He pointed to the blue uniforms of the *Gaviota*'s sailors, yelling out to the men in the picket boat to stand down and holster their pistols. Before the stunned Navy sailors could react to the unexpected sight of blue uniforms on a cotton-laden schooner, Townsend transformed himself into their superior, bullying the junior officer.

"How dare you threaten me," he shouted brusquely through his sea trumpet. "You are speaking with Lieutenant Everett Townsend. I am reporting in as required. This is a captured prize, and we are bound for New Orleans. We were blown off course."

The chastened young officer must have recognized Townsend's midshipman's mannerisms because he didn't question him. Townsend continued berating him.

"Now direct me to the senior officer, Captain John Goldsborough— Where is his ship? I believe he is commanding the USS *Colorado*."

The officer pointed to the east, and Townsend thanked him even as he sharply turned the wheel to fall off again. Townsend's intelligence gathering in Mobile had paid off. As the big sails filled and the schooner picked up speed, he leaned over the windward rail holding his hand up, palm out, in a mock salute to the officer. It was only when Olsen and Red Beard burst out laughing at the confused faces in the picket boat that the Navy men knew they'd been tricked.

Stringfellow, who had been lying flat on the deck, looked up at Townsend with a beaming smile.

"Bravo!" he exclaimed. "Never seen Yankee sailors gulled that way before. Brilliant performance Captain! I had no idea you blockade runners were skilled in the art of the stage as well as the sea."

A volley of pistol shots went off and gun flares signaling "sail running out of channel" were soon rocketing off the decks of several other ships, lighting up the entire fleet ahead of them. Townsend could see there were two heavily armed warships with steam up directly ahead of them, and he quickly changed course. He silently blessed the cat for showing him where the blockading fleet was. Without the flares from the picket boat, he might not have seen how close they were coming to these ships. He would explain to Bertrand later that when a black cat comes on board a ship, it's a sign of good luck. It's only when it falls overboard it's bad luck.

Townsend deftly steered the *Gaviota* through a dark gap in the blockade, away from the flares. One of the big ships started firing one of its howitzers, and Townsend warned everyone to crouch low behind the cotton bales. He could hear shouts and the thudding rhythm and plodding thump of paddle-wheels behind him. He decided to risk overloading the spars with even more canvas to get out to sea as far as possible before daylight. Townsend watched as Higgins released the main topsail and then hung from the spring stay crossing over to the foremast, a dangerous journey, as a fall to the deck some sixty feet below would have probably killed him. In the inky darkness behind them, they could hear several loud booms of cannons, but after that, just the incessant howl of the wind as the ship continued on a southwesterly course toward Mexico.

A dull sky and a chilly, windless air caused the men to huddle around the cast iron stove in the galley for warmth. It had been twelve long days since they left Mobile. Dutch Olsen put on the big coffee pot to boil, and then threw some more coals on the stove. He was baking biscuits and some daddyfunk stew—a concoction of peas, chicken, and hardtack, all cooked in the oven. For two full days they'd been virtually becalmed with puffs of fickle air. The men were restless and to pass time they were telling stories. Olsen threw together the messy ingredients to make the stew, adding generous spoonfuls of molasses and a few more globs of pig fat when Red Beard surprised them all by saying that he owed his life to an oven just like the one in the galley. The Texas sailor explained that when he was a baby, he was small and sickly and the midwife had covered him with fresh sheep manure, wrapped him in a blanket, and put him in the slightly warm oven. The other sailors began snickering and screwing up their noses.

"Sheep shit," Olsen replied. "They covered you in wet sheep dung?"

Red Beard nodded. "From head to toe. Left me in the oven for days, I'm told."

"They left you in the oven?" Higgins said. "They cooked you, same as the daddyfunk stew? Covered in sheep shit?"

"Yes, sir," Red Beard said emphatically. "Like a clump of mud. That's how I came into this world. I owe my life to an oven just like this one."

"Don't forget to thank the sheep," Olsen cried out. "You owe your life to them shittin' sheep as well!"

The cabin echoed with raucous laughter.

"I'm afraid you're still covered with shit, Red Beard," Dutch Olsen said with a hearty laugh. "I guess nothing's changed." Red Beard lunged at the Danish sailor, but Olsen was too quick. The others were soon mimicking sheep, bleating at the Texan mercilessly. At one of the lulls in the storytelling, Olson threw some of the flying fish retrieved from the decks that morning to the cat. Against all odds, the black cat had been accepted by most of the sailors as the ship's pet. She was a double-pawed cat with six toes on each of her paws. These types of cats were known for their climbing and hunting abilities, and were considered by sailors to be extremely good luck when at sea. She was kept in the main cabin house so there was no danger she would fall overboard or get the chickens. Higgins nicknamed her "Look-Out" because she had screeched out the warning about the Navy patrol boat.

At first, the sailors had been mad at Bertrand for his foolish superstitions, but they forgave him when they heard his story about growing up in a New Orleans whorehouse. It turned out when Bertrand was ten years old he'd been trying to pick one of the customer's pockets while the man was in the bed. In the dark, Bertrand stepped on the tail of the house's black cat, and the screeching animal caused the naked man to jump out of bed "hollerin and screamin to beat the blazes." Bertrand said the man thought some kind of demon was after him. He was an old sea captain, one of the establishment's regulars.

"*Sacré Dieu.* When he spied me rifling through his trouser pockets, he swore like a drunken Irishman. *Fou, complètement fou.* He chased me down the hall and gave me a severe whipping with his belt. He then put me on a ship headed for Valparaiso. I've never liked black cats since then."

As the sailors ate their daddyfunk stew, they argued about who was to blame for the weather. They decided Bertrand needed to use some of his New Orleans mumbo jumbo and they sent him up on deck to whistle for the wind. At the helm, Townsend could feel the chilly air bite into his skin. He could hear the gentle lapping of the ocean off to the starboard side, but he could see nothing. The men were still laughing and joking down below. Townsend smiled. Such different backgrounds, but all on the same footing at sea. They'd found common ground among themselves even as his own country seemed incapable of doing so. Even though the men spoke English with different accents, they had found a way to communicate.

Days later, the winds did fill in, and the schooner began making good progress. Townsend estimated they were northwest of Mexico's Alacrán islands, standing as far north as 24 degrees latitude. This was a longer route, but he wanted to stay well clear of the Tortugas, where he knew Van Cortland and other patrolling ships would be waiting.

Unlike the two supercargoes who had kept mostly to themselves in their cabin, Stringfellow had spent most of the voyage talking to the men, learning about the schooner, and hearing about their wild sail to Mobile. During the watch that night, Stringfellow stood next to the captain at the helm. The moon was full and the skies were so light it was almost like daylight.

"Looking forward to Havana, are you?" Townsend asked.

"Indeed I am," the man replied.

"See there now, you better prepare yourself," Townsend told him. "Havana is its own animal, more wolf than dog. You best put your notions of American civilities aside."

"Boh, Havana. Don't I know," Stringfellow said. "I've been there. Back when I worked for the *New York Daily Tribune*. It was about eight years ago. Covered this murder. An English diplomat. Quite shocking."

Townsend and Hendricks looked at each other, both taken by surprise.

"Hulloa! You don't mean Judge George Backhouse, do you?" Townsend asked.

"Yeah, that's right. How did you know?" Stringfellow grabbed on to a stay to keep himself from falling. The boat lurched again, and Stringfellow pulled his slouch hat farther down on his head to keep it from blowing off.

Townsend shrugged. "Just hearsay, is all."

"Well. Like I said, it was a shocking story. English diplomat stabbed to death in his own home. Fellow was some kind of anti-slavery judge. It was all the talk in Havana. By the time I got there, the police had picked up several suspects. We all thought there would be a public execution—at least of two of the men. After all, the Spanish have been known to execute people for a simple robbery. But the mystery was nothing happened. The Spanish authorities released the men. Insufficient evidence, they said, or some such truck. I don't remember. None of us believed it."

"What do you think happened?"

"Hum! I don't rightly know. The case was closed. Nothing was ever recorded. We reporters were never given the names of the suspects. They just disappeared. But it was the limeys that caught my attention. We expected tensions to break out between the British and the Spanish governments. With no execution for me to write about, I tried to interview the British consul general."

"You mean Joseph Crawford."

"Yeah, that's him. Crawford. Silver hair and powdered white moustache?" Townsend nodded.

"A cagey old fox, that one," Stringfellow said as he stroked his beard. "Slippery fellow. I almost laughed at the old diplomat when he told me the British government would be offering a two-hundred-pound reward for any new information about the murderers. Is that what Judge Backhouse's life was worth to the British Foreign Office? I asked him. Nothing more than two hundred pounds?"

"What was his reaction?" Townsend asked, raising his eyebrows.

"He lost his temper. I admit I might have been a little too brash, but I was looking for a dramatic quote. A scoop. My editor at the time loved any opportunity to tweak John Bull's nose. Crawford started shouting and shoved me out the door. I think he wanted to kick me down the stairs. That was the end of the interview."

"Who do you think did it?" Townsend asked as he tugged thoughtfully on his lower lip with his thumb.

"A deuce of a question, that one. There were a lot of rumors going on at the time. Everything from a simple burglary to a political assassination. The police wanted us to believe it was just a robbery. Some even claimed it was a ritual killing by Negro slaves on the docks. Some kind of secret society where the blacks have to kill a white person with a knife to become a member."

"Ñañigos."

"Yeah, that's the name. I never believed that."

"Why not?"

"Because the intruders didn't kill the man who was with Judge Backhouse that night. Fellow by the name of Callaghan, another Britisher. They just tied him up. If it was a ritual killing, I think they would have stabbed him too."

"So who do you think did it then?"

"Only Callaghan saw everything, and he didn't see much. The two men who attacked them had covered their faces. There were suspicions about an employee, a former clerk at the Consulate. Backhouse had just fired him, a most disagreeable drunken scoundrel named Dalrymple, who was known as a gambler and a thief. He left the island not long after the murder. No one made any serious attempt to stop him. Heigh-ho! Just one more mystery."

A weighty silence fell over the quarterdeck.

"I will tell you one thing that mightily intrigued me at the time. I was covering the funeral ceremony in Havana, and one of the younger clerks at the British Consulate let slip that Judge Backhouse's journal had gone missing from the house. It was never found."

Townsend raised an eyebrow. "Maybe that's why Backhouse was killed. To get the journal, I mean."

Stringfellow shrugged and looked out at the cresting waves. The wind was picking up. He turned back to face Townsend.

"No one really knows. Any further investigation is probably pointless. It's ancient history. It's been eight years, and Havana's skeleton pile is ever deeper at this point." He shrugged. "I will say I've always wondered about Backhouse's widow. She was back in England with the two children at the time of the murder. I felt sorry for her. Imagine, your husband murdered, knifed to death in your own home in far away Cuba. Even her own government seemed not to care. Sad story. She never returned to the island. I always wanted to interview her."

Stringfellow patted Townsend on the back. Just then the shadowy figures of Salazar and Nolo walked up the companionway and joined them. Nolo had his knife out, and was whittling away. It looked like he was carving a handspike with a sharp, crowned top to it. As always, there was a certain menacing hostility in Salazar's stare.

"*¿De qué hablan?*" asked the Spaniard brusquely. "What are you talking about?"

"Just a private conversation," Townsend replied. He glared at the two Spaniards, who he made no pretense of liking. Salazar's glance now rested on Stringfellow.

"Haven't I seen you before? Your face is familiar."

"Don't believe so," Stringfellow replied.

"Ever been to Havana?"

At this point, Townsend interjected.

"Mr. Stringfellow was just telling me about the last time he was in Havana eight years ago. He was assigned to write about the murder of an English diplomat. Name of Backhouse. Heard of him?"

Just by looking at the Spaniard's pale blue eyes dart from Townsend to Stringfellow and back again, the young captain knew these two Spaniards were quite familiar with Backhouse. It wasn't just a coincidence either that they'd come up on deck when they did. They'd heard something. After an awkward pause, Salazar asked him how many more days until Havana. Townsend replied that it might take three more days as it was hard sailing into the Gulf Stream chop. The two Spaniards turned their backs and retreated into the cabin house. An uneasiness swept over the young captain as he stared after them. The Backhouse case and its recent investigator, Michael Abbott, were anything but ancient history for these two men.

18

May 10, 1863

In the sweltering sun, Townsend stood alongside Don Pedro and the Confederate agent Helm on the Havana docks as the last of the bulky cotton bales were hauled out of the ship's cargo hold. Ever since arriving the week before, they had spent several days at anchor in the harbor waiting in line for dock space, and the last two days unloading the cotton bales. They were almost done. Salazar and Nolo had handled customs officials and completed the paperwork, making sure that their departure city was listed as Matamoros, Mexico, not Mobile. It was mid morning, and the docks felt like a furnace to Townsend, the tropical sunlight reflecting off the red-tiled roofs of the warehouse buildings. The wooden decks of the *Gaviota* were so hot he could feel the sizzling heat burn his skin through his thin-soled shoes.

Townsend glanced at Helm, wiping sweat from his sloping forehead, as the diligent Confederate agent jotted down observations in his notebook about this latest batch of cotton. Helm pulled on his tufted beard, and Townsend thought to himself that he looked like a banker counting his money. A fitting image, he mused, given that the South's only real currency was cotton. He could tell the man was making quick calculations about how many British weapons the Confederate government's share of this shipload would buy.

"It's a sizeable haul," Helm said with a warm smile as he patted Don Pedro on the back. "I'm glad you made it, as we have word that the USS *Huntsville* just seized another schooner, that one with over two hundred bales of cotton.

Despite that unfortunate news, I do believe cotton schooners like yours are the South's secret weapon. Thanks to this fleet of sailboats we are getting cotton out of some of the most difficult places to navigate, everywhere from the Suwannee River in Florida to the Brazos River in Texas."

Townsend said nothing. The Confederate agent was either misinformed or being overly optimistic. Even he knew the blockade was ever tightening. More steamships were added to the Navy's Gulf Squadrons every month. They had been lucky toward the end of the voyage. A gunship had fired at them when they approached the western tip of Cuba, the ball striking a glancing blow on the ship's hull. They'd been fortunate to be able to patch up the damage and reach Spanish territorial waters. But it was only with the arrival of a patrolling Spanish gunboat that the Navy warship had given up the chase. Running the blockade under sail was becoming increasingly dangerous.

Just then, a cannon blast from El Morro signaled a new arrival into the harbor.

At the sight of a British steamer filled with military supplies arriving from Nassau, the Confederate agent rushed off. Don Pedro left him and Red Beard to oversee the rest of the unloading. Townsend picked up his telescope and looked over across Havana harbor at the wharves at Regla. Two newly arrived British-flagged blockade-running steamers were still loading up with military supplies for a run to Galveston or Mobile. He'd heard news from their captains, who had been running the blockade from Nassau to Wilmington, that faster British-flagged steamships were on their way to Havana. Word had gotten out about how much cheap cotton there was to be had in the Gulf of Mexico.

The sound of Africans singing brought his attention back to the ship. The head dockworker, a powerful, thickset man with glistening muscles, called out a pulsating work rhythm, slapping his thighs and clapping his hands as a chorus of dockworkers chanted a mournful, melodic response. The black stevedores sang as they shoved the big rectangular white bales down the ship's wide gangplank to the docks. There the cotton bales were loaded onto rugged two-wheel carts and flat bed drays pulled by donkeys and mules.

To Townsend, the repetitive, rhythmic chants of the dockworkers now were like a narcotic, lulling him into an indolent daze. There was something primordial about the work songs on the docks, something ancient and constant like the wind blowing through leafy trees or waves crashing against the shoreline. His mind wandered to Emma. He couldn't stop thinking about her. No matter how hard he tried to forget her, he found himself lost, conjuring her wavy hair, her intelligent brown eyes and smiling face.

He remembered dancing with her, feeling the curve of her waist as it gently moved with the music.

Townsend had hoped she would send him a note. He thought the favor he'd done for Stringfellow might have prompted her to write him. Anything would have been fine, but nothing had arrived. Maybe Stringfellow had just looked at her drawings and nothing else? Maybe the reporter hadn't told her he had come on board the *Gaviota*? Townsend considered writing her a letter, but had changed his mind. Part of him said he should stop being a fool. She had rejected him. There was no reason to expect she felt differently now. He was still a blockade runner. He told himself he just wanted to share with her the information Stringfellow had given him about Backhouse. That certainly was true, but deep down he knew, he really wanted to see her again.

A call from Red Beard snapped him out of his moody trance. An all too familiar brigantine was sailing into port. He felt his stomach tighten. Townsend looked out over the shimmering harbor at the USS *Leopard* slide by with her graceful gray hull and long bowsprit. He could see the stocky figure of Van Cortland on the quarterdeck, and he knew the naval officer had seen him, but he did not look his way. The *Leopard* rounded up in the center of the harbor next to a fast topsail Union Navy schooner called the *Nonpareil* that had come over from Key West earlier that day, ostensibly to pick up the mail. Everyone knew these Navy mail boats had another purpose. They were carrying secret dispatches, and they would return to Key West with a packet of intelligence information gathered by the US Consulate about the Confederate activity in Havana. All the spying was not surprising. He remembered what Mrs. Carpenter had said: Even the walls have ears in Havana.

The next day they hired a steam tug to tow the schooner across the bay to Casa Blanca to the shipyard docks. The crew was soon busy recaulking portions of the deck with tar and resin, replacing worn fastenings and applying a coating of pine tar slush and black paint to the stays. Townsend was taking inventory down below. From inside the cabin house, he could hear the banging of the mallet. He looked through the porthole to see Bertrand installing a new shackle to one of the mainsail's eight-inch-by-four-inch blocks. Out of his sailor's bag, Olsen was pulling his knife, some twine, and small swaths of canvas to start patching some of the sails. With the loading done at the wharves, they were waiting for a haul out date to repair some splintered planking in the hull. This work could take weeks, but Don Pedro had been pleased there weren't more problems. The winds at this time of year were fickle and light—it was a good time to take a break from blockade running.

Don Pedro had been insistent that they visit the plantation of Doña Cecilia de Vargas for a few days.

"The last of the sugarcane is being harvested now, and they've begun plowing and planting for next year. We'll go by steamship next week."

Townsend had nodded in agreement, but had made no mention to Don Pedro of his mother or his interest in finding the place with the strange name of Mambi Joo. His search for his mother's roots was a personal, private quest—and he didn't trust the Spaniard. He worried that Emma might try to contact him when he was away. As he watched his crew hard at work, the thought that he might lose the opportunity to see her —to make amends with her—caused him to make an abrupt decision. He knew an unannounced visit wasn't a good idea, but he was determined. He left Red Beard in charge and told Salazar and Nolo he was going back across the harbor to the Cabarga ship chandlery.

When he arrived at Mrs. Carpenter's boarding house after stopping at his rooming house for a change of clothes, he first made sure he wasn't followed. He was let in by one of the Irish maids. He was surprised at how friendly and welcoming she was. It seemed like she was expecting him. She did not ask his name and he did not give it. She dashed off and he heard her say, "The gentleman you were expecting 'as arrived, Mrs. Carpenter." That's a good omen, Townsend thought, and breathed a sigh of relief.

The rustle of bustling petticoats came from upstairs. He heard Mrs. Carpenter call—Emma, and the faint echo of footsteps of someone coming down the marble stairs. Then Mrs. Carpenter came around the corner. He moved to greet her, but instead of a friendly welcome, she seemed to be frozen in place, her face uncertain, frowning.

"You're not," she stammered. "I wasn't expecting you, Mr. Townsend. We were expecting . . . never mind. Please do come in to the courtyard."

Townsend's chest deflated. "I'm sorry to have come unexpectedly. I was hoping to see Emma."

Mrs. Carpenter didn't reply at first, giving him a hard look. "Certainly, certainly. Did you have something in particular. . . ."

This was not going well. Townsend always thought Eleanor Carpenter had liked him, but now the older woman was cold and distant.

"I don't know if your daughter told you, but I brought over from Mobile one of the writers for Frank Leslie's paper on my ship. A Mr. Stringfellow. He seemed quite keen to look at her sketches, and I was wondering if she—"

"Oh yes, Emma was so pleased," Mrs. Carpenter said abruptly. "Mr. Stringfellow stayed here for a couple of days, and only yesterday left on the steamship for New York. He took several of her sketches. She was delighted."

The older woman looked anxiously toward the stairs. Her deeply creased brow revealed her irritation. "I don't know where my daughter has gone off to. Let me go find her. If you will excuse me."

Mrs. Carpenter rushed off, calling for Emma in a shrill voice as she went. He could hear Emma's familiar voice and then a flurry of frantic whispering in the hallways. It sounded like an argument. When Emma finally came into the room, he was transfixed. She was in an elegant yellow and green crino-line dress. She was stunningly beautiful. But instead of a glittering smile, the expression on her face was stiff. No words were spoken between them. He felt the weight of the room's silence settle on him.

"Miss Carpenter," he finally began. "I'm afraid I'm interrupting some-thing. I am so sorry."

She didn't reply.

"I just wanted to hear how your meeting with Mr. Stringfellow went. Was he excited to see your sketches?"

Emma busied herself at a table where there was a vase of flowers. To Townsend's consternation, she showed little reaction. It was almost as if she hadn't heard what he said, until finally she replied.

"I was intending to write you and thank you, but we have been busy around here with so many guests. I am sorry. It was very kind of you to bring him on your ship. Mr. Stringfellow spoke highly of you and your men. I heard your passage through the blockade was quite dramatic. I understand you were chased and fired on by a Union gunship."

"Yes," Townsend replied. "Actually several gunships. I guess we were lucky. Did you sell your sketches?"

"Mr. Stringfellow was quite pleased," she said. "He particularly liked the one of your ship leaving the harbor. It was such a stormy day. Your ship sailed out of port so quickly I was almost unable to do the sketch."

Townsend held his breath, his heart suddenly beating more rapidly. "I thought I saw you on the rooftop."

She looked surprised. "I didn't know you were watching," she said. He detected the faintest of smiles. "Yes, that was me. It turned out that was the sketch he liked the most. I even gave it a title. I called it, 'No Safe Harbor'."

She turned to him and seemed—softer toward him.

"I am glad to have a chance to thank you in person, Captain. And I would like to hear more about your time in Mobile, but I just can't."

"I just need a few minutes to tell you something."

"I am sorry. I just can't as my mother and I are expecting company."

"Of course, of course. I understand," Townsend said. He put his hands in his pockets to hide his awkwardness. "I have more information about the Backhouse murder." He could see her eyes open wider in interest.

"Yes?"

"Mr. Stringfellow covered the story. He told me some interesting facts about the murder."

She nodded, but instead of letting him share his news, she began to whisper.

"There is something I need to tell you. I was going to put it in a letter, but now you are here, I suppose I should tell you in person. I know you won't like it."

Townsend grimaced and prepared himself for the worst. Her calm, remote gaze only added to his concerns.

"About a week ago I went to see the US vice-consul general, Thomas Savage. He is an old friend of my mother's, an honorable, decent man. I told him about Abbott."

"You did what?"

"I know you urged me not to, but I think you are wrong. I have finally done it. It's the right thing to do."

Townsend felt a sinking feeling in his stomach. The name of Michael Abbott kept resurfacing in his life like an apple bobbing up in a barrel of water. Just hearing the name again unnerved him.

Emma looked at him with a forthright stare. By now, he knew her well enough to recognize her fixed determination.

"Mr. Savage was working at the US Consulate when Mr. Backhouse was here. I thought he should know, and I thought he would understand my concern. I believe he intends to file a missing person's report with the Spanish government. I mentioned your name and your involvement with Abbott."

"Why would you do that?" Townsend hissed. "It's been months now."

Townsend tried to compute what this would mean for him. The Spanish police had imprisoned him because of his ties with the Englishman. He was lucky to be alive. For all he knew it was some kind of assassin hired by the police who had knifed Abbott and clubbed him unconscious.

"You realize involving the American consul general might complicate my life," he said with a hint of anger. "I'm the captain of a schooner running the blockade. I'm the enemy as far as he's concerned."

Emma's eyes didn't waver.

"I know the risks, but it is a question of right and wrong. I felt someone in a position of authority needed to know about Abbott's disappearance."

Townsend put his hands up to his head.

"Mr. Savage has requested you come by the Consulate to see him."

"Does the American consul general know that I helped Abbott escape from El Morro?"

She nodded. "And he knows you are a blockade runner. I felt it was best to tell him everything."

Townsend hadn't thought she was capable of such cold indifference. He was about to say so when a tense Mrs. Carpenter came bustling into the room.

"Emma, your guest will be here shortly. Mr. Townsend, I am sorry to chase you off. I would invite you to stay longer, but I am afraid it would be most inappropriate."

Townsend apologized again for coming unannounced and was about to show himself out when the same Irish maid came rushing in, delivering a quick curtsy before she spoke.

"Excuse me, Madam. I don't mean ter interrupt. Another gentleman caller is 'ere for Miss Emma."

"Thank you, Mary," Mrs. Carpenter said. "I will be right there."

"I will show myself out," Townsend said. "I will use the other door."

Mrs. Carpenter nodded. "Thank you, Mr. Townsend."

"Goodbye, Miss Carpenter," he said, bowing slightly. "When could we talk more about this?"

Emma shook her head. His eyes lingered on her a moment, searching for some sign, but she was looking anxiously toward the front door where her guest was.

Townsend could hear Mrs. Carpenter talking to someone in an ingratiating voice.

"Welcome, welcome," she said. "Do come in and I will introduce you to my Emma. You can tell us all about the dangers and the hardships on blockade duty. Emma, our guest is here! Hurry, dear. You don't want to keep Lieutenant Van Cortland waiting."

Townsend felt his heart race out of control even as his stomach seemed to get jammed in his throat. Blood rushed to his temples. Van Cortland there in the boarding house, paying his respects to Emma and her mother. How could that be? He could hear voices and footsteps coming toward the courtyard, and he stepped back into the shadows. Van Cortland's haughty voice echoed through the hallway.

"When my mother discovered I was likely to be stationed in these distant waters for the duration of the war, she immediately began to inquire after the American families found in Havana. Of course, she was told about Emma

Carpenter, who had impressed so many of the ladies in Philadelphia during her recent stay there."

"I am so pleased," replied Mrs. Carpenter.

"The pleasure is mine. Thank you for your gracious invitation. I wrote my mother to let her know about it and I'll write her again as soon as I leave to thank her for the introduction."

Townsend stayed out of sight behind one of the pillars and watched as Van Cortland was ushered into the garden courtyard. Tea was brought to the table. Mrs. Carpenter seemed to like the young Navy officer with the blonde hair and the blue eyes. She was smiling and flirtatious, mentioning the names of high society figures in Philadelphia and New York. Townsend stood frozen in the shadows, hardly daring to breathe. He felt like a ship's lead being hurled overboard, plunging to the bottom of the ocean, deeper and deeper. His head swirled with bitterness and resentment. When he heard Mrs. Carpenter say how she longed to tread on the decks of a US Navy war-ship, he clenched his teeth.

Townsend was going to leave, but he couldn't pull himself away. It was Van Cortland's attitude that most disgusted him. He was nodding formally to Mrs. Carpenter even as he devoured Emma from the tresses of her hair to the heels of her shoes. He watched from the shadowy sidelines as Van Cortland's gaze roamed from Emma's shapely shoulders to her fine figure. He wanted to charge in and hit the man. The familiar rage built inside him. His breathing quickened. His face pounded. His neck was taut. But somehow he restrained himself. He knew he would only hurt his chances with Emma if he did that. He looked at Emma's face, calm and pale, revealing little. She was polite and smiled demurely at Van Cortland.

"Tell us some stories about the blockade," Mrs. Carpenter said. "Have you captured some of the Rebels yourself? Any exciting chases at sea?"

"I am pleased to say that the noose around these Rebel boats with their British and Spanish allies is tightening," Van Cortland said with a surly smile. "Traitors, that's what they are. And they are men of few scruples."

"Pray tell us more. Continue with your story, please," said Mrs. Carpenter as she rested her hand underneath her chin. "No need to worry. You can speak with confidence here. All the servants have been given the afternoon off except Mary, and she is quite trustworthy."

"We spotted one of those profiteering traitors off the Florida coast. He was flying the Spanish flag, and we knew immediately he was a runner from Havana. After a good chase we had our guns on him and his men and he surrendered. He was our prize. But the man had no honor. A wind came up and he fled, capsizing our boat launch. We fired on him and hopefully some lead bullets found their way home. But make no mistake about it, they are scoundrels."

"Who was it?" asked Emma. "Was he well known?"

"A man I am ashamed to say I knew before the war," he grunted. "He was at the Naval Academy with me. His brother was a Rebel, and so was he. He was kicked out of the Academy before he could do any damage."

Townsend saw that the Irish maid had spotted him. He panicked, thinking that she would call Mrs. Carpenter, but instead she smiled at him as if she recognized a kindred spirit. He nodded to her, and quietly slipped out the door just as he heard Mrs. Carpenter tell her daughter to play one of Mozart's sonatas for their heroic guest.

19

May 13, 1863

It was a wet, windy, squally afternoon three days later when Townsend arrived at the US Consulate adjacent to the central wharf area. Sheets of water flowed down the sides of the street, rushing toward Havana Bay in streams, carrying with it the debris, refuse, and sewage of the city. The summer rainy season had come early.

Townsend had taken even stricter precautions than usual to make sure he wasn't followed, taking a wide detour through Old Havana, walking north from his rooming house to Lamparilla Street, and then losing himself in the crowds on Mercaderes before reaching Obispo Street. He thought for a moment he'd seen Salazar, but when a sudden squall unleashed buckets of water, he had ducked into a shop and came out through the back door using a newly purchased, steel-ribbed umbrella to hide his face. He hoped the rain and the umbrella had kept anyone from identifying him.

He looked up at the shiny brass sign on the colossal front door that read "United States Consul General, #1 Calle Obispo," and he felt a hot shiver of apprehension. The heavy raindrops were pelting the rooftops so loudly he couldn't even hear the clattering of the wheels from a passing horse and carriage. He had procrastinated about coming because he knew he would be perceived as a Rebel sympathizer, an enemy of the Federal government. He girded himself for a hostile interview. Just that thought made him want to turn around and walk away. But what choice did he really have? Emma had told the consul general all about him. For better or worse, Townsend knew he needed to give his account of what had happened to Michael Abbott, and what had happened to him. He needed to tell the truth.

Inside the Consulate, the ceilings were over twenty feet high with open rafters. There were about five or six people in the larger office, clerks and translators as well as deputies. The attendant at the desk took his name and told him to take a seat. Townsend had only been waiting for about ten minutes when a large door opened and a well-dressed man in a white linen suit and a small black tie walked over to him. He had a thin face, and curly black hair and a bookish, priestly smile.

"Good morning. You are Captain Townsend, I presume?"

Townsend nodded a reply.

"I am Thomas Savage, vice-consul general. I should explain that I am currently serving as the acting consul general."

The young captain found himself in an office, surrounded by walls of bookcases with leather-bound books, and two large windows where a brass telescope had been strategically mounted on a table-top tripod. There were a few mahogany chairs with caned seats and backs next to a red leather-topped campaign desk, which gave an elegant polish to the room.

"Please sit down, Captain Townsend." He pointed to the windows and the telescope. "As you can see this is my watchtower. Havana is at a strategic crossroads for the American war. Among my tasks here are to listen, watch, and monitor this harbor. From here, I know what ships are coming and going. Each day there are more blockade runners flying the British and Spanish flags, and each day new ones arrive, faster and bigger. I have even seen your schooner, Captain. She is aptly named, *Gaviota*. She sails just like a seagull. I watched you come in with a full load of cotton last week. It looked to be about two hundred bales."

"Two hundred and twenty-five," Townsend said as he gulped, wondering where this conversation was going.

"I understand you were chased by our Navy."

Townsend nodded. "Yes, we were hit by a cannon ball, a glancing blow."

"So I was informed. That was probably the USS *Sagamore*," the vice-consul general said. "She is patrolling the waters off Cuba now."

Townsend thought of telling the diplomat that the US gunship had pursued them within Spanish territorial waters, but he thought better of it. A young Cuban brought the coffee, and Savage spoke to him in perfect Spanish with no trace of an accent. Townsend studied the American diplomat more closely. For some reason, he reminded him of his father, something about his mannerisms. He was direct and straightforward.

"*Desea azúcar?*" Savage asked in clear Castilian Spanish.

"*Sí, una cucharada, por favor,*" Townsend replied without thinking what language he was speaking. "One spoonful, please."

"I see you speak Spanish."

"*Un poco,*" Townsend replied, his face reddening. The man was adept at extracting information. A spoonful of sugar had caught him out.

"Captain, let me get right to the point," Savage said as he slowly stirred the sugar into his cup. "I had a pleasant visit the other day from the daughter of one of my wife's close friends. The young woman's name is Emma Lozada, but I believe she goes by her mother's family name of Carpenter. You do know her, I presume?"

"Yes, I do," Townsend replied, even as he squirmed in his chair.

"My wife, María Dolores and I have known her mother Eleanor for many years. We have observed Emma grow up to be a delightful young lady. She mentioned that you have a story to tell."

Townsend could feel the diplomat's eyes on his face, an earnest, penetrating gaze. For some reason, the man's quiet manner disarmed him. Perhaps it was his reassuring smile that made Townsend less guarded. Whatever it was, instead of becoming defensive, the young captain told his story with ease. He related how he came to Havana, the rescue of Michael Abbott from the sharks off El Morro, the knifing and what he presumed was the murder of Abbott. Then he described being put in prison, the contract with Don Pedro. He found himself unable to stop talking. He even told Savage what happened to him at the Naval Academy. When he had finished, Townsend breathed out a long deep sigh. He felt vulnerable and exposed, but strangely relieved. It was like he had been speaking to his father.

"That's quite an extraordinary story, young man," Savage said as he got up from his chair to walk around the office. He paused a moment, as he fixed Townsend with an intense gaze.

"As the top American diplomat here in Cuba, I am particularly interested in the fact that you attended the Naval Academy. That speaks to your intelligence and your ambitions. I also am drawn to the fact that your mother is Cuban. That explains your interest in Cuba and your knowledge of Spanish. That is a huge benefit. But before I ask you any other personal questions, I would like to know more about this Englishman, Michael Abbott. Emma Carpenter seemed quite concerned. She said he came here to investigate new information about the murder of the English diplomat George Backhouse."

"Yes, that's what Abbott told her. He was sent here by Mrs. Backhouse."

"And he went to see the British consul general here in Havana and was turned away?"

"That's what Emma said."

Savage shook his head in disbelief.

"Such a sad story, the Backhouse murder. So sudden. So shocking, and so unexplained. I was a deputy in the US Consulate in the 50s so I am quite aware of it. I respected Judge Backhouse a great deal because, like me, he had a special loathing for the institution of slavery and the trafficking of human flesh. We shared a mutual abhorrence for what we saw happening here in that regard. His position as the British judge on the Mixed Commission for the Suppression of the Slave Trade put him on the front lines of England's effort to stop slave trafficking to Cuba. But even with his good intentions, sadly he did not accomplish much."

"I have heard he made many enemies here," Townsend said.

"That would be a fair statement. Backhouse did not realize how much his principled crusade against slave trafficking was perceived here as a threat. I should know. My own efforts in detecting and putting a stop to the shameful number of American ships prostituting our flag for the purpose of slave trading created considerable hostility and anger toward me over the years."

"I didn't realize . . . "

"You have to understand, Captain, slavery is the backbone of the Cuban economy. Without it, the plantations fail and so does the economy. Here in Cuba, the Spanish and the Cuban planters live in fear of slave uprisings, and ever since Lincoln's Emancipation Proclamation in January they are increasingly worried about what our war means for them. There's a background here you should know. It goes back to some slave rebellions in the early 1840s."

"That's when my parents were both here."

"Then they lived through a painful period. It was frightening. Talking slave drums tore through the night throughout the Cuban countryside." Savage took a history book in Spanish from a shelf.

"You won't find many of the worst details mentioned in Spanish history books so I will tell you about it as someone who lived through it. It was brutal. Slave revolts broke out in several plantations. Sugar estates were torched. Planters were wounded and killed. It was a time of fear, and all this led to a harsh government crackdown. They called it *La Escalera*, the ladder. Do you know why it was called that?"

Townsend shook his head.

"Many Negroes—both free and slave—were arrested by the government, stripped naked, tortured, tied to a ladder with their heads pointing downward, and then whipped until they confessed or died."

Townsend was horrified.

"I mention this dark period in Cuban history because many of the planters blamed the British consul general, David Turnbull, an activist with the most extreme abolitionist beliefs. The planters and the Spanish government thought he incited the rebellion. They blamed England. And when ten years later George Backhouse came here and signaled that he would champion many of the same causes as Turnbull, he touched a raw nerve."

"I see," Townsend said. "That explains why he had many enemies."

"Indeed so. He was working hard not only to bring known slave traders to justice, but also to document freed Africans who were enslaved here in Cuba against their will. He was trying to gain their freedom."

"How many are being illegally held?"

"Probably thousands. The Africans on board captured slave ships off the coast of Cuba are not routinely returned to Africa. Instead they are issued what the Spanish government calls a certificate of freedom here on the island and then forced to sign seven-year work contracts in which they receive practically no pay. The unlucky ones become field laborers. Even the planters in the British West Indies are involved although that illegal commerce is shrouded in mystery. They sell their black contract laborers to sugar plantations and slave traders in Cuba in what becomes a lifetime of slavery."

Townsend grimaced.

"Ironically, these workers are called *emancipados*, the freed ones, but they might as well be called the condemned ones. It's shameful. A shocking scandal."

An awkward silence settled over the room as both men sipped their coffee. Savage offered him a cigar. He had several brands, but Savage pointed to the Partagas and suggested he try them for their strong and intense flavor. With the cigar in his fingers, Townsend struck a Lucifer match, and then slowly twirled the cigar in the flames before puffing on it.

"I see you have been taught how to light a cigar properly, *estilo cubano*, in the Cuban style. What do you think of the flavor?"

Townsend coughed as he felt the smoke burn the inside of his mouth, but he bravely smiled and nodded appreciatively. Savage stood up, puffing on his cigar. His face appeared more morose and thoughtful as he blew out a thick cloud of smoke toward the beamed ceiling.

"Captain Townsend, whatever dirt there was about the unsolved Backhouse murder has long ago been swept under the carpet. The Spanish authorities don't want to talk about it. Nor does the English consul general. We will almost certainly never know what happened to Mr. Backhouse. As for Mr. Abbott, who knows? I am sorry to tell you there are dozens of cases like his here in Havana where people just disappear. Frankly I am somewhat surprised I hadn't heard something about this man before. As you may have observed already, this city is really a small town. Rumors and gossip, particularly about foreigners, tend to travel like fast-moving blackwater through the streets of Havana."

Townsend was confused. "Will you file a report with the Spanish government?"

"I had considered it, but now that I hear your story I don't think so. Given what you have told me, I am afraid there is not likely to be a great deal of assistance or interest about Mr. Abbott's disappearance from the Spanish government. It would appear they want no one talking about it."

"Nothing could be done to try to find out what happened to Abbott?"

"I have asked some of my informants in Old Havana to make some inquiries about anyone who might fit Mr. Abbott's description, but I am not hopeful. That is all I am prepared to do."

The two men smoked their cigars, neither speaking. Another sudden squall had moved across the harbor. Havana Bay was gray and stormy, dotted with angry whitecaps and covered with wispy black smoke from several departing steamers. Townsend could see the black smoke from the British-flagged, Confederate-owned steamship *Alice* hanging over the masts in the harbor. The big ship with its large sidewheel paddleboxes was picking up speed for its latest run to Mobile.

Savage walked over to the window and spoke with his back to Townsend, his body a silhouette against the gray light.

"We live in dangerous times, Captain Townsend. Our country is being torn apart by civil war. Our relations with France and England could result in hostilities at any time. The French appear to be close to capturing the Mexican capital. We have had reports that the Emperor Napoleon III may be interested in acquiring Texas. The British, in the meantime, are doing everything in their power to make sure the United States is caught up in a costly war. They would like to divide our nation in two. Mr. Crawford of the British Consulate is handing out free sextants and chronometers to any blockade-running captain sailing under the British flag. It seems there is no end to British treachery."

Savage shook his head sadly as he walked back toward Townsend, his eyes flashing determination.

"You might say, Captain, the New World is on fire and the Old World is busy fanning the flames. To be honest, this war of ours could still go either way. But sadly, more bloodshed is likely to be the state of affairs for some time. To win this war we will need to close off the South's supply lines. We have doubled the number of ships on blockade duty here in the Gulf in a little more than a year. We have blockaded every major port from Florida to Texas—Galveston, Matagorda, Mobile, Sabine Pass, Suwanee River. Scores of ships have been captured. But we need more information from Havana's docks on what the enemy is planning. Do you know what our Navy fears the most?"

Townsend shook his head.

"More Confederate warships. Here in the Gulf we know the Confederates are well on the way to building two large gunships up the Apalachicola River in northern Florida, and we have blockaded that river port. But their Secret Service agents have been seen here in Havana searching for more ships to seize, or to buy."

Savage vigorously puffed on his cigar, blowing out clouds of smoke as he gestured at the rain-swept harbor.

"Let me be more specific with you, Captain. You are uniquely positioned to help the Union cause."

Townsend didn't say anything. He was too stunned by the man's words. Savage walked over and sat across from Townsend.

"Your value to us is that you are in good standing with Don Pedro Alvarado Cardona, the man you work for, and we need more information about his business dealings. We know Don Pedro is working closely not just with Helm, but with other Confederate agents."

Townsend found his voice. "You want me to spy for you?"

"Spy is not a word I would choose, but yes, I would like to use you as my eyes and ears."

The thought of trying to be a blockade runner and a Union spy gave Townsend considerable pause.

"I don't know if I can help. I have no desire to be a spy."

"Why not? There are many others willing to do the job. Havana is a harbor of spies. Everyone from the sailors to dockworkers, bar women to boatmen, postilions to street peddlers. They're all informing on somebody. Consider what's at stake, Captain. There are some here and in the United States who believe if the South is victorious, and they form a new Republic, there will no doubt be greater interest in forming the Golden Circle."

"The Golden Circle?" Townsend asked.

"A mad, wild-eyed dream of some of the firebrands in the South. They want to form an alliance of slave states extending from South America to Central America and Mexico to as far north as the Mason-Dixon Line. Cuba would be the centerpiece of this swath of hell. God help us if that happens. A victory of the South will breathe new life into that vile serpent of slavery. It is time for you to take a stand, Captain, for what you believe in."

Townsend said nothing for a moment. Finally, he asked, "But why me? How do you know what I believe in?"

"The truth is, Miss Carpenter suggested it. She mentioned you were quite conflicted about blockade running and that you were opposed to slavery. Perhaps I should say, she thought you would like to take a principled stance."

Townsend's head was spinning. He had thought Emma was done with him, and had forced him to go to the Consulate out of spite, only to punish him. Now he allowed himself to think that maybe he was wrong.

"Captain, you have been here several months. You speak Spanish. Have you not heard the Negroes running in the streets with their chants, '*Avanza, Lincoln, avanza.* Forward, Lincoln, forward?' I can assure you the Negro population here in Cuba is watching the war in America closely, and with good reason. They realize slavery's days are numbered. Our fight is not just to quell a rebellion and preserve the United States, but to end the institution once and for all. Liberation of the slaves will come to this island someday, but right now we're fighting for that same cause in our country."

Townsend gulped. "Suppose I agreed?"

"As I said, we would like you to watch Don Pedro closely, make yourself more useful than ever so he trusts you. Become one of his closest men. We want to know with whom he meets, and ultimately who might be providing ships to the Southerners. We know he is a close financial advisor to some powerful, influential people here. The point is he can connect Confederate agents with the wealthy sugar barons of Cuba, and that is a worry. It boils down to observe, take note, and then report what you learn."

Townsend realized he was about to make a decision that would mean stepping out of one dangerous life and into an even more perilous one.

"I will, of course, have to get full approval from Secretary Seward in Washington," Savage told him, "as well as to speak with the naval attaché from Key West. But those are formalities. You can expect that we will pay you three hundred dollars a month, which is what I am accustomed to paying some of my other informants. Needless to say, we would insist that you not tell anyone about our arrangement."

20

Townsend woke to the noise of the clanging and banging of the passenger steamer as it let out steam in the lower harbor of Matanzas. He heard the splash of the anchor, the rattling of the anchor chain rumbling through the hawse pipe. It was three in the morning. The sixty-mile trip on board the night steamer from Havana had taken less time than he thought, slightly less than six hours. All night long he had struggled to sleep on the cane-bottomed berth, but the throbbing rhythm of the screw propeller and the pulsating tremors of the old steamship had kept him awake.

He had spent the night thinking about Savage's proposal. He had almost said yes to the vice-consul general's offer in person, but at the last moment a sense of caution had told him to wait. The thought of being a spy was troubling. He kept thinking about the time in the bar when he and Red Beard had been accosted by that Confederate rabble rouser. It would be difficult living behind a mask, playing a role. Still, Savage's words about staying true to himself and supporting the Union cause had touched a nerve. Emma had said the same thing. He should stand up for his own convictions. Just the thought of Emma made him realize what an emotional muddle he was in. His feelings toward her were a tangle of knots. He'd told Savage he would contact him when he got back from this trip to the countryside. He just needed some time to think about it.

Part of his uncertainty came when Savage told him he would have to say nothing about this to his crew. "One thing you will learn in the spy business," he had said to him, "is never to share sensitive information with anyone—

unless you have to." That seemed like a betrayal to Townsend. He thought of the double life he would have to lead. He would have to sleuth around, lie to keep secrets from the men he now felt a bond with. In the two passages through the blockade they had made, a sturdy web of mutual respect had begun to weave together. To hide something from them—to outright lie to them—seemed wrong to him, and just the thought of it left him unsettled with a gnawing worry that he would regret it.

Townsend had left the men at the Casa Blanca shipyard to oversee the repairs to the *Gaviota's* hull. It was a more complicated procedure than they thought. Two new chain plates had to be installed. In addition, a sizable area of planking amidships would have to be pulled out and new planks scarfed in. It was going to take two weeks of work, if not more. As he lay there in the dark, his thoughts turned to Hendricks. He worried about the Bahamian. When he returned to the ship after seeing Savage, he'd seen Don Pedro huddled together with Salazar and Nolo, their dark stares cast in Hendricks's direction. He had walked up to them and asked if anything was wrong. Don Pedro had pulled him aside and explained that Salazar had some unfriendly things to say about that "worthless Negro." He thought he might be a spy.

"Who would that be?" Townsend asked, knowing full well who it was.

"The Bahamian," Don Pedro replied. "Salazar doesn't trust him."

"I'm sure there are spies about, but they're not on my ship," Townsend had retorted calmly even as he tried to control a telltale twitch in his lower lip. "Hendricks is a veteran sailor. I can assure you he is not a spy."

Don Pedro had stared at him long and hard without saying anything. "Salazar also informed me that you had a passenger on board, some kind of reporter who was talking about the Backhouse murder?"

Townsend nodded.

"My advice to you is to curb your curiosity, Captain. Here in Cuba some matters like the Backhouse murder are better not discussed. It makes some people uncomfortable."

Don Pedro had put his arm around his shoulders and thrust his face close to Townsend. It was more of an intrusive gesture than a reassuring one, and Townsend found himself cringing as the man squeezed his shoulders with an iron grip.

"*Siempre fiel*, Captain Townsend. Always be faithful. That's what I insist on. We have done well with this first round trip, but we cannot afford to have any rats on the ship. ¿*Me comprende?* Understood? As the priests say, *Semper Fidelis.*"

Maybe it was the man's musky perfumed cologne or being too close to his coal black eyes and his deeply pockmarked face, but Townsend felt a strange sense of repulsion overwhelm him. The ship's whistle blew, a final wake-up call for the sixty passengers on board. From the top deck of the two-decker steamer, he could see the ship had come to anchor a mile from the pier, providing a wide panorama of Matanzas Bay. The big harbor was filled with the shadowy silhouettes of trading merchant ships, large and small, and several Spanish ships of war. Cool winds swept across the ship, gently rippling the surface of the bay. The dark water in the harbor was alive with fiery phosphorescent stars. He found himself falling into the embrace of these silvery, flickering lights. He listened to the gentle lapping of the water against the hull. His mind drifted to a memory of his mother. He thought of the evening he'd spent with her when she was reading Emerson by the fire. He thought of her words of advice, "It's important to know yourself, *mi hijo*, and be comfortable with who you are."

In the distance he could see the dark shape of the high mountain called *Pan de Matanzas*, which he had seen from the sea when they had first sailed to Havana. He looked toward the gas-lit docks and the surrounding town. Somewhere near here his father must have met his mother. He took a deep breath of the cool night air, and a sense of calm came over him. He had so little information to go on, but he thought with his mother's first name, and the old family name, Carbonell, perhaps he could find a relative, or maybe even the place called Mambi Joo. Such a curious phrase, he thought. After several months in Cuba, he knew it wasn't Spanish. He thought it must be African.

Townsend got a whiff of a distinctive sweet musky aroma, and he knew Don Pedro had come up behind him on the ship's deck. The Spaniard greeted a group of men well dressed in their flared Spanish black and tan felt top hats and a colorful assortment of linen suits. They seemed to know Don Pedro and warmly greeted him in Spanish, asking him how the cotton trade was going. They were grousing that Sr. Lincoln with his Emancipation Proclamation and his talk about freeing *los negros* was causing the plantation slaves in Matanzas to get restless. They were worried. Once again Townsend was struck by how many people seemed to know Don Pedro.

As they prepared to step down the ship's ladder to the lighter that would take all the passengers ashore, Townsend noticed a group of eye-catching young women kissing each other on both cheeks. The daughters of some of the local sugar aristocracy, he presumed. From the dangling gold earrings to the ruby-encrusted pendants, it would appear they were returning from a shopping excursion in Havana. Some of them were already smoking cigarettes, their eyes glittering behind their fluttering fans. A few of the girls looked his way. He tried to imagine his mother in this covey of flashy, flirtatious young ladies with their smiles, lace, and jewelry, but the image he had of his serious mother with her modest dress and quiet manners did not fit.

"I see some of the fashionable young *princesas* of Matanzas have you in their sights," Don Pedro said. "Perhaps they like *Yanqui* captains. You should go and introduce yourself. Don't let me get in your way, Don Juan Tenorio."

Townsend just shook his head. "Not my type," he said.

"Have a cigar then?" Don Pedro said as he lit one of his personal cigars. "These are made especially of the choicest tobacco."

Townsend shook his head.

"Are you sure?" Don Pedro asked as he pulled one of the long cigars out of a finely oiled silk wrapping and held it up to his nose appreciatively. "These cigars have been rolled by my own personal roller," Don Pedro said proudly, "not too loose, and not too tight. *Y huelen de maravilla*. They have a wonderful aroma."

Don Pedro lit the big cigar and rolled his eyes in the direction of the young ladies.

"Those *princesas* of Matanzas seem eager to meet you. Are you sure you would not like an introduction. There's no better way to improve your Spanish, you know."

The merchant blew a large cloud of smoke in Townsend's direction.

"By the way, I had no idea you understood as much Spanish as you do. Are you sure you aren't hiding something from me? A secret Spanish girlfriend perhaps? Someone you haven't told me about?"

Townsend enjoyed the brief glimpse of the small port city of Matanzas with its weather-beaten warehouses and the two rivers that emptied into the bay. It looked like a smaller Havana, but with wider streets and bigger shops. There were more signs of American and English merchant houses with names like Churchill and Safford than in Havana, an indication of the foreign involvement in the lucrative sugar trade business. It made him wonder if his father had come here long ago to look for work.

The next day Townsend and Don Pedro left Matanzas before dawn to take advantage of the cooler air. They hired a covered *volanta* and postilion to take them into the Yumurí Valley to the plantation of Doña Cecilia de Vargas. The winding road followed a river to the foot of some hills that looked out onto a rolling valley of green foliage. The darker green patches farther up on the hillside indicated coffee estates. Townsend noticed how Don Pedro had softened toward him. He felt more like his travel companion than his forced employee.

"Matanzas is crowded with Yankees and John Bulls," Don Pedro declared, "and English is more commonly spoken here than French. Not just merchants but planters, plantation overseers, and engineers for the mills. Some of the British banks are also heavily invested here."

Don Pedro laughed bitterly as he puffed more vigorously on his cigar, sending plumes of smoke into the air.

"The English," he spat with a sneer and a dismissive snort.

"What about the English?" Townsend asked, surprised by the sudden vindictive tone in Don Pedro's voice. The Spaniard's face, which normally was hard to read behind the constant smile, was resolute and determined.

"*Hipócritas*, hypocrites, that's what they are. The English are all too fond of expressing their hatred for slavery, but they don't own up to their complicity."

Townsend's eyebrows shot up in surprise. He hadn't seen this side to Don Pedro's personality before.

"All my life here in Cuba I have witnessed the arrogance of the highminded British. With one hand, they send out their anti-slaving gunboats, and with the other they import increasing amounts of our slave-grown sugar. With one hand, they punish Cuba and Spain for bringing in slaves, and with the other hand they give the planters high interest loans so that they can take on more debt and buy more slaves. Nothing but *hipócritas*."

Townsend was again surprised at Don Pedro's single-minded vehemence. The Spaniard's teeth were clenched tightly as he continued to puff vigorously on his cigar and lecture the young captain as if he were his student.

"I would say Mother England's fight against slave trafficking is a rather muddy canvas, wouldn't you? Rather like one of those swirling seascapes by that English painter, Turner. You never know quite what you're looking at, do you? Not when it comes to the English."

Don Pedro fell silent. His eyes which often had a melancholy droop to them, glared with animosity. Townsend simply nodded.

The road into the interior was a mushy mountain riverbed littered with loose stones, causing the *volanta* to lurch from side to side. They shared the rough road with heavily laden sugar carts pulled by three yokes of oxen and men on horseback. The small Cuban horses carefully climbed over the rocks like goats, their hooves thudding and thumping. Even with all the jolts, Townsend found the views captivating. It was all open country, scattered with tall palm trees, leafy mangoes, and small farms with thatched roofs. The surrounding hills were covered by a dark green canopy of tropical hardwoods with the occasional *ceiba* trees that shot up above the forest like looming giants among dwarfs.

When the sun was high up in the sky, and the dusty air was like a furnace, they stopped for a quick meal at a small thatched roof country cottage with dirt floors. The walls were made of brushwood and dried river mud. They sat down at a rough-hewn wooden table next to some sweaty farmers whose leathery faces and thick calloused hands spoke to their country ways. They were served boiled meat, yucca, roasted plantains, and a yellow cornmeal mush. This was a different Cuba than the one Townsend had seen in Havana. He didn't mind the food, but Don Pedro only picked at it, calling it *comida de los bozales*, slave food.

After a brief rest and a cigar, they were on their way again. Don Pedro told him they were not far. The *volanta* bounced along on the rough dirt road, but despite the jostling Townsend did not find the ride too uncomfortable. The air was ripe and thick with the smell of dirt, but there was also a fragrant odor of boiling sugarcane juice in the wind. Soon they could see the tall, whitewashed chimneys of sugar houses and red-tiled roofs stretched out to the horizon. They passed long straight avenues of royal palms that led to more towering chimneys of sugar estates. Scattered around these clusters of white and yellow buildings were the dark green patches of banana trees, and the lighter green of waving coconut palms.

Don Pedro breathed in deeply. "What you smell is the pungent aroma of money." He opened his arms wide to the land around them. "You are looking at what makes this island thrive, Townsend. This is where fortunes are made. What you see all around you tells the story of Cuba."

Don Pedro seemed intent on telling him about the area, the heart of Cuba's sugar economy where there were scores of sugar plantations, many over five thousand acres, each with hundreds of slaves. He explained that the harvest and grinding season for the cane was almost over, and planting had already begun in some fields.

The heat was oppressive, and Townsend tried to imagine what it would be like to be out there with the sun baking down on him, searing his skin like a skewered pig over an open fire. In the distance, he could see the glistening backs of the slaves bent over in the broad plains of sugarcane, cutting the last of the year's harvest. An overseer on horseback wearing a wide-brimmed straw hat cracked a fifteen-foot whip dangling from his right hand. The natural beauty of the land with the cane fields shimmering in the sun stood in sharp contrast to the harsh reality in those fields.

Don Pedro stroked his slicked, well-oiled hair with both hands. He seemed to know what Townsend was thinking.

"None of this would be possible, of course, if it were not for the slaves. The land is important, so is steam machinery, but to make the profits you still need free labor, and to grow and thrive the planters need a greater supply of slaves. *Así es la realidad.* That's the way it is, my young friend."

21

The *volanta* continued to lurch and heave along the rutted dirt road. To Townsend, the sprawling flat terrain seemed vast and the journey unending. It was a windless day. The mid-afternoon sun was punishing, causing him to sweat profusely. He was thirsty, but there was nothing to drink. He could feel a headache coming on. He looked for any sign of coconut trees, but there were none to be found. After several minutes of silence, Townsend asked if they were getting close. Don Pedro smiled and nodded.

"I see you are eager to get there. You have a young man's impatience. What do you know about Doña Cecilia de Vargas?"

"Nothing," replied Townsend. "Actually I am not certain why she invited me. I assumed it was her friendship with you."

"I think she was quite taken by you," Don Pedro said. "That's what she told me after she saw you at the Paseo. When was that? Two months ago, wasn't it? She is quite eager to see you. Do you wish you had not come?"

"No, I wanted to see the countryside. That's why I accepted."

"I see." Don Pedro paused for a moment, and lit another cigar. "Well, Doña Cecilia is a formidable lady of some pedigree here. Her husband Rafael Espinoza Vargas died many years ago of yellow fever, leaving her to run the plantation on her own. She is very proud of her family heritage. On one side, her family is Spanish with more than one hundred years of history on the island. She's a Quintana, not one of the oldest family names here whose ancestors were given grants of land by the Spanish Crown, but a rich aristocratic family nonetheless. On the other side of her family tree, she is

French. Her mother married a French plantation owner whose family fled Saint-Domingue to come to Cuba after the slave insurrection there. So you could say that her family is well rooted in Cuban soil, but from an admirable European pedigree."

Townsend was only partially paying attention. The heat had exhausted him so that he was in a dazed state. But Don Pedro's next words would capture his full attention.

"There is something I must confess to you, Captain. It is something I should have told you before, but I never found the right moment." The Spaniard paused his incessant puffing, revealing his ever-ready smile. He almost looked guilty. "All these months we have known each other, I'm afraid I have not been completely honest with you, Captain. We all harbor unexpected secrets from time to time, don't we? I have one secret that I have kept from you."

Townsend felt a sudden uneasiness. "What are you talking about?"

"There's no easy way for me to say this," Don Pedro replied with an uncharacteristic blush on his face. "You see, I'm not quite the stranger you think I am. I knew your mother."

Townsend almost leapt to his feet in the covered carriage. The blood rushed to his head. "What the hell!" he cried out, not making any effort to hide his surprise and confusion. "What is this, some kind of game? How could you know my mother?"

"It's not a game, I can assure you. I knew Esperanza long ago when she lived here. Before you were born."

The sudden mention of his mother's name, Esperanza, felt like a slap in the face.

Townsend wondered if he could be dreaming. He stared at Don Pedro with eyes wide open. "I don't understand. Is this some kind of cruel joke? You knew all this time who I was? Ever since I was in prison?" stammered Townsend.

"Finding you here in Cuba was a shock and a surprise. When I came to the prison three months ago I couldn't believe it at first. I merely needed a new captain for my latest ship. I never dreamed the man in the prison cell would be Esperanza's son. Then I heard your name and began speaking to you. And I realized it was you."

"Why didn't you say something before? Keeping that from me . . . it isn't right."

Don Pedro shook his head. "I know . . . I know, I've had to bite my lips these many months, but I felt my silence has been for your own good. I didn't think it would be wise to tell you. I wasn't certain I could trust you, you see.

I thought you might run off, first in Havana, then in Mobile. To be honest, I had hoped you would confide in me. It would have been easier that way. That's why I kept complimenting you on your Spanish. I hoped you would tell me about your mother, and how you learned your Spanish from her. But you didn't, and I came to realize you are a very cautious, secretive young man. But that's the past. Now we need to look to the future."

Townsend glared at the Spaniard with accusatory eyes.

"Perhaps I should ask—who exactly are you?"

"I am a close friend and business associate of your mother's family. I suppose you could say I was like an older cousin to her. I even knew your father. Of course, none of us who knew your mother have seen her since she left Cuba in 1843. But we did get news of her from time to time from a Spanish merchant living in Baltimore, a man by the name of Joaquín Nuñez. He befriended your parents, I believe? He was the one who wrote to me that your mother had died and your younger brother had been killed in the war."

Townsend remembered the man, a small bookish Spaniard with an owl-like face, balding hair, and a pencil-thin moustache. He would occasionally visit their house in Havre de Grace. He always brought a gift, and he and his mother would go into a side room and speak only in Spanish. Townsend remembered how sad and silent she always was after he left.

"So tell me, what would you like to ask me? What would you like to know?"

Townsend didn't know where to begin. "I know nothing about my mother's past."

"You know nothing about her family? Her own mother?"

Townsend shook his head. "To be honest, she never told my brother and me anything about her past. I think she grew up in Matanzas. That's what I was told, but I don't know where. I don't know when or how she met my father."

"I had no idea Esperanza was so secretive," Don Pedro said as he puffed appreciably on his cigar. "It seems you share a similar trait."

"Do I have relatives you know of? Do they live near here?"

The Spaniard looked upwards as he blew out a large cloud of smoke over his head, and then watched it slowly drift away. His face had a detached look. "Your mother grew up near here, just like those young ladies we saw on the Matanzas passenger ship. She was a *princesa* just like them. Wealthy and educated to be a cultured lady. *Una de las joyas de Cuba*, one of Cuba's jewels, you might say."

Just then, the postilion began reining in the horses, slowing their pace down. They were approaching the entrance to a large estate.

"Well, here we are," said Don Pedro. "This is the entrance."

The horses clattered through the open gates onto a long driveway lined on either side with tall royal palms. Townsend saw the ornate iron lettering of the plantation's name.

"Mon Bijou," the Spaniard said, one eyebrow slightly raised. "It's a French name meaning, my jewel."

Townsend whispered to himself, "Mon Bijou," pronouncing it as Don Pedro had. "I don't believe I have ever heard of it before."

"I'm surprised," said Don Pedro with a sharky grin. "You see, this estate, my friend, is where your mother grew up."

Townsend stared at him.

"Maybe your mother never spoke of it?"

"It can't be. This can't be. She called it Mambi Joo? I thought maybe that was the name of a small town!"

"Here in Matanzas, Mon Bijou has a more African sound to it. I suppose it's because the English overseers, engineers, and Africans couldn't pronounce the French so the Mon Bijou plantation came to be called Mambi Joo. Growing up here, your mother learned to refer to it that way. She was born here, you know, so she grew up playing and conversing with the African slaves. She was a *criolla*, born and raised in Cuba."

❖

Townsend remembered every detail of that ride up the avenue of tall, stately palm trees leading to the Mon Bijou estate. There must have been more than a hundred trees in a row, all lined up perfectly with short flowering trees planted alongside. In the distance off to one side he could see the tall chimney of the sugar house and long lines of slowly moving ox carts winding their way through a field of partially cut cane. The dust-laden air, the faint glow of the afternoon light, barefoot, naked black children waving and yelling as they ran alongside the clattering *volanta*, and then the elegant round circle outside the stone manor house—he concentrated on each and every detail. All he could think was that his mother had been here. She had grown up here. This was Mambi Joo.

He was in a daze as they stepped out of the *volanta*. Every muscle in his back hurt from all the jarring jolts. The one-story house was surrounded by a mixture of palm trees, poinciana, and red and yellow hibiscus. A soft breeze moved through the branches of a large tamarind tree that shaded the front of the house. There were a dozen black servants looking at them from the wide stone veranda surrounded by an iron railing: cooks, maids, three white-coated butlers, all there to greet them. Don Pedro yelled in Spanish for them to tell their mistress, *la ama*, that her guests had arrived.

"There is something else I need to tell you, Captain, something about Doña Cecilia de Vargas you should know before you see her."

"And what might that be?" Townsend asked.

"She also knew your mother."

Townsend gasped.

"Is she a relative?"

"I will leave that for her to explain. I think it's fair to say you will find out soon enough."

Townsend spotted the older woman he remembered from the Paseo striding out onto the veranda. Doña Cecilia was dressed more simply than when he had seen her last. She stood in front of the heavy wooden doors and solid wooden shutters like a medieval queen at the castle door, a long white ruffled cotton dress with a black lace mantilla draped over her shoulders. She waved at Don Pedro and beckoned him to come up onto the veranda even as she motioned for the servants to get back into the house and get to work.

Townsend watched as she kissed Don Pedro on both cheeks. Her dark hair with streaks of gray had a certain elegance with the black lace falling down her shoulders. He was surprised at the tenderness she showed. Her eyes lingered on Don Pedro for a moment, and he thought he saw him nod ever so slightly to her. She told Don Pedro which bedroom was being prepared for him, and he left to get washed up. She then turned to Townsend slowly with an odd expression that turned to a faint melancholy smile.

"I am so pleased you are here at Mon Bijou. Come, let me show you around. We have fifteen servants in the house—cooks, maids, laundresses, seamstresses, and butlers—so you will not lack for anything. But it is quite a lot to manage, as you can imagine."

She walked with him through the front door into a large parlor with open jalousie windows that were protected by iron bars. With the three-foot-thick walls and the high ceilings, the house was much cooler than it was outside. The rooms off the parlor were filled with the hustle and bustle of black servants who scurried around on their bare feet, making hardly a sound.

He kept looking around as if he would find some clue that would answer his many questions. The house had the feel of another era. The floors were a mix of old chipped terracotta tile and faded white marble. Most of the furniture was dark mahogany, large bureaus and cabinets with scrolled feet and planters' chairs and sofas with cane seats. Townsend couldn't stop thinking of his mother. He tried to imagine her here. This was her childhood home. This is what she had left behind.

Doña Cecilia looked him over with a lingering stare. There was something about her features that captivated Townsend. The thin face, the tightly compressed lips, the dark eyes. She reminded him of his mother. Townsend almost blurted out a question, but he restrained himself out of fear that he might embarrass himself. She lapsed into French, which he didn't speak. "*La maison est à vous*," and then realizing he didn't understand, she repeated it in English and then in Spanish. "The house is yours. *Esta es su casa*." She smiled.

"You do speak Spanish, don't you?" she asked apologetically. "I thought Don Pedro told me you did."

"*Sí, hablo un poco*," he said. "Yes, a little."

"*¡Que bien! ¡Me alegro!*. I am glad your mother didn't totally forget her Cuban heritage," she said with a touch of bitterness.

Townsend was struck by the edge in her voice. He heard resentment. But there was also a suggestion of intimacy. He was about to ask about his mother when she led him into a sitting room with stuccoed white walls. In a corner, she showed him a portrait of a young girl, dressed like a princess, in white ruffles, lace, and satin, her shiny dark brown hair in tresses decorated with ribbons. The girl was looking upwards, smiling hopefully. Her eyes had a quiet melancholy to them. A shiver of excitement passed through Townsend. He was looking at a painting of his mother.

"My Esperanza, she was such a beauty," Doña Cecilia sighed. "*Una belleza*. This portrait was done when she was just thirteen years old."

Townsend froze, and looked at her with shock and amazement.

"Are you . . . ?"

She laughed and gently touched his shoulder with her hand.

"I thought you would have guessed by now," she said in a soft, disarming voice. "I know it must seem strange. It's strange for me as well . . . but yes, I am your grandmother. You must call me *Tata Cecilia*. That sounds better than *Abuela*. Come, let me show you more of the house. May I call you Everett?"

Townsend nodded. This was the woman he had heard his mother curse time and again. She was real. She was alive. He wondered if this was a dream. His grandmother seemed so gracious and welcoming, so different than what he had expected. His mother's version certainly did not match the person he now followed. She showed him the room where the family would play cards and his mother would entertain them with the piano.

"Esperanza was so talented with her music," she said. "She was very proud when she learned to play the score for Bellini's 'Norma.' *¿Sigue con el piano?* Does she . . ." She corrected herself. "Did she continue with the piano?"

Townsend nodded. "Yes, she did. She often played in the evenings after supper."

He looked over at his grandmother, who hadn't taken her eyes off him. He knew that she was taking measure of him, and he couldn't help but feel ill at ease. He didn't tell her that playing the piano had often made his mother teary-eyed. Nor did he say that when she had one of her outbursts, she would angrily pound the keys, her eyes flashing with malice. His grandmother took him to his mother's old room, which still had a few of her old dolls, all made out of coarse linen with smudgy painted faces. There was an old mahogany bed with a green damask cover, and a blue and white porcelain pitcher with his mother's name inscribed on it, perched on top of a bureau. Townsend walked around the room slowly as he thought of his mother, imagining her in this room as a young girl and then a young woman. Time seemed to have stood still here. A chipped gilded mirror on the wall revealed a reflection of her dolls propped up in a cane lounge chair. His grandmother rearranged them.

"As you can see, I have the servants clean and dust here every day."

Townsend picked up some carved miniature figurines of horses that were on a marble table next to a candlestick.

"Your mother loved her horses. As a young girl, Esperanza would ride all over the plantation. Your mother had everything she could have ever wanted in this house," she said softly. "Three maids to attend to her every need. She went to school here. I had tutors come to the plantation. She was a happy girl." She sighed audibly.

They walked to an open courtyard in the center of the house that was filled with flowering bougainvillea surrounding an old stone fountain with a large tiled basin. The sun had mostly gone down so they stood in the gray light of dusk listening to the water splash. Townsend could feel a quiet tension hover over them. A cloud of unspoken questions. This was all too strange to be real. When she stared at him, he kept looking away. He kept hearing his mother's voice in the background. He watched her gaze out at the increasingly shadowy courtyard lost in her memories. Townsend could feel her loneliness, and her sense of loss after all these years. He began to feel sorry for this woman his mother had hated. What had caused such a great rift between them?

"Please hold onto my hand, Everett. I sometimes trip when it's getting dark like this."

Townsend took her hand and helped her down a couple of steps.

"As a girl, your mother would come here and spend many hours reading her books. This was her favorite place. She was always dreaming about adventure and travel. I used to tell her the world is not as glorious as she might imagine."

She paused for a moment and then continued.

"Ay, *de mí*," she sighed. "Esperanza and I had our differences, but I never imagined she wouldn't return. She was so proud and so full of her ideals . . . but enough of that." She took a deep breath and wiped the sadness off her face with a broad smile. Some of the slaves who had stood motionless around the perimeter of the patio now lit the oil lamps, fixed in pairs on each of the columns of the arcade surrounding the open courtyard.

Doña Cecilia caught the eye of one of the older black women with a red turban around her head.

"Mercedes, bring me the *cocuyo* lantern."

"Yes, Mistress."

"She speaks English," Townsend said.

"Ah yes, there are English Negroes in these parts. Mercedes was sold to me years ago. She's from Jamaica, I believe. I don't remember what her original English name was. She has no way back to her home, of course, so it's best that she forget it."

She smiled at him as she reached out and squeezed his hand.

"Now Everett, there's so much for us to talk about. I want to hear about you and your life in Havana. Tell me about the excitement of running through the Union blockade."

Just then Don Pedro walked into the courtyard followed by one of the male slaves, who carried three steaming, frothy cups.

"I'm delighted to see you both are acquainted and are getting along so well. I told you, Captain, that you would soon have all your questions answered. Now it's time you embraced your Cuban heritage," Don Pedro said, shaking his cigar in a slightly regal way.

"Un *brindis*. Let us toast the strength of family ties. This drink is called a *guarapo*. It's my personal version, a mixture of rum, brandy, fresh hot sugarcane juice and an egg. Drink up and welcome to Mon Bijou."

Don Pedro chatted with Doña Cecilia about the harvest, which was going to be better than expected, and then announced he would be leaving early the next morning and would be gone for the next several days. He had to visit some of his business associates in the area to try to keep them investing in his blockade-running ventures. He told Townsend to take the time with his grandmother. He would be back to take him to the coast before they returned to Havana.

"I'm going to bring you to an important event that will attract scores of the most wealthy planters. It's something peculiar to Cuba, *una cosa cubana*."

Townsend hardly paid any attention as the Spaniard walked away. His grandmother was holding an eerie lantern filled with swirling fireflies that the slave had brought her. Doña Cecilia explained to Townsend that in Cuba these fireflies are called *cocuyos*. Townsend looked more closely. The insects were about the size of cockroaches, and their black eyes suddenly lit up when they spread their wings.

"It's a Cuban custom. The *cocuyos* light up as bright as candles," she said with a beaming smile. "These creatures look like they want to fly away, but they are content. They get used to being inside the lantern and soon forget about trying to escape."

Townsend thought the scene was oddly dream-like with the darkness of the maid's skin contrasting with his grandmother's pale white face, the silvery glow of the lantern gleaming with a ghostly light. He noticed that the maid was looking at him closely, but when he returned the stare she averted her eyes.

"That will be all, Mercedes," Doña Cecilia said.

"*Sí, l'ama.* Yes, Mistress."

22

Townsend looked with amazement at the breakfast table in the dining room that had been prepared for just the two of them. The small army of white-gloved servants who surrounded the table stood ready with large platters filled with fried plantain omelettes, fried fish in a coconut sauce, stewed tomatoes and lightly browned sugary pastries, *pastelitos de queso y guayaba*. His grandmother said these were his mother's favorite. A black servant poured strong Cuban coffee into his cup and topped it off with frothy, heated milk. He then asked if *el amo* would take sugar. Townsend shook his head. All this attention made him uncomfortable, and he greatly disliked being called *el amo*.

He sipped the *café con leche* as his grandmother spoke about the plantation and her Esperanza.

"She loved the scent of orange blossoms and jasmine, the call of the mourning doves. During the season, she would go out and pick mangoes, her favorite fruit. She loved this land. She was truly a daughter of Cuba."

The other servants stood by silently with their arms folded, ready to respond to any request. Townsend could sense his grandmother's probing stare, and he avoided meeting her gaze—this "*bruja*" his mother hated so.

"You remind me so much of your mother. Something in your expression. I believe it's the mouth, the strong chin or maybe it's the eyes? I look at you and I see Esperanza."

She laughed and reached out to touch his hand, and he wasn't sure why, but he impulsively jerked it back.

"Everett, I won't bite you, you know," she said. "I can tell you are uncertain about me. I want to ease any concerns you might have."

"No, it's nothing," Townsend replied, flustered and embarrassed. "I have no concerns. I was just wiping my chin."

"I know your mother was terribly angry, and I imagine she may have said terrible things to you two boys about me. I was afraid of this. I was afraid you might think poorly of me. That's why I didn't say anything to you at the Paseo. I had considered it, but then my friend the Condesa joined me in the carriage unexpectedly. It was not the right moment, and Don Pedro said I should wait a little longer. Give you more time to adjust to Cuba."

Townsend nodded even as he fidgeted in his chair. He could sense that she was carefully studying him.

"Enough of that," she said abruptly as she finished her coffee. "We have so much to do. I want to give you a tour of the plantation."

Townsend walked with his grandmother out the front door where an open chaise *volanta* was waiting for them. The postilion was a small slave boy who helped Doña Cecilia into the carriage. He had a big smile, and large dark eyes—an easy manner about him. He looked like he was about thirteen years old.

"Take us out to the chapel, Julio," she said in her soft voice.

"*Si l'ama.*"

"Julio is the son of Mercedes."

"The one who spoke English."

"Yes, that's the one. She's trying to buy his freedom now, something the laws allow here in Cuba. He could be free in a few years. My hope is he will stay here at the plantation. He likes animals, and he's a quick learner."

They soon were bouncing along the plantation's rutted roads. In the distance, Townsend could see a team of oxen plowing the fields. His grandmother told him how she was born and raised at Mon Bijou. She'd lived here all her life except for the years she spent in Paris for her education. For Townsend, the landscapes of undulating green on the three-thousand-acre estate were enormous, but the core of the plantation seemed like a small village. It was home to four hundred slaves and little more than a handful of white people. They arrived at a small community of yellow and white houses for the sugar makers and the engineers. There was a certain beauty in the austere simplicity of the terracotta-roofed buildings, but in the distance Townsend could see the slaves laboring in the fields, and the cruel crack of a whip reminded him that there was nothing charming about plantation life.

Just below the sugar mill, she pointed out a small stone chapel with its steeple and a cross, and asked Julio to pull to a stop.

"This is what I wanted to show you. My grandfather built this. This chapel represents why this land is so important to me. My parents were married here. So was I. My children were all baptized here. There has been happiness and sadness within those old stone walls. The funeral services were held here for my husband, Rafael Vargas—your grandfather. And then a few months later for my two daughters, your mother's two younger sisters. They all three died from a yellow fever outbreak. We call it the black vomit here. ¡Que tragedia, verdad! What a tragedy! They are all buried over there in the family graveyard."

She pointed over to a small cemetery surrounded by a stone wall. A cluster of tightly packed bamboo trees grew near there amid some palm trees. Townsend could hear the quiet moan and wail of the wind through the bamboo.

Tears filled her eyes.

"So I think you can see why every tree, every cane field here at Mon Bijou is like part of my soul. I thought your mother felt the same way. She was born here like I was. But I was wrong."

"What happened to change things?" he asked.

Doña Cecilia paused and then sighed.

"In 1840, suddenly Rafael was gone, and I had to manage the plantation on my own. It was a terrible time. There were slave rebellions mounting. But I managed. A couple of years later when your mother was eighteen years old, I needed to find a suitor for her. A sensible marriage. I chose an appropriate Spanish gentleman, a merchant, who I remain quite fond of. As you know in Cuba, those who are from Spain have more privileges than those of us born here. Esperanza could have lived well. He was wealthy and highly ambitious, and would have supported her in a grand way. I thought it was all settled. They were to be engaged. Then your mother found your father. Imagine, he was nothing more than one of the temporary engineers on the plantation. He was an American ship captain who had taken seasonal work with us as an engineer. Of course, I was horrified. Your father was beneath her."

Townsend was silent at this insult. He noticed that she didn't make the connection with his own life as a ship captain.

"I still do not know why she did that to me," she said, shaking her head.

"I guess they were in love," Townsend answered simply.

Doña Cecilia raised her eyebrows and then looked away. An awkward silence descended on them, and she told Julio to take them back to the house. As the volanta thumped along the rougher sections of the road, Townsend again heard the crack of a whip and one of the slave drivers yelling. Then came the melodic chanting of the slaves and the grinding noise from the sugar mill.

"I still believe as a daughter of mine, her first duty was to her family, but your mother was stubborn and willful. Hot-headed," she said emphatically. "Julio, *Más rápido*. Go faster."

"*Sí l'ama. ¡Arre! ¡Arre!*," he cried out as he whipped the horse in a way Townsend thought unnecessarily cruel. His grandmother didn't seem to notice and turned to Townsend with an ingratiating smile. He noticed there was a slight quiver on one side of her mouth.

"When she eloped with your father, she told me she never wanted to see me again. *Dios mío, no sabes el dolor que sentí.* You don't know how painful it was. I sat in her empty room for days. I was sure she would come back." Her voice cracked.

"When I found out your mother lived near Baltimore in the town of Havre de Grace, I wrote her time after time. She only wrote back once and that was to tell me she no longer recognized our family name, Vargas. Every year I would write, but I never received a reply." Townsend remembered his mother's distress as she crumpled up letters and threw them in the fire. He could see her face even as he looked at his grandmother's.

"Did she ever mention my letters?"

He lied and shook his head.

At that moment, Townsend almost wanted to comfort his grandmother, but didn't, and she breathed deeply and composed her face.

"I have arranged for the overseer to show you the mill and the slave quarters over the next two days. He knew your mother well. It's important for you to see how the plantation works. *¡Ay, Madre de Dios!* I am so glad you are here. You remind me of my former husband with that handsome face of yours."

It was still dark outside at 5:00 a.m. when the plantation bells at Mon Bijou began clanging, signaling another work day had begun. Townsend sat up and sipped the *café con leche* the servant had brought him. Outside he could hear the night chorus of tree frogs chirping away. After three days at the plantation, Townsend was beginning to know the routine. He heard the clopping of hooves outside the manor house, dogs barking, and then the crunch of heavy footsteps followed by the squeak of the front door opening. It was the overseer, who had come to fetch him before he made his early morning rounds of the estate. Townsend did not like the man, a powerful, thickset

Scotsman with a full gray beard. The young captain found him to be surly and garrulous. He had already spent one day with him at the sugar mill. He'd seen how the cane was thrown into steam-powered crushers, squeezing out a steady stream of clear greenish liquid that was then boiled and skimmed in large copper cauldrons. He could still hear the clank of the steam engine and the grinding of the cane and in the background, the rich mournful voices of the slaves.

This was Townsend's last full day at Mon Bijou. As usual, he and the overseer, whose name was William McKintyre, set out on horseback past the barracoons where the slaves lived. The big Scotsman led the way on his small gray horse with a pack of four Cuban bloodhounds following behind.

They came upon teams of slaves with broad-brimmed palm hats trudging out of the thatched-roof barracoons as they were loaded onto sturdy ox carts with high slatted wooden walls. A few of them had iron manacles around their ankles, a chain connecting them suspended from the waist. A collar with three hooks was around their necks and a coupling chain was secured to each collar. McKintyre laughed with a sadistic gleam in his eye and let his whip loose. Townsend flinched at the cracking sound and the sight of the bloody scars on the men's backs.

"Runaways," said the overseer with a cold sneer. "Fear is whit these Africans understand. T'ain no kindness to be given niggers. It's th' only way they can be kept in order." The Scot seemed unaware of Townsend's discomfort. "Twenty-five lashes th' first time they run an' they'ur sent ta th' fields in chains," he snarled in his distinctive Scottish brogue. "If they da it again, fifty lashes an' solitary confinement. Cayenne pepper an' rum keep th' wounds from gettin' infected."

Townsend grimaced in disgust. Slavery came from the devil. That's what he wanted to tell the man, but he decided to keep his thoughts to himself. He turned away, his gaze settling on the fields in the distance. He could see the unwieldy carts heavily loaded with their human cargo as they lurched down a muddy path, tumbling and swaying, into a sea of tall sugarcane. Spanish slave drivers called contra-mayorales, each armed with a pistol and a cutlass, long whips dangling ever ready at their side, followed closely behind on horseback. "What a fine piece of hell this is," Townsend murmured quietly to himself. What he saw was filling a blank page for him. This had been his mother's home. It was another world entirely from their life in Havre de Grace. This was what his mother had grown up with. This is what she had left behind, and had never wanted to return to.

By the afternoon, the garrulous Scotsman was more friendly than usual— likely thanks to the flask he kept swigging from. It was Townsend's last chance to question the man. "My grandmother said you knew my mother. What was she like then?" he asked.

"Ah, yes. Indeed I did know Esperanza. A pretty lass, your mother was. High-spirited. Always wanted the last word."

The Scot paused for a moment as he looked away, and then brought his gaze back to Townsend.

"I don't mean no disrespect, but your mother an' I didn't see eye to eye on many things. I suppose you know, she fought wi' yer grandmother. Like two cats they were, howlin' and hissin' at each other. I knew your father too. Oh yes, I knew him as well. He was one of the seasonal engineers here. He was of th' same mindset as yer mother. They both wanted to help the niggers, givin' those black monkeys all kinds of expectations. I think he was a bad influence over yer mother, if I may say so. The two of them would go and talk to some of th' slaves, spreading all sorts of foolish notions."

"Foolish notions? That's hardly the way I think of my mother or my father."

"Ha! They thought the slaves had th' right ta be free. We had some English slaves then, you know th' ones taken from th' Bahamas and Jamaica twenty to twenty-five years ago. Well, yer mother was encouragin' them ta run away. We couldn't have that so we sold most of those English slaves off. The ones we kept, we gave them the names of dead slaves so they no longer had their old identities, or any rights either."

McKintyre chortled with a dry, weary laugh. Townsend remembered his mother telling him why she volunteered to help the runaways that came through Maryland. She had talked about the hard road ahead for the black people. They have no way back, she told him. They have to find a way forward.

"Would ye want to know somethin' else about yer mother?" asked the Scotsman, his voice beginning to slur and his eyes hardening. He pulled out his flask again. His face was getting redder.

"No, I don't think so," Townsend replied, sensing that the man was drunker than he realized.

"Well, since you been askin' about her, let me tell you something. She broke your grandmother's heart. Plain and simple. It was a cruel thing to do, leavin' th' way she did. This land means everything to Doña Cecilia."

The man took another long drink from his flask.

"But then yer here now. The poor woman needs a grandson like you to help manage things. I haven't seen her this happy in years. Come with me, laddie. I am gonna show you where these darkies live."

It was the first time Townsend had been taken inside the walled slave quarters. McKintyre walked in past a heavy wooden door guarded by four chained bloodhounds with whip in hand, a pistol and a Bowie knife attached to his broad leather belt. Some of the women were tending a small charcoal fire outside in the center of the quadrangle where they were boiling water. They lowered their eyes as McKintyre approached them. When the Scot cracked the whip, some of them got down on their knees and began pleading for him to have mercy. Small, naked children clutched their mothers' calico dresses, their big eyes filled with fear at the sight of the white man.

McKintyre made his rounds, inspecting the small dark rooms with their clay floors and dirty walls to make sure there were no field slaves hiding out. For a moment Townsend thought he was back in Havana's city prison, but the difference was he was now one of the jailors. Entire families huddled in a cramped space no bigger than what he'd been put in. He looked at some of the women apologetically, wanting to let them know he was not part of this cruel system, but he could tell they saw him as one of the overseers—just another cruel white man.

McKintyre showed Townsend how he was training a new batch of young dogs. They were not like American bloodhounds, but looked more like English mastiffs, tan, brindle-colored with a solid build and a short muzzle. The Scot called a slave boy over who was playing with a puppy. Townsend couldn't believe his eyes. He knew the boy. It was Julio, his grandmother's postilion.

"Over 'ere boy, show this gentleman how you can train th' dog."

Townsend could tell the boy recognized him, but he remained silent. McKintyre threw the boy a stick and told him to beat the dog and then run away. "Sí, l'amo," Julio replied, his face transforming from a smile to a sneer. With no word spoken, this mild-mannered boy tied up the puppy with a short leash and began beating it with the stick. Again and again, he struck the animal, causing the dog to yelp and howl in pain.

"From th' look of it, that nigger boy, he will nat want ta play wi' that dog too much longer," McKintyre chortled with a throaty laugh. "He's learning the rough and tumble of the slave business." The overseer explained how the dog begins to associate the beating by the boy with all Negroes, and then pretty soon it will just want to tear any black man apart.

"That's how we train our dogs," he said proudly. "Those Southern planters in Mobile pay good money for our dogs."

Townsend could take it no longer.

"See there now, this cruelty has to stop," Townsend shouted to Mc-Kintyre. He grabbed Julio's arm and took the club away from him. The dog was growling and snarling.

"You're nothing but a brutal animal, McKintyre!"

The overseer glared at him, and told Julio to run off. The Scot didn't say anything to Townsend as they walked out of the barracoon quarters together. Townsend was never happier to hear the sound of the plantation bell, signaling the break for the afternoon meal. He mounted his horse, and pushed him to a fast gallop, cursing McKintyre as he rode. At the stone manor house, he gave his horse to one of the stable boys waiting outside. His anger was muted by the sight of his grandmother, and the bounteous meal awaiting him. Well-dressed butlers in their white jackets had put the steaming platters of food onto a table on the stone veranda—everything from a richly spiced planters' meat and vegetable stew called *ajiaco* to roast pork garnished with olives and raisins and smothered in onions. The side dishes were equally appetizing: yellow saffron rice, fried green bananas called *mariquitas*, black beans with chopped onions, and ochre and tomatoes glistening with lard. All this was served with a Spanish red wine.

Townsend suddenly felt guilty at the sight of all this food. He was troubled by how in just three days he had grown accustomed to this pandering, with house servants tending to his every need from dawn to dusk. He could see how easy it would be to fall into this sleepy, languid rhythm of a planter's life where servants hovered everywhere. It was like a narcotic, gently numbing his senses so that he could no longer feel empathy. He picked at his food.

"Is there something troubling you, Everett?" his grandmother asked. She clapped her hands and called on one of the servants to remove the plates, and then beckoned to another to bring the dessert.

"It's your overseer, McKintyre. He's a monster! The punishments for runaways are severe, way too harsh. Even the training of the dog I witnessed— your young postilion boy ordered to beat a puppy until it became vicious! I have never seen such cruelty. The way the man treats your slaves will produce the same result. They will attack the hand that beats them."

He had expected his grandmother to be shocked at what he told her about the Scotsman, maybe even to be appreciative of his observations. At first she glanced up at the servant bringing the bowls of *guanábana* ice cream, and then she turned to him with a sullen stare. She seemed transformed, the sides of her mouth turned down, her expression brooding and furtive. The silence at the table seemed to go on forever. Finally she gave a great sniff and lifted her head as she took her first spoonful of the sweet, fragrant ice cream.

"Why, Everett, you remind me of your mother. She also couldn't stand the sight of disciplining slaves, but in fact here at Mon Bijou we are just following tradition. Mr. McKintyre learned everything from my husband, your grandfather, who was more lenient than some here on the island. In fact, I don't know what I would do without the Scotsman. He manages everything so well. As for Julio and the training of the dogs, that is for the boy's own good. Mr. McKintyre wants young Julio to learn how to be a field slave driver, what we call a *contra-mayoral*. He is just trying to teach the boy how to be tough. Julio will need to learn how to be hard-nosed if he's going to handle the whip and discipline field slaves as his job."

She reached for her coffee, her face tight-lipped, revealing what he thought was the tiniest touch of contempt. Then she smiled ever so faintly. Her voice was soft.

"I should tell you something about the sugar business, *querido*. It's unfortunate, my dear, but true. The overseers may be cruel and unreasoning, perhaps crude in their methods, but what choice do they have? If you had seen the plantation uprising here twenty years ago, you would understand. Any plantation owner will tell you that it's more important to be feared than loved."

Townsend had not expected this. He looked at his grandmother as if she was a stranger. To hide his disgust, he brought the coffee cup up to his face. At that moment the trees began to rustle with a sudden gust of wind. Black clouds darkened the sky. A rain squall was coming.

23

Before dawn the next day, Don Pedro and Townsend mounted two horses from the stable and rode to the coast. It was still dark, but Doña Cecilia had come out to see them off, kissing Townsend warmly on both cheeks. Don Pedro had told him they were going to meet two important investors, wealthy planters on an estate near the coast. The Spaniard had said he would be discussing an important transaction with the two men that might prove profitable. Without meaning to, Townsend found himself slipping into the role Savage wanted him to play.

"What kind of transaction?" he asked.

"I'd rather not say," Don Pedro replied.

"Something involving cotton and the blockade?"

"Not exactly, but it could prove to be beneficial to our trade with the South. And it might involve you at some point."

As they rode by the light of a full moon, Townsend's thoughts sifted through his tangled mix of emotions. He started making excuses for his grandmother. Her support of McKintyre's brutality was shocking to him, but he told himself these methods of harsh discipline were normal in Cuba. She felt an obligation to keep the family plantation going. It was her heritage, and she was dependent on the overseer to keep things stable. But even as he excused her acceptance of cruelty, another voice inside told him he was kidding himself. He could almost hear his mother caution him . . . be careful where you step, *mi hijo*. And he wondered if his grandmother's defense of

McKintyre was just a brief glimpse into a much more complicated woman—a much more amoral culture.

As the hazy gray of early morning emerged, they passed through small villages of thatched houses causing the dogs to bark, and some angry *guajiros* to shake their fists at them. Dawn arrived with a blazing hot white sun revealing that they were now traveling through a coffee farm. They slowed the horses down to an easy pacing gait, what the Cubans called *la marcha*. As far as the eye could see, Townsend looked out on a rolling carpet of dark green bushes, some of them covered with small white blossoms. When they came upon a stream they stopped to let the horses drink.

Don Pedro took the opportunity to tell Townsend about the man whose plantation house they were going to visit.

"Don Eugenio Hernández is one of our investors with the *Gaviota* and two other ships that I own. He likes to get a progress report on his investments, and this time he is bringing to the table a highly important man."

"Who is that?"

"I'll introduce him to you when we get there. I am glad to see you are showing such an interest, Captain. I believe this trip to Matanzas has done you a world of good. I understand you have had a very educational three days at Mon Bijou. Your grandmother told me she had McKintyre give you a management course on the harvesting of sugarcane."

Townsend nodded, only vaguely aware that he was scowling. "I suppose you could call it that."

"Well, you'll learn more about the sugar trade from Don Eugenio. He took me in when I came here from Spain as a boy without any money, and he made sure I learned the business of being a merchant. He was my patron. He is like an uncle to me."

"I see."

"He knew your mother, and is good friends with your grandmother. So you see, he is almost like family to you as well. Unfortunately, he is quite ill now. For me, it is heartbreaking. I don't like to see good people suffer."

When they arrived at the plantation house in the late afternoon, they were led along a corridor and were taken into a smoke-filled library with floor to ceiling bookcases filled with leather-bound books. Townsend noticed that many of the books were English titles, including complete collections of the works of Charles Dickens, Milton, and Shakespeare. A newspaper on a nearby table was open to the *Esclavos* section—which Townsend could see was an entire page filled with news of recent sales of slaves on the island. Someone had underlined the prices. One thousand dollars for a healthy field slave. Townsend hadn't realized slaves were that expensive in Cuba.

At the far end of the library, two men were seated in mahogany plantation chairs with rattan seats. Townsend scrutinized them. The older man's head was covered with a silk handkerchief. He was dressed gaudily in a blue striped linen suit with a scarlet silk scarf around his waist. Townsend guessed this was Don Eugenio. The other man, with silvery black hair and a sharp aquiline nose, seemed familiar. It was Don Julián Zulueta. Townsend hadn't seen him since Don Pedro had pointed him out walking along the promenade at the Paseo outside the old walls. He'd called Zulueta one of the wealthiest planters on the island.

Don Pedro immediately embraced Don Eugenio, and then formally shook the hands of Zulueta. As glasses of claret were passed around by one of the slaves, Don Pedro addressed the two men, respectfully calling them "distinguished gentlemen."

"*Distinguidos caballeros*, allow me to introduce Doña Cecilia Carbonell de Vargas's American grandson from Maryland, Everett Townsend. He is one of my blockade-running ship captains." Townsend found himself bowing to the seated men who both were carefully scrutinizing him.

"What do you think about this American war, young man?" Don Julián asked. "I will tell you, most of us here in Cuba of our class, particularly those of us who are Spanish born, would like to see a new Confederate States of America. We have much in common with the American South. We intend to hold onto slavery. So what do you think? Will we have two Americas?"

Townsend stared at the man's deep-set black eyes. He knew how he was expected to respond, but instead he remained noncommittal.

"It would be presumptuous for me to say, Señor Zulueta. I am just a ship captain, and have no inside knowledge from the battlefield. I think the war could still go either way."

"But the South will gain its independence, will it not? Tell me, which side would you put your money on? North or South?"

"If I were a betting man, I would venture to say the Union will probably prevail because of the South's weak economy which is far too dependent on cotton."

Zulueta's bushy black eyebrows arched upwards in a gesture of surprise. "I see. That is a grim prognostication indeed, Captain. Not quite the answer I was expecting."

"*Un brindis por los Confederados*," cried out Don Pedro as if to underline the fact that he didn't agree with Townsend's tepid response. He raised his glass to make a toast and Townsend found himself drinking Spanish claret to the shouts of, "Long live the Confederacy, long live Spain, and long live the ever-faithful island of Cuba."

"*¡Vivan los Confederados! ¡Viva España! ¡Viva Cuba Siempre Fiel!*"

When Don Pedro and Zulueta began conversing about the cotton trade, Don Eugenio turned to Townsend, who was scanning the titles of books in the library.

"I am a great admirer of England's bards. My passion is the translation of some of Spain's classics from the *Siglo de Oro* into English." He pointed to an older black man standing in the corner. "Thanks to Javier Alfonso here, I can keep up with my work. He is my personal attendant, a slave who has been with me for over twenty years. He knows where all my books are. Unfortunately, he is not getting any younger. Working in the fields all those years took its toll."

Javier Alfonso appeared to be about sixty years old and had specks of gray hair and a creased forehead. He had a proud, dignified manner about him. His face remained impassive with no expression, but Townsend thought he detected wisdom and sadness in his piercing eyes.

"Javier, bring us some cigars."

"*Sí, l'amo,*" the slave replied. "Yes master, right away." Townsend jumped at the unexpected sound of English coming from the black man.

"He speaks and writes perfect English. Javier, bring the Fígaro Regalías Británicas that Don Pedro and Don Julián like so much."

As the old slave walked away, Don Eugenio gestured for Townsend to take a seat. Townsend studied the man more closely. He had on white stockings with shiny patent leather shoes decorated with silver buckles. His nose and ears were slightly flushed. His eyes were weepy, and strangely red. Townsend wondered what his affliction was.

"Many of my domestic slaves speak English," Don Eugenio said proudly. "I brought them over from Jamaica and the Bahamas many years ago after England freed their slaves in the 30s. It was easy then. The English had given them their liberty, but most of the wretches didn't know what that meant. We just took them or bought them from some of the white slave traders, and landed them right near here at one of the coastal plantations. They were freemen, but I like to think we saved them from a life as beggars and vagabonds. Javier Alfonso has been here in Cuba almost twenty-five years. We got him when he was still a relatively young man. We think he came from a Baptist mission. He may have received his education there."

At that point, the old slave had come back with a polished mahogany cigar box. He opened it, and Don Eugenio picked out one and gestured to Townsend to do the same.

"Javier Alfonso here has long forgotten his former life in Jamaica, haven't you?"

"*Sí l'amo.* Yes, Master."

"And you are well-fed and well cared for, aren't you?"

"Yes, Master."

"There, you see. He's far better off here in Cuba than in Jamaica. And the fact is English-speaking domestic slaves are in great demand here on the island, particularly among the English and Americans who have bought plantations. Speaking for myself, owning English slaves, *es un toque de distinción*, as we say in Spanish. It gives me a touch of class, just like my library. My collection of finely bound English books is well known here in Matanzas. But so is my collection of slaves."

He laughed heartily, and took another sip of the claret.

"I have a saying about my house slaves—speak English, obey Spanish. Some of the foreign planters near here come to me when they need a well-mannered slave who speaks English. We Spaniards admire the English for their refined aristocratic traditions, their wit, and their art. Constable and Turner are some of my favorites. It's the British government with its abolitionist sentiments that we have our difficulties with. There can be no high civilization in Cuba without slavery."

Townsend nodded, trying to keep his face blank to avoid revealing his true feelings. Don Eugenio moved his hand to his swollen face with an apologetic look. "I am sure Don Pedro told you I am not well."

Townsend nodded sympathetically, not sure what to say. He could see to one side of the silk turban on the man's head that there was a lesion that looked like a blister.

"I am afflicted with what they call *Lazarino.* Leprosy. The early stages."

Townsend flinched, his eyes widening. His face must have revealed what he was thinking because Don Eugenio immediately told him not to worry.

"*No se preocupe, joven.* My doctor, who is Scottish and who worked in India as a young man with the English missionaries there, is familiar with the affliction. He says what I have may not even be contagious. He is treating me with a medicinal oil extracted from the seeds of a tree found only in India."

Townsend stammered his sympathies.

"No one knows where this curse comes from. Some say it is hereditary, but some think it might be an African disease brought here by the slaves.

Fortunately, my doctor tells me there is hope for recovery. And as you can see, despite some of my discomforts, I still manage to stay in the mix of commerce."

Don Pedro chimed in.

"Speaking of commerce, Don Eugenio, we have much to discuss with Don Julián about the steamship that will be arriving off the coast shortly."

"Of course," Don Eugenio replied.

"Should be dropping off its cargo later tonight not far from here," Don Julián replied as he puffed on his cigar. "That's what Don Pancho has informed me."

"When and where will the ship be ready to be inspected?" Don Pedro asked. "Is it in good condition? As you know, that is important information."

"I think those details are best to be discussed in private."

"Naturally," Don Pedro said as he glanced over at Townsend. "I'm sure the Captain won't mind stepping outside into the courtyard to get some fresh air."

Townsend was ushered out into a darkened room with heavy-beamed open rafters, the furniture rich and heavy, dark wood. He made a move to eavesdrop at the door, but then he heard footsteps on the marble floors, and he quickly left to go out to the open courtyard. Outside, his eyes took a few moments to adjust to the darkness. The air was pungent with the sweet scent of night-blooming jasmine. Some of the Cuban fireflies called *cocuyos* were dodging and weaving around the trees and bushes. Unlike the captive ones he'd seen in the lantern at his grandmother's, these *cocuyos* were free. Townsend strangely felt at one with them as he followed the swirl of flying lights cutting through the darkness in the courtyard.

An hour later Townsend found himself back in the saddle, galloping into the night along with Don Pedro and several other unknown horsemen through a grove of coconut trees. The soft thud of the horses' hooves told him the path they were on had suddenly turned into sand. He could smell the rotten odor of mangrove mud, and he could hear the faint roar of breakers coming ashore. There were voices in the distance. They dismounted by a beach cottage under the canopy of a giant banyan tree where a large bonfire was blazing and crackling away. There must have been two hundred people there, many of them dressed in formal clothes and top hats as if they had just come from a dinner party. He looked out toward the sea and he could see the silhouette of a three-masted steamship. It had steam up, and was clearly ready to make a quick departure. A small flotilla of rowing boats was coming ashore.

Don Pedro pulled him along. "Come, let me introduce you to one of Cuba's most distinguished men of commerce. Don Pancho is a highly respected figure in Havana's social circles. I pointed him out to you at the Paseo. Remember he was walking with Don Julián."

Before he knew it, Townsend was shaking hands with a tall older man in his seventies who was introduced as Don Francisco Marty y Torréns.

"Don Pancho, this is the grandson of Doña Cecilia Carbonell de Vargas." Don Pedro said in Spanish. "He is now one of my ship captains. He is completely trustworthy."

"*Encantado*," Marty replied in a friendly, easygoing but formal way. "It's a pleasure to meet you. *Es un placer conocerle.*"

Townsend took a quick measure of the man with his receding hairline and large nose. He noticed the medal he was wearing just below the left jacket collar. Unlike most Spaniards, he was clean-shaven. Like the others, he was finely dressed with white pants, an ivory white silk shirt, and a formal dark coat.

"What can you tell us about this latest shipment?" Don Pedro asked in a respectful tone of voice.

"It should go smoothly, Don Pedro," the older Spaniard replied with a faint smile and an authoritarian air. "With the normal gratuities to the local officials, I have paid fifty dollars per slave to the governor and lieutenant governor here in Matanzas, a princely sum, but they have promised to avert their eyes. So we should have no problems."

"And the steamship is in good condition?" asked Don Pedro.

"Yes, it made the passage with no serious problems. I understand from Don Julián and Don Eugenio that you have an interest in it?"

Don Pedro nodded.

"*Me alegro.* I'm glad to hear that. You can see, the *bozales* are coming in now. A boatload of Congos from Cabinda Bay. One thousand dollars a head. We have a cargo of only nine hundred Africans unfortunately. They had to throw three hundred dead bodies overboard due to sickness and disease. Certainly a loss, but then again that number isn't bad for thirty days at sea. Please excuse me."

Townsend watched him walk away to speak to a group of men by the fire. He couldn't believe how casually the man had spoken about the loss of three hundred people. Clearly the slaves were just another cargo to be handled, the same as sugar, tobacco, and molasses.

"Don Pancho is one of the older generation," Don Pedro said. "He and other Spanish merchants like Manuel Pastor, Pedro Martínez, and Antonio Parejo are legendary slave traders. They have been in the coal trade, running Africans to Cuba for decades. But Don Pancho, he's a master. He even provides *bozales* for the plantation holdings owned by Spain's Queen Mother. He's been decorated by the Crown many times."

Townsend heard the creaking of the oars as the rowing boats edged closer, and the soft wail of human beings. He stood in the shadows and watched in horror as the gaunt black figures of men in chains were hauled out of the boats and hurled onto shore. With their handlers cursing and striking them, the slaves were dragged toward the bonfire where the men could see them more clearly—emaciated corpses barely able to walk, their arms and legs shackled together.

At that moment, Townsend knew he would take Savage up on his offer, and become a spy for the Federal government. He knew why. Like a sailor lost at sea, he needed a lighthouse to guide him. He thought of the *cocuyos* he had seen at Don Eugenio's courtyard. It would have been pitch dark if not for those creatures. He needed to follow his own convictions. They were all anyone had at a time like this. To his astonishment, Townsend suddenly breathed easier. He had made a choice, he knew, that would change his life, not necessarily for the better. But at least he might feel more comfortable in his own skin.

In the flickering light of the fire, the planters inspected the new arrivals. The Africans were now standing in groups of eight to ten. They were being fed some kind of corn mush out of a bucket as if they were pigs or goats.

Don Pedro approached Townsend. "Go ahead, young man—choose five for your grandmother."

"What! . . . No. I can't possibly."

"Come Townsend," he ordered. "Hurry. Which ones do you want?"

Townsend was glad that the darkness hid his shock and dismay. Don Pedro pulled him closer to the bonfire where the slaves were lined up.

"Hurry, before any soldiers or police arrive. The best are being picked now. Choose!"

Townsend crossed his arms and Don Pedro shook his head angrily. The Spaniard chose five slaves and left to work out the details with those in charge in the beach cottage. Shaking and distraught, Townsend turned toward shore. He looked over at a group of planters on the other side of the bonfire who were deep in conversation, studying their faces lit up by the flames. He stared at them angrily, accusingly. Suddenly he gasped, startled by a familiar face. The man had glanced in his direction, and then abruptly looked away. He had grown a beard, and his hair was now dyed solid black, but Townsend thought it could be him. He rushed through the crowd to get to the other side of the bonfire, but there was no trace of him. The man he had seen was wearing a black top hat with a red feather, and he thought, just thought, that he looked faintly like Michael Abbott.

24

The squeal of the brakes and the sudden blast of the train's steam whistle woke Townsend up with a start. He shook himself awake and looked out of the car at a passing lush green landscape of banana and coconut trees filtered by clouds of red dust. The breeze coming in through the open window was the only relief from the oppressive heat of midday. He tried to recall what it was he'd been dreaming. It was intense, he knew that. His mind seemed to be blocked, distracted by the clacking of the train wheels and the rocking motion of the car.

Don Pedro had told Townsend to return to the city without him so as to oversee the work being done on the boat. The Spaniard would be staying on in the Matanzas area for several more days to finalize the transaction. He had seemed to be in fine spirits, and was already talking about the next trip to Texas and Matamoros. Despite Townsend's refusal to pick slaves, he could tell he was winning Don Pedro's trust.

He straightened himself up on the uncomfortable caned seat. As he looked around at the other fifty passengers in the car, all smoking cigars, the horror of the dream suddenly came back to him, in haunting fragments amid the clouds of tobacco smoke. Townsend shook his head to try to forget those disturbing images. In the dream, slaves were crawling ashore, clutching the sand. A ghostly figure stepped into the flames. It was Abbott. He was beckoning Townsend to join him and walk into the fire. That's all he could remember. That's when the train's steam whistle had woken him. He shivered.

One of the conductors yelled out, "*¡San Miguel! ¡San Miguel!*" as the slow train came to a grinding stop. Outside a jumble of naked Negro children ran about, amid shirtless Chinese and Negro laborers waiting to load and unload. He had one stop to go before they arrived at the end of the line at Regla. He knew what he needed to do over the next few days. He would check on the progress on the boat at the Casa Blanca shipyard, and try to find out where his crewmembers were. But first and foremost, he was going to see the consul general. At their earlier meeting four days ago, he and Savage had agreed they would meet that same afternoon.

From the docks at Regla, Townsend hired a bungo boat to row him across the bay to the fish market landing. He thought if anyone was watching him from shore or in another boat he could lose them in the crowded fish market. Once they'd arrived, he paid the harbor boatman, and gave him an extra dime for his wide-brimmed straw hat. He pulled the sweaty, worn hat over his head to help him blend in. On the landing, he walked by some of the fishing sloops that had just returned from the banks of Florida or the Tortugas with their catches still alive in sea water wells in their boats. One of the larger boats caught his eye. It was a square sailing barge about fifty feet long and twenty feet wide. Townsend recognized the type of vessel. A two-masted, scow schooner, the slowest boat under sails ever built. He'd seen these barges on the Chesapeake hauling freight up and down the Susquehanna River. With their flat bottoms, straight sides, and square ends, they were ugly but they could go where other schooners could not. He remembered how his father had hidden fugitive slaves in those boats.

Townsend was surprised to see a scow schooner in Cuba and he spoke with the fisherman, a thin-faced Cuban with a scruffy beard who was busy hauling squid and barracuda out of the boat's hold. When he asked where he got it, the man shrugged. He said he had heard it came from the Sabine River in Texas where it was used to carry cordwood. He had no idea how it got to Cuba. He said someone just abandoned it.

"*¿Quiere comprarlo?* Do you want to buy it," the fisherman asked in Spanish. "*Se lo vendo barato.* I will sell it to you cheap."

"What's cheap?"

"Four to five hundred dollars," the man replied with a hopeful expression. "Good ship to run the blockade."

Townsend shook his head. The fisherman persisted and gave Townsend his name, Raúl Ortiz. "In case you hear of a *Confederado* wanting to run the blockade, I keep the boat in Casa Blanca near the wharf of Lucas Padrón. Just ask for Ortiz. Everyone knows me. By the way, you speak Spanish well. *Como un Cubano*, like a Cuban."

Townsend looked back to see if the boat had a name on its stern. He smiled when he read it. It was called *Vírgen Gorda*, or Fat Virgin. He walked up the steps into the noisy, crowded open-air market that overlooked the harbor. Inside the building, there was a labyrinth of stalls. The tangy, briny smells made Townsend's nose twitch as he watched scruffy-faced vendors chop off fish heads with one quick blow and then wipe their scaly hands on their trousers. There must have been one hundred types of different fish with every color in the rainbow, spiny lobster, turtles, *dorados*, and octopus laid out on square stone tables like mounds of jewelry. He looked at the long sleek bodies of barracuda, their jaws lined with rows of razor teeth lying alongside dozens of yellow and red tail snapper, their dead eyes a lifeless gray. Predator and prey, side by side. At that moment his thoughts turned to the landing of the slaves, the bonfire and Michael Abbott. Had he really seen the man, or was it just his imagination? The visions in his dream had started to blend with reality. He was uncertain what he had seen on that beach.

As if on cue, in the midst of all this noisy confusion, he spotted a familiar face. It was the owner of the fish market, Pancho Marty, who was almost hidden by shadows in a dark corner of the market. Townsend was surprised to see him so soon. He must have come back on an earlier train. He was talking with someone who Townsend couldn't see, and together they looked like they were examining some of the recent deliveries being brought in from the fishing boats. Townsend ducked behind one of the pillars and watched the two men from there.

He was about to slip away when he caught a head-on view of the man next to Marty. The sight of him stopped him dead in his tracks. It was Salazar, and given the concerned look on the two men's faces and their anxious hand gestures, they appeared to be having an intense conversation. They clearly knew each other. Townsend pulled his straw hat down farther, giving them a wide berth. He had no idea what those two were talking about, but he supposed it had something to do with investments in Don Pedro's ships. As he looked down at a tabletop covered with squids still writhing, he was reminded of Don Pedro and his cohorts, slim, elusive creatures adept at spewing out clouds of ink to avoid scrutiny. Slave traders, merchants, and planters all seemed to be close companions in Spanish Cuba.

When he walked into the main office of the US Consulate, Savage got up from his chair to greet him. Before Townsend could even shake his hand, his mouth dropped in astonishment at the person standing beside the vice-consul general. She was the last person he had expected to see. She was wearing a green sleeveless dress, a color he thought suited her.

"Hello, Miss Carpenter," he said awkwardly.

"Good afternoon, Captain Townsend," she replied politely with a faint nod of her head. The sunlight from the window shone through her long brown hair.

"I didn't know you would be—"

Savage cut him short as he stretched out his hand.

"Thank you for keeping your appointment with me, Captain. Have a seat, please. I was worried you might be delayed. The train system in Cuba, despite the help of American and English engineers, leaves much to be desired. Sit down. Please sit down."

Townsend did as he was told, his eyes still on Emma.

"I can see you are surprised to see Miss Carpenter here, Captain," Savage said. "Let me explain. It's about that Englishman, Michael Abbott. I know I said I was not going to do this, but I had a change of mind. It is a serious matter. I took the liberty of mentioning the man's name to the captain general, when I saw him the other day. I was curious to see his reaction. I explained to His Excellency the man had been missing for quite some time."

Emma asked expectantly, "What did he say?"

"Well, I must say I was quite surprised. The mere mention of the name Abbott made the captain general quite nervous. He began squirming in his seat. I could see he was taken by surprise."

"So he knows something?" Emma nodded with a frown.

"He said they have no record of a man fitting that description."

"No mention of his imprisonment and his escape?" Townsend asked incredulously.

"He assured me he knew nothing of such a man with that name or anyone fitting that description, and then he asked where I had gotten my information. Of course I made no mention of you, Captain Townsend, or anything that might make him suspect you or Miss Carpenter or Mrs. Carpenter. I merely said that one of my foreign friends here in Havana had known Abbott and even heard about his imprisonment in El Morro and he was concerned."

"How did he react?" Townsend asked.

"He seemed eager to be rid of me. When I continued to press him on the matter he sent one of his aides to check the records. The aide came back to reassure me that no such man had ever come to Cuba."

"So they are covering it up," Emma said.

"So it would seem. Michael Abbott is someone the Cubans refer to as one of the "disappeared ones." All records of the man appear to have been eliminated."

An awkward silence settled in the room. Emma looked away. Townsend wondered if he should mention the slave landing and the glimpse he'd had of a man resembling Abbott. But something told him to hold off. It was too extraordinary. What would Abbott be doing there, anyway? Abbott was supposed to be gone. Disappeared, as Savage had said.

"My advice to you both is that you close the book on this Abbott matter," Savage stated emphatically. "That was my first instinct, but I allowed my curiosity to get the better of me. It may have been a mistake I will regret. Now the *Guardia Civil* and their agents no doubt are spying on me more closely. When you leave I will show you to a back door that leads through a doctor's office, and out onto an alleyway."

Savage got up and started walking around the room, his pale, thin hands held behind his back.

"However, there is more business to discuss before our meeting ends. I think you know what I am talking about, Captain, don't you?"

Townsend nodded.

"Have you given proper thought to what we spoke about last week?"

"I have. I will do it." He avoided looking at Emma, but he could feel her warm gaze turn toward him.

Savage smiled. "Excellent. I am pleased to hear that. Now that I know what side you are on, Captain Townsend, I can give you the good news we just received. The USS *Huntsville* has captured the Spanish steamer, *Union*, of and from Havana, with a cargo of considerable value. But even more important, the flagship of the Havana blockade runners has also been destroyed."

"Which one?" Townsend asked. "Not the *Cuba*?"

"Yes, the notorious *Cuba*. On May 19th, her own sailors set fire to her to avoid her being taken as a prize. The USS *De Soto* chased her for eighteen hours. Finally caught up with her off the Alabama coast. Reportedly more than a million dollars of cargo went up in smoke before the ship sank to the bottom. Major losses for the merchants, and a major victory for the Union's blockade effort!"

"That is . . . wonderful news," Townsend said, trying to hide his ambivalence about other blockade runners' fates.

"But let me get back to the matter at hand. After much consideration and some initial reservations, I have decided to allow Miss Carpenter to help in our intelligence gathering efforts. She is a stubborn young lady, and does not like to take no for an answer. Like her mother, she seems to have something of the Beecher Stowe woman about her. I have asked her to observe the guests at her mother's boarding house and listen for news about visiting Confederate agents in the city. The two of you will both be working as my eyes and ears."

Townsend glanced at Emma, who had an enigmatic expression on her face. There were so many things he wanted to ask her.

Savage continued his lecture.

"When either of you need to contact me, there is a lottery salesman who is always at the Alameda de Paula. Name of Gutiérrez. I have worked with the man for years. He is easy to spot. He's a dwarf, and is always well dressed. No one should take notice if you approach him. Please choose a code word. Give me a name, any name, but something in Spanish."

"How about, *cocuyo*," Townsend said quickly. It was all he could think of.

"Excellent. I will tell Gutiérrez. If you mention the code name *cocuyo*, he will know you are sending me a message. Just buy a lottery ticket from him with your written note, and even if you are being followed no one will suspect anything. Everybody buys lottery tickets in this city."

Savage called the secretary to bring in coffee and some *guava dulces*. He wanted to hear about Townsend's tour of Cuba's sugar plantations. Townsend paused before speaking and then began his unusual story of how he had come to meet his grandmother. Both Emma and the consul general sat spellbound as they heard the puzzling details of Townsend's family story, and how this connection had been hidden from him by Don Pedro all these months.

"How extraordinary," Savage muttered as he thoughtfully stroked his clean-shaven chin. "How strange that Don Pedro would get so involved in your family affairs. I don't think of him as a person who does anything outside his own self-interest and personal gain."

Townsend remained silent. Savage fixed him with an intense stare.

"Perhaps you feel differently now, Captain," the vice-consul general said. "After all, you are related to a Cuban plantation owner who is openly sympathetic with the Southern cause. Like so many of the Matanzas planters, Doña Cecilia de Vargas is known to be a strong supporter of slavery. As her grandson, it might be difficult to continue to be an informant for me."

"She may be my grandmother, but let's just say I find that I feel more like my mother did about the family business and what's at stake in this war."

"Won't you feel like you are betraying your grandmother?" Emma asked.

"No, I feel like I'm honoring my mother," he replied.

"And Don Pedro?"

"Nothing has changed. I feel no loyalty to him. I have never trusted him, and now even less so."

"What other surprises do you have for me Captain?" Savage asked with a probing stare.

Townsend mentioned the visit to the plantation near the coast and how Don Pedro had met with the owner, Don Eugenio Hernández, and his business associate, Don Julián Zulueta. He also told him about witnessing the slave landing and Pancho Marty.

"You have certainly had a busy week, Captain. In Zulueta and Marty, you have met two of the island's most influential men of business, and Don Eugenio is one of the wealthiest planters in Cuba, a venerable *caballero*."

Savage sat back in his chair with a studied scholarly look on his face.

"Be careful, Captain. Zulueta and Marty are two of Cuba's most notorious slave traders with a reputation for taking the law into their own hands. They see themselves as the island's political bosses. They may look polished but they haven't forgotten how to slit a throat. Just last year, their names came up in connection with the murder of two men who bought Negroes from the slavers, but then refused to pay the full price."

Savage paused to sip his coffee.

"Are slave traders here in Cuba then immune from prosecution?" Townsend asked.

"About ten years ago, Zulueta was put in jail, but only for about two months. Then he was released and he resumed his illegal shipments with even more audacity. His arrest was mostly done for show. The captain general in Cuba at the time, Don Valentín Cañedo, was considered a partisan and friend of the slave traders. But he was pressured by the British to arrest Zulueta. A Royal Navy brig had captured one of Zulueta's slave ships, the *Lady Suffolk*, while attempting to make a landing of three hundred Negroes on the southwestern end of the island in Batabano."

"Was that during the time Backhouse was here in Cuba?" Townsend asked pointedly as he looked over at Emma.

"I suppose it was, now that you mention it. The capture of the *Lady Suffolk* must have been the summer of 1853. The Backhouses had arrived a few months earlier. I don't imagine Don Julián Zulueta had any warm feelings for Judge Backhouse. I am sure he viewed his arrest as a terrible affront. He's a proud man, Zulueta. Rich and proud. And like many of the extremely wealthy Spaniards here, he sees nothing wrong with slave trading."

Townsend remained silent as he and Emma exchanged glances. He knew they were both thinking the same thing. This is the kind of information Michael Abbott had been after.

"Tell me, did you hear anything about what business matters Don Pedro was concerned with, besides buying slaves for your grandmother? What did he talk to Zulueta and Don Eugenio about?"

"He seemed curious about the slave ship. Wanted to know the condition it was in and where it was going next. That's all I heard. They asked me to leave the room after that."

"Perhaps Don Pedro is planning on getting into the slave business?"

Townsend grimaced.

"I hope you're wrong. But you may not be. On my way over here I came through the fish market. I spied Marty speaking with one of Don Pedro's associates, a man by the name of Arturo Salazar. They seemed to be talking business."

"Were you spotted?"

"I don't think so."

Savage nodded slightly. "That's good. On a separate matter, Townsend, now that I know about your connection with Doña Cecilia de Vargas, I would like you to get to know one of her friends, if the opportunity arises. She's a Spaniard and a French countess who knows a great deal about Don Pedro as well. She is a French agent here sent by the Emperor Napoleon III. Word is that she was once his mistress."

Townsend could feel the air thicken with tension in the room.

"Her name is La Comtesse Angélica Fernández de Buisson, but she likes to be called Condesa."

Emma flinched at the mention of the name, her body suddenly becoming rigid. Townsend looked over at her, but she didn't look back. She seemed to be staring at the wall.

Townsend blushed. "What do you want me to do?" he asked.

"Just get to know her," Savage replied. "We are concerned that the French might side with the Confederacy."

"I have met her once already," Townsend admitted with his eyes down-turned.

"I see," said Savage with an enquiring look and a raised eyebrow.

Before Townsend could say anything else, Emma stood up determinedly, her chin lifted slightly, her brown eyes darkened.

"Mr. Savage, I would say that Captain Townsend knows *that woman* quite well already. I, for one, want nothing to do with her. She's sin's own aunt. She may be a countess, but she's no lady. *Es una cualquiera.*"

Emma's glare took them both in. Townsend could see that the diplomat was uncomfortable hearing the Condesa being described as a woman of ill repute.

"If her brand of spying is what you have in mind," Emma continued with a steely look, "then I think we should reconsider our arrangement."

Savage fidgeted as he looked from Emma to Townsend and back again. The American diplomat seemed flummoxed in how to navigate the moment.

"I completely understand, Miss Carpenter. I certainly did not mean to suggest anything—"

"I think I will be leaving now," Emma announced. "My mother is expecting me. Thank you for the coffee and thank you for inquiring about Mr. Abbott. I will see myself out through the back door you mentioned. One of your clerks can show me where to go."

She walked out without looking back at Townsend or Savage. The office door closed without even making a sound, and they could hear her loud, angry footsteps on the marble floor. The two men sat there for several moments gazing at the door.

Savage breathed out a long sigh. "Have a cigar?" he finally said in an effort to dispel the awkwardness. "Perhaps a Londres Superfino from Havana's Upmann house. It is expressly made for the English market. A small size with a mild, pleasant flavor."

The two men quietly lit their cigars.

"I have something for you, Captain. A letter stating that you are working for the consul general in Havana as a Federal agent, serving at the wishes of Secretary of State Seward. Keep it well hidden. I thought it might come in useful if at some point you are apprehended at sea by a Navy gunboat."

Townsend nodded his thanks.

"It asks the Captain to show you and the sailors on your boat every courtesy."

Savage leaned back in his chair as he puffed on the cigar.

"Oh, and Captain Townsend. I am sorry."

"Sorry for what?" Townsend asked, cocking his head to one side.

"I believe I may have inadvertently caused you some problems. I will certainly try to smooth things out with Miss Carpenter. As you know, I have known her since she was a young girl. Emma can be stubborn and strongminded, and she is passionate about her beliefs. Understand that while she is an American, she does seem to have inherited a bit of the fiery Latin temperament from her father. Take it from me. I am married to a Spanish woman. Sometimes I feel like I've been placed in a bull ring without the red cape or the sword."

Townsend laughed.

"If it is any consolation, I understand you are not the only gentleman to be at the receiving end of Miss Carpenter's flash of hot temper. My wife told me that a very eligible young Navy ship captain was courting her. Her mother was quite keen about this suitor. Apparently he comes from a well-to-do family. He invited Emma and Mrs. Carpenter onto his ship for luncheon entertainment complete with a Navy band."

"Oh?"

"Apparently, the young man was . . . a bit too forward. He attempted to kiss her when her mother was preoccupied. My wife said Emma slapped him! Quite hard apparently." Savage laughed. "That was the end of the shipboard entertainment."

Townsend grinned. Savage had no idea how happy this news made him.

"Mrs. Carpenter, of course is devastated. She told my wife when she heard the commotion on the ship's deck she rushed over to see what was wrong. Just from looking at her daughter's black fixed stare, she knew there was trouble, and she tried to smooth things over. But Emma demanded to be taken ashore immediately. Unfortunately for the hapless lieutenant, it is unlikely he will have a chance to apologize, at least not in person. The commander of the East Gulf Squadron in Key West, Admiral Theodorus Bailey, has reassigned his ship, the USS *Leopard*, to patrol the east coast of northern Florida around Jupiter Island and Fernandina. Naturally the ship will still be based in Key West, but those new orders won't bring his ship to Havana any time soon."

"Heigh-ho," Townsend said with a faint smile as he puffed on the cigar. "Sounds like treacherous waters."

"Treacherous waters indeed. Don't I know! My wife says Eleanor Carpenter is bound and determined to patch up this kerfuffle. She's got Cupid's bow and arrow on the ready. Bah! I'll say one thing, Townsend. Feminine reasoning is a mystery to me. And mothers and daughters, why, they're like doves and pigeons. Two close companions, but oftentimes flying in opposite directions."

Part Three

When all has been said that can be said in favour of the slave owner in Cuba, it comes to this—that he treats his slaves as beasts of burden. . . . The point which most shocks . . . is . . . the ignoring of the black man's soul. But this, perhaps, may be taken as an excuse. . . . the white men here ignore their own souls also.

—Anthony Trollope
The West Indies and the Spanish Main

25

June 15, 1863

Three weeks later the *Gaviota* hugged the flat barren coast of Texas under
the cover of night with a full load of cotton from the Brazos River. A fickle
night breeze was filling in from the south, allowing the heavily loaded schooner to move along at a respectable seven knots. Not bad for June doldrums,
Townsend thought as he listened to the drumming of the halyards against
the masts. All that could be seen was the dark sandy shoreline off to starboard. The shallowness off this part of the Texas coast meant that most of
the steamers and the larger tallships in the West Gulf Blockading Squadron
had to remain three to four miles off shore. For the moment they were safe.

Townsend was smoking a cigar at the helm, a practice that had become a
nighttime ritual. Just after they set sail, he had told the crew about finding
his grandmother in Matanzas. They had all joked that he was now a slave
owner—they called him "Master" in light moments, asking him for sugar for
their coffee each morning. Now in the comfort of the darkness, his thoughts
shifted to his new secret role. It was a dilemma for him. Each day as he looked
at their faces, he felt he was deceiving them. Savage had said to tell no one
about their arrangement, but he knew that was impractical. He would need
an ally, at least one person he could confide in. Of all the men, he thought
Hendricks would be the most sympathetic.

On one of their night watches, he had opened up to the man.

"Look, Hendricks, you know I'm not sympathetic to the Southern cause.
Running the blockade isn't a choice I'd ever have made. Even though I know

what I am doing is wrong, I've had an opportunity handed to me to do what I think is right—Are you following me?"

The Bahamian stared at him. "I ain' know what you talkin' 'bout."

Finally Townsend blurted out, "I'm now a paid informant for the Union. I was hired by the US Consulate in Havana."

The Bahamian had said nothing. Townsend wasn't certain if he had made a mistake. Hendricks's smooth black forehead suddenly furrowed. Even the man's one eye that was always sparkling seemed to darken.

"You tellin' me you a spy?"

At the mention of the word *spy*, Townsend's palms started to sweat. He'd quickly looked around to see if anyone else had heard.

"It's a good cause, Hendricks—it's right over wrong."

"Da ain' make no sense. You gon' get yourself killed for sure."

"Well . . . I need your help," Townsend stammered.

"What! You tryin' to make me a spy too? Stop ya stupidness. You mus' be jokin'."

Townsend hadn't expected this setback. He offered to share the pay he would receive from the Federal government. It wouldn't be that risky, he'd said. It was mostly about keeping their ears and eyes open, and report what cargo they were carrying. Keep an eye on what our two Spanish supercargoes do, and report on Don Pedro's activities. To his surprise Hendricks seemed to change his mind when he heard that explanation. Hendricks told him he had grown to have a special dislike for the two Spaniards, and never had any interest in helping the Southern cause.

"Maybe t'ain such a bad thing," he said. "Specially as you gon' pay me."

That conversation was two weeks before. Townsend looked over at Hendricks who was leaning up against the cabin house. As usual, the two of them didn't speak much, preferring to sit quietly and feel the motion of the ship.

Townsend puffed on his Upmann cigar, listening to the wind and the water as he savored the bitter taste of the tobacco. Spying was not a profession he would have chosen, but it chose him. Blockade running was now merely a role he was playing, a disguise. Like a masquerade dance, he was spinning on the dance floor with dangerous unknown partners. He thought of what the Condesa had told him on that memorable ride back to his rooming house. In Havana, the delicate game of spying was frequently played to the rhythm of a *danza criolla*. In his case, it was being played to the rock and roll of the ship and the whistle of the wind. His father had always told him there was a solution to every problem, and maybe not what he expected.

"You might have to look underneath some rocks, son. The answers are not always where you think they are."

Hendricks stood up and said he was going to check the rigging up in the bow. Townsend nodded. They'd been lucky so far. Originally, they were going to run the blockade into Galveston, but in Havana they'd been warned by Helm that Union cruisers off the eastern section of Texas were now as "thick as bees" with no less than eight Union steamers blocking the channel into Galveston. The Confederate agent had encouraged Don Pedro to make use of the shallow rivers in Texas, which frequently were left alone by the Navy patrols. They had chosen the Brazos River because they'd heard there were mountains of cotton bales on the docks from the vast plantations there.

On the passage across the Gulf, they had been spared close encounters by staying to the west, but it had not been an easy trip up the remote Brazos River. It had taken them five days to make their way thirty miles up the meandering river, sailing with the flood tide and then anchoring during the ebb, occasionally working up the river with the oars.

After dropping off several boxes of Enfield rifles, rounds of fixed artillery ammunition and Kerr single action revolvers, they'd picked up two hundred bales of cotton in the town of Columbia. Along with the cargo had come two unexpected passengers. His thoughts turned to the two men sleeping below in the cabin house. He wondered who they were.

Just after they had finished loading the cotton, Salazar had brought them on board with their pistols and their carpet bags. The Spaniard had given no names or explanation. The younger one looked to be around thirty-five years old. He had a thin pale face with side whiskers and black hair. He wore a ready-made suit with a waistcoat where he carried a large knife, with the hilt quite visible. The other older man was called the Colonel and seemed nervous and edgy. He had a moustache and a narrow wisp of a goatee hanging limply from his chin like a dangling piece of Spanish moss. He had the appearance of a hard-edged Southern chevalier with a diamond ring on his little finger and stark, brooding eyes. They were bunking with Salazar and Nolo in their cabin. Townsend knew immediately that these two men needed watching. They had the look of Confederate agents on some kind of secret mission. This was the kind of information Savage would want.

Townsend could hear the muted lapping of water chuckling alongside the hull, and he looked up at the tilting mastheads silhouetted against the dark sky. He found the blackness comforting, and enjoyed feeling the ship—the waves, the motion, the breeze—all in darkness. They would have another eight hours of night sailing to get out to sea before heading on a more southerly course to the mouth of the Rio Grande and the Mexican city of Matamoros, less than three hundred miles away. Salazar had announced they would sell some of their cotton there as a safety precaution. But Townsend wondered if the real reason they were going to Matamoros had something to do with the two mystery passengers.

At dawn the next day, the wind fortunately shifted to the east-southeast and they sheeted in the sails on a direct course to the Rio Grande, the choppy waves striking the hull with glancing blows. With a strengthening breeze, the schooner edged away from the bare and scrubby barrier islands off the Texas coast. A few seabirds cried out as they glided over the swaying mastheads. Olsen had brought Look-Out the cat up on deck to keep the seagulls from snatching up the flying fish that had landed on deck overnight. At the sight of the cat, the seagulls squawked and hollered. Look-Out leapt out of Olsen's arms onto the deck, but she didn't get far. The Dane had fashioned a halter made out of twine and leather around the cat's body, and he gave a tug on the rope leash to remind her she wasn't free. Dutch Olsen told Townsend the cat reminded him of his former wife.

"That woman also had a notion to wander," he said.

"Did she like flying fish, same as the cat?" Townsend asked with a wry smile.

"Well, you might say that," Olsen said. "But no, I believe my wife was more squirrel than cat. She liked her nuts, you see, always liked to gather new ones." They both had laughed.

Townsend shifted his attention to the cabin house and the passengers down below. He curled up his nose at the acrid coal smoke wafting up the stovepipe, but then the pungent aroma of freshly brewed coffee drifted up onto the quarterdeck. Through an open porthole, he could hear the two passengers talking with Salazar and Nolo.

Later that morning Townsend sent Hendricks into the main cabin house to eavesdrop. Hendricks stood outside the Spaniards' door and caught snippets of conversation. He gathered the two Southerners were on a clandestine mission authorized by General John Magruder of Houston. The Confederate general had just visited Matamoros a month earlier, where he had been given the high honor of receiving a formal military salute by Mexican authorities. Magruder wanted these two men to help organize a campaign of sabotage in Matamoros to seize Northern merchant ships, and "destroy the enemy's property at land or at sea." Suddenly the door opened, barely giving Hendricks time to back away.

"*¡Fuera de aquí, negro!* Out of here, Negro," the Spaniard shouted. "*¡Te mato!* I'll kill you!"

When Hendricks told Townsend about the exchange—including the fact that Nolo had pulled out his knife and brandished it at him—Townsend called off the eavesdropping plan. It was Hendricks who came up with the alternative. He reminded Townsend how they had hidden Abbott. The sail locker on the starboard side was just outside the Spaniards' cabin. If he could get in there, he would be able to hear everything that was said. Both sail lockers, port and starboard, could be accessed from the raised quarterdeck through a hatch opening flush on the deck. The only problem was how to cloak the sound of Hendricks clambering over the sails. They needed to create some kind of a distraction.

They waited until nightfall to carry out their plan. The moon had come up, casting a faint glow on the tilting mastheads, the light clinging to the sails like morning dew to a spider's cobweb. The wind had picked up sharply, warning that a squall might be brewing somewhere near. Townsend turned the wheel slightly and brought the heavy schooner dead into the wind. The sails began flapping and snapping like gunshots, and the blocks squealed and banged against the deck in a quick succession of loud reports. The noise allowed Hendricks the few minutes he needed to scramble through the hatchway into the dark sail locker without anyone hearing his movements.

For the next two hours, Townsend could smell the cigar smoke wafting up from below and he could hear the steady murmur of conversation. It was sometime after midnight when all went quiet and Townsend decided it was time to get Hendricks out. As they'd arranged, he again luffed up the schooner into the wind. This was the signal for Hendricks to get back on deck. With the sails making a noisy racket, the Bahamian was just emerging on the quarterdeck when simultaneously Salazar and the older of the two Confederates surfaced up the companionway ladder from the cabin house.

"*¡Qué pasa aquí?* What's going on with all this noise?" Salazar asked menacingly. "And what is that Negro doing?"

"He was just checking on some sails we may need," Townsend lied. "Winds picking up. A storm may be threatening. Might have to change one of the jibs."

Salazar approached Hendricks, grabbed him by the arm, and pushed his body up against the side of the cabin house.

"What did you hear, *negrito?*" Salazar jeered as he thrust his nose close to Hendricks's face, pushing the man's head up against the cabin house. "I know you were listening."

Something snapped inside Townsend's head. He jerked Salazar's hand away from Hendricks and pushed the Spaniard away.

"Lay off, Salazar," Townsend said angrily.

Salazar stepped up, his pale blue eyes visibly glistening in the moonlight.

"This Negro is a spy," he hissed. "He has been snooping outside the cabin door and now like a rat we find him inside the sail locker."

Townsend stood his ground, barely able to control his anger. For months he had been keeping himself in check, but he'd reached a breaking point. Salazar had crossed a line Townsend could no longer ignore.

"Never touch one of my men again, Salazar. And be careful what accusations you make. You may be the supercargo and the shipping representative, but I am the captain of this ship. These men are my responsibility, as is this ship. The next time you have a problem with one of my sailors, you bring that problem to me. ¿Me escuchas? Do you hear me?"

"Perhaps you are a spy as well, Capitán Townsend," Salazar retorted snidely.

Townsend stood his ground as Salazar brought his face closer to his.

"Tengo mis sospechas. I have my suspicions about you, Captain. There has always been something about you I didn't like. Perhaps there is more than one rat on board ship. Maybe this is a ship filled with Yanqui rats?"

The Spaniard glanced over at the shadowy figures of the men who were clustered together in the bow of the ship. The noise had woken up all the sailors in the forward house. Nolo emerged from down below. He was carrying what looked like his carved handspike in one hand, the other hand resting on the handle of his sheathed knife. Higgins and Bertrand stepped up onto the quarterdeck alongside Red Beard, who had one hand on his suspenders. All three held belaying pins in their hands. The air simmered with hostility.

"I smell trouble, Cap'n," growled Red Beard as he pulled and snapped the suspenders.

"Ready to assist, Cap'n," volunteered Higgins.

It was a standoff that seemed ready to spiral out of control. Nobody moved for a few tense moments until the man called the Colonel put a hand on Salazar's shoulder.

"Settle down, boys. It's late. Let's be done with this business, y'all hear me?"

Eventually each man went back to their cabins and their berths until only the Colonel and Townsend stood in the moonlight.

"My friend, that's a right keen-lookin' nigger you got. Might be you spoil him too much, and he needs some lookin' after. If I ketch him prowlin' around our cabin again, I won't give him a whippin'. I'll jest shoot him. You should know I have no great affection for niggers, but I have an even greater disregard for Confederate traitors and Yankee spies. I've got my suspicions that you've got both on this ship."

Townsend clenched his fists. He wanted to hit this man square in the face and let him know that he wasn't about to take orders from some unidentified passenger on his ship. But instead he bit his lip, and thought about Savage.

"I certainly understand your concerns," Townsend replied. "I regret to say I didn't get your full name."

"That's because I didn't give it," the man shot back.

"I will need it when we arrive in Matamoros to present our papers to the Mexican authorities."

"I believe Sr. Salazar will take care of those matters," he replied, cutting off a chew of tobacco from a black plug and popping it into his mouth.

When all was quiet, Townsend slipped a becket on the wheel to assure the ship stayed on course, and then motioned for Hendricks to walk up to the bow where they could speak without any danger of being overheard. Hendricks spilled out what he could remember.

"They wa' talkin' 'bout a ship," he said. "Some steamship they gon' pick up in Matamoros just off the Rio Grande."

Townsend thought about what this meant. A mystery ship falling into the hands of the Confederates in a deal clearly brokered by Don Pedro. Hendricks explained from what he could hear, it sounded like the ship would be reflagged as a Mexican ship with a fake Mexican owner. It would be ready to leave the Gulf to go to sea within two to three weeks. It would come to Havana to recoal, and then sail for Andros Island to exchange cotton for some English cannons. They also mentioned something called *La Compañia*. Townsend mulled that over in his mind. The Company. He had never heard of *La Compañia*.

❖

The next morning they arrived to a staggering sight off the mouth of the Rio Grande. For Townsend, it was unreal. There were at least two hundred ships, a vast fleet of steamers, schooners and tall ships from all nations, all waiting to pick up Confederate cotton that had been hauled across the parched deserts of Texas in ox-drawn cotton wagons. They were anchored three to four miles from land in what looked like the open sea. With the winds picking up, ships rolled and tumbled in the choppy waves, pulling at their anchor chains like runaway rocking horses, their foreign flags snapping and fluttering from the mastheads. He had heard that Lincoln and the Department of State did not want to antagonize foreign powers by attacking shipping off the Rio Grande, but he wondered what the secretary of the Navy, Gideon Welles would say if he could see this. As closely as Townsend scanned the flat sandy shoreline, he could find no trace of a port, only a huge shoal with breakers between the fleet and the shore.

"That thar' is the smugglers' cove of Baghdad, Mexico, Cap'n," Red Beard cried out as he pointed out the masts of some small schooners, indicating where the Rio Grande emptied into the Gulf. "They call that swill hole the back door of the Confederacy. Home to swindlers, scoundrels, drunken sailors, and every kind of no-account mongrel known to steal and pilfer. Matamoros and Brownsville are just upriver, but Baghdad is where the trading and loading is done."

Townsend had heard about this place at the mouth of the Rio Grande from sailors in Havana. As filthy a hellhole as you could find anywhere, he'd been told.

"As you can plainly see, Cap'n, thar's no way we can git through them breakers. The water over the sandbar is only four and a half feet deep. We'll have to stay out here at anchor like the rest of these ships and unload the cotton onto lighters."

Townsend noticed that Salazar was standing amidships with Nolo and the two passengers and they were all looking in the opposite direction from the shore, scanning the fleet of anchored ships with field glasses. They were pointing and gesturing toward a screw-propeller steamship anchored farther out to sea. Townsend picked up his own glasses to take a look. It was a blue water sail-steamer with three masts, a tallship about two hundred feet long with one funnel in the center of the ship. She was flying the Spanish flag. Townsend could see a lone figure on the decks looking back at them through his glasses. Salazar walked back to the quarterdeck and with a resentful glare told him to thread his way through the fleet and anchor near that ship. Townsend asked why. Salazar replied curtly, "Business," but didn't explain further.

They luffed up the schooner and dropped anchor near the mystery steamship. Sailors on board the steamer had already begun lowering one of their launch boats. It was clear the steamship had been expecting them. Townsend had Bertrand and Olsen throw down the ship's rope ladder in preparation. Townsend could see eight sailors in the launch rowing toward them and what looked like the captain standing in the stern. When they pulled in their oars and brought the launch up against the *Gaviota*'s sides, Townsend was struck by how little was said. The captain mumbled something to Salazar in

Spanish. Then he nodded graciously to the two Southerners, who clambered down the rope ladder. All of this had obviously been arranged beforehand. Before leaving the ship, Salazar said he and Nolo would be back in the morning. They were traveling to Matamoros to address some business matters for Don Pedro. He would send the Mexican customs authorities out to the *Gaviota* and would contact the local shipping representative to see to the unloading of the cotton.

Townsend watched as the launch boat disappeared into the swarm of anchored ships, the oarsmen struggling to keep a coordinated cadence due to the choppy waves. Moments later, another launch boat was lowered from the steamship with as many as ten sailors clambering in—shore leave. Townsend decided to release his own men—he and Hendricks would stay behind. Once they'd gone, Townsend turned to Hendricks and announced he was going to row over to the steamship as soon as it was dark to see if he could see the ship's name and homeport. Hendricks tried to dissuade him, but when that effort proved fruitless, the Bahamian sailor reluctantly agreed to go with him.

Together in the darkness they rowed the yawl boat around the big steamship, slowly and quietly, looking up at the high wooden wall of the ship's sides. There were only a couple of lights aboard the ship in the foredeck area. The main cabin that loomed above them was dark. To reduce any noise, they'd wrapped the blades of the oars with some rags from the galley. They dipped and pulled in the darkness, making no sound as they approached the stern. There on the ship's transom he could see that the name had been rubbed out. It was a ship with no name. He could barely make out its homeport, Cadiz, Spain.

They continued rowing quietly, staying close to the sides of the ship so they would be out of sight. Someone on board cursed loudly in Spanish, and they both reflexively pulled down their wide-brimmed hats. They rowed around the side until they came to a rope ladder that had been left down.

"Wait in the boat while I take a look around," Townsend whispered to Hendricks. "Be ready with the oars when I come back."

Townsend was barefoot and unarmed except for his sheath knife and a belaying pin. As he climbed the steps, he could now hear the strumming of a guitar and some of the Spanish sailors singing up forward. When he pulled himself over the bulwarks, he scanned the empty decks. Then seeing no one, he crouched down, walking soundlessly with his bare feet. Lights were burning in the forecastle in the front of the boat so he went back to the main cabin area. The door was locked. He walked to the other side and passed by some open grates leading to the center cargo hold. He stopped to look inside and was greeted by a vile, putrid smell of human waste. He covered his nose with one hand and tried to peer inside. In the moonlight, he could just barely make out the faint gleam of metal. There were hundreds of iron chains and manacles attached to the floorboards. The memory of those poor emaciated souls crawling ashore on the beach with their legs and arms in chains rushed back and he felt his stomach roil.

Townsend barely had time to think about what he was looking at when he heard a shout. "¡Alto!¡ Alto!" Someone had spotted him. "¡O paras o disparo!" Someone was yelling in Spanish for him to stop or they would shoot. Townsend ran to the side of the ship and clambered down the rope ladder, jumping into the boat.

"Row, Hendricks row!" he cried out.

A gunshot tore through the air. He heard yelling and shouting behind them. He could hear the shouts of *ladrones*. They thought they were thieves. Townsend saw a few shadowy figures up against the ship's looming stern looking down at them. He saw one man raise a rifle, and Townsend warned Hendricks to fall backwards on the seat. They heard the crack of the rifle and a splash of water next to them.

"Keep rowing," he shouted as he grabbed one of the oars.

Soon they pulled around to the other side of the *Gaviota* where they couldn't be seen by the men on the steamship. That's when he noticed the rising water inside the yawl boat. They were sinking. One of the shots had hit the floorboards. They pulled alongside the *Gaviota*. Townsend reached for the rope ladder and told Hendricks to start climbing.

"What 'bout the yawl boat?" Hendricks asked.

"Let it sink. We'll say it was stolen."

When they got back on board, Townsend had to catch his breath. "It's a damn slave ship."

Hendricks's eyes grew wider in alarm.

"Wha' kind of trouble you got me in now?"

26

Two weeks later they were back in Havana, and with all the cargo un-loaded, Townsend was on his way to a clandestine meeting with Savage. It was nearly 7:30, and the hot morning sun blazed across Havana's rooftops. *Volantas* filled with finely dressed ladies in colorful silk clattered by, push-ing him onto the two-foot-wide sidewalk. The metallic clanging of church bells echoed through the city's narrow streets. Townsend hugged the walls as groups of black-robed priests holding their prayer books walked by in perfect formation like squadrons of pelicans gliding silently over the surface of the ocean. It was Sunday morning and everyone was on their way to mass.

Townsend hadn't been able to escape the scrutiny of Salazar and Nolo eas-ily. A few days earlier Nolo had followed him all the way to where the lottery vendor was selling tickets. Townsend had heard the salesman's falsetto cry before he saw him. "¡Lotería! ¡Lotería!" Townsend had walked nonchalantly up to the dwarf, who was standing on a box, and asked him in Spanish if he was Gutiérrez.

"Who wants to know?" the short man answered suspiciously.

"A friend of mine named *cocuyo*," Townsend replied.

Gutiérrez extended his hand with a lottery ticket as Townsend handed him a few gold coins. Tucked underneath them was a tightly folded note to Savage. Townsend had kept it simple. "Confederate agents acquiring steam-ship in Matamoros through Don Pedro. Ship en route to Havana soon." All of this had happened under the watchful eye of Nolo, who did not appear to suspect anything. Everyone in Havana bought lottery tickets. Townsend went back the following day and pretended to buy another lottery number for Savage's brief reply. The note said that the vice-consul general would meet him at the old cathedral on Sunday. High mass was always at 8:00 a.m. Townsend had memorized the exact instructions, and then burned them as he lit a cigar. When Nolo approached him to ask why he had bought another ticket, Townsend had shrugged. As he puffed away on his cigar, he smiled at the Spaniard. "The vendor said I would be lucky if I bought a ticket today."

Despite his calm demeanor, the young captain anticipated problems from the two Spaniards. He sensed from Nolo's threatening stares that there was trouble brewing. Clearly they didn't believe his story about the stolen yawl boat. He knew they would be reporting their suspicions to Don Pedro, but he told himself not to worry. After walking in and out of several churches to elude anyone who might have followed him, Townsend emerged in Havana's old cathedral square with its well-worn cobblestones and picturesque arcades. The huge bronze bells in the larger of the two towers were ringing in earnest, calling people to confession. In the opposite tower there was a nearly one-hundred-year-old English-made clock that despite its age was still working. He squinted his eyes to check what the time was. Quarter to eight.

Townsend walked up the stone steps through the massive wooden doors of the old cathedral, pausing for a moment to take in the soaring marble columns and the blinding sunlight pouring through the windows near the top of the huge vaulted ceiling. He stepped to one side and found a shadowy spot near the door where he could look around to see if anyone might be watching him. He noted with interest a few of the early arrivals. Elegantly dressed ladies in flowing, fluted trains of silk and velvet, with their faces veiled, their hair partially concealed by scarves of Spanish lace. They walked in with their black servants dressed in calico with yellow and red turbans following closely behind.

He stood there in the shadows near the big entrance doors, enjoying the symphony of organ music and bells. He watched as the house slaves spread out rugs on the marble floor and brought caned seats for their mistresses to sit on. It always amazed him that there were no pews in Havana's many churches, only a few benches. He heard the sound of soldiers marching outside and he became more alert. His new life was one full of risks. He even put Hendricks in danger. He pushed those concerns aside as he quietly repeated Savage's instructions to himself. His note had said for him to walk up to the chancel and look at the white marble tablet in the wall that marked the resting place of Columbus, gaze at the altar and the frescoes as if he were a casual visitor, and then walk back to the second large column and turn left. He would find him there up against the wall in the shadows.

Townsend slowly walked by the array of flickering candles toward the richly carved mahogany altar. The priests were waving censors of sweet-smelling incense, which sent clouds of aromatic smoke upwards like wispy plumes of sea fog. He focused on one of the priest's glittery fingers sparkling with emeralds and rubies. As his eyes wandered to the old decaying frescoes above the altar and around the church, an image stayed with him—a painting of the Mother Mary holding the infant Child, rising above the flames of purgatory, even as the sinners below reached upwards, imploring her for forgiveness.

Townsend stopped in front of the white marble tablet in the wall as he had been instructed, and reached out to touch Columbus's tomb as any casual visitor might do. Outside he could hear more clearly the sound of a military band marching down the street, a rich mix of trombones, bugles, cymbals, and drums. He wondered what the great explorer would have thought about his remains being left behind on this island, Spain's most faithful colony. He turned and walked back toward the front door entrance, stopping to gaze upwards at the large dome. Townsend scanned the doorway, looking for any sign of someone following him. There were several top hats to be seen, but nothing he found suspicious. In the dark corner up against the wall he could see the shadowy form of a man wearing a formal coat and a top hat. He was standing by a small side altar with a carved statue of the Crucifixion.

"Thank God," Townsend breathed out. "You're here. I don't think I was followed."

"Good. Come with me."

Townsend followed Savage. The large columns and pillars hid them from view of the growing numbers of faithful. Savage walked through a wide opening at the side of the cathedral that led to an oddly shaped courtyard, then through a creaky door. They wound their way up a spiral staircase entirely made of stone masonry mixed with coral rock. Townsend could hear the bells clanging louder than ever, the stairway acting like an echo chamber. They must be in the bell tower. After several turns on the winding stairs, they arrived at a landing and Savage took him to another door. Inside there was a bed, a table, and a couple of chairs. He closed the door so that the ringing wasn't quite as loud.

"We are safely out of sight here."

Savage then took him through another door that led to the chorister's room and the organ loft, and pulled over two chairs.

"These are the bell ringer's quarters," he said. "You may wonder why I brought you here. Crowds are helpful distractions when you are trying to avoid being followed, and gatherings of the faithful are useful sanctuaries."

Townsend turned his attention to a wooden table with a pile of delicate brown wrapper leaves and bundles of loose tobacco. Savage saw the direction of his glance.

"As you can see, the bell ringer is a cigar roller, *un torcedor* as the Cubans say. An exceptional one, I might add. His name is Manuel Escobar. He makes extra money by rolling cigars, and I have long been one of his regular customers."

Savage picked up a bundle of cigars that had been left there. They were wrapped in soft, oiled silk and had a distinct odor. Townsend thought the aroma was familiar.

"I come here once a month to collect a dozen of his hand-rolled cigars. That's how I know this place. I have brought other informants here, and I have sworn Manuel to silence. I pay him quite handsomely so I think he's quite trustworthy."

Townsend described the two passengers they'd picked up and what Hendricks had overheard. At first, the acting consul general was not happy to hear about Hendricks even though the young captain assured him the Bahamian sailor was thoroughly trustworthy. Savage grumbled, but as he heard more details of the tense relations on board ship, he reluctantly agreed with Townsend that an accomplice was needed. The diplomat now listened carefully as Townsend described how they had rowed alongside the Spanish-flagged steamship. And then how he had sneaked on board and found the chains and manacles in the cargo hold.

"A slave ship!" gasped Savage, spitting out the hateful words. "Could this be the ship you saw unloading slaves at the beach in Matanzas? Pancho Marty's ship?"

"Hard to say," Townsend replied. "It was too dark to see much, but he heard them mention something called *La Compañía*."

Savage's eyes grew large. He moved his hands restlessly through his hair.

"¡*La Compañía*! Of course! I should have known. It's Zulueta, Julián Zulueta. He must be behind this."

Savage, clearly agitated, stood up and began pacing the room, his pale, thin hands clasped behind his back.

"*La Compañía*, Captain Townsend, is short for the African Expedition Company. It's a Spanish slave-trading syndicate. The firm owns a large fleet of ships, some say as many as twenty, but no one really knows. Some of these are steamships built at good shipyards in England and then fitted out for the slave trade in Spain. Julián Zulueta holds 50 percent of the shares. And I don't doubt that Marty and Don Eugenio Hernández could also be involved."

"So you think Don Pedro is helping sell one of their slave ships to the Confederacy?" Townsend asked.

"That would be my guess. We know Confederate agents are desperate for ships. About six months ago they almost took possession of a Spanish ship called the *Noc Doqui*, a suspected slaver rumored to be linked to *La Compañía*, but fortunately, and quite by chance, Admiral Wilkes of the Navy's West India Squadron captured it along with the Confederates on board. That may have been the first attempt by the Confederacy to buy a ship from Spanish slavers. I fear that Don Pedro has persuaded the African Expedition Company and the Confederacy to try again—letting him act as the merchant in charge of the sale and transfer."

"Certainly Don Pedro could do that," Townsend said.

"What makes this speculation a distinct possibility is that I received intelligence not too long ago from one of the old established American merchants in town. Charles Tyng. I'm sure you've seen the sign for his company right next to Cabarga's chandlery. He's a reformed and now retired shipper of slave cargoes. He hears the scuttlebutt. He tells me that *La Compañía* is buying new ships. At least four—fast steamships built in England, all intended for the slave trade that can carry as many as two thousand Africans on board each ship. Perhaps the firm is selling some of the older ships. Tell me more about this vessel."

Townsend described it—two-masted screw-propeller steamship, six hundred tons, about two hundred feet long with one funnel, wooden hull. He couldn't tell what kind of engine it had.

"That certainly would make a good gunship. You say they are planning to sail it to Havana?"

"That's what Hendricks thought he heard them say."

"No doubt to recoal. They'd be safe here, particularly if they're masquerading as a merchant trading ship, flying a Mexican flag. Havana is a safe haven for these rebels." He paused thoughtfully, then began to pace again.

"Unfortunately we can expect that within days of the ship leaving Havana Bay, the Confederates will have the vessel fitted with English-made Blakely deck cannons in the Bahamas, and then be ready to raise the Confederate flag. Go to thunder—we'll have another CSS *Alabama* on our hands. We have work to do, Captain. I will need advance notice about the ship's arrival so I can alert Admiral Bailey in Key West. I will also need to know the ship's new name as soon as you find out."

Savage stopped his pacing and looked at Townsend, who had furrowed his brow.

"I am sorry. I have not asked how all your sleuthing has gone. I hope nobody suspects anything?"

Townsend stayed quiet for a moment. The bells weren't ringing anymore. All he could hear was the organ. He pursed his lips and acknowledged that the two supercargoes on board might be a problem. "They've accused Hendricks and me of being spies. They have no proof, but still . . ."

"Sounds like trouble. What about Don Pedro? What does he think?" Savage asked.

"I don't know. He is apparently in Matanzas now, but is expected back shortly."

"You will have to reassure him how valuable and how loyal you are," Savage said. "Perhaps spread a rumor about his two representatives. Maybe they were swindling him—taking money under the table from those two Confederates?"

Savage paused and Townsend let that thought sink in.

"Part of being a successful agent, Townsend, is knowing how to tell a convincing lie. You must be willing to put your scruples aside, particularly when dealing with the unscrupulous."

"What about the crew? I should tell them what I'm doing."

"I urge you not to do that. Only reveal your secrets when you have no choice, or when you can get something more valuable in return. You will learn, my friend."

Savage smiled at him and patted him on the back.

"I should add that I spoke with Miss Emma Carpenter when you were away. I think everything has been smoothed over. Do describe those two agents to her, no doubt members of the Confederate Secret Service. Sooner or later they may be coming here, and they might show up at her mother's boarding house. Lodging is not easy to find now in Havana. I understand Mrs. Bremer's Hotel Cubano is overflowing with Confederates, some of whom are here to discuss future arms deliveries with Helm and Mr. Crawford."

At that point, they were interrupted by a swarthy man with black curly hair and a beard who walked through the door.

"Ay, perdóname Señor," said the Cuban who appeared surprised to see them.

"Ah Manuel, que bueno que estás aquí," Savage said as he rose to greet him. Without introducing Townsend, he thanked the Cuban for the cigars, saying they were just leaving. Townsend noticed that Manuel, who graciously took the money Savage handed him with a deferential nod, was now staring at him with a long, piercing look—as if scrutinizing his face.

"I will show you a different way out of here," Savage said. "We will go up on the cathedral roof, crossing over to the other tower. If anyone has been following us, they will be expecting us to come out the front door."

As they walked across the rooftop of the cathedral, Townsend noticed grass and vines growing in the chinks of the old stone and coral rock masonry. He wondered how that was possible. Then he saw the pigeons on the belfry roof—they must be the carriers of the seeds. The old church had secret hideaways even for the birds.

When Townsend arrived back at the docks, Salazar, Nolo, and Don Pedro were clustered together in deep conversation. It was clearly not casual banter as Salazar and Nolo were gesturing wildly with their hands. As Townsend approached, all of them stopped talking and stared in his direction. For a moment he thought they knew about his secret meeting with Savage, but then Don Pedro smiled.

"Where have you been, Captain? I've been looking for you all morning. Salazar has just been telling me about how flawlessly this trip went."

Townsend could tell from the grim faces of Salazar and Nolo that this was far from what they had been talking about. Salazar's pale blue eyes flashed contempt, and Nolo's scowl left little to the imagination.

Don Pedro put his arm around his shoulders, and Townsend tensed at the first whiff of the man's sweet musky scent. It seemed to envelop him like a ripe fisherman's net.

"It's time for our *almuerzo*, and I thought I would take you to a small French place just outside the old walls called *Les Tuilleries* at the corner of Consulado and San Rafael. It has excellent *camarónes al ajillo*, shrimp with garlic. And then I'll show you my new warehouse in Chinatown where I'm storing some British-supplied arms and ammunition waiting to be shipped. I want to familiarize you with more of our operations. I have told Salazar you have tremendous potential."

Don Pedro hailed his driver and soon they were headed out of the old city, leaving through the Muralla Gates. As the *volanta* rumbled by the sentries, Don Pedro mentioned the news he had read in the *Diario de la Marina* that officials in Madrid had ordered the leveling of Havana's old walls. Work was to commence immediately. The old city and the new city would soon become one.

"It will be a new era," Don Pedro said proudly. "You will soon see Havana being referred to as the Paris of the New World."

Don Pedro offered him a cigar and then casually asked how the trip went. Townsend quickly replied that all had gone well except for an incident in Matamoros when their yawl boat had been stolen by some thieves. Don Pedro lifted his bushy eyebrows in feigned surprise, but Townsend could tell he had caught him off guard and so he continued. He lowered his voice, "There is something else I think you should know."

"And what might that be," responded the Spaniard with a suspicious tone in his voice.

Townsend told him how one night when they were underway he had sent Hendricks below in the sail locker because they needed to change headsails. While he was below he had overheard something there, something important. Don Pedro gave him a lingering stare. Townsend could tell he had the Spaniard's full attention.

"Those two passengers we took on board up the Brazos River were having a discussion with Salazar and Nolo. Hendricks couldn't help but hear one of them in the cabin offering to pay Salazar and Nolo a sizable bonus if they could arrange discreetly for extra weapons to be loaded on the ship at no charge when it came into Havana."

Don Pedro's face froze. Townsend could tell he hadn't been expecting this.

"I'm just passing it on. Thought you should know."

"That *negrito* sailor of yours seems to be skilled at listening to other people's conversations," Don Pedro said, his voice hostile. "What else did he hear?"

"Just that Salazar wanted to be paid in gold. One of them said he would arrange for that to happen."

"That's a far different story from the one I just heard," Don Pedro said. "Salazar told me the *negrito* was spying. He thinks he's an informant for the American government."

"Bah! I think Salazar hates Negroes just like he hates foreigners," Townsend replied. He checked himself so he didn't lose his temper. "Maybe you should take a closer look at Salazar. He may be telling you this cock and bull story about spies as part of his con game. All I know is, Hendricks went down in the sail locker to get a sail at my request, and he came right back up as soon as he got it ready. Couldn't have been more than five to ten minutes. He told me what he'd heard."

Don Pedro studied his face.

"It's not just the Negro, you know," he said in a drawn out, deliberate way. "Salazar doesn't trust you either, or for that matter the rest of your crew. He said he had a rather unpleasant confrontation with you."

There was a touch of menace in Don Pedro's voice. Townsend's breathing quickened as he focused on Don Pedro's crow-like eyes.

"I hate to say this, Captain, but even I have started to have some of my own suspicions," the Spaniard continued.

Townsend felt a bead of sweat crawl down his spine. His lower lip began to twitch slightly. He straightened his back, and thought of his strict midshipman training. He needed to control himself. He would show no fear.

"Given what Salazar and Nolo may be doing behind your back, Don Pedro, I am not surprised they would lie. Salazar is a man who will stop at nothing. He has resentments, and clearly bears a grudge against me. This spy business is just pure twaddle."

Don Pedro looked deep into his eyes, and then after a prolonged pause restored his constant smile.

"You're right, Captain. I am sorry for doubting you. I can't say the same about that overly inquisitive Negro of yours or your crew, but I was wrong to question you. Salazar and Nolo are close, longstanding associates of mine whom I have long relied on, so I am surprised at what you tell me. But then Jesus Christ was surprised by Judas's betrayal, wasn't he? The key word for me is trust, Captain, as you know. That's what I value the most. Remember, *siempre fiel*, always faithful."

Don Pedro smiled, but his face was tense. He took Townsend's hand and squeezed it, bringing his nose close to Townsend's face.

"I need to know, Captain," he whispered. "Can I trust you?"

"How can you ask that?" Townsend replied with a straight, deadpan face. "I have made four successful trips through the blockade for you, Don Pedro. Isn't that proof enough?" He discovered to his surprise that he was beginning to enjoy lying to Don Pedro. "I think I have earned your confidence."

"Of course. Of course," Don Pedro replied. "Yes, you have done your job well. Now tell me what you do know about that ship you saw in Matamoros. It's important you not mention anything about it to anyone."

"Truth be told, Don Pedro, nothing. Salazar kept me and everyone else in the dark. He didn't even say who his passengers were. But from the looks of those two Southerners, it was not hard to discern they were keen as beavers to get aboard that steamship."

"You know nothing about that ship?"

"Nothing," Townsend lied. "Please enlighten me?"

"I'm afraid there is little I can tell you, Townsend. Suffice to say, we are helping those two Southern gentlemen acquire that ship. The discussions are still underway."

"I see," said Townsend. "Will I be seeing those two men again?"

"You might," replied Don Pedro. "They should be coming here to Havana shortly to finalize matters. If all goes well, we may do more business with them."

Townsend tried to keep his lips from twitching, but Don Pedro didn't seem to notice. Suddenly the Spaniard called on the driver to pull off to the side.

"There is something else I need to talk to you about, Townsend. *Un asunto grave y delicado.* A serious and delicate matter."

Now it was Townsend's turn to be taken by surprise, and he faced Don Pedro with a quizzical look.

"When I was in Matanzas I heard rumors about a suspicious Englishman nosing around some of the plantations, asking a lot of questions. What was unusual is that he carried no written introduction as is customary."

Townsend felt a shiver of disquiet run through him.

"This Englishman says he's an investor and wants to buy land here in Cuba, but some people think he is a little too curious. He may not be who he says he is," Don Pedro added as his eyes once again probed Townsend's face. "He may be an imposter. It is a matter of some concern."

"What has that got to do with me?" Townsend asked.

"I wondered about that Englishman you helped all those months ago. The fugitive you helped escape. What was his name?"

"Michael Abbott." Townsend felt his stomach tighten.

"Yes, Abbott, that's it. What else can you tell me about him? How badly was he injured?"

"He's dead, as far as I know," Townsend said defensively. "Stabbed. I was hit on the head. I never saw what happened to him. From the blood on the ground I assumed he must have died. I thought you told me I was supposed to forget that man."

"Yes, you're right. I did. But this Englishman is making people nervous. He's asking questions. Too many questions about some sensitive issues from the past."

"Who is he?"

"The man's name is Rupert Bascombe, or that's the name he is traveling under. He says he is from Bristol. Dresses formally, has a beard. I wondered if he might be an accomplice of Mr. Abbott's."

Townsend felt the air being sucked out of him, but managed to breathe out a question.

"What makes you think this man has anything to do with Abbott?"

"He has a whiff of abolitionism about him. My friends fear he might be an activist, an abolitionist investigator sent here by London's Anti-Slavery Society pretending to be a planter. Some even wonder if he is the same man you saved, the prison escapee. If somehow Michael Abbott did not die, and this imposter turns out to be him, the authorities will have to be notified immediately. Abbott is a wanted man, and considered a grave threat to the island's security."

A wave of foreboding swept over Townsend. Could Abbott really be alive? If he was, he was in serious danger yet again.

"The man I helped never said anything about abolitionism. He never said why he was put in jail. It must be somebody else. I saw Michael Abbott knifed. I am sure he is dead."

27

July 16, 1863

Townsend looked at his reflection in the small mirror in his cabin. He rubbed his smooth chin, and put down the straight razor next to his comb, brush, and scissors. He rubbed some coconut oil pomade into his hair, *estilo cubano*, and began trying to smooth out his unruly hair. Once he'd combed his hair to his satisfaction, Townsend pulled out his new trousers from the closet, and his only pair of nice boots. He looked at the short note from Emma again. It was written in the neat tight lettering he recognized from her illustrations. All it said was, "Important news. Meet me at the corner of Compostela Street and Los Cuarteles outside the small old church of Santo Angel at noon. There will be a covered Victoria cab there waiting for you. You will know it because the Negro postilion will not be wearing his top hat." Townsend was familiar with the old church, which had been severely damaged by a hurricane years earlier. It had one of the most prominent belfries in the city, and was visible from the sea at the entrance to the harbor.

There was something comforting in this simple, businesslike note, something stolid and dependable in its straightforward prose. Just the thought of seeing Emma again made his breath catch. It had been brought to him by one of the small barefoot Negro boys who hung out at the docks. He knew the boy. Rafi was his name and like so many of the abandoned, homeless street urchins in Havana, he was always looking for odd jobs. He supposed Emma had sent someone at the boarding house down to the docks with instructions to find a messenger boy so as to avoid suspicion. Savage would be pleased how quickly she was learning to be an effective informant.

As Townsend scanned the docks looking for signs of Salazar or Nolo, he wondered what Emma's news would be. Something to do with Southern agents, he supposed. Havana was now crawling with Confederates. He'd been told by Bertrand, who spent most of his time in the fandango bars, that some Rebel naval officers had just arrived in Havana from Mexico. They were on a clandestine mission to take charge of new warships on the continent. Word was they would soon board a British passenger steamer bound for England. Townsend asked Bertrand to try to get the names of these men so he could pass that intelligence on to Savage. Maybe these men could be apprehended en route. Maybe Emma knew who they were, and that's why she wanted to meet him.

Apprehensive and tense, Townsend walked up to the hatless postilion sitting on the lead horse outside the church. The black man beckoned him to go inside the carriage. He opened the door and was startled to see an older man, balding with a silvery black beard and dressed simply in a brown robe. He started to back away, but then he spotted Emma's familiar face in the opposite corner of the carriage.

"Hurry. Get in," she said. "Close the door."

Townsend sat down next to her as she banged on the door to signal the postilion to get the carriage underway.

"This is Padre Pablo Uribe," Emma said.

"Oh," Townsend replied as he looked back and forth from one to the other. "I am so pleased to make your acquaintance." He shook the man's hand uncertainly.

The horses quickly broke into a fast gait.

"I'm glad to see Rafi delivered the message as he said he did. My mother and I hand out food to some of these street urchins. Rafi is one of my favorites. He'll do anything for me."

"I was careful not to be followed."

"Good. As a precaution, we are going to put some distance between us and the harbor. I want to show you El Cerro—the neighborhood where the Backhouse family lived. It's just a few miles outside the city. It will also give us a chance to talk with the padre. He has much to tell us about Abbott. Important news," she said with a broad smile.

Emma grabbed his arm, no longer able to restrain her excitement. "It's Abbott! He's alive!" she cried out. "Can you believe that?"

Townsend fell back in the carriage, stunned. So indeed Abbott was alive. He looked from Emma back to the man in the brown robe.

"It was a minor miracle he recovered," Padre Uribe said. "I would like to think our prayers helped him."

Townsend suddenly recognized the man facing him. He remembered the bearded face with the distinctive, slightly hooked Spanish nose. The last time he'd seen him was at the Church of St. Augustine. He was the man staring at Abbott through the barred window, his face lit only by a candle in the darkness.

"I remember when we last saw each other," Townsend added. "Months ago."

The man nodded at him. "*Sí, fué hace mucho tiempo,*" Padre Uribe said, but then quickly changed to English. "Yes, it has been some time now."

Townsend now felt a shiver run down his spine as he remembered that night. The Spaniard explained how he had followed them to the tavern. He had stood in an alleyway, and was about to step out into the street and introduce himself when that street mob appeared.

"Believe me, Captain, there was nothing I could do. I just watched helplessly from the shadows, stunned as those street dancers grabbed you both. As soon as they were gone, I could see there were two bodies. I ran over. I recognized Abbott as the one who had come to the church asking for me, and saw that he was bleeding. Then I heard the sound of hooves clattering on the cobblestone. I dragged Abbott into an alley, and moments later some men were there. They seemed to know what they were looking for. They searched the surrounding streets, looking for any trace of blood, I suppose. Luckily it was quite dark and they didn't see any trail. They came close to where I was hiding with Abbott, but fortunately they never found us behind a shed. I waited. Again I'm sorry I did not pull you to safety as well, but there was not much I could do. I was quite surprised when a group of police threw a bucket of water over you and you woke up. I had thought you might be dead. Then the police took you off in chains to the prison."

"And Abbott—how on earth did he survive?"

"He had a deep wound, but miraculously the knife blade slid into one side of his abdomen and didn't puncture his organs or his intestines," Padre Uribe replied. "He was feverish for the first two weeks. The injuries he'd sustained escaping from El Morro hadn't healed, either. He told me about the sharks. I told him God must be watching over him. I didn't want to take him to a hospital for obvious reasons. I treated him as best I could, frequently dabbing the wounds with iodine solution and giving him laudanum for the pain. It took weeks for him to recover."

"Where is he now?" Townsend asked.

"That's just it," the padre said. "As I told Emma earlier, I don't know exactly where he is. I believe Matanzas. He went there disguised as a planter. Grew a beard. He was wearing a signature black top hat with a red feather. That was to be the code. The way he would find his contact."

"Contact?"

"Yes, the slave who wrote the letter to Grace Backhouse. He wrote that she should have her emissary wear that hat, and that's how he would recognize him. He was an English-speaking slave her husband had been trying to free. This man claimed he knew who killed her husband."

"Rupert Bascombe," Townsend mumbled. His veins felt icy cold.

Both Emma and Padre Uribe looked at him in surprise.

"How did you know that name?" Padre Uribe stammered. "That's it, Abbott's alias."

"You didn't tell me that you—" Emma started.

"Let me explain. I saw a man when I went to Matanzas . . . before I saw you at the Consulate. It looked like Abbott. It was just a glimpse, and then he disappeared. See there now, this is not good news. They have suspicions, Don Pedro and his plantation owner friends, and probably the police. Heigh-ho! This is terrible!"

Townsend put his head in his hands. Once again Michael Abbott was going to cause him no end of trouble. He told Emma and Padre Uribe about his conversation with Don Pedro, and how the Spanish merchant suspected this Englishman named Bascombe was a fraud and somehow connected with Abbott.

"He believes Bascombe could be an English abolitionist—not a comforting identification or safe description to be given in Matanzas."

The air in the carriage seemed to grow suddenly stale, leaving no trace of the earlier enthusiasm. There was no need to say anything. They all knew that Abbott could be in trouble, his fake identity uncovered, and there was little to nothing they could do about it. They drove southward through the working class neighborhood of San Lázaro, passing the public gardens across the far outskirts of the city.

Emma was the one who broke the silence.

"Padre, how did you come to be Michael Abbott's contact in Havana?"

"Abbott had ties with the Anti-Slavery Society in London. Maybe that's how Grace Backhouse found him. I don't know, but before he left London the Society had given him my name as a contact."

"You are with the London Anti-Slavery Society?"

"I am one of their informants here in Cuba. I should tell you that Uribe is an alias. Even Abbott never knew my real name."

"Why would a Catholic man of the cloth like yourself take such risks to help Protestant abolitionists?" Townsend asked.

"In Cuba, there are few alternatives for a man of principle. I was an ordained priest for the Diocese of San Cristobal de la Habana, but the torture that the Spanish government used to crush the slave revolts in the early 1840s changed me forever. I became a member of the Franciscan Third Order and lived for a while in Guanabacoa. Then I came to the Church of St. Augustine here in Havana. At the time I went to the plantations regularly to provide basic religious services for the slaves. I secretly collaborated with London's Anti-Slavery Society to give them information about the *emancipado* workers who were being held illegally, as well as anything I heard about slave deliveries."

"So you knew George Backhouse?"

"Yes. I gave him the names of planters and others who were holding *emancipados* and other Negroes illegally. I trusted him. We would meet discreetly in various places including his house on one occasion. I admired him for trying to enforce the treaty, but I also knew he didn't understand what he was confronting. The system is entrenched here. The so-called *emancipados* are turned over to the state and rented out like property to the planters as field laborers. They might as well be slaves. It is an old story here in Cuba, and I suppose you could say Backhouse paid the price for trying to change it."

"Have you continued to work with the English?"

"Only with the Anti-Slavery Society. Not with the Consulate."

"Why not the Consulate?"

"To be blunt. I don't trust the consul general. Backhouse told me about him. He felt Crawford went behind his back."

"I have heard these accusations before. Do you think Crawford might have—"

"No, I know what you are about to ask. No, I would never say that. I just believe there were rivalries between the two men."

They sat there in silence until Emma finally spoke up.

"Why are you just telling us about Abbott now?"

"Abbott never wanted to involve either of you because of the danger. We agreed he would send me notes, brief notes once a week, but it has been several weeks now that I have not received any word from him. I am worried. That's why I came to see Miss Carpenter."

"Do you know where he is?" Emma asked. "Is there a way to get word to him that his life could be in danger?"

"I'm afraid not. By agreement, he said the less information he sent the better. All I know is he was going to the plantations where there were English slaves. He was making inquiries there."

"I was at a plantation with English slaves," Townsend interjected. "A plantation owned by Don Eugenio Hernández. Not too far from the coast where I witnessed the slaves land—where I saw Abbott."

"Why don't we go?" Emma exclaimed. "We could start making our own inquiries."

"I could tell Don Pedro I want to help," Townsend said, echoing Emma's enthusiasm. "I could tell him I could be useful . . . identifying the man."

The Spanish priest shook his head.

"No, I don't recommend it. Too risky. Don Pedro has his suspicions, but at this point they are just suspicions. We don't know much more than that. Any questions you might ask could lead to unfortunate consequences. If you are too inquisitive, they might suspect you both. Trust me, I know Matanzas. It has its own variety of justice."

As the horses and carriage began climbing a hill, Townsend looked to his left at a sparkling view of Havana Bay in the far distance. Soon they were driving into a neighborhood lined with homes with high, sculpted stone entranceways and massive wooden doors studded with brass knobs. Emma explained that this was El Cerro. She pointed out the expansive private gardens of the opulent villa belonging to Count Fernandina, one of Cuba's wealthy plantation owners, and then, as they turned on Buenos Aires Street, she showed him the Backhouse residence with its large columns shading the front entrance.

"You can see it's a neighborhood common criminals would not idly enter. When I would come and visit, the Backhouses never locked their doors. They felt safe here."

They stopped the carriage and knocked on the door. A maid let them in. The house was currently not rented, and Emma was able to persuade the kindly woman to let them come into the house to look at the view of the city and Havana Bay in the distance.

They walked through the spacious living room where Grace Backhouse had placed her elegant French-Erard piano, and went out to the veranda. Townsend could see the road traffic moving up and down the Calzada de Cerro, and he could scan the bay. The house was all on one floor, with the servants living separately. Emma led them to the small library room where Backhouse and his clerk, Thomas Callaghan, had been attacked. They all stood there in silence as if somehow the walls could speak and tell them what had happened. Townsend tried to imagine the scene, the shouting, the scuffle, the overturned chairs, and then the blood on the floor, the assailants running out the door as one of the servants called for help.

"Who do you think killed him, Padre?" Townsend asked.

The priest reflected on the room. "I have often thought about the Backhouse murder—how the assailants got in and out of here with so little trouble. There were servants working at the time, yet these two men entered without anyone sounding the alarm or intervening. I think they may have walked through the front door. Someone who knew the house must have helped them. The police questioned nine or ten suspects, including two white servants employed here, but that was it. According to Backhouse's dinner companion that night, Thomas Callaghan, two men of color attacked them while they were sipping an after-dinner wine. They had knives. Callaghan was tied up, but not hurt. He couldn't identify them. It was too dark. After knifing Backhouse, they fled immediately. They could have been thieves, but I believe they were hired *matones*. I believe the English word is, thugs."

"Hired by whom?"

"Who knows? Rich planters, slave traders, merchants, police. There are many people who might have wanted Backhouse dead."

Padre Uribe shook his head sadly.

"I tried to persuade Abbott to go back to England. I told him it was useless to continue his investigations. It was too dangerous for him here. He was a prison escapee, a wanted criminal, and would be executed by the government if they found him. I wanted him to leave while he could, but he refused."

"Why?" Townsend asked.

"I think he knew how much suffering Grace Backhouse had been through, and he wanted to try to give her some solace, if not some answers. She believed the murder was carefully planned. And she wanted the British government to recognize her husband's sacrifice, an acknowledgement that her husband had been killed in the service of his country. Abbott felt an obligation to find the man who wrote her the letter. He was determined to find George Backhouse's missing journal. That is, if it existed. He was convinced he could find it."

"I have heard about that journal," Townsend said. "A news reporter who was here then told me it could be important."

"Backhouse was always writing in that journal. When I traveled with him through the countryside, he was always scribbling notes. Given his investigations, it might well have had important sensitive information."

"Sensitive enough to warrant murdering him?"

Padre Uribe didn't answer. He leaned over close to both of them, his voice barely audible. "Abbott told me," he whispered, "that Grace Backhouse is convinced it was slave traders who ordered her husband's death. Apparently she was told that by a merchant who was in Havana at the time of the murder."

The robed padre gave the sign of the cross, and then recited a small prayer.

At his request, Padre Uribe got off the carriage in the southern outskirts of Havana in an area of destitute poverty off the Calzada de Jesús del Monte, not too far from the city's slaughterhouse. He said he went there once every few months to tend to the sick and dying because no doctors or priests dared set foot there. It was too dangerous. It was a human wasteland, a place where Cuba's forgotten, lost souls went to spend their last days. After seeing the elegant mansions of El Cerro, Townsend couldn't believe the portrait of human misery in front of him. Row after row of wood shacks were stacked up one against another. Amid mud and garbage, women and naked children were scavenging for scraps of food next to the pigs and the chickens. Emma and Townsend watched as the man waved farewell and walked into this community of misery with a purposeful stride.

Townsend looked behind them and noticed a closed carriage pulled to one side. The pair of chestnut horses looked familiar. Had he seen that same carriage drive by the Backhouse residence? He hoped they weren't being followed. As they made their way down the busy road toward the old walls of the city, Townsend felt uncomfortable being alone with Emma in the carriage. The sound of the wheels and the clip clop of the horses' hooves only accentuated the awkward silence. He wasn't sure what to say. Each of them looked out their side of the carriage. Townsend rummaged through his mind for something to say that wouldn't be stupid. Emma broke the tension for him.

"Mr. Savage passed on some of your information about the steamship and the two Confederate agents. He said you'd give me a more detailed description."

Townsend was happy to oblige and gave her a full account of them.

"On a lighter note, have you gotten more news about your art work?"

At this, Emma's eyes lit up. "Indeed, the editors at Frank Leslie's Illustrated Newspaper want me to do more sketchings of Havana harbor, in particular the growing number of fast English blockade-running steamships. They may want me to travel to Key West to do drawings of all the captured blockade-running ships there as well as the steadily expanding fleet of Union gunships. My sister lives there with her husband, a local merchant, so I wrote the paper to tell them I might be interested."

"Key West? Only . . ." Townsend stammered. "I mean won't your mother be upset?"

"About what?"

"About your leaving?"

"Not really. It's just for a short time. As I said, my sister lives there and my mother wants to know how she's getting on. She's just opened a boarding house there."

"I see. But won't it be boring there? It's not much of a town compared to Havana. . . . There are some fine homes, but from what I hear it's mostly wooden shacks, a few churches, muddy streets with drunks, soldiers, and sailors wandering about."

She looked at him, confused.

"Is there some reason you don't want me to go there, Captain?" she asked, her sharp-eyed gaze now clouded.

Townsend felt flustered, and began rubbing the back of his neck as he looked away. He felt like an idiot.

"Is there something you wanted to tell me?"

"I suppose . . . ," he stammered, "well, I just wondered . . . if there was another reason you wanted to go there. Maybe your mother wanted you to go there for some other reason."

At that point, Emma's face blushed as it dawned on her what Townsend was trying to say. Her wide-eyed expression revealed a tentative delight.

"I see, Captain Townsend. Now I understand, or at least I think I do. Were you meaning to ask if I wanted to go to Key West to see a particular ship?"

He nodded awkwardly. What a stupid fool he was.

Emma's face lit up with a glow.

"A ship that has visited Havana before? Perhaps a US Navy ship?"

"Yes, *that* ship," he said emphatically. "I was wondering about *that* ship."

"To answer your question. I have no need to see *that* ship or its captain ever again no matter what my mother has to say. I have made that quite clear to her."

Townsend began to smile.

"If I might inquire then, what types of ships interest you?" Townsend asked, as he dared to hope he was reading her signals correctly. "I mean from the point of view of an artist, steam or sail."

"I have a strong preference for sail," she replied with a deadpan face, but then raised her eyebrows. "However, I'm quite particular. For instance, I like one of the ships here in Havana, but given the harbor's polluted water, I think it needs some cleaning, scraping, and painting."

"Oh," he replied with a mischievous hint of a smile. "That's a harrowing job but with proper oversight it can be done."

"Good to hear. There is one other thing I like in a boat."

"What is that?"

"Dependability."

"I see," said Townsend, his mouth wide open in surprise.

"Have you ever heard of the Dutch word *howker*, Captain?"

He shook his head, wondering what she was getting at.

"That's what the Dutch call two-masted fishing boats, but that word has another meaning. It is also used to refer to sailors who have two or more girlfriends. It seems *howkers*, whether they are boats or men, are viewed by some of the Dutch as risky and *unreliable*."

She paused and looked at him, her lips pursed. She brushed her hair off her face. Townsend squirmed under her piercing stare, his face reddening at this not-too-subtle verbal slap—but he was still greatly enjoying this word play with Emma.

"I see what you mean," he replied with a mock serious tone of voice. "Those Dutch certainly understand their boats."

"Apparently they do."

At that point they both laughed, their eyes both twinkling. All Townsend could think of was how much he wanted to kiss her, even if it was just on the cheek or the forehead. He found his arm stretching out toward her across the seat, his fingers lightly touching hers. His heart pounded as he felt her respond to his touch. Slowly their fingers began to weave together until they were intertwined. Townsend hardly dared to breathe. They stayed that way, not moving or speaking, while the carriage rumbled through the Tierra gateway and entered the old city. As they neared the Cristina marketplace in the Plaza Vieja with the throngs of noisy vendors, Townsend finally spoke.

"You can let me out here. I'll walk the rest of the way to the docks. It's better not to risk being seen together."

She banged the carriage twice to signal the postilion to stop. As the closed carriage slowed down near the corner of Teniente Street and San Ignacio, Townsend reached out for her and took her in his arms. He could feel her smooth skin through the thin cambric linen. The tickle of her wavy brown hair and the subtle smell of her lavender scent were intoxicating. He felt like he was floating in a cloud. They kissed each other cautiously, their lips only slightly touching. His breathing quickened and his heart sang. He drew back and looked at her.

"I've wanted to do that for the longest time."

"What took you so long," she replied.

"I almost did months ago on the terrace roof together at sunset."

"It was a moment I'll never forget," she whispered with a happy sigh as she wrapped her arms around his neck.

28

For the next few days Townsend could think of nothing but Emma. He walked around the decks of the *Gaviota* in the hot sun lost in a daze, staring at nothing. The summer heat was far more oppressive than it had been at sea. They were anchored off the warehouse docks, but even out in the middle of Havana Bay, there was no breeze, no relief, just listless muggy air. The newly tarred seams on the wooden deck were a sticky hot paste that burned to the touch. But none of this mattered to Townsend. All he could see was her fixed stare with those brown eyes, and her long black eyelashes, her wavy, dark hair curling down the back of her neck. His thoughts were of Emma's tapered body swaying with unconscious self-confidence as she walked through the old Backhouse residence. He could still feel her elegant thin hands, her fingers intertwined with his on the carriage's leather seat, the light touch of her arms around his neck, the excitement of that first kiss.

With the rest of the crew ashore spending their money in gambling houses and bars, Townsend began to try to take an inventory of what they still needed on board. He wrote down more oakum, tar for caulking seams, extra replacement fastenings, more canvas for patching. To focus his mind, he studied old charts of the Florida coastline. Don Pedro had told him on this next trip they would be likely carrying arms and ammunition to a little-known Florida harbor north of the Suwanee River called Deadman's Bay. But again his mind wandered, and instead of studying currents and tides and plotting possible rhumb lines, he found himself staring idly out the portholes at the swaying masts in the harbor.

Hendricks must have noticed something unusual about him and asked when they would be loading cargo. Townsend didn't hear him at first, not until Hendricks asked the question a second time. Townsend mumbled it would probably be next week, as soon as Helm gave Don Pedro the go ahead.

"Wha' happen to you. You lookin' pale. Unhealthy."

"No, it's nothing."

"Da' cant be true. You pasty white. You getting fevah?"

Townsend shook his head and reassured him there was nothing wrong. But when Hendricks insisted again, he told him what he'd learned about Abbott from Emma and Padre Uribe.

"Lawd bless. I can't believe dat Englishman still deh living," the Bahamian said, shaking his head, his eyes wide in astonishment. "He must be a jumbie."

"A what?"

"A jumbie man. A walkin' dead man. If he be alive, you bes' be thinking of what you gon do. Deh gon' kill him, you know. Don Pedro and his people. They gon' kill Abbott. I might not know much about Don Pedro, but I tellin' you one ting, he's a bad man. And dem two barracudas workin' for him, Salazar and Nolo, deh be worse. They got killin' in the eyes."

Hendricks was right. Don Pedro had connected Abbott with the mysterious Englishman in Matanzas. It was only a hunch at the moment. But hunches were dangerous here in Cuba.

"You bes' be careful. This time they might kill you too."

Townsend didn't reply because the heavy thundering of El Morro's cannons signaled the latest arrival. The well-known Spanish-flagged sidewheel steamer, *Isabel*, was just coming in from St. Marks, Florida. She was one of the fastest of Havana's blockade runners, and had made multiple successful trips across the Gulf. He wondered what information she would be bringing. Most of the news about the war was now reaching Havana by means of ships running through the blockade. Just a few days earlier, the *Alice* had brought in the dramatic newspaper reports from Mobile about the South's surrender at Vicksburg. All the ship captains knew what that victory meant. With the Mississippi now firmly under Union control, more Federal gunships would soon be diverted into the Gulf. The blockade would tighten even more. Word was that the small harbor in Key West was already clogged up with as many as sixty blockade runners, now up for auction as captured prizes. Southern captains on those ships who refused to pledge allegiance to the Union were sent north to prison.

The next day Townsend got an unexpected invitation delivered to his rooming house. It was from his grandmother. She had just arrived in Havana. She wanted him to escort her to the Opera House for a special off-season performance to hear *Maria di Rohan*, a Donizetti opera about a tragic love triangle. It would just be the two of them in her theater box. The hand-delivered note had come with a complete set of formal clothes. Item by item, he laid out the clothes on his straw-filled sleeping cot: fine white pants, an ivory silk shirt, black tie, a burgundy waistcoat, a long dark satin coat with a black top hat, white stockings, and black patent leather shoes. His grandmother clearly wanted to dress him up like a fashionable Spanish Don from Havana.

In his new clothes, Townsend felt awkward and clumsy. He hoped he wouldn't run into any of the sailors he knew. They would laugh at him, he knew. He hailed a *volanta* cab to take him to his grandmother's house on Compostela Street near the Santa Catalina Church. It was on the other side of the old city, and Townsend sat back to enjoy the ride. For the first time, he took special notice of some of the colors and the architectural details of the buildings, the salmon-colored cornices, the light green mouldings, and the lilac trim. Havana was a city filled with many colors, he thought to himself, and many surprises.

His grandmother's house was cream colored with a purple-blue trim painted around the windows. He walked up to a large iron-studded wooden door and a brass hand door knocker. Like all the older houses in Havana, there were floor to ceiling iron-grated windows, which allowed him to look inside. He imagined his mother as a child seated on one of the cane-bottom rocking chairs looking out at him through the iron bars. It was like looking into a painting. In his imagination, she was giving him a disapproving look. He knew she wanted him to walk away, but he didn't.

The maid he'd seen at Mon Bijou let him in, politely nodding her head. He thought about saying something to her, but he couldn't find the words. Her dream was to free her son, Julio, but Townsend knew his grandmother's plans for the boy would mean he would never escape the plantation, free or not. He felt tremendous guilt about his silence. His attire somehow amplified it. He found his grandmother in the parlor, a large airy room with brightly painted fluted columns, black and white marble tiles and dark mahogany furniture. She had on a full-length silk dress with lace around the neck and the arms, a diamond comb in her hair, and six strings of pearls. She greeted him warmly, kissing him on both cheeks, and then stopped to admire his appearance, holding onto his hands.

"¡Ay, *que hombre tan guapo y elegante! Un verdadero Don Juan,*" she said in her soft voice, and then repeated it in English. "Such a handsome gentleman, you are, Everett, and so elegant! A true Don Juan!"

A white-jacketed butler brought him a *guarapo* with freshly squeezed cane juice, and gave Doña Cecilia a cup of Spanish licorice tea with salt that she said was to ward off any illness. As before, Townsend found her quiet, courteous manner disarming. It was still hard for him to understand how his mother had become so angry with her. He looked around the room. On one of the walls was a fresco painting of a plantation with the slaves bent over, working in the fields. On the opposite wall was a portrait of a Spanish-looking gentleman, stout and gray-faced, dark-haired, finely dressed in an older style. He was holding a riding crop with his thumb and forefinger much like a monarch might carry a scepter. In the background was a seaside plantation with its tall chimney, the mill and a cluster of sheds.

His grandmother saw his gaze lingering on the portrait, and she looked up at it.

"That's my mother's father, my grandfather. That would make him your great-great-grandfather. He was a Quintana, one of the old aristocratic Spanish families in Cuba."

She paused for a few moments, her eyes lingering on the portrait. Then she smiled and turned her attention back to her grandson.

"I am so pleased you are here in Cuba, Everett. Fate works in unusual ways to bring people together, families together. *¿Te lo imagines?* Just imagine, if your mother had remained in Cuba. Ay, *Díos Mío, que pena que no haya sido así.* If that only could have happened. You would have been born and raised at Mon Bijou just as she was, just as I was. It was such a joy to have you there. *Me dío tanta alegría.*"

She sipped on her drink slowly. Townsend could see a weariness in the lines in her face.

"Some say you can't make up for lost time, but then maybe you can. *¿Quién sabe?* Who knows? When you are older like me, you will learn that there are some things that cannot be changed. I believe you must look ahead, not behind. That is my way of thinking."

Just then, the butler announced that the postilion had brought the *volanta* around to the front entrance. Doña Cecilia looked at the clock, and said they must be going. It was important to arrive early at the opera house to join the promenade of Havana's prominent citizens.

"All of the city's *beau monde* should be there for tonight's performance."

Soon they were outside the old walls and the horses were trotting alongside the rocky, windblown north coast on their way out of the old city, passing the solid limestone structures that housed Havana's public sea baths. She began to talk about the plantation and how Don Pedro had been such a help to her. She spoke about the hard times of running the plantation by herself, and the difficulties of raising her daughter alone. Townsend noticed how his grand-mother's eyes were wet, but at the same time he could see behind the emo-tional façade, a look of steely determination. She wiped her eyes and turned her head as she restored her composure, and then abruptly changed the topic.

"I am sorry I haven't asked you, Everett. How are you and Pedro getting along?"

Her eyes lingered on his face as if she was searching for something. He wondered what she knew. Again he replied diplomatically.

"Don Pedro and I have a good business relationship, I believe. The voy-ages have all been successful. He's told me how much he values my efforts. I believe he thinks I would make a good merchant."

"Pedro is such a *caballero*. So handsome and distinguished," she said. "I am glad you are getting along with him. Did I mention he is related to a rich planter who is a friend of mine. I believe you met him, Don Eugenio Hernández."

Townsend nodded.

"Yes, Don Eugenio took him on as an apprentice many years ago when as a boy he was sent here from Spain. He paid for Pedro's schooling in New Orleans. Some whisper Pedro is Don Eugenio's illegitimate son, but *quién sabe*, who knows."

She looked reflective and sighed as she fingered the strands of pearls around her neck.

"Many of the young ladies in Havana would have given anything to have been chosen by Don Pedro back then. But not your mother."

Townsend started. He swiveled his head to face his grandmother.

"You never made any mention of this before."

"Yes, your mother turned him down. Handsome and rich was not good enough for her."

"My mother and Don Pedro? Don Pedro never told me. He said they were just acquaintances. Were they . . . were they ever a couple?"

"They should have been. I thought it would have been a sensible arranged marriage, what we call *un buen matrimonio concertado*, but your mother thought differently."

"Was he the older man you said you had found for my mother?" Townsend asked, stupefied, as he shook his head in wonderment.

"Indeed. I thought it was a good match. He was an older man, a success-ful merchant, still young and vibrant enough to meet the desires of a young woman. His wealth would have allowed him to offer your mother whatever she wanted. And, of course, he would have been able to help financially with Mon Bijou. I even announced in social circles that they were to be engaged."

"Engaged!"

"Yes, but your mother already had fallen in love with your father. They were meeting secretly. It was McKintyre who told me what was going on. I confronted your mother. She said she would never marry Don Pedro, and she vowed to marry your father with or without my permission. She accused me of selling her off to pay the plantation's debt. As you can imagine, I was distraught. I threatened to put her into a convent if she didn't stop seeing your father. Then I went to Don Pedro and encouraged him to take matters into his own hands."

Townsend hardly dared to breathe. He could see an angry gleam in her black eyes. The red leather inside the carriage only made her look more intense.

"At the time, I was so mad, I would have been glad if Pedro had locked your mother up in a cell. Those were difficult days then, back in the early 40s. We planters feared there would be a full-scale slave rebellion. It was so frightening. There were rumors that foreigners, English and Americans, were behind this uprising. Many of the American and English engineers working on the plantations were arrested. Don Pedro came to me and said he had a solution to the problem with your mother. I never knew what he intended."

"What did he do?"

"He went to the authorities to report your father and have him arrested."

"Arrest my father. For what?"

"For inciting rebellion. McKintyre said he'd overheard him talking to some slaves, encouraging them to run off."

"Was that true?"

"I never knew."

"So my father was arrested with your permission," Townsend said with a hint of derision in his voice.

"I never gave my permission. But yes, your father was arrested, taken to prison and charged with instigating rebellion. I was furious with your mother, and so was Pedro. I'd already let it be known that they were to be engaged. ¡Me dio tanta vergüenza! It was so embarrassing. Your mother demanded that I withdraw Don Pedro's accusation. I refused. She called me an evil, treach-erous woman. She said she hoped the slaves did burn down Mon Bijou. I slapped her across the face. I wished I had not done that, but I did. And then she left. Somehow through some connections she had with the American or English Consulate, she got your father released. And they left together on his ship a few days later. I never saw her again. *¡Ay de mi! Que horror!* Your mother and I never spoke again."

Doña Cecilia choked back a sob. She wiped her eyes with a linen handkerchief. Townsend did not move. He had no comfort to offer her.

"I only wanted to do what I thought best for her," she added in a thin, remorseful voice, almost like the whisper of a little girl.

"Did you write to tell her that?"

"Yes, I wrote her. Like I told you before, she only wrote me back once. She said she would never forgive me. She never wanted to see or hear from me again. She called me *una bruja. ¡Imagínate!* Imagine calling your own mother a witch!"

Townsend could hear the anger rising in her voice. He didn't say anything even as she dabbed her eyes and collected herself. They remained silent through their arrival at the opera house and their journey into a sea of swirling silk, fluttering fans and bobbing top hats. His grandmother's box was on the second floor balcony. It had comfortable chairs and an open railing, and it offered an ample view of the multi-tiered theater, which held three thousand people. Townsend had never seen anything like this before. His grandmother's enthusiasm for fashionable Havana soon replaced any lingering dark feelings. She trained her small theater glasses on some of the prominent people. She pointed out the red and yellow satin-draped box for the captain general, and the crowded box for the British consul general and his family.

"Look there is old Papa Crawford with his young wife and their sixteen-year-old daughter. She is his second wife, a delightful person. Her family owns a plantation here. He's been the British consul general for so long it's almost like he's from here. That's why some of us call him Papa. To some of us, he's like family."

His grandmother was increasingly animated as she spotted some of the old established families: the Aldamas, the Alfonsos, the Peñalvers. She was particularly interested in the Countess Fernandina, who was wearing a lilac dress.

"So charming, don't you think Everett. Designed to show off her graceful shoulders. *¡Ay, Mira!* Look over there. Don Julián Zulueta's box. Such an important man! My word, Pancho Marty is with him, and so is our Don Pedro. And there's Charles Helm, the Confederate agent. That must be an important meeting of some sort."

She dropped the glasses from her face, and looked at him.

"I wanted to ask you again, *cariño*. Are you sure everything is fine between you and Pedro?"

Townsend had no desire to hear the man's name, but remained civil.

"Everything is fine."

"Just yesterday I asked him what he thought of you. I was expecting to hear a glowing report. But instead Pedro said he was sad to report that he may have misjudged your potential."

"Really. I'm surprised," Townsend said even as he felt a slight chill travel down his spine. He hated the man, but he knew he needed to maintain his trust.

"He said you were too much like your mother."

"In what way?"

"I asked him, but he simply shrugged, and said to me, '*así son las cosas.* That's the way it is.' I was surprised. Perhaps he feels you are too hot headed. Your mother certainly was. I just thought I'd ask again. Is there something you aren't telling me?"

She looked over at him with an expression of caring concern, but in her eyes he saw something else, that same steely iciness he'd seen before.

"I would be careful, *cariño. Ten cuidado.* Pedro is a complicated man. I have a great deal of affection for him. He has been helpful to me over the years, but I am wise enough to understand his motives. It's no secret he would like to own my Mon Bijou."

Just then the crowd started to applaud wildly. About two dozen white pigeons with red and blue streamers tied to their feet were released into the air. To Townsend they looked like tropical forest birds being freed from captivity. The huge curtain lifted, and a soprano's voice pierced the enormous theater. At the interlude after the first act, Doña Cecilia applauded enthusiastically and took her grandson's arm.

"As you can see, Havana's *beau monde* love the opera. It puts them in ecstasy. Are you enjoying it?"

Townsend nodded even though he hadn't cared much for the performance. To him, all this display of emotion was somewhat of a mystery. He liked the music, but he couldn't understand anything.

Doña Cecilia took out her blue and pink fan and snapped it open in one fluid movement like a butterfly opening its wings. "Everett, you are still so young," she began. "Have you thought about what you might do when this American war is over?"

"Not much," he replied.

"Will you go back to Maryland?"

"I'm not sure."

"Know that you have a home here, *cariño*. Mon Bijou could be your home. I would love to convince you to stay. You are my grandson, and you know Mon Bijou will one day be yours."

Townsend's eyes grew wide. The idea of running a Cuban sugar plantation was repellent enough, but the possibility that he might one day be the owner of a Cuban sugar plantation—a sugar baron, was not something he could even consider. He was speechless.

"You don't have to tell me now, but just think about it," she said with her soft voice and the faintest of smiles.

"I don't think I am the right person for that job," Townsend finally stammered. "I would like to stay involved in what I know—ships and the sea."

Townsend could tell from her furrowed brow and pursed lips that she was not pleased at what he had just said.

"Well, I hope you will think about it."

She looked straight ahead toward the stage. Her hands began to finger her pearls like a woman praying with her rosary beads. He thought he saw her eyes begin to tear up.

29

July 21, 1863

Days later, Townsend was still pondering his grandmother's offer. It wasn't just a job. She was asking him to come live with her, to be her heir. The idea of inheriting a Cuban sugar plantation and owning four hundred slaves was repugnant to him. Now that he'd been given a glimpse of slavery, he wanted nothing to do with it. But strangely, he hadn't stopped thinking about what she'd said. He thought of the naval career he'd hoped for, but would never have. The plantation would give him a comfortable life. His grandmother was his family. Other than his father and a few unknown relatives in New England, he had no one else. At the opera house, he had sensed her loneliness, the quiet anguish in her voice, the worry in her eyes. It was hard not to feel sorry for her.

But then he shook his head in wonderment at his poor judgment. How could he possibly be tempted? He wondered what Emma would say. Would she be swayed by the enticement of wealth? No. He thought of Julio beating the puppy under the watchful eye of McKintyre. His grandmother had approved this act of cruelty. His mind turned to his mother, and he suddenly realized why she left Cuba. It wasn't just the rift with his grandmother. Yes, she'd felt betrayed by her own mother. She was bitter and angry, but the reason she left the island was more complicated. She fled and never returned because she knew her own sense of human decency was at risk. She left to save herself. She had seen what Mon Bijou had done to her mother, and she didn't want that to happen to her. If she stayed, her principles would have slowly eroded. She would have become just like her mother, who in the name of preserving her family heritage, had been willing to look the other way all too often and embrace brutality.

The blast of a ship's steam whistle interrupted his thoughts, and Townsend walked out of the cabin house to look at the latest arrival to the harbor. He brought his telescope to his eye to get a better view of the three-masted ship steaming into port, its tall funnel amidships belching out black smoke. She was flying a Mexican flag off her mizzen mast. The ship looked quite familiar. He scanned the dozens of sailors scurrying around the deck, tying down halyards and coiling deck lines, until he spotted two familiar figures wearing slouch hats, the same two Southerners who had traveled with them on the passage along the Texas coast from the Brazos River to Matamoros. The ship was now close enough that Townsend could plainly see their features, the tension and determined looks in their faces.

As the ship steamed by, he focused on her stern. She now had a name painted on her transom, *María Guadalupe* out of Vera Cruz, Mexico.

Townsend called out to Hendricks down below in the main cabin.

"Looks like the phantom ship from Matamoros has arrived," he cried out. "She's flying a Mexican flag now. And she's got a name. *María Guadalupe.*"

Hendricks came out on deck and stared at the passing ship. He held his hand over his eyes to block the sun's glare.

"Them two Confederates, deh on board?"

"Yes, they are."

"Bes' to stay far away then," the Bahamian said with a shake of his head. "I ain' goin' near that slavin' ship."

Townsend didn't reply. His first thought was sending a message to Savage about the ship's arrival, but he was also mindful that he had promised to meet Bertrand shortly at the *Toro del Mar.* The New Orleans sailor had sent him an alarming note, writing it was urgent, and that he had important information for the whole crew. Given Bertrand's reputation as a petticoat chaser, he and Hendricks assumed that it had something to do with the *mulata* he'd continued seeing, despite repeated warnings. But in this harbor of spies, you never knew.

Soon the small launch carrying the Spanish customs and health inspectors made its way to the newly arrived ship. The sun had sunk lower on the horizon, and the church bells were already chiming for evening mass. Townsend went below to his cabin to get his coat and then he and Hendricks hailed a passing harbor boat, taking care to climb down on the side away from the Mexican ship, just in case someone on board had spotted them. Once ashore, they ducked in and out of stores to make sure they weren't being tailed, and then circled back to the street corner near the Alameda de Paula promenade where the lottery ticket salesman was standing. Townsend told Hendricks to wait across the street and look for anyone suspicious.

By now, Townsend was quite familiar with this little man, his contact person, and called him by his nickname, Guti, short for Gutiérrez. Townsend walked up to him and handed him a note hidden under a pile of coins. All he'd written was, "Phantom ship has arrived. *María Guadalupe*. Flying the Mexican flag. Confederate agents on board." Townsend looked around to see if anyone was watching, but he saw no one, just some passing *volantas* and carriages and some street vendors. The lottery vendor's impassive face never flinched or revealed anything as he handed him the ticket in return.

"*El cocuyo trae buena suerte,*" he said. The firefly brings good luck. Townsend nodded. Gutiérrez immediately turned away and began crying out to passers-by to come buy the winning number, the lucky number.

"*¡Lotería! ¡Lotería! ¡Número 21534. Número de la suerte!*"

With the sky darkening, Townsend and Hendricks made their way through the gas-lit streets on the south side of the old city until they got to the familiar sign of *Toro del Mar*. Townsend had grown accustomed to this drunken oasis where foreign sailors drowned their sorrows. He looked in vain for any sign of Bertrand or the other three crewmembers, but he didn't see them. He sensed rather than saw the bar women sizing him up. The women at the *Toro del Mar* were famous for their skills at pickpocketing. He stood next to a table where some rough-looking Confederate veterans were talking in hushed voices. He told Hendricks to stay close to him and if anyone gave him any trouble, to say nothing. He would take care of the rest.

Townsend was still getting used to the darkness when he felt a hand on his shoulder. It was Bertrand, and the sailor beckoned him over to a dark corner table in a small room away from the music where his *mulata* girlfriend, Gabriela Ramírez, was seated. Townsend nodded politely to her as she acknowledged him with a blink of her eyes. He couldn't help admiring the striking good looks of this woman, with her mahogany skin, high cheekbones, and full, sensual lips.

Bertrand's expression was unusually serious, his face taut and strained.

"What's so urgent, Bertrand? Why are you so frazzled?"

"I believe we have trouble, *mon ami*."

"Where are the others?" Townsend asked.

"Coming soon," Bertrand whispered. "*Toute suite*. I wanted you to hear what Gabriela has to say. She will not stay long. It is better you have arrived first, *Capitaine. Tant mieux*. We have problems."

Townsend stared at Bertrand with a puzzling frown and then turned to look at the woman.

"Well then, let's talk."

"Gabriela is the mistress for Captain Reinaldo Gómez, who now reports directly to the captain general about all matters related to security and shipping in Havana port. She hears many things. Gabriela, tell him what you've heard. *Díle al capitán lo que me contaste.*"

Gabriela's eyes nervously darted around the room for several seconds before she began speaking in a hushed voice.

"*Todos ustedes están en peligro, Capitán.* You and your men are all in danger."

"How do you know this?" Townsend asked, speaking in Spanish

"I heard Gómez talk with Captain Vásquez of the *Guardia Civil.* You are being watched. Not just at the docks, but in the streets as well."

"I'm accustomed to that treatment here in Havana," Townsend replied nonchalantly.

"No, it's more than the usual dock informants," she said emphatically. "Now you have policemen out of uniform watching you and your men. It's a special branch of police. These are dangerous people."

"Why would the government care about any of us?"

"They believe you and your men are all spies. Yankee spies working for Mr. Lincoln, and you are trying to gather information harmful to Spanish interests, secret information about the Spanish government's links to the South. They suspect the American government wants to find a reason to declare war against Spain and invade Cuba. The Spanish have always feared an American invasion of Cuba."

"What nonsense," sputtered Townsend. "*Puras tonterías.* Pure twaddle."

"They are worried about a ship called *María Guadalupe.* There is something secretive about it. It's coming to Havana soon."

"It's already here in the harbor," Townsend said. He looked over at Hendricks. The Bahamian couldn't understand Spanish, but he recognized the name of the ship and his face now revealed his concern.

"Then in that case you have even more trouble, Captain," Gabriela said. "The police have been ordered to arrest all of you for espionage as soon as that ship docks and is loading cargo."

"Does the owner of my ship, Don Pedro Alvarado Cardona, know this? Did you hear his name mentioned?"

"No. Nothing. That's all I heard. I must go now."

She looked at him with a frightened expression. "I have told Bertrand you must all leave Havana. Save yourselves and get off this island."

Gabriela put a black lace veil over her head as a disguise. Bertrand escorted her out of the bar to the safety of a carriage, and then returned. As soon as the other three sailors drifted into the *Toro del Mar*, they all wanted an explanation for this meeting. Townsend let Bertrand explain to them what they had just heard from Gabriela, emphasizing that they could all soon be arrested as spies. Townsend's instincts warned him there must be some truth to what she said. In all likelihood, they were now hunted men.

"What in thunder!" cried out Red Beard with a set of his bearded jaw. "I'm damned if I understand that. I'm no spy."

"Why, arrest us?" Dutch Olsen said. "We haven't done anything!"

"It's something to do with a ship that has just come into port," Bertrand said. "The Spanish think we are spying on that ship."

"It must be Don Pedro and his supercargoes," said Higgins. "They must be behind this. What do you think, Cap'n?"

Townsend sat there, his head slumped over, looking down at the floor as he tried to control a twitch in his lower lip. He wasn't sure what to do. He looked up and saw Hendricks staring right at him. At first he didn't say anything, but then he began to speak slowly, softly. He explained everything he knew about the ship, starting with the fact that it was the same ship they'd seen in Matamoros. The two Confederates they'd taken over as passengers to Matamoros were on board. He told them it was a Spanish slave ship that had been bought by the Confederates from Spanish slave traders. It had been reflagged as a Mexican merchant ship, a neutral flag, to get it safely through the Union Blockade in the Gulf. In Nassau it would be outfitted with deck cannons supplied by the British and turned into a Confederate warship."

"A Confederate gunship that has run slap up into Havana harbor," Red Beard whispered, shaking his head in disbelief.

Townsend nodded. "Don Pedro is the broker, and these latest developments suggest he may have used his connections to get the full cooperation of the Spanish naval officials in the port."

"But why in blazes did that ship come here to Havana?" Higgins asked. "It could have gone directly to the Bahamas."

"Most likely to get coal and load a new crew," Townsend said. "Just look at the number of loyal Confederates swarming all over Havana now. Finding a crew is easy pickings here. There may be other business still to be conducted as well. Possibly taking on arms and ammunition."

Red Beard eyed him suspiciously. "You sound like one of them high-tone Pinkerton detectives I read about, spying for Lincoln and the blue bellies."

Townsend didn't reply. The hostile tone in Red Beard's voice was unmistakable, and the accusation had hit him squarely in the face. Higgins stood by silently. Olsen was busy downing a second drink. Townsend could feel the tension simmering. His palms were sweating. He'd grown fond of these men. They made a good team. He had kept his promise to Savage as long as he could, but now that he'd endangered them, he owed them a full explanation. They deserved that. They were his shipmates.

"I have a confession to make," Townsend said. He gulped nervously.

All eyes were on him. He looked at the bronzed weathered features and furrowed brows around him. They came from different backgrounds, but wind and water had given them a common purpose, a special bond of trust. They were all just trying to survive, keeping their heads above water so as not to drown in this outer eddy of the American conflict.

"I was asked by the acting US consul general in Havana, Thomas Savage, before our last voyage to report on the activities of the business dealings of Don Pedro—and I have been doing that."

"A spy for Seward and Lincoln," Red Beard hissed.

"I prefer to call myself an informant, but yes I suppose I am a spy."

"You're a crittur full of surprises, Cap'n," Red Beard said, shaking his head. "I did my part in this war on the Confederit side, but I see you're still engaged."

"I should have told you before," Townsend said. "I wanted to, but I was sworn to secrecy by Thomas Savage. It was safer for all of us. Until now."

"*Sacré Dieu, Capitaine.* I thought you told us you weren't taking sides in this war," Bertrand said.

"I remember that as well," said Olsen. "You said we were all outsiders."

Townsend didn't answer at first but then said, "I never intended to become a spy, but in running the blockade I realized I've been betraying myself. I felt like I needed to take a stand."

"And Hendricks? Is he a spy too?" Red Beard growled.

"I asked him to help me, but he should speak for himself."

Hendricks's face was impassive. He responded without hesitation. "I agreed to help the Cap'n cause I ain' want nothin' to do with them Spaniards. But now that you ask me if I deh a spy, I gon tell you one ting. I ain' feelin' no shame. Dis war up north is a war between Americans, but for me it also deh a war 'bout freedom, not just for slaves but for all Negro people. So I ain' feelin no shame."

Townsend had never heard Hendricks speak that way before, so directly and with such conviction. Nor had any of the others. They sat in silence, contemplating. It was as if the war, its consequences and its causes, had suddenly hit home, with one of their own explaining what was at stake. Townsend knew he had to say something. He reached into his pocket and pulled out the letter he'd been given by Savage with the stamp of the Consulate.

"I know you men feel betrayed by me. It's understandable. The bond of trust we had, I broke it. I know that, and I need to fix it."

Townsend waved the letter in front of them.

"This might help. It's a letter from the American consul general. Before I agreed to do any sleuthing for him, I had Mr. Savage write this up. It may be our ticket out of here. The letter asks any US naval captain who might stop us at sea, to extend to not just me, but to all on board every courtesy and consideration. It goes on to explain that we have provided important help and intelligence to the US Consulate in Havana, and should be considered as loyal American citizens."

"That's a mighty fine gesture," Olsen said, "if some Navy gunboat doesn't shoot us out of the water first."

"*Malheureusement*, we have no way out of Havana Bay," Bertrand said, shaking his head. "*Pas de sortie*. And there is no going back to the *Gaviota*. We would be arrested."

"They'll be watching and stopping all vessels," Higgins chimed in. "We're trapped. We'll need some way to get out of the harbor. We need a new ship."

The thought of a new boat gave Townsend an idea. He began to tell them about a schooner he knew over at Casa Blanca. The owner was a Cuban fisherman by the name of Raúl Ortiz, who wanted to sell it to a blockade runner. He was selling it cheap.

"I think I can get it for four hundred dollars. Fortunately I took my money off the *Gaviota*. I've got a mixture of gold doubloons and bank notes from the Banco Español. Should be enough."

The others were digesting this new information and the bad situation they were in. Townsend could see they were resigned. He looked over at Red Beard, who glowered at him with a resentful stare. He knew the Texas sailor would not forget this betrayal of trust easily. He decided the best tactic was to leave him alone.

They left the bar in groups of two so as not to attract attention. Townsend and Hendricks walked ahead, hugging the sidewalk so they remained in the shadows. They took a circuitous route through a warehouse area, walking quickly with their heads down.

They arrived at the ferry docks, breathless. There was no sign of the others. The harbor was closed to any large boat traffic late at night, but for the right price you could always find harbor boats willing to take the risk. Townsend told Hendricks to wait and keep a lookout for the others. He would find a boatman. He lifted the wide-brimmed hats of several sleeping boatmen, shaking them awake, but then quickly realized they were too drunk. Finally he found a man who agreed to smuggle them across the harbor to Casa Blanca for a high fee. He'd been drinking like the others, but as soon as the Cuban boatman saw the shine of a quarter-ounce Spanish gold coin worth about four American dollars, he jumped to attention.

"Do you know a fisherman by the name of Ortiz?" Townsend asked in Spanish. "*¿Conoce a Raúl Ortiz?*"

"*¿Por qué lo estás buscando? ¿Qué ha hecho?* Why are you looking for him?"

Townsend thought it best to be vague so he said simply that he was an old friend of Ortiz, and wanted to go out fishing with him. The man was like so many of the Cubans working on the docks—a wiry, leather-skinned man with a stubbly beard who spoke a colloquial Spanish. The boatman introduced himself as Junípero Díaz, and said he knew Ortiz, the fisherman. He would take him to the docks nearest the fishing fleet, not far from where the man lived. When the others arrived, Townsend had to reassure him that these were all friends of Ortiz. The man smiled, revealing a gap in his front teeth.

There was a slight night breeze coming from the south as they cast off from the docks and the boatman raised a lateen sail. The small responsive boat immediately heeled over, and the boatman motioned for all of his passengers to move into the center of the boat. Somewhere in the darkness off to their left was the *Gaviota* riding at anchor. Townsend strained his eyes to see if he could spot her masts, but it was impossible to see anything more than a hundred yards away. Townsend could hear the muttering and complaining in the darkness. He knew these men were distraught about leaving Havana. He knew they blamed him. His choices had put them all in danger. He knew they were right to be concerned, but he ignored the disquiet on the boat. They sailed up to the docks at Casa Blanca where the fishing fleet was anchored, and Townsend told the man to wait. There were still some flickering lights on at a late night tavern, and he walked in and inquired about Raúl Ortiz, who, he was told, lived just a block away.

Townsend walked off, leaving the others outside the tavern. Ortiz lived in a small one-storied wooden house painted orange, with blue and red steps that led to the front door. He woke the fisherman up, introducing himself as the *Confederado* who had spoken with him at the fish market. It took two cups of coffee and the sight of gold coins, but within an hour Townsend was the new owner of the scow schooner. Ortiz told him where it was tied up, and Townsend was soon showing off his new boat to the crew, a square lumber barge, fifty feet long and twenty feet wide, two masts and a bowsprit. In the pale moonlight, the crew stood there speechless as they stared at the dim silhouetted outline of this ungainly vessel. Even in the dark, it was clear that the ship had bulky sides, square ends, and a flat bottom.

"She's called *Vírgen Gorda*," Townsend finally said. "The Fat Virgin."

"She may be fat, but I reckon no virgin," Olsen piped in. "This boat is old and she's got a cargo hold smelling of rotten fish."

The sailors all laughed.

"She's certainly no weatherly vessel, Cap'n," Higgins complained. "I'd call her a fat barge."

"She's a scow schooner," Townsend said. "Slow, but seaworthy. Built to carry cordwood and stone up the Sabine River in Texas. What the Texans might call a right smart, sturdy boat. She's heavily planked and with the wind and waves behind her she'll move along. She might do four to five knots, maybe more running before the wind. It's all we've got, I'm afraid."

Townsend again apologized to the men, and told them he intended to make amends. "I'm going to sneak back on the *Gaviota* tonight to retrieve the sextant, telescope, charts, and that Colt pistol. I'm taking requests. Each of you gets one item. Red Beard, let's start with you. What do you want from the ship?"

"Chawing tobacco," the Texan grumbled as he bit off another plug of tobacco.

Higgins wanted his sea knife. Bertrand, a love locket containing a strand of Gabriela's hair. Hendricks, a pocket compass. Olsen said he wanted the cat.

"I doubt I can retrieve the cat, Olsen," Townsend said.

"Could be she will bring us good luck, Cap'n. We may need her. Besides, this stinking ship you've found for us is probably full of rats. Look-Out could be useful. Just put the halter on her."

"I'll do what I can."

Townsend turned to leave, but came face-to-face with Red Beard's whiskery beard.

"Whar' you headed afterwards?" the first mate asked.

"Back to the docks and the city," Townsend replied. "Some personal business."

"I reckon you mean spy business," Red Beard whispered bitterly.

Townsend ignored the remark. He turned toward the men's shadowy faces up against the hull of their new ship.

"I'll meet all of you at the *Muelle de Luz*, the small landing where the fishing boats and harbor boats tie up near the ferry docks directly across from Regla. The boat should blend in there, and not be noticed. I'll be there at four o'clock. If I'm not, you'll know something has happened to me. Just set sail."

30

As Townsend stepped back on board the harbor boat, he could tell immedi-ately from Junípero Díaz's breath that the man had been drinking more. The Cuban had a slight slur in his voice as he demanded a sixteenth-ounce gold coin. At first, Townsend thought about bargaining with him, but then he re-considered his situation. He gave the man another coin. He told him to take him to the *Gaviota* before heading to shore. More than anything, he needed the ship's chronometer, the sextant, and the charts of the Gulf waters, but he also wanted to retrieve the Colt pistol he'd grabbed from Van Cortland. It was a risk he was willing to take. He nodded to the boatman and pointed in the direction where he thought the schooner was anchored in the center of the harbor. Townsend could feel the freshening breeze coming in from the southeast as they quickly pulled away from the fisherman's wharf. The resentful burn of Red Beard's eyes, his anger, and the man's distrust were still fresh in his mind. He wondered if the crew would be waiting for him in Old Havana when he got back. They could just decide to leave him behind. It was another risk.

The small boat with its lateen sail glided through the dark harbor, quietly passing the silhouettes of anchored warships, merchant tallships, and the ragtag collection of schooners and tugboats involved in blockade running. Beyond that, he could plainly see the shimmering lights of Havana, the dark shapes of the church towers and the massive domes dominating the skyline. From the bow, he looked back at the long stream of phosphorescent light trailing in the boat's wake, and he was reminded of the *cocuyos* in the Cuban countryside.

Townsend was still lost in a meditative reverie when he heard voices. His back stiffened. The voices sounded close by. He scanned the darkness.

"*Centinelas*," the boatman whispered. "*Son centinelas de la fortaleza.*" Townsend could barely make out the lonely figures of sentries with their rifles standing high above him on the parapets of the Cabaña fortress. It was 2:00 a.m., and the soldiers were routinely passing on the "stay alert" signal from one fortress wall to the next. In the dark, he listened to the eerie cry of these night guards, echoing across the blackness of the channel. He hoped they didn't spot their small sail.

After tacking back and forth between ships staggered alongside each other, Townsend finally picked out the shadowy hull of the *Gaviota*. There wasn't a sound to be heard as the boatman, drunk as he probably was, skillfully brought his small vessel into the wind and nudged it up alongside the *Gaviota*'s hull. Townsend grabbed the stays and nimbly pulled himself up onto the schooner's deck.

"*Espérame Junípero*," Townsend said to the man. "*Dame unos minutos.* Wait for me. I'll just be a few minutes."

The boatman replied evasively that he had to make another trip, but he promised he would come back. Townsend was wise to that trick. He knew the man had just given him an ultimatum. Pay more or he would leave. He handed the man another gold coin.

"*Suficiente*," Townsend asked. "Is that enough?"

"*Sí, jefe.*"

Before going down into the cabin, Townsend walked up to the bow, scanning the shadowy shapes of ships anchored near them. Just to the windward of the *Gaviota*, there were two Texas blockade-running schooners, their decks stacked high with cotton bales. They were clearly waiting to be cleared to unload their valuable cargo. It didn't look as if there was anybody on watch. Townsend sat on a water barrel near the foremast listening for any strange sounds, anything out of the ordinary. Satisfied there was nothing, he walked into the forward cabin house, lit a lamp, and collected the few personal things the crew had asked for. He then walked back to the stern, stepping down into the main cabin house, breathing in the familiar moldy tar smells of the ship. He lit a candle in his cabin, and began pulling out the old sea charts and books of the Gulf coastline he thought he might need. He wrapped the brass ship's chronometer in its gimbaled rosewood box, and the sextant in its container in some old shirts. He grabbed the nautical almanac and the sight reduction tables he needed for his calculations and then packed all of this into his duffel bag.

Finally he put his hand into the back of his closet and pulled out Van Cortland's .36 caliber Colt pistol. He'd never used it, but he always kept it loaded. He knew it was against the law to carry any guns ashore, punishable with six years of imprisonment and hard labor on Havana's chain gang. But then given Gabriela's warning, what difference did it make if he broke the law. He was pondering how to carry the pistol safely when he heard noises outside. It sounded like the squeak of wooden oars. Then came the thud of a boat bumping up against the schooner. Townsend put the gun down quietly as he strained to hear any other noises through the porthole. At first he assumed the drunken boatman must be stumbling around in his boat looking for another bottle. But then he heard an unmistakable cry of pain and a heavy splash in the water.

Townsend's body stiffened in alarm, and without thinking he grabbed the pistol off the table, cocked the hammer, and rushed up the stairs. He got there in time to see two dark figures pulling themselves up on board the schooner, knives in their hands. At the sight of the glint of the metal blades, something shifted inside of him. For that brief desperate second, he was transported back in time to the street on the night when he and Abbott were attacked. He was hearing the loud rhythmic drums, and he was looking at a knife plunging into Abbott's body. He felt a wild rage sweep through him, and he told himself, *no, never again*.

Townsend raised the pistol and squeezed the trigger just as both intruders climbed onto the deck. The gun went off with a loud roar, and Townsend was surrounded by a plume of smoke and the acrid smell of gunpowder. One of the men cursed and fell backwards, holding his shoulder. Townsend swung the barrel of the gun, his thumb on the hammer, and aimed it at the second figure.

"*¡Quítense de ahí!*" Townsend yelled and then repeated the warning in English. "Get the hell off the boat!" He shook the long barrel at the man as he stood above his squirming colleague, who was screaming in pain. Townsend warned the intruder he would shoot again. He told him to drop the knife and leave the boat with his wounded friend or he would fire again. The one man let the knife fall onto the deck with a clatter as he raised his hands. With the candlelight from the cabin shining through the portholes, Townsend could see the man was white. The man he'd shot was a *mulato*. They were both dressed simply like so many of the dockworkers.

"Who sent you?" he cried out to the shadowy figures, then repeating the question in Spanish.

The intruders didn't answer. He could only hear a faint groan from the wounded man.

"Who are you?" he asked.

No answer. Before he could react, the two men turned and jumped over the side into their small launch boat. Townsend was thinking about firing another shot to scare them when he noticed the floating body, face down in the water. It was the boatman, Junípero Díaz. The man was either unconscious or dead, as there was no movement. Townsend quickly grabbed the long-poled boat hook that was attached to the schooner's ratlines, and climbed down into the small boat. He leaned over the gunwales and reached out with the pole as far as he could. After several failed attempts, he finally secured the hook into the man's belt and began pulling him in. Suddenly something struck the pole, wrenching it out of his hands. He heard a splash in the water. He wheeled around, thinking that his two assailants had returned. His eyes strained in the gloom to see what the noise was. And then without warning, the water around the man's body exploded into a blinding whirlpool of thrashing, splashing, and shaking.

Townsend threw himself back into the center of the rowboat. He could see the black fins as they carved their deadly pattern through the shimmering water, the man's inert body tossed by each lunge. Townsend knew there was nothing he could do. The floating body was surrounded by at least a half-dozen sharks drawn by the smell of blood. They were in a feeding frenzy, and he knew more were probably on their way.

He jumped back on board the *Gaviota* to gather his things. He felt sickened by what he'd seen, and he vomited over the side. He knew he had to hurry. The sound of the gunshot might have drawn the attention of the harbor police. He went below and threw on his linen coat, placing the fourteen-inch-long pistol in one of the interior pockets. He still felt physically sick, and thought he might have to vomit again. He tried to make himself focus. He went to the ship's small library shelf and grabbed the biggest book he could find. It was *The Atlantic Navigator*, Captain Evans's favorite book, a sea captain's guide to the wind and currents of the Atlantic. He felt a pang of guilt as he placed the book in the other side pocket along with the telescope. Now both sides of his coat looked the same.

He tried to think of what else he needed to bring. He was listing the personal items of the crew to himself when he heard some rustling and scratching coming from behind the stove. He grabbed the pistol and pointed it in the direction of the noise.

"Come out from behind there," he yelled.

Just then he heard a meow. He saw a raised shadowy tail that quivered a greeting.

"Holy Cow, the cat!" Townsend exclaimed. "I knew I'd forgotten something."

When Townsend climbed back on deck to survey the harbor, there was nothing to be seen of the body of Junípero Díaz, just the smooth, slightly ruffled surface of the black water. Like vultures, the sharks of Havana Bay had efficiently done their job, leaving no trace of the body or any crime. Townsend carefully threw his duffel into the bungo boat and then clambered over the side, holding Look-Out with one hand. He'd put the cat's halter on and attached the leash so she couldn't escape. Townsend decided to head for the *Muelle de Luz* landing where he'd told the crew to meet him. After drifting into a small pier crowded with tied-up harbor boats and fishing boats, he waited there for a couple of hours, hidden in the dark under the awning of the boat. He would stay there until the sun rose. It gave him time to reflect on what had just happened, and to plan what to do next. He looked at the knives the two men had been carrying. They were long Spanish knives made in Sevilla, similar to Bowie knives, about nine inches long with the notable characteristic that for several inches, the blade cut was double-edged. Who were these intruders, he wondered—thieves, or hired assassins? Most likely, he thought, they were some kind of non-uniformed agents of the police.

Townsend dropped both of the knives into his duffel bag along with the charts, the nautical almanac, the sight reduction tables, the sextant, and the chronometer. At dawn, when the first boatman showed up, he gave him some money and told him to drop his sailor's bag off in Casa Blanca. When he showed him the cat, the man thought he was crazy, but Townsend was able to persuade him with another sixteenth-ounce gold coin, and by throwing the cat into the duffel. Townsend described the vessel and its name, and told him to look for a man named Bertrand. He assured him he spoke Spanish so there would be no problems.

Then he sat down to write a note to Savage. He tore a blank page out of *The Atlantic Navigator* and began writing.

Hon. Vice Consul General, Thomas Savage
United States Consulate, Havana

Sir:

I regret to inform you of some unfortunate developments. I have reason to believe that the Spanish authorities wish to arrest and imprison myself and my crew. It is therefore too dangerous for any of us to remain here. We must flee the island. We hope to be leaving the Muelle de Luz landing near the ferry docks before dusk. We will be sailing on board the Spanish-flagged scow schooner *Vírgen Gorda*, which is a known fishing vessel I have purchased. We hope to sail to Key West. Any assistance you might provide through your regular mail dispatches to Admiral Bailey would greatly be appreciated. Be advised that the Mexican ship I mentioned in my previous note has kept steam up, and by all appearances may be ready to depart soon.

I am, Vice Consul General,
Very respectfully,
Captain Everett Townsend

The early morning sun was already blazing hot when Townsend left the docks at the *Muelle de Luz* to walk into the city. It was 7:00 a.m. The streets were beginning to fill up with *volantas* carrying well-dressed merchants to work. Black-robed priests appeared at every corner, walking briskly toward the chimes and peals of the many church bells that called them to prayers. The cries of street vendors selling milk and bread competed with the firing of cannons from El Morro castle in what by now had become a familiar early morning symphony. Townsend had thought earlier about returning to his rooming house in San Isidro to grab some clothes, but after the sudden attack he knew it would be too dangerous. If the police were sending men with knives to the boat, they would be doing the same outside his room.

The young captain headed to the opposite corner of the Alameda de Paula where the lottery vendor Gutiérrez usually stood. He walked down Oficios Street and then turned toward the harbor at Acosta Street. He breathed a sigh of relief as he saw the diminutive figure of the lottery salesman and heard his high-pitched cry, *¡Lotería! Lotería!* With his hat pulled down over his forehead, Townsend walked briskly toward the little man, bending down to hand him the neatly folded letter underneath a pile of coins. Gutiérrez looked up at him strangely, not recognizing him at first, but then when Townsend whispered "*un mensaje del cocuyo*," a message from *el cocuyo*, he quickly acknowledged the young captain and gave him a lottery ticket.

Townsend locked eyes with the little man and told him he hoped he had the lucky number and would win the lottery this time because his needs were *urgent*. He emphasized the last word, and Gutiérrez nodded that he understood. Townsend then headed across town to Mrs. Carpenter's boarding house. He desperately needed to see Emma, not only to tell her what had happened but also to say goodbye. He wanted to see her face to face, and reassure her that he was not just another sailor. He was dependable. He would miss her so. And he knew she could pass on a more detailed message to Savage on why he and his crew couldn't stay in Havana any longer. He'd been discovered. It was too risky. Townsend kept looking behind him. He thought he heard footsteps, but he saw nothing.

Several blocks later, he heard the rapid clatter of hooves and the squeal of carriage wheels on the cobblestones. He wheeled around, his hand already reaching for the gun. Before he could do anything, he heard his name being called out. A silvery-black-haired gentleman dressed in a white suit poked his head out of the carriage window. It was Don Pedro.

"What good fortune to find you, Captain Townsend. I have been looking all over the city for you. I just came from your rooming house where it's clear you didn't sleep last night."

Townsend's first instinct was to run, but Don Pedro's warm greeting seemed disarmingly friendly.

"I've been making the rounds of the taverns," Townsend replied.

"I can tell," the Spaniard said and offered him a cigar. "From the look of your crumpled shirt, you slept in it."

Don Pedro said he was going to see *una pelea de gallos*, a special cockfight that had been organized by the captain general. He insisted that Townsend should join him to see this most Cuban of sporting events.

"It should be quite a spectacle. Please join me. Get in the carriage. Otherwise we'll be late."

Townsend did not see that he had much choice. He decided he would play along. Maybe he could bluff his way through this encounter. He was not certain what information Don Pedro could have on him. He hoped it was still just suspicions.

As the carriage made its way through the gates of the old wall, Don Pedro revealed nothing about his state of mind. He was strangely silent. He smoked his cigar quietly as the wheels clattered along the Calzada de San Rafael into the working class community of San Lázaro. They were headed for the Campo de Peñalver in the outskirts of the city where the main cockfight arena was located. Finally the Spaniard talked about the probable next trip to northern Florida where Helm had said arms and ammunition were sorely needed. They would be sailing to a little known harbor in Deadman's Bay just to the north of the Suwanee River that was not likely to be patrolled by the Navy. The harbor entrance would be staked or buoyed. Only small, shallow draft ships could get in there.

Townsend nodded, knowing full well by the determined look on the man's face that this was not the only matter he wanted to discuss. Townsend sensed something purposeful in the Spaniard's hooded gaze. After a long silence,

Don Pedro told him there had been some important developments since they had last spoken. Townsend feared the worst, and his hand slowly reached into his coat pocket to find his gun.

"We caught him," Don Pedro said. "The Englishman. The same man who you helped to escape from El Morro, the English spy."

"Michael Abbott?"

"Yes, *ese hijo de puta*. That same son of a bitch! He was in disguise, pretending to be an interested investor in Cuban sugar plantations. He came to Don Eugenio's estate, calling himself Rupert Bascombe, asking a lot of questions about English-speaking slaves. At first Don Eugenio was intrigued, because as you know he prides himself on his slaves, but this Englishman began asking about the Backhouse case. That's when Don Eugenio grew concerned."

"Why didn't he confront the man?" Townsend asked.

"The Englishman ran off, and took Don Eugenio's personal house servant with him. You may remember him, Javier Alfonso."

"Yes, the servant in the library, who spoke English."

Don Pedro nodded.

"Yes, that traitor. For Don Eugenio, Javier Alfonso's disloyalty was a bitter blow. They took a valuable book from his library. Don Eugenio set the dogs after them, and they caught them just before they were about to board a train for Havana."

"Are you certain this man is Michael Abbott?"

"Quite certain. It took a little effort, but he confessed. It seems he is a detective who is linked in with the London Anti-Slavery Society. He was sent here to find out more about the Backhouse case. The authorities are most interested in discovering who his associates are on the island."

Townsend feigned indifference.

"Any ideas?" Don Pedro asked.

"About what?" Townsend asked, his lower lip twitching slightly.

"Who his contacts are on the island?"

Townsend shook his head.

There was a heavy silence in the carriage as they rumbled along the Calzada de Belascoaín Boulevard at the outer edge of Havana.

"I'm truly surprised about that Englishman," Townsend finally said as he turned toward Don Pedro. "I never thought he could have survived. I saw him get knifed in the stomach."

Don Pedro remained silent.

"Where are they being held?"

"A safe place," Don Pedro replied tersely, "a place where they can be dis-creetly interrogated without any possibility of escape. We will soon find out who Abbott's associates are on the island, all of them."

Townsend said nothing at first, finally breaking the silence after a few moments.

"What do you think will happen to them?"

Don Pedro at first didn't answer, but then he mumbled a reply.

"*Sólo lo que se merecen.* Only what they deserve."

After a half an hour drive, they arrived at a circular two-storied framed building at the Campo de Peñalver on the far outskirts of Havana. Townsend could hear the raucous shouting and cheering from inside. With the audible roar of the crowds, Don Pedro seemed to become more animated, and quickly got out of the covered carriage. The Spaniard began telling him about the finer points of cockfighting and how in Cuba the custom was to either put detachable spurs on the birds or to sharpen the natural spurs, all to make the fight deadlier and quicker. Inside the building, Townsend came face to face with an enclosed ring filled with sawdust where two men held fighting roosters in their bloody hands. One of the birds, a small one, was already blinded by an injury to its eye from the first round, and the handler was wiping the blood from its head, and then squirting some rum into its eyes.

Townsend looked up in the stands at hundreds of leering faces, people of all skin colors, black, white, yellow, and brown. This was clearly one of the few places where the races on the island were allowed to come together. He wondered if this would ever be the Cuba of the future, a place where people of every shade of color had the same rights, the same opportunities. Somehow he doubted that vision would be possible in the rigid structure of Spanish rule. As if he could read his mind, Don Pedro pointed to the mix of Chinese and Negroes in the crowds.

"Look around my friend. Cuba is an island of opportunity. The ones you see here are the lucky ones who have bought their freedom or completed their work term. Now trying their luck with *los gallos.* These lucky ones dream of winning here and earning enough to go home. They may not know it, but they will never leave this island. Lady luck has a fickle hand."

Don Pedro and Townsend took their seats on worn wooden benches. The men in the stands were shouting and making their bets. "Four to two on the blind one," someone yelled out in Spanish. The crowd roared its approval as the roosters were freed and went at each other again with a fury, clawing, nipping, flapping, and dodging.

The air was ripe with the smell of sweat, unwashed bodies and the vinegary odor of dirt and urine. There in the midst of the confusion, the shouting, the wagering, and the bloodlust of the crowd, Don Pedro explained why he liked the sport, because the winning birds won by stealth and speed.

"You see it has nothing to do with strength or size. It's about tactics and strategy. The small bird frequently prevails. It's like our schooners, isn't it, Captain? We run through the blockade against the big ships. They have the guns, but we still outsmart them."

The crowd roared as the two birds flew at each other in a violent flurry of feathers, lashing at each other with their spurs. The screams and shouts continued until one bird was dead. The owner of the triumphant fighting cock proudly held up the winner into the air to the cheers of the onlookers. The small, blind one had unexpectedly prevailed. Townsend looked forlornly at the crumpled heap of bloody feathers in the center of the circle. Such a cruel sport.

The fighting seemed to calm Don Pedro. He was quiet and melancholy, concentrating on the pit and smoking his cigar. Then his head jerked up at the sight of someone in the crowd, and he beckoned to the man. "Ah, Manuel. Por fin has aparecido. Ven aquí. It's Manuel," Don Pedro said with a smile. "My personal cigar roller."

Townsend felt a cold chill run down his spine as he recognized the familiar figure of the man he'd met with Savage in the belfry tower of the cathedral. This couldn't be a coincidence. The dry taste of fear and panic exploded in his mouth even as his mind quickly began to assess his situation. Manuel must have informed on him. He knew he should run. Don Pedro must know everything about his spying for Savage. His face felt flushed. He couldn't think clearly. He was trapped.

The crowd was once again yelling out their bets as people came back and took their seats in the stands. He heard someone shout to "clear the pit." Another cockfight would soon begin. Townsend took off his linen coat and folded it over his left arm as Manuel got closer. With his left hand he felt for the Colt pistol, his thumb strategically placed over the hammer. He could feel Don Pedro's eyes on him as he introduced his ship captain to Manuel.

"Captain, I want you to meet my good friend Manuel Escobar, one of Cuba's finest cigar rollers. He's bringing me some of my specialty cigars."

Townsend nodded and shook hands with the Cuban even as he pretended not to recognize him. Manuel, his stare both piercing and solemn, also revealed no overt sign of recognition, but Townsend thought he detected a subtle signal between him and Don Pedro. It was something in the way the man's eyes blinked. He was certain he had been discovered. *The cigar roller,* he thought to himself. Who would have imagined that this simple-looking Cuban, who had been so deferential to Savage, was actually a double agent. He saw Don Pedro momentarily glower as he turned from Manuel back to Townsend, the Spaniard's fake, lazy smile almost immediately returning.

"You already know Manuel, I believe?" he asked Townsend with an insouciant tone of voice that was at odds with the Spaniard's menacing stare.

"No, I don't believe I do," Townsend replied.

"Oh, I see. I just thought the way you were looking at each other. I thought you might have recognized each other. I guess I was mistaken."

Don Pedro was already beckoning to someone else across the pit. Townsend could see the man coming toward him. Just the man's aggressive posture told Townsend he had to act quickly. He grabbed Don Pedro by the arm.

"I need to talk with you now," he whispered in his ear. "It's urgent."

"What about?" Don Pedro asked, clearly taken by surprise.

"It's about Manuel," Townsend said with mock seriousness. His imploring eyes implied he had sensitive information to tell Don Pedro. "There's something you should know about him. It's important."

Don Pedro seemed reluctant at first but then, still somewhat uncertain, walked with Townsend away from the pit. Townsend kept his right hand firmly on the handle of the Colt pistol. He brought the long barrel, hidden in the coat pocket, closer to Don Pedro.

"What is it you want to tell me?" Don Pedro asked. "Some problem with Manuel?"

"Yes," replied Townsend. He shoved the gun into Don Pedro's waist, causing the Spaniard to gasp audibly.

Townsend whispered to him. "Yes, it's a pistol, a Colt pistol, .36 caliber. At this range it should blow your insides apart. Tell Manuel, your two-headed snake, he can go away now. And whoever the other monkey is, you can tell him you were mistaken. Everything is fine. You do not need him anymore."

Don Pedro waved them both away. He was practically spitting as he hissed at Townsend.

"You disappoint me."

"I'm sorry you feel that way, Don Pedro," Townsend replied in a hushed whisper. For some reason, with the gun in his hand he felt calm. Any fear had disappeared. He had a score to settle with this man. He wanted revenge.

"We're going to walk out of the cockpit fighting arena together, slowly and calmly, and then get into your carriage. I want no protest, no cry for help. I hope you understand I won't hesitate to shoot."

"Where will we be going?" Don Pedro asked, his ever-present, condescending smile returning.

"To the docks," Townsend replied. "I will tell you where."

31

Like a dutiful priest holding a bible under his vestments, Townsend held the hidden Colt pistol with the hammer half cocked under his crumpled linen coat. He walked alongside Don Pedro, keeping the barrel of the gun aimed directly at the man's midsection. They passed a long line of private carriages, and clusters of *volantas* for hire. Don Pedro walked with his head erect, looking straight ahead, his face guarded and secretive.

"It makes me sad, you know."

"What makes you sad?" Townsend snapped back.

"Your betrayal," Don Pedro replied. "I trusted you, Townsend. I saw great potential in you. I refused to believe Salazar when he said you were a spy. He said he suspected your whole crew was contaminated. I should have known he was right."

Townsend said nothing. He looked over at Don Pedro's sallow, pockmarked face which now had a deep crease between his eyebrows.

"I knew something strange was going on when you were spotted first at the cathedral and then buying lottery tickets," the Spaniard continued. "I see you are surprised. Yes, I had several men following you. Even before you returned from Matamoros, I suspected something, but I must admit I never thought you might be spying for the Americans, not until Manuel came forward, and told me where the US acting consul general, Mr. Savage, was getting his intelligence from."

Townsend was silent. He knew all too well what this meant. Townsend spotted Don Pedro's postilion. He shoved the gun's barrel into Don Pedro's side as a reminder that he wouldn't hesitate to shoot.

"Tell your servant we are going to the docks. I will tell you where to stop when we get closer."

The Spaniard's face remained impassive, but the stiffness of his neck and his rigid jaw conveyed his sentiments.

"*Al muelle,*" Don Pedro said to the postilion who was standing next to the lead horse.

"*Sí l'amo,*" the man replied. "*Vamos al muelle.*"

Don Pedro looked smugly at Townsend as the postilion closed the door of the covered carriage. Townsend instructed Don Pedro to tell the driver to take the longer coastal route along the Calzada de San Lázaro. They were headed for the docks by the ferry landing where Townsend hoped he would find his crew on board the scow schooner. He calculated it would take them twenty minutes. Townsend could see the postilion crack his whip high in the air, and he fell back on his seat as the carriage suddenly lurched forward.

Townsend glared at Don Pedro. "Now tell me where you are holding Abbott and Javier Alfonso."

Don Pedro, who was gazing out at groves of palm trees off to the left, paused for a few seconds before he answered.

"By now they should both be on board the ship."

"What ship?"

"You surprise me, Townsend. The *María Guadalupe*, of course. I'm sure you've noticed the big ship in the harbor getting resupplied with coal and cargo. Well-guarded too, I might add. From Manuel's description of your conversation with Mr. Savage, I gather you know quite a bit about this ship, and my dealings with our Southern clients. You see it was a relief to me that our hospitable Confederate friends were kind enough to offer us a safe house in one of their cabins on board. It has made it considerably easier for Salazar and Nolo to question these two abolitionist saboteurs, and naturally it offers a convenient method of disposal."

"You son of a bitch!" Townsend cried out. "*¡Hijo de puta!*"

Don Pedro sneered at Townsend.

"I'm glad to see you are improving your Spanish, Townsend. In fact, let me just say that your accent has improved. You could be Cuban. But perhaps you are right, disposal is too crude a word. I'm sure there are better words to express myself, but as you can imagine, the Spanish authorities want this man Abbott to be dealt with in the most inconspicuous way. He escaped once, as you well know. The authorities don't want to risk that happening again."

Townsend gripped the pistol handle tighter, and lightly touched the metal trigger with his finger. He'd never killed a man before, but as he looked at Don Pedro he knew he was capable of it. He thought about how little this man had revealed about himself. He was like a sphinx, the near-constant smile, his studied silences and his leering glances. He was sickeningly adept at manipulating others. He was as malevolent as he was repugnant.

"Who are you? You and your two vile thugs. Why are you so involved with this case?"

"I am simply a patriotic Spaniard, *siempre fiel*, forever faithful, who wants to serve his country on the island of Cuba. Is that something difficult for you to understand, Captain Townsend? Faithfulness, and loyalty."

"Enough of your bunkum, Don Pedro," Townsend said as he shoved the gun's barrel into the man's stomach. "No more of your worthless bullshit. What have you done? Who are you working with?"

"I suppose it is fair to describe me as someone certain people call whenever sensitive issues must be tended to in a more discreet manner." Don Pedro's cat-like smile returned. "I deal with matters that others would rather not be associated with."

"So you are some kind of enforcer, like those *rancheadores* in the country with their dogs, paid to run down runaway slaves. You do the dirty work even the police don't want to do."

"That's a crude description. I would put it differently. I prefer to think of myself as a problem solver for the government and the planters. My unique skills have given me many useful connections in places of influence and power. Open doors, my friend. To do well in business you must not only have important friends in high places, but they must owe you favors."

"Is that how you put my father in jail under false charges, all those years ago? You called your connections in high places to jail an innocent man?"

Don Pedro's left eyebrow cocked upward.

"My, my," exclaimed Don Pedro. "You are *un gallo de pelea bravo*, a feisty fighting rooster, aren't you? I didn't know how much you were aware of your family's shared history with me. I suppose your grandmother has been confiding in you."

"I know what you did, and I know why you did it," Townsend growled. "You wanted to get rid of my father so you could take over Mon Bijou. My poor mother was just a means to an end, wasn't she? You have lied to me from the beginning. Nothing that comes out of your mouth is the truth."

Don Pedro tensed up, his voice now bristling with hostility. "You have learned some of the serpentine ways of doing business in Cuba, I see. I may have taught you more than I realized. Yes, it's much easier to become rich by marrying into a fortune than by working for it. I thought Mon Bijou would be mine long ago. As I am sure your grandmother must have told you, I was engaged to be married to your mother. We were *una pareja comprometida*. Sadly fate went in another direction. Your mother ran away and eloped with your father, and with that went my chances to own the plantation. My dream of owning a sugar estate was lost, but then in a wonderful twist of fate so many years later you fell right into my hands. It was as if it was meant to be. I could hardly believe my good fortune."

The familiar, ever-present smile now returned to Don Pedro's face.

"When I learned from the captain general the name of the ship captain they were holding for further questioning, I was quite astonished. It was relatively easy to persuade him to release you. The authorities were concerned that Abbott might have accomplices. The captain general wanted you watched in case Abbott or any of his informants on the island tried to contact you. The police weren't sure whether Abbott was dead or not."

Don Pedro pursed his lips. "But I have to admit there were other more personal reasons I wanted you freed from prison."

"Which were?"

"For one thing, I knew your grandmother would be forever grateful to me. She would be in my debt. I also realized you would be useful to me as a ship captain. You could make me some money. But do you know what my biggest incentive was?"

The Spaniard paused, his mouth contorting into a twisted grin. "My biggest reason was revenge. I wanted to have you in my power. Your mother hurt me terribly, you see, and I have not forgotten that embarrassment. Fate, it seems, intended for the two of us to be intertwined, at least for a short while. So for all these months I have entertained our business partnership. I must say it has been profitable having you work for me, but now our arrangement must come to an end. You might as well put the gun down, Captain. It's useless."

Townsend stared long and hard at Don Pedro. "Why do you say that?"

"Because if you shoot me, the sound of the gun will bring police."

"Why should I care? You want me dead whatever happens. I might as well take you with me. If I kill you first, you won't have the satisfaction of knowing what happened to me."

A brooding silence hung over the two men like a dead calm settling in over a sailboat. The windows were open and the hot, dust-laden air filled Townsend's lungs. The heat was making his hands sweat, and he could feel his wet palm slip over the pistol's grip. Don Pedro's arrogance only served to stiffen his resolve.

"When does the ship leave harbor?"

"Quite soon. Just after dusk I believe. As you know from experience, that's the best time to avoid the Union blockaders. They're loading the last of the cargo now. The new crewmembers are already on board, all loyal Confederates. Soon that steamer will leave the harbor and disappear. The Captain of the Port has been instructed to record nothing about this ship. The arrival and the departure of the *María Guadalupe* from Havana Bay will be an illusion, a shadow, nothing but a dream."

Don Pedro cocked his head to one side to get a better look at Townsend's face. "If you are thinking of trying something foolish, my friend, I would advise you to forget about Mr. Abbott and the English slave, and worry about your own safety. You do realize there is no way for you or your men to escape from this island. The harbor police, the *Guardia Civil*. They're all looking for you and your men now."

They were on the north shore road, clattering along the boulevard that looked out at the blue-green Gulf Stream. He was trying to decide what his next move would be.

"Tell your man to take us to the landing just beyond the ferry docks at the *Muelle de Luz*. We have another ten minutes before we arrive. Why don't you tell me about your involvement with the murder of George Backhouse? Did you kill him?"

Don Pedro smirked and then laughed.

"What makes you think I had anything to do with the Backhouse murder?"

"If not you, who was it then? Was it slave traders? Zulueta? He certainly had a motive, revenge against the English for forcing the Spanish authorities here to put him in jail."

Don Pedro glowered at Townsend, but said nothing. Townsend pressed on like a prosecutor summarizing his case.

"Or was it your good friend, the fishmonger-slaver, Pancho Marty? He also had motive, didn't he? He was angered by Backhouse's interference in his slaving ventures and his investigation of the *emancipados*? Perhaps it was Don Eugenio Hernández, your patron? Or should I call him your father, as I hear you are his bastard son. Maybe he was worried that Backhouse would try to free his English slaves? Which one of your business associates was it? Perhaps it was all of them. A grand conspiracy by the shareholders of *La Compañía*."

"You are quite the Grand Inquisitor and prosecutor aren't you, Townsend," Don Pedro sneered. "I see you have formed some strong opinions. That is quite an indictment of the island of Cuba, and an insult to the highly respected individuals you just mentioned—not to mention an affront to me personally."

"Which one was it, Don Pedro? No matter who it was, the trail leads back to you. That much I am sure of."

The Spaniard paused to look out the window as the carriage glided by the massive walls of La Punta fortress and entered the old city gates.

"Even if I did know something, I have nothing to gain in telling you, Townsend. You're not even English. What do you care about Backhouse, that *gusano sinvergüenza*, meddling, shameless worm that he was. George Backhouse has been forgotten by his own government and his countrymen. He is nothing anymore. I repeat. He is nothing. His death is ancient history, one of Havana's many unsolved murders. So I ask, why are you so curious?"

Townsend ignored Don Pedro's question. "Was it his journal? Is that what Abbott took from Don Eugenio's library?"

"How perceptive of you, Townsend. You have good instincts. Yes, the book the Englishman took from Don Eugenio was indeed the journal. After it was taken from the Backhouse residence that night eight years ago, it was put in Don Eugenio's library by me for safekeeping. I gave it to him as a gift, *un obsequio*, a kind of trophy. And now that you have guessed the importance of the journal, I suppose I might as well tell you the rest as you'll never leave this island alive. It's a wonderful story filled with irony. You see, Backhouse's own notes in his journal helped gain the freedom of his murderers."

Townsend stared at the Spaniard with a puzzled look.

"Let me explain," Don Pedro replied, his face now revealing a certain pride and satisfaction. "Backhouse's journal contained the names of plantations and planters who were holding freed slaves. Also some of the English-speaking slaves, many of whom had been kidnapped. Some of the owners were the wealthiest patriarchs on the island. Not only that, but he had compiled a complete record of the level of corruption from the captain general down. This was quite a complete record, local officials, mayors of all the coastal towns, priests, Spanish navy captains, governors of the various provinces, all paid to look the other way. All of this would have been very embarrassing to Spain as well as to some very important and wealthy people here."

"A damning document."

"Yes, indeed. Both the journal and an accompanying folder were filled with names. It was quite a surprise. All of these were notes he'd made, intended no doubt to be used in a letter to be sent to the Foreign Office in London."

"How did the assailants know where to find it?"

"A disgruntled former employee of the British Consulate."

"You mean Dalrymple, his former clerk? He betrayed Backhouse?"

"Yes. Dalrymple, a useful idiot. He bore a grudge against Backhouse for firing him. He was a gambler and owed a great deal of money to Pancho Marty. Dalrymple couldn't pay up so instead, as payment, he offered Don Pancho information on Backhouse's journal. He told them where to find it and how and when to get into the house."

"But why did they need to kill Backhouse?"

"That was indeed unfortunate. The hired men who broke into the house were under orders to rough him up, and then steal the journal. He was supposed to be beaten. Beaten badly enough so he would want to leave the island for the safety of his family. It was supposed to look like a robbery. Unfortunately Backhouse struggled with his attackers, and the hired man used his knife."

"So what was your role Don Pedro?"

"Like I said, I was the problem-solver. I was asked to make this awkward situation go away."

"By whom?"

"Some highly important individuals here in Cuba, men of power and influence."

"And?"

"I began by reading Backhouse's journal from beginning to end, and I found something quite unexpected. It seems Mr. Backhouse, principled man that he was, not only had been documenting the illicit money trail of the slave trade, he had also been investigating the extensive English ties to slavery here in Cuba. He even had a rough draft of a letter he was planning on sending back to the Foreign Office to Lord Clarendon himself."

"What did it say?"

"He wrote how it troubled him to report that British private money was all too evident in Cuba to aid and assist the export of slave-grown sugar. He felt that this should be looked into, as it was squarely in conflict with Britain's long-held opposition to slavery and slave trading."

"I see," Townsend said. "And this was never sent?"

"Apparently not."

"No doubt, you brought this to the attention of Mr. Crawford."

"How perceptive of you, Townsend. Yes, I read all of this to the British consul general, and my candor was not appreciated. I pointed out to him that making relations more tense with Spain would not serve England's interests. He asked what I was proposing. I gently suggested that if England did not cooperate, I might have no recourse but to take Backhouse's journal to the members of the press. Imagine the headlines, I said. 'The murdered Backhouse speaks from the grave, condemns England for helping to finance slavery.' I read him other portions of Backhouse's draft letter to Lord Clarendon, which I warned him were quite personal."

"How so?"

"Backhouse wrote that 'it pained him to report to his Lordship that, in his mind, Mr. Crawford, while diligent in performing such duties as the reporting of sightings of slave ships, may over his many years of service in Havana have become too appeasing to some of the wealthy interests on the island.'"

Townsend's eyes opened wide. "A personal attack on Crawford! How was that received?"

"By then, Crawford lost all control. He called me a Spanish pirate, *hijo de puta*, son of a whore, and threatened to kick me out of his offices. What do you want, he finally asked, and I told him. Spain wants England to acknowledge that the unfortunate tragic death of Mr. Backhouse is declared the work of thieves, an unsolvable crime. England will promise to withhold any formal protest when the police release the suspects for insufficient evidence. In short, the matter will be closed. So you see, Captain, that's how the problem was resolved. It was Backhouse's own words and his diligent research that ironically provided the key to free his murderers."

"So that was it," Townsend said. "You used extortion to outwrestle the English. It was a cover-up."

"I would prefer to say that England and Spain both agreed that there were some mutual interests that needed to be hidden from the glare of the press and the public. Mr. Crawford tried to demand the return of Backhouse's journal, but I told him that would not be possible. It was safely in private hands. And indeed it was in safe keeping in Don Eugenio's library until that troublesome Mr. Abbott came along. His appearance upset a goodly number of people. No one imagined that Don Eugenio's trusted personal servant would betray him."

Don Pedro took a deep breath, and paused a moment.

"But now it gives me great relief to know that once again the journal has been restored to a safe place in a library where it can gather cobwebs and dust away from enquiring eyes."

Townsend hated to admit it, but part of him had to admire Don Pedro's cunning. He took a quick look out the window. They were now in the old city clattering down Oficios Street. They would soon be passing the Plaza de San Francisco and the main landing area.

"You still haven't answered a most important question," Townsend said. "Who ordered the attack on Backhouse?"

"I am afraid, my friend, I have told you enough. I can't give you names. Suffice to say, an important decision like that is not made by one person. You seem to have grasped far more than I realized. You have been busy during your short stay here in Cuba. But there is one thing, Townsend, that I can tell you. Besides Abbott and the slave, we also are holding a young woman involved in this case. Someone you know, I believe."

Townsend felt a sudden surge of panic. His face became swollen and hot. His breathing quickened.

"Yes, I believe you are well-acquainted with her," Don Pedro said, his face lighting up. "Salazar and Nolo were supposed to pick her up today. They are taking her to the ship. Perhaps she's there already. I believe her name is Miss Emma Carpenter."

Townsend's heart pounded.

"We would have picked her up earlier, but it took me some time to find out who the mysterious young lady was. It was only after considerable effort that Mr. Abbott divulged her name under visible duress. It appears he was hoping she would help in his escape. I'm afraid you will never see her again. Such a shame. Quite a handsome young woman. My Southern clients have been most accommodating in agreeing to take her with them when the ship leaves this evening."

Townsend was speechless.

"I don't know what I would do in your predicament, Townsend. Perhaps if you turn yourself in and give us the whereabouts of your crew, I can find some way to lessen your suffering. We also need to know the other contacts Mr. Abbott had on the island. Abbott did divulge a priest, but it appears he gave us a false name."

32

Townsend tried to control his rage, but he couldn't. He grabbed Don Pedro by the throat and shoved the pistol hard into the man's stomach. The thought of Emma's predicament was too awful for him to contemplate. As for Abbott and Javier Alfonso, they might not even be alive. It sounded like they'd been brutally tortured, no doubt by Salazar and Nolo.

"Say your prayers, Don Pedro."

His finger pressed against the trigger. He could feel the man flinch and squirm. He started to squeeze, but just then the postilion cried out.

"*Hemos llegado, l'amo, al Muelle de Luz. We have arrived, Master, at the Luz landing. Sooooo. Esperan, esperan.*"

The postilion continued to talk reassuringly to the horses as the carriage's wheels shimmied to a stop. Townsend released his grip on Don Pedro's throat and let out a deep breath. He realized how close he had come to pulling the trigger.

There was no sign of the scow schooner anywhere, and no sign of any of his crew at the landing. Townsend told a fearful Don Pedro they were getting out here, and he should order his driver to go back to his warehouse in the Barrio Chino.

"Here?" Don Pedro asked with a slight tone of uncertainty. "Where are we going?"

"We're going to take a boat trip across the harbor to Regla," Townsend replied. "You and I are going to have a tour of that steamship."

"I see," said Don Pedro with a barely disguised hint of satisfaction.

285

Townsend looked over across the harbor at the deep-water Regla docks where the Mexican-flagged Confederate steamer was tied up. Black clouds of smoke billowed from the ship's raked-back funnel. The ship was clearly ready to make a quick departure. He gulped as he thought of Emma and the other two captives on board. He tried to imagine the horror and fear they were experiencing, and that helped him focus.

"Are you going to continue to hold me at gunpoint, Captain?"

"You're my hostage, Don Pedro. If you give out a warning, I'm happy to kill you."

Don Pedro didn't reply, and stepped out of the carriage with Townsend close behind. They both watched the driver and the carriage clatter away on the cobblestones, headed toward the old wall and the *Barrio Chino*. Townsend pushed Don Pedro forward with one hand even as he fought off a wave of panic. He looked around at the shabby fleet of harbor boats and fishing boats at the Luz landing, and headed for the ones with less blistered paint. Sweat was pouring down his back. His shirt was soaked. He knew what he was contemplating was sheer folly. It was not so much a plan as it was the lack of one. A rescue might be feasible if his crew had shown up, but he saw no sign of the scow schooner anywhere. He was alone. In the back of his mind he wondered if the other sailors had just decided to take the boat and leave without him. He shook his head to try to banish that thought.

As they approached the last harbor boat, Don Pedro seemed to recover his composure and he asked Townsend what he thought he could accomplish.

"For your grandmother's sake, why don't you give yourself up? You need to think what you can do to save yourself."

Townsend wanted to pull the trigger and be done with this man, but he kept that violent impulse in check. He knew that he alone offered the only thin strand of hope left for Emma. He needed to keep a cool head. He ignored Don Pedro as the man continued talking.

"If the police capture you, they will no doubt imprison you in El Morro, torture you, and then kill you. If the Confederates seize you, they will accuse you of being a Yankee spy, and probably hang you from the yards while at sea. It's useless, Townsend. It's over."

Townsend glared at Don Pedro with a hateful stare. With his folded coat still covering the pistol, the young captain kept the barrel tightly pressed into Don Pedro's lower back, right where his kidneys were. He approached one of the boatmen he thought he recognized, and hired the man to take them over to Regla as quickly as possible. They both stepped into the boat and they were about to leave the docks when Townsend heard his name being called out in Spanish. Someone wanted him to wait.

"*¡Espere, Capitán. Espere!*"

A chill went down his spine, his body tensing up. His hand clutched the pistol more tightly. He was about to order the boatman to cast off and row away, but then he saw a shirtless, barefoot Negro boy running toward him. It was Rafi, the homeless street urchin who had given him Emma's message before. He was waving his arms. Townsend told the boatman to wait.

"*¿Qué pasa, Rafi?* What is it?" Townsend asked as soon as the boy arrived, breathless and winded.

Rafi hesitated, looking with suspicion at Don Pedro before speaking.

"La señorita Carpenter . . ."

"What about her?" Townsend asked.

"*Venga, es urgente.* You must come. It's urgent."

"You've seen her. *¿La has visto?*"

The boy nodded.

"*¿Dónde está?* Where is she?"

Rafi explained she was just a block away in a covered carriage under a tree alongside the Alameda de Paula. She wanted to meet him there. Townsend felt a rush of emotions sweep over him like a freshening breeze rippling across the water. It was as if some miracle had just occurred. She was alive, and she wasn't a prisoner.

"I can't believe it," he blurted out. "Is she all right?"

He glanced over at Don Pedro whose face was glowering. He was not pleased to be foiled.

"*Venga conmigo, Capitán.* Come with me. I will take you."

Townsend told him to run ahead and tell her that he was on his way. As Rafi ran off, Townsend scanned the landing area for any signs of police. He paid off the boatman, and negotiated the purchase of the man's wide-brimmed palm hat and some rope. He and Don Pedro walked quickly down the road adjacent to the Alameda de Paula. Townsend's mouth was twitching with anger. Don Pedro had played him for a fool. He had used the lure of a captive Emma as a way to get him to the ship. It had been a trap Townsend had narrowly avoided.

"Your lies fall out of your mouth like dung balls from a donkey's ass, Don Pedro. I don't know what bit of hell was waiting for me on that ship, but I'm pleased I have disrupted your plans."

Don Pedro kept his reptilian gaze forward and refused to look at Townsend. When they reached the carriage, Townsend could see the shadowy form of Emma inside. His heart quickened. He scanned the area. The postilion was nowhere to be seen. No one else was around except a scattering of parked *volantas* for hire at the other end of the harborside promenade. When Emma spotted him, she smiled and raised her hand. She was about to get out of the carriage, but he signaled her to wait, turning and nodding his head toward Don Pedro. She had never met the Spaniard, but she knew who he was.

Townsend shoved Don Pedro forward with a jab of the gun. The Spaniard paused before he moved to take the step up into the carriage. He stumbled and fell, reaching for his ankle as if he'd hurt himself. Townsend leaned down to help him up, but then in one sudden fluid motion Don Pedro pulled out a small hidden knife from a leather sheath strapped to his lower leg, whirling around as he placed the double-edged blade against Emma's throat.

"¡No me jodas, Townsend!" the Spaniard hissed. "Don't play games with me. I will cut her throat. Now drop your gun."

Don Pedro pulled Emma to the opposite end of the carriage away from Townsend.

"Shoot him, Everett! Shoot him!" Emma screamed as she struggled to get free.

Don Pedro jerked her head back with a wrenching motion.

"One slice and she will bleed out, Townsend."

The Spaniard pressed the blade of the knife against Emma's throat causing her to gasp, her eyes filling with terror. Townsend held the pistol firmly, still hidden under his coat. His face was pounding. He blinked in hesitation. He realized how powerless he was.

"Drop the pistol, Townsend," Don Pedro repeated with a satisfied sneer. He pointed with his free hand at the carriage seat. "Put it right here beside me, and then step away."

Townsend was about to comply when he spotted Rafi out of the corner of his eye on the other side of the carriage. The boy was signaling with his hands that he would open the carriage door. He was pointing at Don Pedro whose back was leaning up against the door. Townsend needed to think quickly.

"Do it now," Don Pedro ordered. "I will cut her."

Townsend saw a trickle of blood travel down Emma's neck. Without thinking, he shouted out in Spanish so Rafi could hear him.

"Don't harm her, Don Pedro! Before I do as you wish and give myself up, you should know one thing."

"What is that?"

"My men are looking for me right now at this very place."

"¡Pura mierda! That's bullshit," the irate Spaniard exclaimed.

"Over here, Red Beard," Townsend suddenly shouted, beckoning with his head as he looked over at Rafi. "I'm over here, Bertrand."

Somehow the boy recognized his cue. He yanked open the door of the carriage, causing Don Pedro to fall back and twirl around to see who the unknown intruder was. Townsend reached inside the carriage, knocking the knife from the man's hands even as he pulled Emma outside to safety. Snarling and cursing, Don Pedro turned and hurled himself at Townsend, reaching for his throat and hauling him back inside the carriage.

The Spaniard grabbed the fallen knife off the floor and wildly swung it upwards toward Townsend's torso. Townsend brushed it aside, using his coat as a shield, but Don Pedro leapt up and thrust the sharp knife again. This time it stuck something solid. Townsend grunted and fell backwards. Don Pedro threw his weight forward and drove the blade into his target as far as he could. But Townsend recovered quickly. The blade had found its mark in the thick navigation book inside his coat.

Don Pedro pulled the blade out and drew the knife back over his head to strike again. Townsend slammed the heavy handle of the Colt pistol into his jaw. Before Don Pedro could react, Townsend hit him again, hard on the top of his head, not once but twice, causing the Spaniard to fall backwards onto the carriage seat. Townsend hardly knew what he was doing. He struck him again. He had lost control. He might have continued beating the unconscious man with his pistol if it weren't for Emma. She pulled him out of the carriage.

Townsend backed away, breathing heavily. He put his hands over his face. Emma reached out to comfort him, He hugged her, letting her embrace calm his rushing blood. Once he caught his breath, he took the rope, tying up Don Pedro's wrists behind his back, and then tightly binding his ankles. He tore some pages from the navigation book, rolled them up, and stuffed the large ball of paper into Don Pedro's mouth. He then blindfolded the unconscious man by tying his bandana tightly over his eyes.

Some pedestrians had stopped and were looking in their direction. Townsend pulled Rafi aside and whispered something to him. The boy darted off, and Townsend started crying out. "¡Ladrón! ¡Ladrón! Thief! ¡Deténganlo! Stop him!" The attention of all the passers-by was soon directed away from Townsend and Emma toward the disappearing boy.

Townsend drew Emma into his arms again as he gave a quiet thanks. She responded by hugging him tightly.

"I am so glad you are safe," he whispered. When he looked at Emma's teary eyes and stricken face, he knew there was something else deeply wrong.

"What is it?" he asked.

"Abbott," she said in a hushed whimper.

"What about Abbott? Is he . . ."

"Yes, he's dead. And so is the other man. They killed them both."

"How do you know for sure they're dead?"

"The consul general told me last night. He came to the boarding house. A Union spy on board that Confederate ship, one of the engineers, spotted Abbott and Javier Alfonso being brought on board as prisoners. He told the consul general that he overheard the Confederate captain speaking to the Spaniard with pale blue eyes."

"That would be Salazar," Townsend seethed.

"The Spaniard told the captain the two prisoners were dead. The Confederate captain assured him the bodies would be thrown overboard as soon as the ship reached international waters."

Townsend closed his eyes, his chin resting on Emma's head. He felt a sudden sadness, and a deep, speechless helplessness.

The sound of church bells announcing the top of the hour made Townsend snap to attention. The bells had tolled four times.

"It's four o'clock. I have to escape from here," he blurted out as his eyes darted from left to right. "I have to go."

"I know," she said.

"You are in danger as well. You do know that, don't you?"

"Thankfully Savage warned me in time," she replied. "His spy told him I was in danger. I went to St. Augustine's to warn Padre Uribe, and he insisted I stay there. I guess it was lucky I did leave the boarding house since they must have been looking for me. I met with Savage again this morning, and he told me about getting your note. That's how I knew I would find you here."

"Where is the padre now? They're looking for him too."

"He has gone into hiding."

There was silence as they both pondered their predicament, and then Emma nodded her head in the direction of the unconscious Don Pedro.

"What are we going to do with him?" Emma asked.

Townsend thought for a second.

"I should throw him in Havana Bay for the sharks. That's what this lizard would have done with me. What do you think?"

Emma thought for a moment, and then whispered coldly. "That might be too good for him. Let's have the driver take Don Pedro to the shantytown."

"You mean, off the Calzada de Jesús del Monte amidst all the mud hovels?"

"Yes, right there. Dump him in some heap of roadside rubbish," she said. "He is a monster and deserves much worse. Perhaps the starving dogs can be his judge. I imagine he will be lucky to come out of there alive or without serious injury."

Townsend nodded his head, and mumbled almost to himself. "It's probably a fate he deserves."

As Townsend watched the carriage clip and clatter away from the harbor with the trussed-up Spanish merchant on the floor of the cab, he wondered if he would ever see that man again. Emma pulled her hair back and gazed up at him with a determined look. That's when he noticed a carpet bag at her feet. He looked down at her and saw her dress. It had an overskirt in front and a bustle draped at the back. The hemline just over the ankle was what caught his eye. The style of dress suggested she was planning on some kind of trip. So did the carpet bag. Her gaze lingered on him.

"I want you to take me with you." Emma stepped backwards, her features set.

"I want to go with you. I have a letter of introduction that Mr. Savage has written on my behalf to the head of the Navy in Key West, Admiral Theodorus Bailey. The letter mentions you and the crew. I also have a Stars and Stripes ensign Savage gave me. It's for you."

She reached down to the carpet bag and pulled out a neatly folded American flag.

"All of this sounds and looks like you've carefully planned it," he said with a smirk.

She simply nodded with a broad smile.

33

Townsend suddenly remembered the harbor boat of Junípero Díaz, and he grabbed Emma's hand. Amazingly the small boat he'd left behind earlier with its oars and small sail was still there at the landing, tied up where he had left it. He helped her on board and took out his telescope to scan the docks and the shipping in the port. Out toward the entrance of the harbor, he could see the Spanish navy patrol boats checking all vessels leaving the bay. There was no sign of the scow schooner or the crew. It was now past five o'clock. The sun was low on the horizon. He swung the telescope back to the central dock where several recently arrived blockade-running schooners were unloading cotton, and he could see the large numbers of police. Security was tighter than he'd ever seen.

He moved the telescope to the nearby ferry landing and almost fell backwards into the water. Through the lens, he came face-to-face with Salazar and Nolo, their mouths tight-lipped and their snake eyes darting from one side of the docks to the other. They were just a few hundred yards away, walking quickly and purposefully in his direction along with a number of plainclothes police officers.

"Get down, Emma," Townsend whispered in a panic.

"What is it?"

"It's that animal, Salazar. He's coming our way. Stay out of sight under the awning."

Emma scrambled to the forward section of the boat, adjusting her cumbersome bustle as she crouched under the awning. Townsend was about to push the boat off from the landing when the two Spaniards suddenly veered away to another dock and boarded a steam launch. Townsend pulled his wide-brimmed palm hat farther down on his head and lay flat on the bottom of the boat. He whispered to Emma to stay quiet. He could hear the launch's engine getting nearer, the paddlewheels chugging directly by them. He thought he could hear Salazar's voice describing who they were looking for. Townsend held his breath, fearful that at any moment they would be discovered, but the engine noise faded away.

After waiting for another ten minutes, Townsend poked his head over the gunwales of the harbor boat. He could just barely make out the smoke from the small steamer. He held the telescope up to his eye and watched as the steam launch tied up to the sides of the *Gaviota*. An explosion of sparkling sun reflections suddenly blinded him. He saw three or four silhouetted figures board the *Gaviota* with what looked like knives in their hands. He couldn't be sure, but the slender and stiff shape of one of the men looked like Salazar.

Just then, Emma hissed, "Hurry. We need to leave here. I think I see more police. They're searching the boats."

Townsend scrambled to get the oars ready and untie the docklines. He tore off his shirt so that he was bare-chested like so many of the other boatmen, and pulled his palm hat down firmly on his head. He pushed the boat off and grabbed the two oars, inserting them in the thole pins. He decided not to unfurl the sails. He didn't want to attract attention. Once out in the middle of the harbor, Townsend stopped rowing and swept the telescope to his right across the bay over the roofs of Regla's warehouses. It was then he spotted the bare poles of the scow schooner's two masts far off in the eastern section of Havana Bay. After rowing furiously, Townsend brought the small boat up alongside the scow schooner and called out to his crewmembers.

At first, the sailors didn't know who he was with his dirty palm leaf hat and his bare chest, and they told him to go away. They thought he was just another banana boat vendor. Townsend had to call out several times before Hendricks recognized him. Townsend scanned their faces to try to ascertain the mood. From their expressions, it seemed as if they had all weighed their choices and thrown their lot in with him. They knew they all had to leave Cuba. They had no choice.

"Did you get the sailor's bag I sent with the sextant and the chronometer?" Townsend asked.

"We got all of that," Higgins replied. "Even the cat." He gestured toward the boat's cabin. "What we was wondering 'bout are those two long-bladed Spanish knives. Care to tell us how you came by those?"

At that point, Townsend gave them a hurried description of what had happened to him since he'd last seen them. He was just getting to the part where he'd pulled a gun on Don Pedro at the cockfighting arena when he noticed their eyes straying way from him over to something on his right, directly behind him. He quickly swung his head around, prepared for the worst, only to come face-to-face with Emma. His frown turned to a warm smile. She had emerged from under the canopy, straightening her overskirt and bustle and was standing right behind him. Townsend sheepishly looked back at the other sailors.

"May I introduce you to Miss Emma Carpenter. Like all of us, she is in grave danger, and has requested safe passage to Key West."

Hendricks was the only one of the men who knew about her, so he showed little reaction, but the others, who were well used to "running up a woman with a glance" were leering at her with curious eyes. It was Bertrand who offered Emma a hand to come aboard.

"*Bienvenue*. Welcome on board Miss Carpenter. This is the *Vírgen Gorda*."

Emma stood there speechless as she took measure of the boat she had agreed to sail on. Even Townsend gulped as he realized how basic this vessel was. The scow schooner was little more than half the size of the *Gaviota*, and most of the stern area was covered by a large square deckhouse just aft of the main mast. What alarmed him most was that the stubby ship's rail was just three feet off the water. The only consolation was that she was fully decked, and her rigging with a mainsail, foresail, and a jib appeared to be intact.

Townsend could tell that Emma was having second thoughts. He hadn't told her much of anything about the boat. He immediately took her inside the deckhouse, which seemed to make matters worse. The inside of the cabin was nothing more than a roofed shack that had been built over the deck.

"This is not what I expected," Emma said simply.

"What's the matter?" he asked. He had to admit, the cabin was sparser than he had imagined, ten feet by fifteen feet. There were only two small windows, a small iron stove in one corner, and four stacked bunks on the other side.

"There is no privacy for a woman. Where am I going to sleep?"

"Don't worry," Townsend said as he tried to console her. "As soon as we get out of the harbor, I will fashion a private area. Maybe use some old sails. The men will sleep outside on the decks."

Emma walked around the cabin, tight lipped with a brave smile, but said nothing. Townsend looked around the space as if he could somehow improve it.

"Well, at least there are two lanterns," she finally said. "I won't have to sit here in the dark."

Townsend took one look at the two gimbaled lanterns attached to the walls and he rushed over to smell them. It was what he thought. The beginnings of a plan began forming in his mind of how they might get out of the harbor. He told Emma to stay in the cabin, and he bolted onto the deck, shouting for Red Beard and Bertrand.

"Where are the ship's supplies?" he asked.

They took him forward past the smelly, fishy cargo hold to a small fo'c'sle that was used as the boat's storage area. He jumped inside and was soon taking inventory of what was there, bags of old tattered and worn sails that had been patched so many times they looked like they would tear with the slightest pull. He threw those sail bags on deck. There were crates filled with cordage, twine, and oakum and a replacement anchor. He spotted a couple of wooden sea buckets with lines attached to their handles, and he handed them to Bertrand. Suddenly he found what he was looking for, a large wooden barrel marked turpentine oil. The fisherman had used red paint to emphasize how flammable it was.

"What you aimin' to do now?" Red Beard asked. "This harbor is crawlin' with patrol boats. One of them will stop us for sure if we try to go out the channel."

The other sailors had gathered to see what Townsend was doing. They were all glum-faced and pessimistic.

"Even if we somehow get out of the harbor," Higgins groaned. "they'll probably come after us. This barge is slower than a lame mule. We can't possibly escape."

Townsend looked at the five sailors and explained his plan.

"Hendricks will come with me in the harbor boat," Townsend said. "That is if he's willing?"

Townsend took a hard look at Hendricks. He'd chosen him because he knew the Bahamian was the best sailor of the bunch, and unlike the others, the two of them could communicate without speaking. He wasn't sure if Hendricks would say yes—the plan was a dangerous one, filled with high risks.

"I ain' got no quarrel with that," Hendricks replied finally. "The onliest ting I know is the faster we get off this island the better."

Townsend nodded approvingly.

"The rest of you can row this whale barge back over toward Casa Blanca. Drop the anchor in the shallows at the Feliciano shoal area off the docks. There's only six feet of water there so it's not likely the patrol boats will bother you. Wait for us. No lights. We'll find you even though it will be dark. We won't be long once the commotion starts."

Townsend put the telescope to his eye and studied the heavily loaded Texas schooners he'd seen the night before, their decks piled high with cotton. His eye focused on the thick hemp anchor lines. He wanted to make sure the cables were hemp, not chain. He swiveled the glass to his left in the direction of the *Gaviota*. There was no trace of anyone on deck. Whoever had boarded the ship must be hidden below. Slowly he nudged the glass back following the shear of the ship until he reached the door into *Gaviota*'s main cabin house. A man was peering out. It was Salazar.

Townsend told Hendricks to tack the small boat back and forth away from the city lights until darkness fell. He wanted to stay hidden amid the anchored ships away from the docks. The breeze was blowing steadily from the southeast as Townsend had anticipated, and the small boat skipped across the rippled grooves of the water like a flying fish. Under the boat's awning, Townsend was busily soaking the old tattered and patched sails from the scow schooner in the barrel of turpentine. With Hendricks at the tiller, he poked his head over the gunwales. He noted with satisfaction that it had gotten dark quickly. Nightfall was not far off. Off to the right less than fifty yards away, he could see the familiar shape of the *Gaviota*, and the two other cotton schooners anchored next to her. Townsend pointed his finger at it, and Hendricks nodded. That was their target.

Both he and Hendricks closely studied the schooner as they sailed by. There was a dim light in the aft cabin house, but it was dark up forward. A five-foot-high wall of stacked cotton bales extended from the foremast all the way back to the mainmast, effectively separating the bow from the stern. With a subtle nod of his head, Townsend signaled to Hendricks to bring the boat into the wind, dropping the small sail at the same time.

The breeze and the slight current now carried them back toward the schooner, drifting slowly and silently in almost complete darkness. At a signal, Hendricks snagged the ship's anchor cable and pulled them in closer to the schooner's bow. Clasping the schooner's whisker shrouds with both hands, Townsend gingerly got off the small boat and stepped onto the schooner's bobstay. The taut large chain was a perfect near vertical walkway from the water up to the end of the bowsprit. Holding on to the whisker shrouds, he cautiously edged his way forward. He couldn't see anything. The blackness of the night had come more quickly than he'd expected. Suddenly his feet slipped off the chain, and Townsend found himself dangling over the water. He hung there for several haunting seconds looking up at the shadowy bowsprit above him before he was able to swing his feet back onto the chain.

Like a tightrope acrobat, Townsend inched his way upwards. Then with one hand he grabbed the secured canvas sails tied down on top of the bowsprit and pulled himself upwards. The faint sound of an accordion and a banjo drifted back from the stern of the ship, but Townsend couldn't see anything. Someone laughed on another boat. Frozen, his body molded into the sails. He waited for another minute, and then, straddling the bowsprit, he began wiggling his way toward the ship's bow.

Once he had a solid deck underneath his feet, Townsend looked down at the shadowy form below him in the harbor boat. He signaled with his hand and Hendricks threw him a line, the other side of which was tied to the turpentine-covered sails. Townsend hauled the turpentine-soaked canvas on deck. He stuffed the wet, tattered sail around the cotton bales, and then began hauling up sea buckets filled with turpentine oil from the harbor boat. He dumped the smelly liquid on top of the stacked bales of compressed cotton. The strong vapors were almost unbearable, making him lightheaded. He was woozy and dizzy, and he began to worry he might faint. There was no time to waste. He pulled out his box of Lucifer matches and struck one inside the turpentine-soaked wooden bucket and watched the flames quickly leap up. He stuffed a corner of the sails in the burning bucket, and then quickly crawled over the side of the schooner, sliding down the anchor line until he dropped into the harbor boat.

"Cut the line, Hendricks," Townsend said breathlessly.

Hendricks swiped his knife across the last remaining strand of the four-inch-thick hemp anchor cable, freeing the schooner to drift with the current. Pushing off into the darkness, they quickly raised the sail, and headed to windward away from the cluster of ships.

"We're in the shoals now," Townsend said in a hushed whisper. "It's all open water here. Let's head for the lights of Casa Blanca."

Townsend could see the orange flames flickering up at the bow of the drifting schooner. The turpentine-soaked sails were burning, but the cotton bales had yet to catch fire. The big schooner was now floating down on the *Gaviota*, pushed along by that southeasterly breeze. As they sailed over the shallows, Townsend looked back and saw the midships section of the Texas cotton schooner suddenly burst into a ball of flame. The cotton cargo had finally erupted into a roaring bonfire. The harbor filled with the popping and crackling of burning wood along with much shouting and yelling and screams of alarm. The stern of the burning schooner, now adrift, hit the anchor cable of the *Gaviota* and soon the two boats had swung together, their rigging becoming entangled. The flames spread quickly to all the furled sails, flickering up the masts like an uncontrollable wildfire.

Townsend brought the telescope to his eye and trained it on the *Gaviota*'s decks. The light from the intense flames lit up the ship's decks like a lighthouse tower. Part of him grieved for his old ship, but another part of him wanted the schooner to burn. He saw four men rush out of the main cabin house, which had now caught fire, and hurl themselves into the water. Again he thought he saw the familiar silhouette of Salazar. Soon the burning hull of the *Gaviota* was locked together in a fiery dance of flames with three other ships. "Heigh-ho," Townsend whispered quietly to himself. It was hard for him to fathom the reality of the chaos he and Hendricks had caused, an inferno of burning cotton and wood in the middle of Havana harbor.

The Bahamian sailor didn't say anything through all of this. By the time they reached the others aboard the *Vírgen Gorda*, there was mass confusion throughout the harbor. The fires had spread to even more wooden ships. Sailors all around the harbor were ringing fire bells and blowing their ships' whistles. Spanish naval ships from all over the bay were rushing over to try to put out the fires and rescue dozens of sailors who had jumped into the water. Townsend and Hendricks clambered aboard the schooner, and set the empty harbor boat adrift into the darkness. They waited there in the safety of the shoals for several hours, watching the drama unfold. At the first sign of the mauve sky of early dawn, Townsend gave the signal to begin rowing.

"Head for the channel," Townsend whispered in a hoarse voice. "Stay close to the eastern shore. We want to be the first vessel out of the harbor."

Slowly and quietly the men rowed the scow schooner along the shoreline, passing through the anchored ships off Casa Blanca and then rowing close to the looming walls of the Cabaña fortress. They rowed for what seemed like an eternity to get out of the harbor entrance, and then Townsend looked up to the sheer, gloomy black walls of El Morro castle. They were so close they could smell the cooking from the fortress's kitchen. There was an appetizing aroma of fried fish and garlic that caused Look-Out to cry out with a loud meow.

Suddenly a voice cried out.

"*¿Quién vive?*"

Townsend froze as he felt a wave of panic sweep over him. It was the sentry guard calling out who goes there. He must have heard the cat. Without thinking, Townsend cried out that he was Ortiz, the fisherman, and he had brought along his cat for good luck. He spoke quickly, blurring his words together, trying to sound like a Cuban.

"*¿A dónde se dirige?*"

The guard wanted to know where he was going.

"*A Cayo de Sal a pescar.*" Townsend replied that he was headed for the Salt Cay Banks to fish.

"*Tenga cuidado.* Be careful," the guard said. "There are Yankee spies in the harbor committing sabotage. They may be lurking outside the harbor as well. Have you seen any sign of them?"

"*Ni uno.*"

Not a one, Townsend replied, and the guard wished him a safe journey. Townsend pulled his palm leaf hat farther over his face and let out a shuddering sigh. It had been a close call. They were lucky the guard let them leave before dawn. Somehow the sentry didn't detect that he was a foreigner. Six months in Cuba had left its mark. Townsend marveled that he could now imitate the way a Cuban fisherman talked.

As the schooner pulled out of the protective harbor, they raised their sails and headed out into the choppy Gulf waters. Soon they were sailing on a northeasterly course, allowing the Gulf Stream to propel them forward. At the first sight of sunrise, they heard the distant thunder of cannons from El Morro behind them, signaling that the harbor was now officially open.

Later that morning, Townsend went into the cabin house and found Emma sitting on one of the bunks with her carpet bag open and a pen in her hand. She was clearly about to write something down on paper. He looked at her with an enquiring expression and she explained she was writing a letter.

"A letter to whom?" he asked. It would still be another ten hours before they arrived in Key West. The scow schooner was incredibly slow.

"To Grace Backhouse," she replied. "I can't stop thinking of her. I thought I should write because I'm sure she will remember me."

"Oh," he replied in surprise. "How difficult. Yes, you should write the letter. What are you going to say?"

"I know what to write about Michael Abbott and Javier Alfonso," she said with a determined look. "I will try to be as faithful and true to the facts as I can, but what should I write about her husband? We don't have the journal. It will most likely never be found again. Whatever Abbott had uncovered will never be known. What can I write that might console her?"

She looked up at him helplessly. Much to his own surprise, Townsend found himself speaking with a certain clarity, summoning an inner voice he didn't know he had. It was as if he was speaking for Michael Abbott, the words spilling forth as naturally and unexpectedly as water gushing out from a freshly dug well.

"Tell her she was right. Those responsible were in the slave trade, just as she'd heard. It was a conspiracy of powerful Spanish slave traders acting in collusion with some of the island's most wealthy sugar barons, all leading citizens on the island. Those who ordered the attack on her husband most likely are tied to the Spanish slave-trading syndicate called *La Compañía*."

Townsend paused to let Emma write all this down.

"Tell her, she should know her husband documented some inconvenient facts on the island of Cuba. Compromising information that neither the Spanish nor the English wanted revealed. It was decided by both governments that it would be better to stop any investigation of the murder. Tell her there is little information to offer her solace, except for the fact that many of those in Cuba who want to end slavery still remember her husband as a principled man, whom they hold in great respect. To them, he is not a forgotten soldier in Britain's fight to end the slave trade."

"There's a steamer coming toward us, Captain," Higgins called out. "Could be a gunship. She's steaming southwest by west."

Townsend quickly went out on deck and looked through the telescope. He could see the thread of black smoke on the far distant horizon to the north. He thought he could just barely make out the Marquesas buoy. He looked up at the masthead where the Stars and Stripes ensign was now fluttering. His eyes lingered there as he absorbed the fact that once again he was sailing under the American flag. He was already thinking about what to write his father. He had much to tell him. He hoped he could make amends.

Townsend turned to walk back to the scow's stern rail, scanning the horizon in the direction of Cuba. Earlier he thought he could still make out a faint line of shadowy mountains, but now he couldn't see anything except the whitecaps and bright blue sea of the Gulf Stream. The island had disappeared. He thought of his grandmother, her anguish and her loneliness. He knew he might write her, but he doubted they would ever see each other again. Their lives might be linked, but they would remain separate. Townsend looked down at the water. He thought he could see the faint outline of coral heads. Shallow water ahead. He gave a quick nod to Hendricks, but the Bahamian had already seen the shoal ahead and taken the precaution of raising the centerboard.

Townsend stood there gazing at the greenish-blue water as he thought about the cruelty of fate. Saving Abbott from the sharks that night now seemed like another lifetime. Yet it was only six months ago. It was like an illusion, some part of a shadowy dream. He and Emma had been so hopeful. It was as if Abbott had a guardian angel. Twice the Englishman had cheated death and had sidestepped a violent end. Yet despite these moments of hope, the end result had been the same. In hindsight, it all seemed so pointless.

A strand of brown, curly hair suddenly brushed against his cheek, and he smelled the familiar sweet scent of lavender behind him.

"How many more hours?" Emma asked.

"Not too long," Townsend replied with a smile. "Should make Key West by nightfall, maybe sooner if that Navy ship steaming our way gives us an escort."

A warm hand with gentle fingertips touched his, and he responded by loosely pressing his fingers over hers.

"What will you do in Key West?" she asked.

"Try to join the Navy in some capacity, I suppose. Savage's letter might help. This war shows no signs of ending so maybe the Navy will have some use for me. We shall see. And you?"

"My sister, Elizabeth, will be glad to see me. She knew I wanted to do some illustrations of the blockading ships stationed at Key West. She will be expecting me. Just not quite this soon."

"And your mother? Will she be all right?"

"I'm going to write her as soon as we get to Key West. Tell her to come and visit. Close the boarding house for a short while."

At that moment, Townsend spotted a pod of dolphins off the ship's bow, leaping and surfing and then darting ahead of the scow schooner as if they were showing them the way. Townsend allowed himself to feel like one of them. He thought of that quotation from Emerson. "Live in the sunshine, swim the sea, drink the wild air's salubrity."

Emma whispered in his ear. "You know I have spent a lot of time over these past months trying to decipher who Everett Townsend is, the real one, I mean."

Townsend turned to look at her. "And what did you find out?"

"It's been difficult. Finding the real one, I mean. Everett Townsend is an elusive character."

"I see. Somewhat of a sphinx, is he? That does sound challenging. I suppose you will give him a tepid review?"

"No, not really. It turns out he has some truly positive attributes. I believe I understand who he is now. He's like the bottom of a ship. Quite the mystery. You have to scrape the wood to find out the condition of the hull. Fortunately for him, underneath all the sea moss and barnacles, the original planking seems in good shape. Just needs a fresh coat of paint."

Townsend looked over at her with a beaming smile. He felt her fingers press more tightly over his. The two of them stood side by side, gazing to the south toward the island they'd left behind.

Acknowledgments

First and foremost, I would like to thank my wife Tamara for her tolerance in listening to my daily musings and mutterings. She was always willing to patiently listen, and to read the first rough drafts, chapter by chapter. As any author can attest, early feedback from a discerning reader is perhaps the most important help you can receive. Special thanks are due to my editor, Alexandra Shelley, who from the beginning of this project kept me on the right compass course with her constructive criticism. Her early advice to keep the story focused on Havana proved to be wise. When it came time to clear out the brush and deadwood, I want to thank Julie Miesionczek for her well-honed editorial skills.

On the research end, I have many people to thank. I'll start with Tom Hambright, the senior librarian at the Monroe County Public Library in Key West. He introduced me to some unpublished journals from that time period as well as the published naval records from the Civil War. On matters related to the US Navy, I would like to thank James Cheevers, the senior curator at the US Naval Academy Museum, and the Civil War naval historian and author, Robert M. Browning Jr.

Regarding Cuban history, I would like to express special gratitude to Dr. Luis Martínez-Fernández, a Latin American historian and author specializing in nineteenth-century Cuba at the University of Central Florida. He helped me with many of the details about the Backhouse murder, and kindly read parts of the manuscript, offering valuable historical insight. I would also like to thank historian and author Dr. Louis A. Pérez Jr. at the University of

North Carolina, and Sylvia Crane, a family friend, who sparked my imagination with her story she had heard from her grandmother in Cuba about an ancestor's escape from El Morro prison.

On the maritime side of things, I want to extend my utmost appreciation to Captain Ray Williamson, who owns three traditional wooden schooners in Maine, all part of the state's historic windjammer fleet. He was kind enough to take me out sailing for several days on the *Grace Bailey*, a restored cargo schooner originally built in 1882 which now carries tourists instead of lumber. For information about the Dry Tortugas, Kelly Clark of the National Park there helped me with historic details about Fort Jefferson. She also provided old sea charts of the Dry Tortugas. Don and Cheryl Barr, the authors of *Yacht Pilot's Cruising Guide To Cuba*, offered their expertise on the Gulf Stream. Veteran Caribbean navigator and maritime expert Donald M. Street Jr. kindly read one of the final drafts of the manuscript with his nuanced eye for nautical detail and history. Susan Fels, the author of *Before the Wind: The Memoir of an American Sea Captain* was also extremely generous with her time, offering informed suggestions and welcome editorial polishing. Finally I would like to thank Gail Lelyveld, who spent many days in the Manuscript Room of the Library of Congress gathering documents on my behalf, Elizabeth Brake at Duke University who helped with access to Grace Backhouse's letters, and Stacey Warner of Warner Graphics who worked on the presentation of the various images. Also thanks to Luis Carrasco and Debbie Davidson who helped clean up my untidy use of French and Spanish.

Author's Note

The seeds for this novel started with my desire to write about the role of sailing ships during the American Civil War. A little known fact is that during the early years of the Civil War, a large portion of the blockade running in the Gulf of Mexico was carried out by shallow-draft sailing schooners that could navigate the treacherous rivers, bayous, and inlets that define the coast there. An inspiration for me was the entertaining memoir by the Scottish blockade runner, William Watson. Watson wrote about his adventures as the captain of a schooner running through the Federal blockade fleet into various ports in the Gulf of Mexico. His book, *The Civil War Adventures of a Blockade Runner*, is an excellent firsthand look at the men who ran the Union blockade under sail, their passages through the blockade sometimes under cannon fire, and the business syndicates that were behind them.

An important primary historical source for me were the official records of the US Navy's Gulf Blockading Squadrons, which contain hundreds of pages of highly descriptive dispatches written by all the Navy's captains from the beginning to the end of the Civil War. I soon realized in doing my Civil War–era research that my story was largely going to be set in Havana, the supply depot for blockade-running ships in the Gulf of Mexico. As a former Latin American correspondent for NBC News, I knew Havana fairly well. I had traveled to Cuba on assignment on many occasions in the 1980s and early 90s to report on political developments there. I had gone to many parts of the island, usually under the watchful eye of government agents, but occasionally I could slip away unnoticed from the government minders. As a result, I got to know some of the historic areas of Old Havana relatively well. But all these years later as I did my research for this book, I quickly realized my familiarity with contemporary Havana was not going to help me too much. Today's Havana is a far cry from the city as it was in the nineteenth century.

The city in 1863 was flush with wealth and opulence from the export of sugar. It was still defined by the trappings, customs, and architecture of old Spain, but the island's elite had lofty ambitions for Havana to be known as the Paris of the tropics. This was the era when steamships and square-riggers were anchored side by side. Havana was a bustling harbor with plenty of swagger, filled with vessels of all kinds. It was a crucial shipping crossroads, and as a result, it became a strategic diplomatic watchtower for England, France, and Spain. Extremely helpful in providing details about Havana at that time was a little known traveler's handbook to Havana published immediately after the Civil War entitled *The Stranger in the Tropics*, by C. D. Tyng. Details on commercial operations and protocol in Havana Bay came from a document published in 1858 by Charles Tyng & Company, commission merchants and underwriters in Havana.

My visualization of the city was inspired by studying the old maps of Havana and reading many published and unpublished journals from visitors to Cuba during the mid-nineteenth century. These journals were not only descriptive, but in one case helped me develop an important strand of the plot. A traveler's journal written in 1861 by a Mrs. William Nye Davis from Boston described visiting a sugar plantation in Matanzas where she found that strangely all the slaves spoke English. Like her, I wondered how that was possible. The answer is shrouded in mystery, but certainly there are numerous accounts of English-speaking Negroes taken to Cuba by force from the Bahamas and Jamaica after the slaves were freed from those islands in 1834. Once in Cuba, they were enslaved, their identities frequently changed by Cuban plantation owners, and their life stories forever lost.

From my research, it became clear how important a political and economic role the various consuls general played in Cuba. There was still no underwater telegraph to Cuba, so all correspondence to and from the island was by letter. To get a firsthand sense of the concerns of the Federal government, I read all the original handwritten letters of the acting US consul general in Havana, Thomas Savage, which are in the Library of Congress. Savage was diligent in reporting a list of blockade runners, and frequently specified what ships were in port. These details allowed me to describe known blockade runners such as the *Alice* and the *Cuba*. His letters mention specifics about how much he paid an undercover informant on a Confederate ship. He also reported the fascinating detail that Cuban slaves could be heard in the streets of Havana chanting pro-Lincoln slogans.

The correspondence from the Confederate agent based in Cuba, Charles Helm, revealed that he was pressing hard to persuade the Spanish to support the Confederacy, emphasizing the shared belief in continuing slavery. He made it clear how friendly he was with the British consul general, who was eager to reflag blockade-running Confederate vessels with the British flag. From his letters, I learned his job was to keep close records of all blockade-running ships, and their cargoes, and persuade the European powers that the Union Blockade was a farce.

With regard to the British viewpoint, some of the correspondence of the British consul general, Joseph Crawford, points out how much the slave-trading issue was of paramount importance and concern. In one of Crawford's dispatches back to London, he reported in January 1863 that a Confederate emissary had been seen in Havana who was linked with a steamship fitted out for the slave trade. That vessel was the *Noc Doqui*, one of the slave ships owned by the Cuban slaver Julián Zulueta, who was the primary shareholder in the Spanish slave-trading syndicate known as *La Compañía*. The *New York Times* reported in January 1863 that the US Navy had captured this steamship off the Mexican island of Isla Mujeres. By then, it had been transferred into Confederate hands. That startling detail gave me an important thread for the plot. It made sense. The Confederacy needed ships, and the slave-trading interests in Cuba, who openly favored the South, had a fleet of fast ocean-going steamships.

The first mention I found of the African Expedition Company was a report written by retired US Navy Captain R. W. Shufeldt in January 6, 1861, about "the secret history of the slave trade" in Cuba. In the report, Shufeldt described how "an organized company exists in the city of Havana with a capital of one million dollars whose sole business it is to import Negroes into the island of Cuba." He identified the head of the company as a well-known Spanish merchant. Julián Zulueta's and Pancho Marty's involvement in slave shipments is well documented in British consular records as well as in the consular reports to Washington from acting US consul general in Havana, Thomas Savage.

Finally a book written about the experiences of one of the British diplomats living in Havana in the mid-nineteenth century, who was knifed and killed in his home, provided an essential thread for this novel. This was an actual murder that was never solved. The book, *Fighting Slavery in the Caribbean* by Luis Martínez-Fernández, is a well-written account of George Backhouse and his time in Havana as the British representative in the joint

English-Spanish Commission for the Suppression of the Slave Trade. The book tells the poignant tale of this man's struggle in Cuba to enforce the Treaty laws against slave trading, and how he was attacked by unknown assailants in his own home and murdered in 1855.

In the collection of Backhouse letters at Duke University, I was able to read newspaper coverage about the murder as well as some of the letters to and from Grace Backhouse in the months after her husband's death. One of the letters stood out. Mrs. Backhouse writes a poignant plea to Lord Clarendon at the Foreign Office requesting greater financial help as "her husband lost his life in the service of his country." In that same letter she writes that his murder "may in reality have been the result of a slave dealing conspiracy." Her pleas for more financial help from the Foreign Office were politely received, but strangely seemed to fall on deaf ears in London. She ends the letter with a heart rendering appeal. She wrote, "Were it not for my children, I would have been, not only content, but most thankful to have borne my sorrows in silence." Another mystery was a missing journal. The letters sent from the consul general's office in Havana to Grace Backhouse some months after her husband's death mention that no trace of her husband's journal could be found.

A man's escape from El Morro castle into the sea seemed like a good way to begin. I'd read accounts of how the Spanish authorities in the nineteenth century would hurl the bodies of prisoners, who were executed, over the walls of El Morro castle to what they called a sharks' nest below. The bodies were also thrown down chutes built inside the fortress walls. What triggered my imagination was a story I had been told about an escape from El Morro. This story had been passed down in one Cuban family from generation to generation. As I wrote that first chapter, I was thinking of John Singleton Copley's painting, dated 1778, now in the National Gallery in Washington, DC, of the actual rescue of a young British sailor, Brook Watson, from a shark attack in Havana harbor.

—Robin Lloyd
July 25, 2017